MAGICKS & ENCHANTMENTS

ENCHANTED TALES ~ 1

DEANNA KNIPPLING   LEAH R. CUTTER

ROBERT JESCHONEK   DEBBIE MUMFORD

ANNIE REED   REI ROSENQUIST   ALICIA CAY

JAMES PYLES   GRAYSON TOWLER

JAMIE FERGUSON   DAYLE A. DERMATIS

THEA HUTCHESON   LESLIE CLAIRE WALKER

SHARON KAE REAMER   STEVE VERNON

Edited by
JAMIE FERGUSON

BLACKBIRD
PUBLISHING

COPYRIGHT

"But what can I do?" cried she, spreading out her arms helplessly. "I can not hew down trees, as my father used; and in all this end of the king's domain there is nothing else to be done. For there are so many shepherds that no more are needed, and so many tillers of the soil that no more can find employment. Ah, I have tried; but no one wants a weak girl like me."

"Why don't you become a witch?" asked the man.

— From "The Witchcraft of Mary-Marie" by L. Frank Baum

CONTENTS

INTRODUCTION

Growing up, I loved reading stories about magic. And about space-ships, and adventure, and a zillion other things—I read anything I could get my hands on. But I've always have a special affection for stories involving anything magical.

As an editor, I'm able to create anthologies filled with the kinds of stories I love to read. I edit A Procession of Faeries, an anthology series with a focus on the Fae and related mythology, and it's been *so* much fun to put those collections together that I decided to create another series with a broader magical theme. *Magicks & Enchantments* is the first issue in the Enchanted Tales anthology series. Each issue will have a unique focus, and all of the stories will involve some aspect of magic, spells, or sorcery.

So far I haven't met any mythical creatures, found secret passageways or magical amulets, or come across fairies dancing in the forest...but there's a part of me who thinks maybe, just maybe, I will one of these days...

For now, I'll settle for creating more collections of stories full of enchantment, mystery, and magic!

Introduction

—Jamie Ferguson
Editor

THE COFFEE SHOP GHOST

DEANNA KNIPPLING

IT WAS SUPPOSED to be a simple cleansing at the Red Eye Coffee and Breakfast Bar. I had planned to come in, take off my shoes, open all the doors and the windows, sweep the floor with a bristle broom, clean everything with vinegar and/or baking powder and/or decalcifers and/or salt, burn some sage, ring a bell, leave old copper pennies and pieces of selenite on the windowsills, and then get down to my real work.

Look.

Magic exists and it pervades the world. But I'm not a witch; I just pretend to be one. I dress in long, diaphanous black dresses, wear my flamingo-colored hair in a witchy bun, enchain myself with oodles of silver skull jewelry, appear in public only with a pair of killer eye-wings, and speak in a low and seductive voice.

But I don't do it because I'm a witch. I just like wearing that stuff. I'm a goth, that's all. One of the night folk.

I *do* have a power, though.

A cup of coffee, some swirling steam, a few choice words under my breath to focus my energy—and then I close my eyes and inhale.

And suddenly I can taste the room.

My sense of taste includes but is not limited to: ghosts; spirits; devils; demons; the fae; vampires; werewolves (but who can't taste a fucking werewolf inside an enclosed space, though?); different types of cigarette, marijuana, wood, and other smoke; a variety of goblins, ghoulies, and wee beasties that creep in the hidden spaces; enchantments; lost things; secret identities; ancient, multi-generational tragedies; psychopomps; psychopaths; drag queens (yum); a bunch of disabilities that are based on genetics; cancer; fear.

It sounds like I have a smoker's voice, but I don't smoke: it's all the spirit traces I've inhaled over the years, settled into the back of my throat.

But, in order for me to get anything useful out of my talent, first the place has gotta be cleaned. The daily detritus of chemicals, pollution, and foot traffic makes it hard to be sure what I'm picking up.

I've had good readings off hot tea, cocoa, hot toddies, Alka-Seltzer tablets in a mug of hot water, and even a "cappuccino" out of a Keurig machine in a hospital waiting room once. It just has to be hot enough to steam.

I don't do cleansings full-time. Like other practitioners of the unusual and strange, I put together a living out of a hodge-podge of activities. I also read palms and tarot cards, assist ghost hunters in a more-or-less legit capacity, sell soaps, perfumes, and tea online, and work at one of the local haunted houses every Halloween. Plus about a hundred other things. Satisfaction, or at least a job well done, guaranteed.

The Red Eye was in the Highland neighborhood in Denver. It was nice. Small boutique shops and corner stores that had been around for generations. One-story brick houses with porches and decorative wrought-iron bars over the windows, terraced yards, brick sidewalks with teeny-tiny flowers growing in the cracks—interrupted by modern two-story condos with steel-tube balconies overlooking the street.

In a few years, a decade maybe, all the charm would be gone.

The Red Eye itself was built into part of an old corner store that had been split into two separate businesses: a tavern-slash-sports-bar called The Jester's Tavern, and the Red Eye.

The interior of the Red Eye was mostly the crumbling, raw brick of the old building itself. A garage door covered half the frontage; in warm weather, the baristas would open the big door to let the fresh air in. LED lights hung off the roof supports. A narrow aisle between tables led from the front door to the humming refrigerated bakery counter in the back. The shop was narrow but long, with chipped wood tables and painted metal chairs. The coffee bar was lined with mismatched swivel stools filled with long-haired brunettes in puffer jackets and stocking caps typing away at their laptops in the winter, or middle-aged dude-bros in t-shirts and backward baseball caps in the summer.

The owners were a couple of hipsters in their thirties, skinny black jeans, button-up shirts, and black-framed glasses. The guy was balding and wore a trimmed beard. The chick wore combat boots and had her hair in a sleek ponytail. They looked like siblings. Whenever one of them was talking, the other would tilt their head to the side to listen. They had handed me a cup of coffee, no cream, no sugar, in a heavy hand-thrown mug with a fingerprint at the top of the handle as we sat down. The coffee itself spoke well of their dedication.

"Hi, I'm Tiff Cordero," I said.

They blinked at me, probably expecting something like "Raven Blackcraft" or something. But I like my name, the same way I like my hair to be aggressively pink.

"What we want," said the guy, "is to have you do a cleansing."

The chick said, "It's not—we don't believe in ghosts. It's just that—"

"—Things have been going strangely here lately."

"Yes. Strangely."

I asked, "Strangely how?"

A flicker crossed the woman's face. "I'd like to see what you can pick up on your own," she said firmly.

Which was fair.

"I won't be able to pick up much until after I've started the ritual," I warned her. "There are just too many influences, good and bad, floating around."

"I understand—" said the chick.

"—But we don't want to prejudice you with our impressions," said the guy.

They both looked at me hopefully. I was "on."

I lifted my coffee cup in front of my face, breathing in the steam for a few long seconds. I picked up Axe body spray, brand-new sneaker soles, floor wax, a few rancid coffee grounds, and something burnt and truly nasty. I held the scents in my mouth for a second, then exhaled. "I'm not sure that you're haunted," I said, "but there's *something.*" It wasn't the first time I'd said that sentence, and it wouldn't be the last. "Not historic," I added, in case they were concerned about an old ghost haunting the place. "Something recent."

They looked at each other. "No one has died here recently, that we know of."

I shook my head. My earrings jingled. "It almost smells like plastic. Burnt plastic."

Their noses both wrinkled up, as if on cue. I couldn't have gotten a better reaction if I had planned it. *Plastic.* To a certain type of person, that was a dirty word.

"Should we call an electrician?" the chick asked.

Hm…

A pregnant pause.

Then the chick shrugged. "I can't actually smell anything."

"Burnt plastic of the spirit," said the guy. They both chuckled.

"Can you do anything about it?" the chick asked.

"I can try," I said. Then I hefted my black leather bag with the bats onto the table, pulled out my tablet, and said, "If you would just sign here…"

WHEN I ARRIVED at one p.m. to get to work, they both looked ashamed and somewhat horrified. The sign on the front door read *CLOSED FOR REPAIRS/OPEN BY FOUR.* They assured me, at length, that they'd cleaned the ice machine—thus, the shame and horror—scrubbed out the air pots, run the descaler on the espresso machine, cleaned the bathrooms, and taken out the lunch trash, as requested.

I thanked them, brought in my equipment from the car, and asked them to help me open up the building. Then I put on some Dead Can Dance, took in a moment to soak up the vibes, and got to work.

I kept catching the burnt plastic smell as I worked.

As I swept, as I wiped everything down in the bathrooms, as I mopped out the storeroom, as I cleaned the computer screen in the office, as I ran clean the dishwasher and cleaned around all the fittings: burnt plastic. There was definitely something going on. I kept trying to figure out where the smell was coming from, but it seemed to come from nowhere and everywhere all at once.

Almost like it was following me around, trying to get my

attention.

I don't do windows, but sometimes I do mirrors. On the wall opposite the coffee bar, where a barista could look up and see their face reflected back at them, was a head-sized round mirror with an old-fashioned wood frame, the kind that's usually gilt. This one was painted white.

I cleaned it with vinegar and water while sitting at the coffee bar, testing a small spot on the frame to make sure I wasn't about to wreck the paint. What felt like a thousand years of dust came off, both on the frame and the glass. How anyone had been able to see themselves in the mirror, I don't know.

When I was done, I looked deep into the mirror.

And saw nothing odd. Just myself: silver hoop earrings in a half-dozen piercings per ear, pink hair, a zit near the corner of my mouth. I wasn't wearing any foundation; it screws with my sense of smell.

I let my eyes go soft and unfocused. I'm no scryer, but anybody can do that trick.

Out of the corner of my eye, I saw movement, which I deliberately did not look at. Something *was* here. I caught the impression of softness rather than harshness, something that didn't want to be seen—or that felt bad about being seen.

On impulse, I went around the counter, pulled a double shot of espresso, and poured it onto the mirror, which promptly drank it.

I *had* been intending to make a simple scrying mirror. You can also make one by painting the back of a regular mirror with black instead of silver, or pouring ink into a dish of water.

Having the mirror drink my impromptu ink was not what I had been expecting.

Cautiously, I lifted the mirror and checked underneath to make sure the espresso hadn't just soaked through. But no: not a trace of liquid anywhere. The mirror silvering had gone darker, though, adding a chocolatey haze to the world. I put the mirror back down, then let my vision go soft again. I held out my hands on either side of the mirror, tried to channel some of the actual witches that I knew, and relaxed.

After a few moments, a presence tapped softly on a wood door-frame from somewhere behind me, and whispered, "Are you done yet?"

I repressed a smile and said, "I still need to do the sage smudging."

"Okay. Fifteen more minutes? It's four o'clock."

"Ten more minutes."

"Okay. Sorry!"

The presence was gone.

I banished the distraction, let my eyes go soft again, and waited, still holding out my hands.

A soft touch brushed against one of them, cool and smooth—someone's hand. I couldn't quite see who was there, and knew better than to try to look.

"It's okay," I said. "I'm a friend of the dark. Do you need something? I can get you out of here, if you need to go somewhere else."

The hand seemed to linger for a few more seconds, then withdrew itself. I waited for another moment, but I knew the spirit had retreated.

"I'm going to smudge some sage around, ring a bell, then open the front of the house back up for customers," I said. "You okay with that?"

A dark flutter out of the corner of my eye. Then it was gone.

I started a pot of coffee, then smudged the front and back of the house. I didn't sprinkle salt across the thresholds or anything, just laid out the pennies and the crystals. I walked around ringing my bell, an old, tuned bell like they used to ring in churches, that I had picked up at a rummage sale. It was a B-flat. Then I went out back where the cook, both owners, and a barista were all waiting for me to wrap things up.

"All done? How did it go?" the guy asked.

"There's definitely a spirit on the premises." I told them about the mirror and the presence that had visited me.

"How can we get rid of it?" the guy asked. The chick gave me a *look*.

I said, "If it's okay with you, I'm going to hang out and drink a couple of cups of coffee and see what happens when you have customers here. I didn't actually see the spirit doing anything disturbing or problematic. Maybe it's something the customers are bringing with them."

"With them?"

"You know, like when someone's wearing strong perfume and it irritates everyone around them. Mortals can affect the spirits too, you know."

"Huh," said the guy.

The chick still wasn't talking. Then, deciding to trust me, she said, "You can hang out now if you want. But the incidents have been happening after sundown, mostly."

I agreed to come back later that night, no extra charge, if they fed me. They said it was no problem. I hung out at the table under the mirror for a while that afternoon, then got up and took a position near the front counter where I could look into the mirror, which had been rehung.

It weirded out some of the customers to see a goth standing in front of the pre-bagged coffee shelves, but most of them looked at me like I was part of the ambiance, a performance artist in a world of high-priced sneakers, cheap bike locks, and blank-eyed toddlers in jogging strollers.

I wondered what the spirit was doing to them that had made the owners call me in.

THAT EVENING I RETURNED. It was a good evening, cool and dry, with a clear sky fading from one jewel tone to the next. The garage door was open, and a light breeze sauntered through like a black cat with its tail up. The conversations happening on the tables near the sidewalk seemed suppressed, though, as if everyone had just heard of a death in the family, or were hung over. I walked in and pondered the chalkboard menu: parsley-garbanzo salad with lemon chicken, or a green chili refrito burrito? The air inside was thick with smells, not all of them bad, but all of them quickly becoming confusing: golden retrievers, Vibram shoe soles, bike tires, car exhaust, grass clippings, body sprays (ugh), cinnamon, garlic, grilled chicken, and, yes, coffee.

I ordered the salad and brought a cup of drip coffee back with me to an empty seat. While I was in line, I had looked into the mirror and hadn't seen anything—but scrying wasn't my specialty. As I waited, I noticed that every conversation stopped as soon as new customers walked through the door. The newcomers' faces turned ashen and pale, and one little girl pulled her shirt up over her face, crying when her mother made her pull it back down.

What was going on here?

I leaned back against the bricks and let my head clear. Whenever I do that, I become aware of just how much tension I carry around on my head and neck. I also hear just how loud my tinnitus really is: I have it constantly, and there's not much that can be done about it, but I don't usually *hear* it. It's like having a TV on static in the background, most of the time.

When I felt sufficiently relaxed and clear, I lifted my cup of coffee and took in a deep breath of steam and scent.

It was like inhaling a migraine.

I whimpered and lowered the coffee to the table, then put my hands over my face. It was all I could do to keep from sobbing. The pain was bad. The visual aura was terrible. The ringing in my ears was *gone*. In exchange, the volume on every sound in the coffee shop had been turned up to eleven. The dim little LEDs on their strings seemed to bore through my eyelids.

A moment, and then someone was crouching next to me. The chick.

"Are you okay?"

I shook my head.

She helped me to my feet, then brought me behind the pastry counter and out the back, where the cook, who I hadn't seen before, was on a smoke break. The chick sat me at a little picnic table and gave me a napkin. I began sobbing uncontrollably.

After a few minutes, I was able to get it together again. The migraine had faded: the ringing in my ears had come back like a comfortable, shimmering muffler of sound. The streetlight still pricked at my eyes and my stomach still lurched, but at a level I was used to.

The chick had disappeared, but the cook was still there.

"You got it pretty bad," he said.

"Yeah." I took a breath. "Is it like that for everyone?"

"Nah. Not that bad. Most of the customers who come through here aren't exactly sensitive, you know? The ones who are, don't come back."

"I can see why."

He grinned. He had a mustache and arched eyebrows—devil's eyebrows—and deliberately unruly, frothed-up hair. He smelled of American Spirit cigarettes, cooking oil, cypress, and peppermint. "The migraine ghost. *La Migraña.*"

"Is that a thing? A Latino thing?"

"No, I just made it up."

I laughed. "Good name, though. You can feel it?"

"Oh, yeah. I told them about it months ago. Did they listen to me? No. They needed to consult a goth chick for that."

He laughed, I laughed with him.

"Okay, okay," I said. "I'm sorry that I didn't get to talk to you earlier. What do you know?"

The cook's name was Dante. He had started working at the coffee shop about six months ago. There had been nothing then. A couple of months ago, though, the migraine ghost had started its horrible work, driving off a bunch of regulars and some of the servers. The owner chick could feel it, faintly; the owner guy had passed out a couple of times, it had been so bad: he had stopped coming in the evenings entirely.

"And you?"

"Me? I take a lot of smoke breaks," he said.

"I don't mean to be offensive but—"

"Oh, here it comes," he said. "Something offensive."

"*But,*" I said, "are you a witch?"

"A witch?"

"Or something."

"I'm an 'or something.'"

"Me, too," I said. "I have clairalience." When his face didn't resolve into an "aha" expression, I added, "Psychic smelling abilities."

"That's why you cleaned everything. They said you were talking about burnt plastic."

"Yeah. You?"

He shrugged. "I don't like to get involved in that stuff."

I suspected that he had been a lot more involved in that stuff than he wanted to admit. But that was none of my business.

I asked, "Do you smell burnt plastic?"

He grimaced. "No, it smells like leaking antifreeze to me. Turns my stomach."

"Any sense of threat or attack? Any weird moodiness?"

He licked one corner of his lips, then the other. "I wouldn't say it's an attack. It feels like a constant state of depression. The kind that goes on and on, like drizzle."

The chick came out of the back door, bringing me a different mug of coffee. "You don't want that salad, do you?"

I shook my head. "I am feeling better, though." I took the coffee, held it, cleared my head, and inhaled. Outside, under the hum of a greenish streetlight, I didn't catch more than a moment's dizziness and nausea. But the smell was stronger: burnt plastic.

"Hey, don't—" said the chick.

But I was already up and walking toward the back door, following the trail of scent. Dante got up and opened the door for me, and I walked in like a black-clad ghost, seeing nothing, eyes closed, skin pale from the migraine.

I stepped inside and the pain hit me. I was ready for it this time, and didn't clear my head fully. The ringing in my ears was loud, insulating me from a terrifying spike in my senses. (Why this works, I don't know, and it's kind of the opposite of most people with migraines.) I walked through the back of the house and into the customer area.

The trail of scent led me forward, past the end of the bar and through the line of customers.

Then straight into the shelves of roasted, pre-ground coffee. I didn't quite literally run into them, but it was close. Dante caught my shoulder and stopped me before I could run face- and coffee-first into the shelves.

Hot coffee sloshed over my hands and left a wet, but invisible, spot on the front of my black dress.

"It's coming from the tavern," I said, turned, and walked out the garage door and onto the street.

THE JESTER'S TAVERN wasn't as cool as the name implied. Despite the bare brick walls and restored hardwood floor and nice scavenged-materials bar, the vibe was pure Sports Bar, with about a hundred flat-screen TVs hanging from the walls, a variety of team jerseys hung everywhere else, and the reek of fried cheese and onions hanging in the air. The name of the bar apparently came from a black velvet painting hanging above the bar, a neon jester in cap and bells. Next to it hung—of course—a velvet Elvis and a velvet Elvira: quite the triumvirate.

I said, "I'm looking for some friends?" to the bartender, who waved me inside. I walked over to the spot on the wall opposite my near-faceplanting on the other side.

The smell was strong. The booth along that part of the wall was empty, so I slid into the seat, still holding my mug of coffee from next door. Dante, who had followed me, took the seat opposite mine, then jerked his head at me twice. I switched seats and grimaced: it was definitely the seat where it had happened, whatever *it* was.

The reek of burnt plastic was so strong it surprised me the fire alarm wasn't going off.

I felt a presence beside me elbow me in the side. "Sorry," I said. Dante and I slid apart almost automatically, making room for an invisible third between us.

A waitress in an orange crop top came up to us and said, "Um…would you like to order?" Her nose was wrinkled up.

"Do you smell anything?" I asked.

She made a face. "No? Nothing weird, anyway."

"Have people been getting migraines here lately?"

Her eyes widened. "Oh, yes! The regulars who used to sit right here did! Now they never come back. And they were good tippers, too. And a lot of the people who sit near this table get them, too."

"Can you give me their names? The regulars, that is?"

She made a face and walked away. I shrugged at Dante. *Oh well.*

"Now what?" he said. "Exorcise the place? Talk the owners over here into paying you for a cleansing? What?"

"I'm not sure," I said, tapping one short, chipped black nail against my teeth. I couldn't force the owners here to hire me. I could tell my clients about the ghost crossing back and forth from one side of the building to the other, but what could *they* do about it, if the problem was on this side? I could take the laborious path of researching local ghost stories, contacting those two patrons (some-how), going from door to door around the neighborhood and finding out who had migraines…

I turned to the spirit next to me and said, annoyed, "I wish you could just tell me what you wanted."

Dante said, "Uh…a date?"

I blushed. I hadn't been expecting *that.* I ducked my head, mumbled, "I meant the ghost," and tried to disappear into my black clothing. It wasn't working.

Dante stared at me, half-panicked.

I straightened up, took a breath, said, "A date would be lovely, let's do that. But right now, I need to see what I can do about this ghost."

Dante blinked. "'Let's do that,' she says."

I rolled my eyes. "The ghost?"

"Maybe it has a headache and wants an aspirin."

I reached past the ghost and punched him on the shoulder. "Maybe it comes over here to get drunk, then crosses back over to sober up."

"That's not a bad idea," he said.

"Migraines aren't the same as hangovers," I said.

"That doesn't mean that a ghost's hangover can't give a sensitive mortal a migraine."

"Point," I said. "But neither of these businesses has been there that long, and the owners didn't report that anyone had died recently. And I think they would have known if anyone had died next door." I paused, trying to relax and let my eyes soften, in case I was able to see the spirit sitting between us. It didn't feel threatening, and I, at least, wasn't getting a migraine. "Have you ever heard of having phantom smells during a migraine?"

"I'll look it up," Dante said, pulling out his phone, the screen flashing bright.

It hit us both like *that*, the wretched pain of a strong migraine. The sounds of the TVs instantly became the shrieking of demons. Every clink of silverware or glass was torture. My stomach lurched.

Dante gritted his teeth and searched for the information. In a choked voice, he said, "Yes. Phantom smells. This one guy even described it as burnt plastic. It's called *phantosmia.*" He turned off the screen.

And the pain stopped.

I turned toward the spirit, frowning. It went back and forth between alcohol and caffeine all day with a migraine. *Both* alcohol and caffeine were triggers for migraines.

The regulars who had sat in this seat had had migraines.

I had assumed that the regulars had had migraines because they were sitting in this seat. That the spirit had given them the migraines.

But what if they had given the migraines to the spirit?

I waved at the waitress. She came over again. "I'm not allowed to give out customer information."

"If I really need it, I'll have the owners next door ask for it," I said. "What I want to know from you is whether the regulars who sat here ever played cards or games at their table, or ever laid jewelry or smoked anything weird here."

The waitress seemed taken aback. "Um, yeah! How did you know?"

"What did they do?"

"It was the last time they were here. They took some paper and wrote on it with these big fancy red feather pens with gold tips and ink in a little jar, then tore the paper up and burned it in an ashtray. It was weird. They had a bunch of silver jewelry that they laid out all around the ashtray, like, silver charm necklaces with oval charms about the size of a dime, and they were chanting weird things as they burned the paper, a lot of mercy this, mercy that. I would have kicked them out, but it was just a little piece of paper. It didn't set off the fire alarm or anything, and anyway, after that, they stopped showing up."

I said, "Thank you. With any luck, this table should be cured in a couple of days, no migraines."

"Really?" the waitress asked. "That would be cool. What are you going to do, magic? Are you a witch?"

"Yes," I said, thinking, *close enough.*

BACK IN THE COFFEE SHOP, I told the owners about the spirit, and what I thought had happened: "It sounds as though what they were doing was some sort of Christian magic. The silver ovals sound like saint's medals, and Christian invocations generally start with 'Lord have mercy on me, Christ have mercy on me,' and so on."

The guy looked at me, puzzled. "Christians don't do magic."

"They do," I said. "They just call it something else: *thaumaturgy,* or the working of miracles. Several of the saints were known thaumaturges, Saint Andrew Corsini, Saint Menas of Egypt, even good old Saint Nicholas, Santa Claus, has been considered a thaumaturgist. I think what these two were doing were invoking the intercession of a saint. I did some research. I think they may have been trying to invoke Saint Gemma Galgani, the patron saint of migraines, while saying an exorcism rite. They treated their migraines like demons and exorcised them…right onto a harmless local spirit."

The chick said, "Doesn't an exorcism have to be in Latin, with a chalk pentagram on the floor?"

"That's only on the *Supernatural* TV show," I said. "The important thing is that you have faith, and that you have a talent for that type of magic."

"Could you do an exorcism on someone's migraine?"

"I'm not that kind of girl," I joked. "I'm a negotiator, not an expeller. Plus, doing an exorcism where you don't care where the spirit ends up is, let's just say, less than ethical."

"I guess what we need know is…can you fix all this?" the guy asked.

"What I need," I said, "is for the names of those two regulars. If you can get the names…probably, yes. The waitress wouldn't give them to me. But maybe you could talk to your next-door business owner. They're avoiding using that booth, which has to be costing them money. They'd probably go in halvsies on my fee, too, if you pitch it right."

No business owner can resist temptation like that.

AFTER THAT, it all went quickly.

The customers' names magically appeared in an email. I tracked them down, hired a friend of mine who's an actual witch to curse them in such a way that it mostly just reversed the exorcism of their migraines onto the poor spirit, then sent an updated bill to the coffee shop owners, who promptly split it with the bar owner. I got a nice tip, which I split with my witch friend.

Everyone breathed a little easier. The migraines faded, the ghost stopped suffering, and everyone at the coffee shop swore that the owners had done something to the place to make the coffee taste even better. I think it was just that the spirit was pleased to be able to drink in peace.

Dante and I are still together. For our first date, as a thank-you for his help with the ghost, I took him to one of my favorite places— a place for the night people to gather, a gastropub named Ligeia's where the werewolves like to hang out.

The date was a smashing success—but that's a story for another time.

ABOUT THE AUTHOR

DeAnna Knippling is always tempted to lie on her bios. Her favorite musician is Tom Waits, and her favorite author is Lewis Carroll. Her favorite monster is zombies. Her life goal is to remake her house in the image of the House on the Rock, or at least Ripley's Believe It Or Not. You should buy her books. She promises that she'll use the money wisely on bookshelves and secret doors. She lives in Colorado and is the author of *The House Without a Summer: A Gothic Novel*, and other books like *The Clockwork Alice, A Murder of Crows: Seventeen Tales of Monsters & the Macabre*, and more.

As always, this story is dedicated to Ray,
without whose love none of this would be possible.

Find out more about DeAnna at:
wonderlandpress.com

f facebook.com/deanna.knippling

twitter.com/dknippling

instagram.com/deanna.knippling

g goodreads.com/goodreadscomdeannaknippling

BB bookbub.com/authors/deanna-knippling

a amazon.com/DeAnna-Knippling/e/B0049HF320

pinterest.com/dknippling

DREAMS OF SAFFRON AND LACE

LEAH R. CUTTER

REGINA VICTORIA EDMONDSON sat on the storytelling chair—the same one that Mum had always used to sit on, that they'd brought with them all the way from London—and regally waved her hand at her brother, Tobias.

"You have my permission to leave," she said, keeping her nose in the air. She resisted the urge to run her other hand over the rough taffeta of her black mourning skirt, or to fidget. She kept herself as still as Mum's portrait of old Queen Victoria in her dark blue dress, with the small diamond crown and light blue sash.

The one Mum had had over her desk. From before the war. Before their flat in London had been destroyed by the nasty bombs the stupid Germans dropped.

"Do I, now," Tobias said, rolling his eyes.

"Yes," Regina said hotly. "It's my turn to be in charge. Not yours," she reminded him.

She wished there was a place in the new nursery that she could set up as a dungeon for him, someplace where she could punish him. Leave him in the cellar with the spiders and cold concrete, as she had back in London. Or maybe make him sit completely still and watch as the ants followed the line of honey she'd drawn, coming closer and closer to his bare leg.

But the new nursery was in a much smaller room, crowded with five ancient wooden school-desks, a steam trunk full of old-fashioned toys that both of them had long since out-grown, and a tall wooden podium that a teacher or parson might lecture from.

The room always smelled of musty books, even though the shelves held nothing but dust. All of the windows had been wired shut, so they couldn't air out the place. No colorful drawings livened up the walls, like in their old nursery. No red-and-white rose tea set just for them to use, smaller than an adult set but more sturdy.

Bare-branched trees crowded close to the second story windows that covered the eastern wall. Maybe come summer they would make the room delightfully green and cool, but for now, in that awkward time between winter and spring, when the wind blew, it felt to Regina like skeletal hands tapped at the glass.

Making her want to turn and look, then blink her eyes until the ghostly faces she was sure she'd imagined disappeared.

"It's always your turn to be in charge," Tobias complained.

"That's because I'm older," Regina said. And she was. Though they were twins, she'd been born eleven minutes and some seconds before her brother, ten years and one hundred ninety–six days before. "It will be your turn when you're older," she added.

"But you'll always be older than me!"

Regina shrugged. It wasn't her fault that he'd been such a slug-gard. That she mostly chose their games and his punishments.

"I don't like this stupid game," Tobias added.

"You like it well enough when you get to play Raj," Regina pointed out. She mostly did what he said when he was the Raj and they pretended to be in India, riding on elephants or hunting tigers.

It was only fair that he should do what she said when she was Queen.

Even if he was right and she got to be Queen much more often than he got to be Raj.

Tobias crossed his arms stubbornly over his chest. "I want to play something else."

"Like what?" Regina asked. As Queen, she could afford to be magnanimous. That was a word she'd only just learned the week before. On the day before the funeral. When the Vicar had been talking about Mum and what a kind, giving person she'd been.

He'd been right. Their mum had been the best. When she'd been around, of course, and not off working on one of her charities or lunching with Someone Important.

"We could pretend we live at Misselthwaite Manor," Tobias suggested. "Go searching for the secret garden."

Regina couldn't hide her shudder. "The gardens have their own secrets," she whispered, afraid to speak out loud about the strange things she'd seen.

Particularly the back garden. The one far behind the house, at the edge of the estate property.

A fountain that never had any water in it, filled with a green-bronze statue of turtles, sat at the back of that garden. Old fieldstone walls separated it from the other gardens. Sharp white rocks made up the pathways. They gleamed like bones in the dim winter daylight. Nothing grew there, though maybe that was just the season and they'd see green shoots poking above the earth soon.

Time moved there, but not in an orderly fashion. Instead, it flowed against the current, then seemed to turn and overflow the banks, pushing both backwards and forwards.

An icy silence passed between Regina and Tobias.

Tobias liked that garden, giggled at the things he saw.

Regina…didn't. And knew she never would.

"I still want to go outside. And play," Tobias said. "I'm tired of wearing black all the time. And being quiet and still."

Though it had been a week since the funeral, they still got dressed in their mourning clothes every day, her in her long black taffeta skirt and tightly buttoned black blouse, him in a black suit and tie, with a white shirt that barely fit him anymore.

Mum would have loved to see how he'd been growing and told him what a big boy he was becoming. But Regina couldn't tell him those things.

"Don't you miss Mum?" Regina asked instead, her sadness crossing over her like a dark cloud spreading above green fields.

"I do, Reegy," Tobias said, coming closer, even though she'd told him that he should leave, that she wanted to be alone. He used his pet name for her, the name he'd given her that almost rhymed with his own, REE-gy, and TOE-by.

No one else had permission to use that name, and Regina didn't allow Tobias to call her that very often.

"I miss Mum. I miss London. I miss our friends and everything from before the war," Tobias assured her.

Stupid war. Stupid German bombers who attacked every night. Stupid Mum who'd gone and gotten herself blown to bits. Stupid Da who'd gone off to fight in the war and hadn't returned for them, not even after Mum had been killed.

Stupid grandparents who lived out in the country who'd taken the twins in, even though Regina and Tobias had never met them before.

Mysterious grandparents who the twins never saw, even after they'd come out to live with them.

Were they Mum's parents? Or Da's? Regina had never been quite certain. She'd thought for a time it was one of each, Mum's mum and Da's father, though that didn't seem right either.

But there was no one to ask. The twins were mostly left on their own. Meals appeared on a regular basis in the smaller of the two dining rooms, and their beds were made and their clothes cleaned by silent servants who faded into the hallways and woodwork unless there was a particular need.

Though there was a school they could go to, and lessons they should be learning, they mainly spent their days exploring the rambling old house—not quite large enough or grand enough to be called a manor, more like a small country estate—and gardens that were easily four times the size of the house.

Maybe even bigger. The borders seemed to fluctuate at times.

"Please," Tobias said. "Let's go out."

"Very well," Regina said, granting her (one and only) subject his wish.

She would have to change out of her mourning skirt and into something that no one would fuss over if she got it dirty. But she could dress herself—she'd never been as spoiled as having servants see to her that way.

When the twins had been younger they'd often exchanged clothes, with no one the wiser, her in Tobias' short pants and shirt, him in her long skirt. They both had the same soft brown curls from their mother, the same pale skin and sky-blue eyes as their father, the same rosy-apples in their cheeks when they got excited.

Though maybe Mum had known and could tell them apart, and had just played along and pretended not to notice.

Tobias' hair was too short now for him to be mistaken as Regina, though Regina had threatened more than once to chop all hers off, viewing it as a nuisance, at best. Particularly now that she always had to brush it and wash it herself.

Still, she would go outside with her brother, to the detested garden in the back.

Then maybe she'd make him lay very still in a corner of the nursery, playing at hiding while she played at being the big, bad German spy who "accidentally" destroyed his books, searching for him.

So she dressed in brown, loose pants that she'd insisted were decent, playing Queen with the old Vicar's wife who'd been sent with her to get her some appropriate clothes for the country, as well as a gray wool blouse and a heavy, navy blue pea-coat. Warm, uncomplicated clothing. Clothes that would have been comforting if she'd been going out to a picnic with Mum.

Instead, they were clothes that she wrapped around herself like armor.

Spring wouldn't be arriving for another month or more and she didn't like the winds that blew from the fields surrounding the estate.

Though she suspected that it was the garden itself that kept the air unnaturally chilly.

Regina met Tobias just inside the grand front entranceway. An unlit chandelier hung above the marble floor. It had two hundred and thirty-five crystals hanging from its graceful silver boughs. Dark paneling covered the walls, full of ninety-six knots that reminded Regina of black eyes staring greedily at her, sucking at her soul. A staircase leading up to the second story waited just beyond the hall-way, with wooden stairs that creaked all night, as though ghosts held races on them.

She'd often thought that stepping inside the door of the estate was like stepping into a cave, chilled and unchanging.

The doors leading outside stood almost a story tall. The tops slanted into each other, forming a sharp peak at the center. The doors were new, made of a light-colored wood. They smelled sweet, like lemon oil, and were sectioned together in long panels.

Regina had seen an old painting of the original doors in one of the picture galleries. A couple dressed in old-fashioned clothing had stood in front of the doors, staring darkly into the distance. Regina supposed they must have been relatives of hers, as they seemed to have the same eyes and hair as Regina and Tobias.

She hadn't paid that much attention to the couple, though, and instead, had studied the doors behind them.

The panels on the original doors had been full of carved animals cavorting with each other. There appeared to be lambs dancing with chickens, wild geese nesting with boars, even goats and horses poised on their hind legs.

Why had the old doors been taken down? Why had the new doors been put up instead?

What had the old doors allowed in that the new doors kept at bay?

"Ready?" Tobias said with a grin as he slipped on his warm black mittens.

Regina gave him a sharp nod. She supposed they were sharing the rule now, as the outdoors were really more of Tobias' domain than hers.

She braced herself as he swung open the door on the right, pushing it out into the cold wind and air.

At least the wind smelled fresh, of wet earth and burning peat from a nearby cottage. Not stale and moldy, like the house or the nursery.

"Let's go explore," Tobias said, the high red of his cheeks showing his excitement.

"Very well," Regina granted, still playing Queen in her heart and holding her head high as Tobias led the way around the house, toward the back.

In truth, her heart pounded with fear. But Queens didn't show their terror and dread.

Regina never knew what she would find in the back garden.

Or what would find them.

Neither of them did.

THE GARDEN in the far back seemed to be feeling its age that afternoon. Or at least that was how Regina would have described it. The fieldstone walls looked smoother, as if time wore heavily on them.

The leafless ivy that covered the walls looked cracked and broken, as if the stems had weathered an icy winter. The rock pathways glittered, as if frost had been sprinkled across them.

Tobias crouched down when they first came through the grand archway. He tugged on Regina's arm, trying to get her to crouch down with him.

"What?" Regina asked crossly.

"Don't you see the wolves?" Tobias asked.

"No. I don't," Regina said. She refused to be pulled into this game. She didn't like this talk of wolves, or any other kind of wild animals.

Not in this garden, at any rate.

With a sigh, Tobias stood up. "Then what do you see?"

Regina looked around. The turtle fountain stood at the back of the garden. Orderly plots of bare ground, four on either side of the main path, spread out before her. The rock pathway divided just inside the entrance, three-pronged like a trident, with the main path going straight and smaller paths to the left and right, marching along the walls, all meeting up again at the fountain.

The fountain itself was round, made of gray, cold stone. The turtles stood in the cement bowl, the lip rising just past Regina's knee.

She knew what it felt like to sit on that cold stone, to stick her bare legs into that cool water, the shock and delight of showing that much skin and how improper it was, though it had never been *her* here.

All the time *she* had lived here, the fountain had never worked.

The servants had been very clear when she'd asked. The fountain hadn't worked in many, many years.

A large tortoise stood at the very bottom of the graceful column that rose up from the bowl. More turtles stood on its back, each getting smaller and smaller until the very last turtle at the top, no bigger than Regina's hand. They all had their necks extended, their mouths pointed upward. The column of turtles rose up far above Regina's head. Even a tall man would need a ladder to reach the top.

If the fountain worked, Regina knew that all the turtles would spout water. It would be a lovely, splashing sound. She could hear it carried on the wind, a cool summer breeze from long ago.

When she stared long enough, Regina could see that day, feel the warm summer sunshine on the back of her head, smell the roses blossoming behind her, taste the lovely clotted cream and scones she'd been served for tea, run her fingers over the bumpy lace of the gloves on her hands, still hear the falling water.

"I don't see anything in the garden," Regina lied. "Nothing but dead plants and a broken fountain."

That day in the summer was long past, and it hadn't been her, not really.

She refused to see the blooming garden spreading before her, the gray parting like mist. Refused to step into the summer sunshine and a more uncomplicated time.

"Nothing?" Tobias asked, disappointed.

"No, it's all dead. Everything in the garden. It's dead," Regina insisted.

Dead, like their mum. Dead, like their da would be before the end of the war, or so the garden assured her. Dead like the ivy covering the walls and the fountain.

As dead as their previous lives were, their new lives yet unformed.

"You don't know dead," Tobias fumed as he stormed toward the fountain.

"I do so," Regina insisted. Mum was dead. London was dead. All the bombs from the Germans. So many other people dead.

"Do not," Tobias snapped as he started to move.

"Don't go," Regina ordered.

But it wasn't her place anymore. The Queen didn't rule here.

The Raj didn't rule here either, but she suspected he didn't know that.

"Don't," Regina whispered as Tobias marched forward into a past she didn't want to see.

She followed after him, helplessly drawn in his wake though she really didn't want to take another step into the garden. She didn't like the way the bare plots wavered, one moment green and covered in growing things, the next, the branches all withered and dying, and then back to bare ground again.

Tobias reached the fountain. "It doesn't have to be dead," he told her. "See?" He dipped his hand into the sparkling (ghostly) water and playfully flicked it back at her.

"It is dead," Regina insisted. Her face was dry, not wet. If there was any moisture there, it was from tears forced from her eyes by the wind.

Today, here and now, there was no water. The fountain was broken, had been dusty and disused for all of her ten years and one hundred and ninety-six days, or even longer.

She refused to see any water in it at all. Refused to hear the tinkling sound of falling drops. Refused to feel that far off summer sunlight.

Refused as only the Queen could.

"It is dead," she insisted again.

Tobias nodded sadly. "Does your majesty demand that it be dead?"

"I do," Regina said as regally as she could muster, given how her bones shook and her blood ran cold and the wind suddenly seemed to howl, summer complaining at being issued so abruptly off stage.

"How could I fight that?" Tobias asked. "Being merely a Raj."

Two stone benches curved around the fountain. He walked to the right hand one and laid down on it. "Then let us be dead." He put his hands over his chest, in prayer position, like how the old sarcophaguses of the knights did.

"NO!" Regina screamed, running over to where Tobias lay. "The Queen commands that you not be dead. That you not play this game. That you don't have to lie still."

But it was too late.

He'd already turned to stone, as gray and as old as the fieldstone wall behind him.

REGINA WAS ONLY ten years and one hundred and ninety-nine days old at that point, she knew how to get her own way when she needed to. When it was most important.

When she truly had to be Queen.

She won the fight with the Vicar and had her brother buried in the far back garden, where he'd gone ahead and died despite all her tearful condemnations and pleas.

Or maybe he'd just traveled to some other time.

Regina could never be quite sure.

Heart just gave out, or so the old country doctor claimed.

It didn't matter why.

He was gone, leaving her utterly alone, and she would mourn him every day.

Until he returned and started to haunt her.

REGINA SAT in her stiff mourning clothes in the formal dining room, spreading orange marmalade on cold, buttered toast, when she heard Tobias ask her, "Pass the tea, could you Reegy?"

Startled, Regina dropped her knife. The heavy silver clanged loudly on the white-and-red-flowered porcelain plate. Slowly, she turned her head.

No one sat to the right of her, as she had known. Tobias was dead. He'd been gone for eight days, now. The Vicar had finally left her alone in the great estate house, with only the servants, though he promised (threatened?) to visit her every fortnight.

Regina looked around the rest of the room. No one occupied any of the other seven chairs pushed properly into their places around the table. The ancient wainscoting that rose from the floor up one yard (made up of seventy-two strips of wood on the long walls and only forty on the shorter ones) looked solid and couldn't hide anyone. A servant hadn't come in and didn't stand next to the serving board to her left.

Slowly, Regina bent her head to the side. A ghostly figure didn't give her a skeletal grin from underneath the table, either.

No, she must have imagined it. Just as she imagined the faces in the trees, the splash of the fountain, the sound of hooves in the hallway at night.

She was quite, *quite* alone.

And wanted to remain that way, thank you very much.

REGINA SAT in the storytelling chair in the old nursery, reading an old fairytale about a pauper and a horse-spirit—a Púca—out loud. Brisk spring winds made the tree branches tap softly on the windows like moss-covered fingers. Even through the glass, the smell of green growing things seeped into the stale room.

"Come outside and play!" came Tobias' voice, carried on the breeze.

Regina read the next sentence louder, trying to drown out the voice. It had grown harder over the last thirty-two days to pretend she didn't hear it. To stay inside all day, every day. The old manor house held secrets too, old memories that teased Regina with their persistence.

"Reegy, come out siiii-de," Tobias called in a song-song voice.

"The Queen demands that you be silent!" Regina yelled.

The laughter that followed didn't surprise her. Tobias had gotten quite full of himself now that he was dead and she could no longer punish him as she once had.

She longed for the old days when tying him up in a closet was an option, when she was the Queen and must be obeyed.

"The Raj wants you to dance!" Tobias replied.

Regina shuddered. She remembered her dreams from the night before, dancing with a talking goat in the back garden. He'd stood quite nimbly on his hind legs, and wore glasses perched on his long goat face. The fountain had sprung to life, the splashing water accenting their steps.

It had actually been delightful until the goat man had tried to kiss Regina, his foul breath like sewage, his flabby lips and long tongue dripping slime on her skin.

"No dancing," Regina said firmly. She felt like washing her face again, though she knew it had just been a dream. Her skin was still dry and smooth under her fingertips when she reached up.

"But the Raj wants to dance!"

Regina sighed. "Dance with the leaves, then, fool." She primly picked up her book and started to read out loud again about the silly man fooled by the horse-spirit.

She refused to look out the window. She didn't smell the lime-stone ashes and earth of the grave carried on the breeze.

In particular, she did *not* see the ghost of her brother tripping lightly along the budding branches, swirling up higher with the wind, laughing at her all alone in the dim nursery.

"REEGY, just come out for a little while!" Tobias said cheerfully.

Regina shuddered and pulled her pillow more tightly over her head. "It's late!" she complained. "I can't go out at night." She shivered in her bed, more annoyed than afraid. It didn't matter if she left the lights on at night or not, Tobias' voice still came whispering —or occasionally yelling—in her ear.

He'd come to haunt her every night for the last week, keeping her awake for most of the night.

"Please, Reegy," Tobias said, a pleading whine in his voice. "Just for a little while."

"No, Tobias," Regina said. "I need to sleep."

She wore her long wool nighty, the white one with the three lines of lace that ran across her chest. It kept her warm as summer held off for just a little while longer. She'd look like a ghost herself if she went out and skipped along the pathways of the garden, as she had in dreams that had been so real she'd had to wash her feet twice in the morning to remove the imaginary mud caked there.

"The Raj commands you!" Tobias said, giggling.

"The Raj can go to hell," Regina retorted. "The Queen needs to sleep, young man." She tried to sound as firm as Mum had when she'd been angry with them, and not whiny, though she was afraid she missed the mark.

"Reee-gyyy," Tobias called. "Reee-gyyyyy."

Regina shivered again when she felt…something…tugging at the comforter.

"No!" she wailed, unwilling to look. "Go away!"

The tears that she'd cried when Tobias had passed had been the last that she'd shed. Now, she felt them coming back. "I'm so tired!" she said.

Something tugged at her cover again, harder this time.

"NO!" she screamed, throwing back the pillow and sitting up.

She was alone in her bedroom, of course. The lights showed a plain room with gold-and-white ribbons swirling through the wallpaper, the wooden floor covered with a faded, red-and-black Chinese-patterned rug, an old wooden writing desk shoved in one corner, and a tall matching dresser standing in the other.

Thankfully, she couldn't see through the windows behind her, that framed the iron bed, couldn't see the white ghostly figure of her brother floating out there.

Regina pulled her knees up and wrapped her arms around them. "Please," she moaned. "Leave me alone. Let me sleep." Despite how she tried to harden her heart, tears still leaked from her eyes, soaking into the soft duvet.

Her heart pounded hard in the ensuing silence. Had Tobias finally left her in peace?

"You must come visit me," Tobias finally replied. "In the back garden. The Raj commands it."

Regina pushed her legs down flat and sat up straighter. "If I come visit you, you must stop haunting me," she said. "The Queen demands it."

"You must visit once a week," Tobias bargained.

"Once a month," Regina instantly replied.

"Once a fortnight," Tobias said. "As a compromise."

Regina sighed. She supposed it was only fair. She'd go visit her brother, keep him company, then he'd stop bothering her.

Maybe he was lonely too.

"The Queen proclaims that she shall visit the grave of Tobias Sebastian Edmonson once a fortnight from this day forward," Regina said as formally as she could. "In return, the Raj shall give his word of no more haunting."

The audible sigh of Tobias almost made Regina smile. How did he make such a breathy sound when he was just a ghost?

"Fine," Tobias finally said. "The Raj agrees. As long as the Queen keeps her promise, the Raj will keep his."

"Thank you," Regina said. She closed her eyes and laid back down. She was still on edge, her ears waiting for that next scream or cry or laugh.

She nearly missed the whispered words, "Then we shall see who is oldest. And who has to obey who."

She pulled her comforter tighter over her. She'd show *him*. It didn't matter who was oldest.

She was still the Queen. And that was all that counted.

GREEN SHOOTS SPRANG up in all the flower beds. Ivy leaves unfurled, hiding the cracked and dried stems. The early morning air smelled fresh and good. It had been forty–three days since Tobias had passed away (that afternoon, just before tea, would mark forty–four). Spring had been late in coming. If Regina had been the poetic sort, she might have said that it was in mourning as well.

Instead, she suspected it was just the manor. Spring might have already arrived in the surrounding countryside. She already knew that summer would be late arriving here as well, and wouldn't be very warm.

Still, it felt good to leave the manor house. To walk along the brick paths swept clean of the last of the autumn debris by invisible gardeners or fairies. The wind tugged at her navy-blue pea coat, urging her along. She even heard robins singing from the hedge, their bright song cheering the day.

Regina dawdled walking along the hedge. If only she didn't have to keep her appointment! Could a robin show her the way?

But that only happened in books. No bird hopped along, chirping and asking her to follow. No secret path opened up for her to escape into, no hidden door revealed itself.

Very well, then. Queens could be soldiers when need arose.

Regina straightened her shoulders and marched herself to the entrance of the back garden, dread filling the pit of her stomach, her mouth gone dry.

The white rock path that went down the center of the back garden glittered in the morning sunshine, as if still covered in dew.

It also worked as a sharp dividing line.

On the left, the normal spring progressed, with roses still budding, sleepy leaves unfurling.

On the right, spring had gone mad. All the flowers bloomed— crocus, daffodils, snow drops, geraniums, and tulips—their heady scents carried on the breeze. The green of the leaves and grass was so bright and young it hurt her eyes. Bees busily buzzed between the blossoms, intent on their work.

The fountain at the back remained silent, the turtles with their mouths uplifted, like choirboys awaiting the sacrament. It seemed to be in its own time, not rushing forward or leaning back.

Of course, Tobias' grave stood on the right side.

Regina hadn't wanted her brother planted close to the fountain. She'd wanted to bury him near the entrance of the garden, so that she could merely walk past the gate and see his final resting place. However, she'd been overruled on that. No one else wanted a grave next to the grand arch that led to the garden.

Regina continued her march into the garden, going down the center path, the rocks crunching under her shoes. Warm, then cooler breezes pushed at her. At least the plant beds stayed fixed in their states, instead of passing quickly from one season to the next, as they had the last time she'd been there.

Two stone benches curved before the fountain, one on either side of the main path.

Regina shuddered as she passed the one on the right, the one that Tobias had died on. It gave off a cold air, as if the sunlight would never be enough to warm the stone.

Just past the path, in the flower beds next to the old fieldstone wall, Tobias lay. Statues of angels sat at the foot of the grave. One appeared to be shushing all onlookers, while the other had tears on his chubby cheeks, his wings pulled tight for comfort. The statues were no longer white, but appeared aged, the stone grayed as if it had withstood many spring rains already. They came up to Regina's shoulders as she stood at the foot of Tobias' grave, like guards preventing her from taking another step.

Soft green grass covered the grave, looking more like summer than spring. Flower urns at the other cardinal points brimming over with azaleas, geraniums, and daisies. Now, Regina heard the fountain's cheery splashing despite how dry and broken it appeared. Warmer winds caressed her cheeks.

Regina wasn't sure what she should do next. Say a prayer for her brother's soul? Surely it was already lost. Beg for their dead mother to find her son? But Mum had already moved on and forgotten them.

Instead, Regina reached down to the stone path beside her and picked up one of the hard white rocks. It lost its glitter in her palm and quickly grew warm.

"I hope you find your way home," she whispered as she placed the rock at the foot of the grave.

If she was being truly honest with herself, though she didn't want to believe (and refused to see) the strangeness in the garden, the reason she'd wanted Tobias buried close to the gate was so that he could find a way to escape the garden's clutches.

However, she knew in her heart that he never wanted to leave.

When Regina turned, she found the ghost of her brother standing beside her. He also stared mournfully at his grave.

He wore the clothes she'd last seen him in, warm jacket and pants, and not the black mourning suit the Vicar had insisted he be buried in. He looked like a solid cloud, all white and gray, though he didn't cast a shadow. He gave off a chill like the curved stone bench in front of the fountain. The smell of the grave wafted from him, limestone and freshly buried things.

After a few moments of silence, Regina finally told Tobias, "The Queen has fulfilled her promise."

Tobias turned and looked at her. His eyes seemed, well, haunted.

Had she misjudged him? Did he want to escape the garden? To flow along with normal time again? To leave the sunlit days of the past that weren't really his?

Then his smile turned cruel—much more like the smile that she saw in the mirror when she was playing Queen.

"The Queen doesn't rule here," Tobias announced, his whispery ghost-voice very strong.

"Neither does the Raj, fool," Regina hissed at him.

Too late. The garden had heard his boast.

Great winds pushed against Regina, trying to flatten her. They blew *through* her brother's form, turning the ghostly shape translucent, the garden apparent behind him.

Sparkling water filled the fountain, golden like Champagne, fizzing with bubbles, like washing powder gone mad. The sounds of wild laughter swirled around Regina. She smelled burnt pork and long-rotted melon. Hooves pounded nearby.

Tobias reached for Regina greedily, his eyes turned into dark, sucking holes.

Or was it her brother? Had he lost his will and become one with the garden?

Tobias grabbed Regina's forearms. Arctic cold fingers slipped *through* her coat, wrapping themselves around her bones. Ice shredded her soul, freezing her in place. Life drained from her limbs, spring growth replaced with winter chill.

No!

Regina refused to submit. She was still the Queen. She would *not* be torn in two.

She raised her hands up sharply, twisting her arms and breaking free of her brother's grasp.

Then she turned and ran up the side garden path.

Roses with thorns as big as her thumb scratched her coat, trying to snag her. Birds pulled at her hair. Fat white worms sprang up in the middle of the path. They gave a disgusting squelching noise as she stomped them.

Instead of following the smaller path all the way to the end of the garden, Regina cut across one of the paths between the flower beds to the main path. The winds died down, but she kept running.

How far away was the entrance? Had the garden just doubled in length?

It didn't matter. She was determined to leave.

And never come back.

Suddenly, the grand garden entrance loomed ahead of her. She broke free with a soft *pop*, as if she'd just burst a soap bubble. The winds died down instantly. Spring (and sanity) returned.

Regina stopped. She took a deep breath, her heart instantly calm. Surprisingly, her blood wasn't pounding anymore. The spring chill returned, her skin cool to the touch.

She held up her head, stiffened her spine.

The Queen returned.

She ran a hand over her wild mane of curls, pushing them down. She'd have to repair the rip in her jacket. She could still smell the gross white worms she'd stomped. She would have to clean her shoes too.

Regina took another breath, then turned around.

The garden seemed perfectly orderly, now. The same amount of spring stood on either side of the center path. No water filled the fountain, no mad winds threatened to tear her to pieces.

Suddenly, Tobias stood just on the other side of the garden entrance. He looked sad but determined.

"Remember your promise," he told her.

Then he disappeared.

Regina stood stock still for a moment. She wished she knew more curse words.

She would have to return to the garden in a fortnight. The Queen had given her word. Otherwise her brother would haunt her terribly.

Would she be able to escape the next time? Or the time after that? Or the time after that?

With a shuddering breath, Regina turned and walked back toward the dark manor house, scared but determined to figure some way out of her predicament.

REGINA PRESENTED herself at the grand gate to the back garden the next day. The tricksy spring had fled, leaving behind showers and gray. Though it was only misting, rain had already beaded up on the shoulders of her pea coat. Her curls still defied the water, spreading out like a mane around her head.

She hadn't been able to eat any of the porridge she'd found waiting for her in the formal dining room that morning. Though her dreams had been pleasant, and no ghostly voice had disturbed her sleep, she didn't feel rested, either.

Inside the back garden, rain fell harder, masking whatever madness lay there.

"Tobias," she called as she stood at the gate. "Come here," she demanded.

Tobias appeared in front of her. He wore a summer outfit now, with short pants. His feet were bare and his sleeves were rolled up.

Behind him, a wave of change rippled out, the garden growing sunny and green. "Why?" he asked, sounding petulant.

Did he look older? As if the garden had aged him? Or was he not moored in time anymore?

"I cannot visit you if I'm afraid for my life," Regina told him. "The Queen does not have to put herself in danger. Not that way."

"It wasn't me," Tobias assured her. He tried to sound innocent, but she didn't believe him.

"The Raj *must* guarantee my safety," Regina said. "That is paramount for any visit from a head of state." She'd read about Queen Elizabeth visiting bombed areas, but only once the East End had been declared safe.

Tobias turned and looked behind him, as if consulting with some unseen presence. The fountain at the back of the garden sprang to life, bubbling clear water splashing loudly enough for her to hear. Laughter followed, a young girl's, mingled with a young man's.

Regina's heart lurched. Could that be her and Tobias?

She pressed down firmly on her hope. No. That was those other people, whose lives were not hers.

She was alone with a bratty ghost of a brother who'd grown as cold as she was.

"If you came more often, the garden wouldn't be so angry," Tobias said, finally turning to look at her again.

Yes, he was definitely older than she was now, no longer eleven minutes younger.

"We have our agreement," Regina said firmly. "Is the Raj so pathetic that he cannot maintain order in his realm?"

The flare of anger that washed through Tobias made him seem much more human, much more like the brother she loved to torture. If he'd been alive, the apples of his cheeks would have turned bright red.

"Fine," he said. "You will be safe when you enter my realm."

"Thank you," Regina said stiffly. "I will see you in a fortnight."

"Until then, dear sister," Tobias said with a little bow. Then he vanished, and another ripple went through the garden, changing it from green summer to ashen winter.

Regina hurried away. That had gone much better than she'd hoped.

She still didn't trust Tobias. Or the back garden.

Who knew what other secrets lay hidden there?

A FORTNIGHT LATER, Regina returned to the back garden. The spring rains had stayed steady most of the time, the sun only peeking out every two or three days. Regina had felt as ashen as the clouds, unable to go outside even if she'd wanted to. While not a speck of dust dared gather inside the manor, Regina felt as though she'd grown covered in it, with spiders building cobwebs in her hair.

Even with the gas lights in the bathroom turned all the way up, she still felt as though she looked gray.

Her hunger had never returned either, and she found herself frequently skipping meals, though her appearance remained the same and she hadn't grown as gaunt as she'd felt.

That morning, however, the sun had returned in all his glory. The robins sang carols of joy. Spring breezes carried the smells of freshly plowed fields, newly mowed grass, and sweet heather. Regina actually skipped along one of the brick paths, surprised at how far she could go without losing her breath once.

Then she turned the corner. Up ahead lay the entrance to the back garden.

She stopped, the winds suddenly cold. Her palms felt clammy. The grayness she'd felt the past two weeks doubled.

She could do this. The Raj had given his word. She would be safe in his realm.

Well, safe enough.

Regina ran her hands over her hair, trying to press down on her curls. She really was going to cut it all off someday. Then run away, maybe all the way to America.

Except that she suspected no matter where she went, her brother would find her.

Regina paused at the entrance of the back garden. It looked to her as if the garden couldn't make up its mind, the seasons changing as she watched, the flower beds winter bare, then filled with autumn stems, then sprouting with the green folly of spring.

"You promised," Regina said out loud as she stepped into the garden.

No rough winds accosted her. No wild thorns tried to detain her. The flower beds continued their backwards dance through the seasons. The birds sang out in a merry song, and the sunlight beat down warm on her head. She might have to take off her coat before too long, though she still found herself carrying the spring chill, despite how she'd skipped and skipped.

The fountain stayed still, a silent reminder of happier times. Tobias stood to one side of it, next to the bench he'd died on.

Chill winds sprang up as Regina approached.

Or maybe that was just air from beyond the grave.

Tobias had grown older, still. He stood taller than her, now. He wore old-fashioned trousers, held up with an unfamiliar black belt. His shirt seemed to come from an early era as well, with wide stripes in a color she couldn't guess.

"Greetings, dear sister," Tobias said formally. "Please, won't you come sit with me?"

Regina refused to allow her uncertainty to show. "Of course," she said, walking forward to sit on the bench, then not moving when Tobias sat beside her.

"How have you been?" Regina asked after a few moments of silence.

The smile Tobias gave her chilled her very soul. "That's the wrong question," he said. "The real question is how do *you* feel?"

Regina wasn't about to tell him the truth, or to try to explain how wan and worn out that she'd felt. "I'm fine," she said, raising her chin defiantly. Stiff upper lip and all that.

Tobias just shook his head. "Ah sister," he said. "You still don't know."

Behind him, the fountain sprang gently to life. A summer sun shone down on the sparkling water. Regina could almost feel the soft spray on her bare legs.

A young woman approached the fountain from the far side. She also wore old-fashioned clothes, a long sheath dress with cap sleeves in a pattern of small flowers on it. She was barefoot, and sat on the curve of the fountain, dipping her toes in the water.

Regina felt the water as the woman did, felt the warm sunlight and the lazy, slow time.

"No," Regina said, tearing her eyes away from the apparition that was *not* real, could not be real. "You say I still don't know. Don't know what?"

"The fountain caught you the last time you were here," Tobias explained.

"What do you mean?" Regina said, standing.

Her blood should be pounding. Her heart trying to beat its way out of her chest. Why was she still so cold? So calm? More silent than any portrait of the Queen?

"That's the real you," Tobias said, pointing at the fountain and the young woman—the older Regina—sitting there. "You're the ghost, now."

"That's not possible," Regina said. She held her hands out in front of herself. She wasn't as pale as Tobias. Wasn't gray like a ghost. Wasn't just a shade of her former self.

Despite how dim and lifeless she felt.

Tobias laughed, sending chills across her shoulders.

Surely she shouldn't be able to feel goosebumps if she no longer had flesh? *She* was the real Regina. Not that specter over there.

"I promised to look after you, keep you safe. And I can do that, now," Tobias told her. "But you've forgotten what kingdom the Raj has command over."

Regina gasped. Tobias was right. He didn't have control over the garden. Neither the Raj or the Queen ruled here.

The Raj's realm only included the dead.

Tobias rose and walked away, slipping into that happier summertime, sitting down next to her alter-ego on the fountain. She heard the tinkling laughter as he splashed her.

Stormily, Regina turned and started marching up the main path. Figures traipsed along the other paths, ghosts that she refused to see: the Púca and the goat man, the Vicar and his wife, even the servants who she occasionally caught a glimpse of in the estate.

She was *not* the lone ghost remaining on the estate, haunting the schoolroom and reading fairytales out loud to herself. She would prove Tobias wrong. She *would* age beyond her ten years and one hundred and fifty-eight days.

She would find colors other than gray in her life. Would do more than just dream of yellow saffron and black lace.

ABOUT THE AUTHOR

Leah Cutter writes page-turning fiction in exotic locations, such as a magical New Orleans, the ancient Orient, Hungary, the Oregon coast, rural Kentucky, Seattle, Minneapolis, and many others.

She writes literary, fantasy, mystery, science fiction, and horror fiction. Her short fiction has been published in magazines like *Alfred Hitchcock's Mystery Magazine* and *Talebones*, anthologies like *Fiction River*, and on the web. Her long fiction has been published both by New York publishers as well as small presses.

Find out more about Leah at:
https://leahcutter.com

goodreads.com/leah_cutter

facebook.com/leah.cutter

bookbub.com/authors/leah-cutter

amazon.com/Leah-R-Cutter/e/B001H6WDEM

A SPICE MOST DEMANDING

ROBERT JESCHONEK

"ONE MORE, PLEASE, HOMAN."

The middle-aged, overweight man at the corner of the bar slides another hundred-dollar bill across the polished mahogany, then follows it with two more.

It's five minutes till closing time, but I figure what the hell. I'll give him another shot of what he needs.

"Another of the same, then, Ron?" I smile as I walk the length of the bar, straightening my button-down black shirt. He's one of my best customers, and a very decent man; there's no need to make him feel bad about his addiction.

The desperate look in his slightly bulging eyes tells me he suffers more than enough because of those appetites of his. "Make it a double, Homan."

"A double it is." Turning, I admire my face in the mirror behind the shelves—wavy salt-and-pepper hair, smoldering dark eyes, angular cheekbones. As vices go, vanity isn't so bad; I like the way I look, so sue me. The confidence helps me handle the customers here at my place, The Unicorn's Egg in downtown Philadelphia. It helps me, as I serve them, to give them a little show, which frankly is a big part of what I deliver.

Done checking myself in the mirror, I grab what I need from the shelf and turn back to Ron, who is watching my every move. A fine sweat appears on his forehead, and he wipes it dry—but then *presto chango*, it moves to his upper lip.

I put the item I've retrieved on the bar and wave my hands over it—a candle that lights with nothing more than a few whispered words from my lips. Some more choice words, and the candle flame flares brightly, forcing Ron to shield his eyes with one thick arm.

When the light fades, the bar is alive with what he *really* wants —*magic*.

This time, it comes in the form of tiny dancing girls in diaphanous silk costumes, gyrating across the mahogany. There are a dozen of them, double what I conjured for Ron fifteen minutes ago...and every one of them is stunningly beautiful behind her rippling veils.

"P-perfect." Ron's voice quivers as he speaks. His glittering eyes never budge from the undulating beauties before him. "Homan, you have *outdone* yourself!"

"Good to hear it, Ron." Part of me is happy about his praise; after all, magic is my game, and helping those with a taste for it is my business. But another part of me pities him, because I know his desires will forever control him. Some folks shake the magic monkey off their backs sooner or later, but Ron Hockenberry will *never* be one of them.

Neither will I, though *my* monkey—the reason a very strong warlock has exiled himself to running this back-alley magic bar—is quite different. *My* monkey has more to do with not letting go of an unforgivable and costly mistake of the past.

"Just *look* at them." He can barely control his delight. "Each one is *different* in her own way. And they all look like they *adore* me."

"They do, Ron. Every last one of them." I reach for a little canister on the shelf and pry the lid off. Sticking three fingers inside, I pinch out some of the gold and silver glitter and sprinkle it over the dancing girls. They glow and twinkle in the low light of the bar, and the tempo of their sensuous dance increases.

Ron's voice drops to a whisper. *"Dear God!"* He leans his arms on the edge of the bar and rests his chin on top of them, gazing at the hypnotic scene playing out in front of him.

"Five more minutes, Ron. Then I'm kicking you out."

"Uh-huh." I know he didn't hear a single word I said. All he thinks about, all he sees, are those hypnotically gyrating bellies, those beautiful faces.

He is *lost*, under their spell. *My* spell, technically…but magic just the same. Does that make me an *enabler?*

Walking out from behind the bar, I head for the door to lock it, keeping out additional customers for the night. "Just don't make a mess when you *snort* them."

"Uh-huh."

Just as I reach for the doorknob, it glides away from me. The door opens outward, and I find myself face-to-face with two strangers I'll have to turn away.

"Sorry," I tell them. "We're closed for the night."

"Why?" One of the newcomers, a dark-haired young man who looks like he could be in his twenties, smirks back at me. Between his red-and-black flannel shirt, his bushy Van Dyke beard, and his black disk earrings, he looks like a hipster to me. "*Booze* is not what *you're* selling, is it, Mr. Teatree?"

"As I said, we're *closed.*" I push forward, making a grab for the door.

"But why?" says the young man.

"Because it's *my* place, and I *said* so." I get my hand on the door and tug, but it goes nowhere. The newcomer has an iron grip on it, though he doesn't look as if he's making the slightest effort.

"Of course." The young man's tone changes, losing some of its smirky edge. "Nevertheless, I hope you will hear me out. My name is Oliver Box." He makes a slight bow, then gestures at the withered old man beside him. "And this is my friend, Mr. Lockhart Whittle."

Whittle shook as he nodded behind his long white beard. He looked either baffled or troubled, I couldn't tell which.

"I've heard you occasionally do some *pro bono* work," says Oliver. "In the interest of helping the truly needy, like Oliver here."

"Okay, listen." I let go of the door and step forward, intruding in Oliver's space. "Unless you want me to strike you down here and now — which I *can* do—you'll walk away and come back some other time…or *never.* We are *closed.*"

No sooner do the words leave my lips than I'm standing alone in the doorway, looking out at an empty sidewalk. Whirling, I look back into the bar, and there they are—Oliver and Lockhart, gazing admiringly over Ron's shoulder at the dancing girls.

I can't believe it! The son of a bitch played a *trick* on me! In the doorway of my *own place.* Clearly, he has some *magic* up his sleeve.

"Hey!" I storm back into The Unicorn's Egg, fit to be tied. "Now I *know* I want you out of here!"

Oliver's expression when he looks my way is one of complete innocence. "Wait, why? It was just a little *misdirection…*"

"Meaning you're a magician in your own right!" I clamp a hand on his shoulder and pull him away from Ron. "You don't need *my* help."

"I totally *do*," says Oliver. "All I know are a few *parlor tricks*. You're a full-blown *warlock!* You can do shit like *that.*"

He gestures at the dancing girls, just as Ron pulls The Big Straw out of the pocket of his suit jacket. It's a large-bore silver straw, about the size of a straw used to drink bubble-tea, carved with intricate scrollwork and inlaid with tiny multicolored diadems.

"Wait, what's *that* all about?" asks Oliver.

Without a word, Ron sticks one end of the straw in his nose and leans forward, directing the other end at the dancing girls. They never stop shimmying as he suddenly inhales, funneling all of them into the straw in one swirling, rainbow stream.

Ron's head bumps back as the burst of magic hits home, and he gasps. Eyes glazed over, he wipes his nose with the back of his hand, then lowers the straw to the bar and vacuums up any residue that remains.

"Oh, I see." Oliver turns and puts his arm around Lockhart, pulling him close. "All the more reason to do some *pro bono* work for Lockhart here. Make up for some of the *magiholics* you've been keeping *hooked* as a *dealer.*"

Just as I'm about to say something to shut him down, Ron jumps up from his bar stool and runs after one of the dancers who somehow broke away. She's not really running, just wriggling across the floor, and he quickly catches up.

Then he *steps* on her, smashing her flat, and drops to his knees. He jabs The Big Straw into the smashed, twitching body of the dancing girl and snorts it up with one mighty huff and a cry of orgasmic ecstasy.

The sight gives me just enough of a pang of uncertainty that I back down the rage in my chest. When *was* the last time I did anything *pro bono*, like helping a customer kick the magic habit he or she developed in my establishment? Maybe it wouldn't *kill* me to do someone a favor.

"All right." I sigh and keep watching Ron scrabble around on the floor after a few last mystical wisps. Wish I could say it's the *first* time I've seen him do that. "Tell me what Lockhart wants, and we'll see."

"Thanks," says Oliver. "I swear, this will be easy. All he wants to do is *remember* something he's *lost.*"

When Ron finally leaves, I lock the door, switch off the outside lights, and dim the inside ones. Then I switch off the ringer on my phone and meet Oliver and Lockhart at the bar.

The place looks different with the lights down, more like a darkened cellar than a den or study. The walls are painted with sigils and lined with magical artifacts above the mahogany wainscoting—a battered top hat and magic wand here, a bust of Anubis there. Those walls have a lot of power on them, though hardly anyone who looks at them fully realizes it.

What about Oliver? Too soon to tell. I stand behind the bar and stare into his eyes, probing with all my strange senses, and I get nothing. He's just *there*, with the old man at his side for reasons I've yet to fully fathom.

"So what have you lost?" I ask Lockhart.

"Almost everything," says Oliver. "There isn't much of him left, thanks to the Alzheimer's."

Lockhart narrows his eyes at me. His mouth works, but no audible words come out.

"I'm no dementia specialist." I fold my arms across my chest and shake my head. "I don't know of any workings that can restore a mind so damaged at this stage."

"What about retrieving *one* memory?" Oliver reaches into his shirt pocket and brings out a white ring case, as if he's about to propose. "Perhaps with some *guidance* to help his focus?"

Suspicion shoots through me like a stray shot through my front window. "Why only *one* memory? What makes *that* memory special?"

"It's his favorite." Oliver smiles warmly and plunks the ring case down on the bar. "He wants to experience it one more time before the end."

"How does he *know* that, if he can't *remember* it?"

"He remembers a little. Enough to want the rest with all his heart." Oliver taps the ring case with his index finger. "*This* sparks fragments for him. I'm hoping you can use it to channel the rest."

He pushes the ring case across the bar, and I take it. "No promises," I tell him. "I haven't done anything like this in a very long time."

"Give it a shot," says Oliver. "It'll mean the world to him if you can do this."

With a noncommittal grunt, I open the case—and there's no ring in there at all. Instead, tucked between satiny white folds, I see an Indian arrowhead carved from shiny gray flint.

"His favorite memory?" I pull out the arrowhead and hold it up for a closer look. The flint fizzes a little in my fingertips, effervescing with traces of magic. "Got any clues for me?"

Oliver nudges Lockhart, waking him from an unexpected nap. "Remember this?" He grabs my hand and pulls it over in front of Lockhart's face.

The old man makes a gargling sound in his throat and nods off again. Oliver responds by grabbing Lockhart's left hand and smacking it down on top of my hand holding the arrowhead.

"It happened when he was a boy," says Oliver. "Something about an old woman who took him in and gave him the arrowhead."

Suddenly, Lockhart's eyes snap open, and he whispers a name. "Henrietta."

The fizzing from the arrowhead becomes prickling, like needles jabbing my fingers. When it turns from that into stabbing jolts of pain, I jerk away from Oliver's grasp.

"Ah." Oliver nods knowingly. "You're getting something."

"Getting *stung*, maybe." Turning, I put down the arrowhead and rummage through the shelves behind me, pulling out a few ingredients I need. There are best practices to be followed for every working under the sun, and going in unprepared isn't part of any of them.

Of the three items I place on the bar, I open the little silver tin first and pinch out just enough powdered wolfs bane. Sprinkling the powder in a hexagram form on the bar, I open the vial of foul-smelling liquid next. Dabbing a drop of that on each point and the middle of the hexagram, I finally open the blue-lidded Tupperware bowl full of mummified monkey-paws and take one out. When I wave it over the hexagram and whisper the right words, the whole design glows with a gentle green flame.

"Let's try that again." I reach for Lockhart's hand and hold it above the heart of the pentagram. He yelps softly as I score his parchment-thin flesh with the arrowhead, letting droplets of his blood drip down to mingle with the pungent liquid below.

This time, a strong tingle flickers up my arm and lingers without becoming jolts of pain. Our hands blur together, and the porous borders of his mind give way to gentle pressure from my own.

His memory, when I reach it, is like a gray garden of dusty still lifes—faces, places, and objects hanging frozen like Spanish moss from the boughs of crooked trees. They thicken as I move deeper, many broken and incomplete like statues in the ruins of a Roman villa. Finding the one memory we seek is the proverbial hunt for a needle in a haystack.

"Lockhart." I tighten my grip on his hand, squeezing his blood between my fingers. "Remember the arrowhead. Remember when you *got* it."

Lockhart crushes his eyes shut and tosses his head from side to side. Under that long white mane, I feel him casting about for the arrowhead memory, flailing—finding only random still lifes and firefly flickers of pain or pleasure.

Then, without warning, a memory flares to life within him, around me. I know without a doubt that this is it, the right one, and I transmit it back to the pentagram on the bar.

It plays out there like Ron's dancing girls, and Oliver is trans-fixed. As for Lockhart and me, we watch mostly in the confines of Lockhart's mind, where everything's a little more high-def than the version playing in the dim light *outside* his head.

In the memory, a heavyset old woman lies in bed, eyes shut, panting for breath. A little boy stands beside her, frowning at her form under the blankets. Judging from the room's furnishings and the boy's attire, the scene is set sometime in the early 20th century.

A middle-aged doctor with wavy red hair and dense freckles walks over and steps in front of the boy, who backs away. The doctor places the bell of his stethoscope on the woman's chest and listens, then shakes his head.

Not much longer now, Lockhart. That's what the doctor says. *I'm so sorry, but your mom is about to pass.*

Foster mom. Lockhart's words are loaded with hate. *Never my real mom.*

The doctor pulls a cigarette from the pocket of his old-fashioned black vest and lights it with a match. *Do you have anyone else to stay with?* he asks the boy.

Little Lockhart shrugs. *I'll be fine, Doctor Donnelly. I'll be just fine.*

You're a brave one. Donnelly smiles and ruffles Lockhart's fine blond hair. *Call me Ronan. And, you know, there might be one more thing we can try.*

Dr. Donnelly plugs the cigarette in his mouth and undoes his black-and-white-striped tie. Then, he unbuttons his white dress shirt and reaches behind his undershirt to pull out a crystal vial hanging by a gold chain around his neck.

I got this from a gypsy woman back in Ireland, and I've been saving it for a special occasion ever since. She said it has the power to bring the almost-dead back to life.

Dr. Donnelly unclasps the chain and lifts the vial clear of his throat. He flicks the cap off and passes it under Lockhart's nose to give him a whiff.

The gypsy called it silphium. An ancient spice treasured by the Romans and lost in the mists of history. It hasn't grown on the face of the Earth since the Roman Empire fell, she said.

Lockhart's eyes light up instantly. He has never smelled anything like it—a spice so aromatic and powerful, it mesmerizes him. As soon as the faintest wisp of it drifts into his nose, he immediately wants more, wants to rub his whole face in it.

But Lockhart never gets the chance. Dr. Donnelly whisks the vial past him and holds it over the old woman's open mouth, then taps in a few grains of it.

Little Lockhart doesn't want the doctor to waste it on her, wants it all for himself, but it's too late. The grains disappear between her lips, and her tongue flickers out to taste them.

Will she wake up? Lockhart prays the answer will be no. He prays she won't go back to beating the living shit out of him every time a whim strikes her.

Dr. Donnelly caps the vial and returns it to his neck. Then he pulls something out of his vest pocket and hands it to Lockhart with a warm smile.

The Indian arrowhead.

This is for you, Lockhart. Try not to worry about your mom.

I won't. The arrowhead fascinates Lockhart.

All we can do is pray, says the doctor.

I'm praying already, says Lockhart, though the truth is, he is praying for her to die.

"THANK YOU," says Oliver after the memory has run its course and faded away. "He *knew* that arrowhead was important somehow, but he couldn't remember *why.* It was driving him *crazy.*"

I wipe off the bar with a ward-embroidered cloth, cleaning up the residue of the spell I cast. Lockhart, meanwhile, just sits there and stares at my hand as if he's torn between kissing it and stabbing it.

"V-very important," he mumbles.

"That was wonderful work." Oliver grins and shakes his head admiringly. "You are *extraordinarily* talented, my friend. I heard you were *good,* but not *this* good."

I shoot him a scowl. "You heard it from *whom?*"

He doesn't answer the question. "You recreated that memory in full 3-D, complete with *audio* and *emotional resonance.* All that from the Alzheimer's-riddled brain of one infantilized old man. I can still hardly believe the *quality* of your constructs."

"Thanks." I enjoy flattery as much as the next person, but it's four in the morning at this point. I'm more than ready for the two of them to leave. "I'm glad I could help."

As I walk out from behind the bar to urge them on their way, Oliver throws an arm around my shoulders. "I've never seen someone as good as *you* are doing *pro bono* in a joint like *this* before."

"It's *my* joint, all right?" I shake off his arm and head for the door.

"I'm just saying, with that kind of *power* and *control*, you could be king of the *warlocks* or something."

"Who says I'm not?" I turn it into a joke so we can end this on a happy note. "Maybe I just like keeping a low profile."

Oliver laughs and fetches Lockhart from the bar. As he leads him out the door, he pauses for one more question.

"Have you ever done anything more…*lifelike*, Homan?"

"Good night, Oliver. Safe travels home." I shoo him and Lock-hart a little further out the door.

"I'm talking about *from scratch. You* know. Like what you just did in there but *bigger.* More *real.* More *permanent.*"

"Thanks again for stopping by!" I physically push Oliver clear of the door. "Have a great morning!"

Then I shut the door hard behind him, breathing a sigh of relief that I'm finally alone again—even if his last words continue to haunt me more than I'd like.

How DOES a warlock live out his days? You might be surprised.

I sleep, I work, I eat, I binge-watch Netflix, just like you. I drive a car, I go shopping, I pay my bills, I answer the phone, just like you. The magic I use and the things I can do don't make much differ-ence in the grand scheme of things.

It doesn't change the feelings I have, either. I'm still just a person, capable of happiness, sorrow, anger, despair…and regret.

Sometimes, when I look back at some of the things I've done with my power, I feel a *lot* of regret, in fact. It doesn't matter that

I'm not the same person, that I've learned from my mistakes. They keep coming back to me, day after day, no matter what I do. There's no spell in the world that can change that. It's beyond the reach of magic and science together, for once.

Especially because the *price* was so high. The price of my greatest mistake, the one Oliver made me think of, continues to haunt me. It makes my existence a twisted shadow of what it once was.

All because of something brought to life at my hands, conjured from *scratch*, as Oliver said.

"HOMAN! HELLO AGAIN!"

One year and one month later, Oliver enters my bar again, all smiles. This time, he's pushing a wheelchair with another old man in it—a man even older and more decrepit than Lockhart.

"Oliver." I don't bother shutting down the multiple magic shows I've got running for various customers around the place, as I'd do if someone uninitiated walked in. Oliver already knows the deal in here; the minotaur on the bar and the blue, six-armed goddess chanting on a table are no surprise to him.

"Up for some more *pro bono* work, my friend?" Oliver gestures at the withered form in the chair—a veritable bag of bones in a hospital gown, milky eyes lolling in a bobbing, bald skull. "This is my friend, Ronan Donnelly."

I frown at the name, which sounds familiar. "And once again, you've chosen closing time to revisit my establishment."

Oliver winks. "Not an accident, Homey." He moves a chair from a nearby table and pushes Ronan up as close to the edge as he can.

"Leave it at Homan." I sigh and shake my head, not at all in the mood...but he hasn't bothered me for over a year, so at least I'll hear him out. "So what exactly do you want?"

"Same as last time," says Oliver. "He needs help remembering his favorite memory. Could you find and bring it to life like you did for Lockhart, God rest his soul?"

"I don't know," I tell him. "If there's nothing *left* of it, no amount of *working* will bring it back."

"Understood, understood." Oliver, who's wearing a black business suit with black vest, black shirt, and crimson necktie and ear disks, reaches into a pocket of his vest. "Here's a little something to help the two of you focus."

I start to protest, then give up and take the object from him. It's a single playing card, the six of spades, with an elaborate design of dark blue curlicues and clock faces on the back.

I hold up the card in front of Ronan, and he shows no recognition or even awareness of its presence. The man is so far gone, I'm frankly surprised he's still breathing.

That said, I still feel the need to balance my enabling of addicts with a little genuine *pro bono* for those in need...so I make up my mind to take a shot.

"Just give me a few minutes." I pocket the card and head off to close the joint for the night. "We'll see if anything develops."

AFTER EVERYONE HAS GONE but us three, I map a pentagram on the table, then take Ronan's hand and focus in on the world in his head —what's left of it.

Interestingly, his mind is much more crowded than Lockhart's was—but the contents are less well-defined. There are people without faces or identifying characteristics...objects of indistinct form or function...and places of unsettling vagueness and monotonous gloom.

If anything, the lack of detail and abundance of content makes my job more difficult. It's like wading through an ocean of pie dough and cotton, trying to find a single piece that can be teased into any kind of color and life.

But the playing card provides a guiding tingle that leads to something glowing faintly in a distant corner. Ronan, who barely seemed alive until now, reacts with sudden agitation; his excitement provides the energy and certainty I need to coax detail from the dough, making it rise as if by yeast and attain definition and the fire of life.

As soon as the moment is fully baked, I shunt it to the tabletop between us. It plays out there in miniature, complete with sound and true-to-life lighting and movement—just like the scene that had played so well over a year ago for poor Lockhart.

In the memory on the table, a woman sits by a campfire near a gypsy wagon in the woods of West Virginia. She wears a colorful dress—all reds and purples—and covers her hair with a silken scarf of scarlet and yellow.

As she sits before the dancing flames, a teenage boy steps into the shot. He wears a torn and blood-stained white t-shirt, mud-caked blue jeans, and damaged sneakers.

Please won't you read my fortune, Madame Zaba? asks the boy. *Just a little bit of it?*

I read it before you got here. When the gypsy waves a playing card over the flames, they dance more energetically. The card is the same six of spades that Oliver handed me earlier. *It makes me shiver to think about it.*

Why? What do you mean? The boy shifts uncomfortably from one foot to the other.

The gypsy gazes up at him with eyes narrowed. *I know what lurks inside of you. I know the terrible things it drives you to* do. *And I know the far worse things you will do in the future because of it.*

I don't... Young Ronan doesn't finish the sentence. *What kind of things in the future?*

You already know. You have big *plans, don't you?*

Young Ronan scowls and doesn't answer.

What if I told you there is another way? says the gypsy. *A way with just as much blood, hundreds of times as much death, and none of the horror. A life you would spend as something other than a monster, while still meeting the awful needs inside you.*

Old Ronan's eyes seem to clear, and he leans closer to the memory playing out before him. *"Neeeed."* He whispers the word like a prayer, like an oath, like a term of endearment.

Tell me more. In the vision, young Ronan sits down in the dirt across the fire from the gypsy.

I'll do better than that. I'll give you this. The woman tucks the playing card under her head scarf, then lifts a vial on a gold chain around her throat. *It is an ancient substance, capable of miracles and wonders you cannot imagine. If you* slip, *if you fall back into your darkling ways, it will enable you to bring* life *to that which is* dead.

Really? Young Ronan's eyes widen.

But only a few times. Only a few grains of it remain. And this is the last of it in the world. There is no more of it anywhere on Earth.

Then why give it to me?

It has given me a very long life, but the goddess who gave it to me said the day would come when I would have to give it to someone else. I give it to you now to prevent your darkness from coming into its full flower. To keep you on the path of saving more lives than losing them.

Saving lives how?

By practicing medicine. Becoming a doctor. And this precious substance will undo your excesses when they come. This precious silphium, last of its kind.

Slow on the uptake as I've been, it's only now that I finally remember and understand. It's the same vial from Lockhart's vision a year and a month ago, the one used by the doctor to save the dying foster mother…and the boy in *this* vision *is* that doctor.

Doctor Donnelly. The boy sounds it out. *Maybe.*

Already, your future is changing. The gypsy flutters her hands, and the jingling of the little bells on her sleeves mixes with the crackle of the jumping flames. *Say it one more time. Tell me what you will become!*

"Doctor Donnelly," says the ancient man in the wheelchair. "Call me Doctor Donnelly."

"Explain yourself."

When the memory runs its course and dissolves, I drag Oliver away from the table, leaving Ronan to scrabble feebly at the now-empty air where the gypsy was briefly recreated.

"Thank you, my friend." Oliver nods gratefully. "You've done that old man a world of good."

"He was the *doctor* in the memory I dredged out of *Lockhart*. The two are *connected*." I grab Oliver's lapels and wrench him closer. "What's the *real* story behind this so-called *pro bono* work?"

"Of *course* they're connected." Oliver smiles calmly. "They're both from the same part of West Virginia. It makes perfect sense."

"There's a *reason* you *brought* them here. There's something you're not *telling* me. A *secret* of some kind."

"Not at all." He shakes his head. "But have you given any more thought to what I asked you about last time? Doing something more *lifelike* and *permanent?*"

"Never," I tell him firmly. "That's something I'll never do again."

"And why is that?" asks Oliver. "You never did say."

"None of your business."

"*Now* who's the secret keeper?" Oliver winks and turns away from me, going back to the table to retrieve Dr. Donnelly.

Leaving me to wonder what his game is, and how I might possibly find out.

MAKING something truly lifelike is like being God, with all the amazing joy and gut-wrenching horror you might imagine could come with it.

I only knew the *joy* of that experience until I got around to making a fake *wife* for myself. I think about her again as I close the bar and return to my upstairs apartment for the night.

Her name was Marissa, because that was my *real* wife's name. She was much like Real Marissa in many ways—yet *different*. *Prettier. Younger. Flirtier. Flashier.* A better *dancer.*

Think Marissa 2.0.

This was years ago, back when I *had* a wife…when I worked a full-time job and owned a house and kept my powers pretty much under my hat. Fake Marissa was the exception to that tendency, and a rare one at that. I only conjured her up on special occasions, when I wanted to make an extra-special splash. When, in my opinion, the original, unenhanced Marissa just wouldn't do. I only brought her back when I needed to make a great impression on a client or a boss. I hardly ever had her around much at all.

At first.

THREE MONTHS after I recreated the fateful meeting with the gypsy from Dr. Donnelly's memory, Oliver comes back to The Unicorn's Egg. This time, he's back in flannel (blue and gray plaid) with white ear disks and has an old woman with him, again in a wheelchair—so ancient in appearance that it seems a miracle she is still drawing breath.

After the last time, I don't want anything to do with either of them. Oliver has been keeping secrets from me; I have no desire to get caught up in something about which I know so little.

"Find someone else to reconstruct memories for you," I tell him. "I've got a bar to run."

"Please, Homan, please." Oliver winces and squeezes my arm. "She's so far gone, she can barely remember to keep breathing. Won't you give her just one more moment of remembered happiness before the end?"

"Maybe if you tell me your *secret*. Maybe if you tell me why you're *really* doing all this."

"I already *have.*"

"*Bullshit.*" I hiss the word between my teeth. The three patrons still in the bar pay no notice, preferring instead to continue watching the magic creations I've conjured on their tabletops or the surface of the bar. "What's your game, Oliver? What are you looking for?"

Oliver sighs. "If we find it, you'll be the first to know, all right? I promise." Reaching into a pocket of his suit jacket, he pulls out a weathered gray coin the size of a nickel and hands it over. "This ought to help you excavate the memory we need."

Holding up the coin, I see an image of the two-faced Roman

god Janus on one side. On the other, there is an inscription in Latin and a faded engraving of a plant with broad leaves and bunches of flowers.

"This is ancient." I turn the coin over and over between my fingers. "I can *feel* its antiquity."

"Let's see what it brings to light, shall we?" Oliver takes my arm and tries guiding me toward the old woman.

I hesitate. Could this be another step in a *trap* whose outlines I still can't see?

"Come on." Oliver gives my arm another tug. "I'll even *pay* you, okay? Forget *pro bono*. I'll pay you five hundred dollars."

"It's not about money." I stare at the coin, then the woman, then Oliver. "Why should I *trust* you?"

"Why *shouldn't* you?" Oliver smiles and shrugs. "What have you got to *lose?*"

Nothing, perhaps. Oliver gives off no waves of magical power that I can detect; I can't imagine he poses any threat to me. Plus which, he *needs* me to perform these memory probes. Why would he hurt or kill someone who's giving him what he needs?

I'm still edgy about this whole thing, but I decide to try one more working on his behalf. He might be hiding something, but maybe I can solve the mystery myself…and in the process, satisfy my curiosity.

"Once more." I let him guide me to the table where the old woman waits. "Once more and then I'm done with this."

"Thanks, buddy." Oliver pats my back affectionately. "Hopefully, the third time will be the charm."

AGAIN, I swim deep through a damaged mind, this one the emptiest and quietest yet. You might think it would be easier to find what I'm looking for here, but it's not; it seems to take forever, poking through the ashes and mist for the slightest signs of life.

Eventually, though, I come across something that is stirred by the coin—something in seemingly the furthermost quadrant of the wasteland…and therefore, the most ancient.

I have to coax it from the faintest spark, like blowing a glowing ember back to life as a flame. It takes most of my considerable talent and power to make it rise, give it any kind of substance and shape. Even then, parts of the memory are missing, distorted, or out of synch; it takes even more of what I have to patch and correct it, hold it together, and make it watchable. Then I carry it out carefully like an unsteady wedding cake and deposit it on the table between us.

And it plays. For the first time in what I think might be thousands of years, the memory plays and is witnessed.

The scene takes place in what looks like an ancient temple with columns all around. A dark-haired woman in a toga kneels in supplication before an altar littered with fruits, vegetables, and flowers, her head bowed and arms upraised.

As we watch, a female voice rises and echoes in the temple, calling out in Latin, which I translate into English. *Zaba. Zaba, arise.*

Even before the dark-haired woman lifts her head and rises, I know who she is. I recognize the name from Oliver's last client, his last visit to my bar.

The woman with the long, dark hair, clad in a toga, is the same woman who played the role of a gypsy in Dr. Donnelly's memory… only much younger, in her twenties perhaps. Zaba and Madame Zaba are one and the same—and the woman in the wheelchair across the table from me is what's left of her now.

O beloved Ceres. Zaba speaks also in Latin, which I also translate. *My husband, governor of Cyrene, is in great danger.*

What does this have to do with me? asks the voice of Ceres from all directions in the temple.

You are the goddess of growing things, says Zaba. *I come to beg you to restore the crop of* silphium *to our city. If it continues to die out, we will lose our livelihood, and my husband will lose* everything.

Silphium. As Ceres says it, she fades into view behind the altar, manifesting her physical form as a beautiful blonde woman in flowing robes. *Do you think your faithless people truly deserve this wondrous herb?*

Faithless?

Many of you turn to the Nazarene, says Ceres. *You betray your true gods and the ancient rites in favor of the charlatan Jew. Do not expect the gifts of the gods of your ancestors to continue in the face of such blasphemy.*

Please, my lady. Give us another chance! Bring the silphium back to life, and I will do anything!

Anything?

I will pay any price, says Zaba. *No sacrifice is too great if it means that miracle plant will grow again in the fields of Cyrene.*

I should give you people nothing. Ceres' voice is flat. *You are truly a feckless and wicked lot. Do you even* know *what triggered the decline of your precious silphium?*

Our loss of faith?

Try murder! Ceres' voice booms like thunder and rattles the wind chimes hanging between the stately columns of the temple. *For the mystic herb to grow, it had to be specially tended by an* avatar *spun from the very substance of the plant! I gave this avatar life, and she wandered the fields night and day, keeping the delicate spice healthy and plentiful. For centuries, the balance has been maintained, until last week, when my avatar was cravenly murdered!*

Milady Ceres, please don't punish us all for the crimes of a few.

I will punish whom I choose! At Ceres' cry, the temple shakes, and the ground beneath it rumbles and splits. *You, of all people, do not command me!*

M-me?

Your husband is the killer! When you found out, you covered it up!

Eyes wide, Zaba cowers before the rage of Ceres, who proceeds to float up toward the high, domed ceiling.

You do not deny it? howls Ceres.

Zaba looks away, then back. *I deny only that all of Cyrene should suffer for this crime. Please answer my prayer and punish only* me.

You are mad! says Ceres.

If one must die, let it be the one who cannot keep a roof over our children's heads or food in their bellies.

69

What do I care about the children of a killer?

Because one of them is your granddaughter!

The temple is quiet for a long moment. Then, Ceres floats back down to Earth—in front of the altar this time. *You are raising...the child of my avatar...as your own?*

Yes, says Zaba. *The child whose mother was murdered by my husband because she was carrying* another *of his spawn, and she refused to stop its birth with the nectar of the very plant she tended.*

Silphium. Ceres stares into space for a moment. *How is it that I did not know this child was my own granddaughter?*

Your daughter hid the truth from you with spells from a Bacchanalian witch. She feared you might be angry if you found out she'd consorted with a mortal man—a married one, at that—and take the child away from her.

She was right to do that, says Ceres. *I* would *have taken the child.*

Yes, milady.

Ceres thinks for a moment, then extends her hands over Zaba. *Very well. You have convinced me your cause is just.*

Thank you, great lady, says Zaba.

One more avatar then...but only one. Ceres weaves her hands through the air, leaving an intricate trail of golden light. *If any harm comes to her, silphium will vanish from the face of the Earth forever.*

I shall pledge myself to her protection.

Yes, you will. Forever. Ceres claps her hands together, and a shower of sparks rains down over Zaba. *You are immortal now. And* she *is your charge.*

Ceres' hands swoop and slash overhead, then flare with blinding light. When the light fades, a beautiful young woman stands before Zaba, her long, brown hair draped over a glittering gold tunic.

She is the female of the species, says Ceres. *Only she can keep the species, the silphium, alive and thriving.*

Thank you, great Ceres! cries Zaba. *I will guard her the rest of my days! I will never break your trust!*

You lie, as all mortals do, says Ceres. *But for today, it is enough. Meet your charge, woman. Her name is* Proserpina.

Proserpina offers her hand, and Zaba takes it.

I swear, says Zaba, *I shall protect you, dear Proserpina, for as long as my heart shall beat.*

Then, Zaba kisses the hand, and all the wondrous flavors of fabled silphium rush into her in one incredible, disorienting gust.

Just as that happens in the memory, I feel the barrel of a gun pressed against my right temple, and hear the voice of Oliver whisper behind it.

"Whatever you do, don't stop tapping this memory," says Oliver. "I need you to use it to bring Proserpina back to life."

REMEMBER MY FAKE WIFE? How I only brought her to life on special occasions when the *real* Marissa couldn't live up to the demands of my vanity?

Eventually, that all changed. Fake Marissa was so much *better* than the real thing that I kept her around more and more. Eventually, I stopped un-working her altogether, and set her up in an apartment that I visited frequently.

Only to realize, one night, that she wasn't where she was supposed to be. Only to find, when I went home, that she'd gone there instead, and murdered the Real Marissa with her bare hands.

Because, of course, she was in so much better shape than the real thing, wasn't she?

At least until I undid her forever. At which point, as I watched her melt away like a snowflake, I swore *never* to make another person so lifelike, so imbued with free will, that such a terrible thing could happen again.

Forcing *me* to do such a terrible thing and live thereafter with the memory of seeing my wife die *twice* because of my mistake.

"I DON'T *DO* that kind of working anymore," I tell Oliver, but the gun against my temple doesn't budge. "You *know* this. I *told* you."

"Do it or die," Oliver says matter-of-factly. "It's that simple. And don't bother trying to *magic* your way out of this. I know a few *parlor tricks,* remember?"

I do, and he has a point. As powerful as I am, can I be sure that whatever I try against him won't be countered? Can I take the chance he won't slip a bullet in my skull in the breath it takes to conjure my way to freedom?

Unfortunately, the answer is pretty clear to me.

"This is a mistake," I tell him. "I know from experience. Whatever you're trying to fix, this will just make it worse."

"You know *nothing.* This will make it *better,* trust me." Oliver cocks the gun. "Now do it."

"No." I'm afraid to shake my head. "I won't do it."

"Reach into that memory," says Oliver. "Dig *deep.* Sense the *shape* of her...the sound of her...the smell and feel and *taste* of her."

"Shut up." My concentration is rattled by his voice, not to mention the gun. "Walk away from this while you still can."

He presses the gun harder against my skull. "Gather up those details and knit them together. Weave them into a facsimile of the person who used to be."

"It won't be the same as that person," I tell him. "It will *never* be the same as that person."

"Based on a memory like *this?* A first-hand memory from a direct *eyewitness?* It'll be close *enough.*" He grunts. "Why do you think I searched so hard? Brought the old-timers to you? Followed the trail from one to the other until we found someone *living* who had had first-hand contact with Proserpina?"

Finally, I understand his end game, if not the motivation behind it. His *pro bono* work makes sense now, as do his questions about conjuring lifelike subjects. His only goal from the start was resurrecting Proserpina, avatar of Ceres, tender of the ancient miracle herb silphium.

"But why?" I ask. "Why *her?* Why try to bring back Proserpina?"

"Quit asking questions and do it. Do it or *die.*" His voice is icy and grim, utterly convincing of the consequence he threatens. "Do it *now.*"

I don't want to die. That's what it comes down to. That's why I end up breaking my own promise to myself to never do what he wants me to do.

"I said *do it now!*" Oliver is running out of patience.

I holler right back at him. "It won't *happen* if you keep wrecking my *concentration*."

It's true. I'm having a hard enough time keeping the memory in play, let alone extracting and resurrecting the remembered essence of one of the figures it depicts.

"I'm not moving the *gun*," snaps Oliver. "Not till you're *done.*"

"Which will be *never* if you don't leave me *alone.*"

That quiets him down enough to let me make an effort. I do pretty much exactly what he told me to, reaching deep into the memory of the scene from ancient Roman times and gathering up the details of Proserpina as portrayed therein.

The sight of her is easy, and so is the sound. She talks to Zaba in the memory, exchanging insights on the growing of silphium. The feel of her is easy, too, as she and Zaba continue to hold hands.

As for the taste and smell of her—they are *vivid* from Zaba's memory of kissing her hand, vivid and utterly unlike *any* taste or smell or sensation I've ever known in my life. They are *remarkable* in ways I cannot even properly describe, ways that leave me spinning in circles and gasping for breath. And I realize, as I process all this, that for the first time in my life, I've experienced the flavor and fragrance of pure silphium, a substance that no longer exists in the world.

A substance that comprises the blood, bone, and sinew of Proserpina in the memory I've hotwired.

"Where is she?" asks Oliver. "How much longer?"

Instead of answering, I fight to stay focused on the task at hand. Embracing the multitude of details within Zaba's memory, I bolt them together, assembling a version of Proserpina in my mind. I imbue that version with all the magic power at my command, bathing it in electrifying force. Then, with every last iota of strength and belief in my arsenal, I fuse this new Proserpina into something that *might* yet live, and I hurl it from its birthplace into the world outside our heads. I make it part of the world, and I wonder how long it will live.

She. How long *she* will live.

"Oh my God." Oliver pulls the gun away from my head. "You did it. It's *her.*"

Suddenly, the replica of Proserpina draws a sharp breath and opens her eyes. She looks at me, then Zaba, then Oliver—and her eyes stay with him.

"Thank you." Oliver puts the gun on the table and goes to her. He breathes deeply, inhaling her fragrant scent, the aroma of a spice long lost to the world. "Thank you for bringing back the *female* half of the silphium equation."

"There's a *male* half?"

"Oh, yes." He takes her hand kisses it softly, beaming. "You're looking at him."

Six months later, I drive up a winding dirt road in southern California, dappled sunlight streaming through the leafy oaks on either side of my rental car. I roll along a loop that guides me up the gentle rise, and the trees suddenly give way to a vast, open field.

I park at the edge, where Oliver and Proserpina greet me with cheerful waves. Each wears denim overalls, tan work shirts, and broad-brimmed straw hats...not exactly the togas of ancient Rome, but better suited to labor in the fields.

"Glad you could make it." Oliver moves in for a hug.

I twist around and turn it into a handshake. I'm still not sure how I feel about all this. I definitely don't appreciate being used and threatened at gunpoint, no matter what the end result is.

"Hello, Proserpina." I nod to her.

"Hi, Homan." She casts a broad smile in my direction, looking regal as ever. Her skin has tanned and her brown hair has gone blonde from all the time she's been spending in the sun.

"So what do you think?" Oliver turns and spreads his arms to encompass the field. It teems with squat plants bobbing in the soft

June breeze, thick with bunches of fragile little yellow flowers. "Isn't that a sight for sore eyes?"

"Pretty amazing." I might not like how it came to pass, but I can't deny how wondrous it is.

"There hasn't been a field like this in thousands of years." Oliver plants his hands on his hips and shakes his head. "Silphium hasn't grown *anywhere* in the world since the death of the Roman Empire."

"Since the death of *me.*" Proserpina says it matter-of-factly, her dark brown eyes scanning the yellow-flowered horizon. "Since Zaba, commissioned by Ceres to protect me, failed so dismally...and without *my* protection, the silphium of Cyrene also perished."

"By which point, the plant's mother goddess, Ceres, was also long-gone," says Oliver. "Lost to the modern monotheistic age that had no room for such specialized pagan goddesses."

I walk up to the nearest row of the crop and crouch down to take a closer look. The plants look just like the one on the coin Oliver gave me months ago to help me focus on extracting Zaba's memory.

"You've brought it back." Reaching down, I gently stroke the herb's flowers and deep green leaves. "The two of you managed to regenerate it."

"Male and female together was the only way," says Oliver. "And we have you to thank for making it all possible."

Frowning, I get to my feet. "But where exactly did *you* come from, Oliver? You never did say. If *she* was dead since Roman times, and all the silphium was gone, how did *you* as a male avatar of the herb come to be?"

"Would you believe I was a kind of *refund?*" Oliver laughs. "Some woman excavated a *wishing urn* from the sunken ruins of Thonis-Heracleion off the coast of Egypt and unwittingly read out the spell of undoing engraved on its shell. It turns out the original wish, meant to ruin the silphium-growing capital of Cyrene, was to wipe *me*, the crop's original male avatar, out of existence...but the spell of undoing *reversed* it.

"I popped back up after millennia of nonexistence, only to find that my beautiful *plant*, a gift from the gods with the power to save the *world*, had been nonexistent, too. The female avatars who'd come after me—Proserpina's mother and then Proserpina herself—had kept it going for a long time after my vanishing, but *their* deaths had sealed the deal. No more silphium...so my purpose was clear. As soon as I'd acclimated myself to the modern world, I set out to *restore* it."

"Which is where *I* came in." I can't help glaring at him a little. "Not that you bothered to just *ask* me to help instead of *tricking* me."

"You were his last chance." Proserpina's unwavering voice leaves no room for doubt. "He could *not* risk that you might refuse him."

I tip my head to one side as my glare deepens. "Last chance?"

Oliver shrugs. "You weren't my *first* choice, all right? I tried every other warlock and witch I could find with proven mastery of life-generating magicks, and none of them worked out. You were the *last stop*—but hey! Look how great it all turned out in the end!" He sweeps an arm around to indicate the vast field of silphium.

A surge of indignation rolls through me, but I let it go. He's right about the ends being worth the means in this case.

And maybe I don't mind being tricked and used, after all, if it makes up in some small way for what I did to my wife years ago. Maybe it's only right that the same damn power of mine that got her killed brought back this legendary herb that might possibly do some good in the world.

The ancients used it to cure almost everything, and the gods meant for it to cure so much more. This time, maybe, instead of being wiped off the face of the planet, it might help turn things around in ways I cannot yet fathom.

"So what now?" I ask. "Harvest your crops and head down to the farmer's market?"

Proserpina shakes her head imperiously. "Nothing so mundane." She lets a little smile play at the corners of her mouth. "*Our* work shall operate on a *grand* and *unprecedented* scale."

I scowl. "I don't know what that means."

Oliver reaches out with both hands. "It means we need a *partner*.

Someone with great *power* at his command and a real *knack* for managing *addiction* and *illusion* in pursuit of *redemption.*"

It's not exactly what I expected to hear him say. "Is that so?"

"We have a product that could save the world," says Oliver, his smile as free and easy as ever. "What do you say about helping us *market* it?"

"So to speak," clarifies Proserpina.

"Exactly," says Oliver, still reaching. "What do you say, Homan?"

I shrug. "What've I got to lose?" Then, alongside the acres of silphium plants, their yellow flowers bobbing harder as if in silent ovation as the wind kicks up, I go ahead and give him a damn hug...during which I must confess I pat him on the back a little harder than I have to.

ABOUT THE AUTHOR

Robert Jeschonek is a *USA Today* bestselling, envelope-pushing author whose fiction and comics have been published around the world. Robert's work has appeared in *Galaxy's Edge, StarShipSofa, Fiction River, Pulphouse,* and many other publications. He has written official *Star Trek* and *Doctor Who* fiction, as well as comics for DC, AHOY, and others. His young adult fantasy, *My Favorite Band Does Not Exist,* was named a Top Ten First Novel for Youth by *Booklist* magazine. He also won an International Book Award, a Scribe Award for Best Original Novel, and the grand prize in Pocket Books' Strange New Worlds contest.

Find out more about Robert at:
robertjeschonek.com

facebook.com/usa.today.bestseller
twitter.com/TheFictioneer
instagram.com/jcschonek
bookbub.com/authors/robert-jeschonek
amazon.com/Robert-Jeschonck/c/B0037B7E2G

THE SOLITARY SORCERESS

DEBBIE MUMFORD

CHAPTER 1

KAITLYN FELT HIM DIE. Felt his spirit depart this world, though it had been years since she'd seen his beloved face.

She stumbled, though the path through the white-barked aspen trees was well known to her and the morning clear and bright.

Fear and grief assaulted her mind.

She felt his power return to the reservoir of ambient magic. Felt a cresting wave of urgent desire break against her will as the magic in the very air around her ebbed and flowed, seeking a new balance.

The Firestone awoke, scrabbling for energy as it tried to claim more magic, claim more of her life.

She collapsed to the bare ground, bracing herself against the rough trunk of an aspen. Dropping her gathering basket, she hugged her knees beneath scrunched and disheveled skirts and petticoats.

"No," she whispered through gritted teeth, sweat beading her forehead. "No. You will not advance. I refuse to allow it."

Closing her eyes, her brow furrowed in concentration, she weathered the magical spike, struggled against the fingerless golden glove that covered her right hand and forearm, against the slender tendrils that sought to extend toward her elbow. With gritted teeth and clenched fists she fought for control…and won.

The fine tendrils retreated, the golden glove quieted. The magical storm calmed.

Tears slid down her heated cheeks. Partly in relief that she'd once again mastered the Firestone, but mostly in mourning for her dead friend. Aelfric, the master sorcerer to whom she had once been a contrary and headstrong witchling.

She rested her head on her knees and reflected for a moment on her loss while her pulse slowed and her breathing quieted, becoming even again. Aelfric was gone, the master who had guided her through the turbulent adjustment after she'd so rashly used the Firestone to defeat the evil wizard, Darius. She'd won a war and saved her brother, but at a terrible personal cost.

King Lorien had hailed her a hero, but the common folk had the right of it—they named her the Solitary Sorceress.

For that was the price the Firestone had demanded of Kaitlyn, that headstrong fourteen-year-old witchling. She had dared to summon the powerful talisman from its resting place and it had come to her in its quiescent state, a simple gold ring. But when she had claimed its power to defeat Darius, when she had placed the ring upon her finger, it had bonded with her flesh, sending tendrils into her very bones, wrapping her hand and wrist in a golden sheath that had extended to her forearm before the battle ended.

The Firestone made her invincible.

It also made her untouchable. Literally.

For once she was bonded to the talisman, no other human could lay so much as a finger on her, nor she on them.

Sighing, Kaitlyn wiped her eyes on her linen apron, and picked up her gathering basket. Time to put away memories and push grief to a remote corner of her mind. Ten years had passed since that fateful battle. Nearly nine since she'd left Aelfric's side and gone into seclusion. She would mourn the passing of her counselor and confidant, but not right now. Now there were preparations to be made.

CHAPTER 2

SHE'D EXPECTED King Lorien to summon her to court. She hadn't expected her brother, Gavin, to be the messenger.

"Katie! You look wonderful!" Gavin dismounted and handed the reins to his squire, a jug-eared youth with bowl-cut tawny hair and eyes that looked ready to pop from their sockets.

"And you as well, Gavin. How is Lydia? And little Kathryn?" Kaitlyn smiled at her older brother, amazed at the calm tone of her voice, when her heart was pounding and her pulse roared in her ears. She wanted nothing more than to throw herself into his arms and be hugged and petted. She loved Gavin more than life itself. It was for his sake that she'd committed the folly which had cost her the ability to touch him, or to hold his little daughter.

He reached toward her, remembered himself, and let his hand fall. "They're fine," he said, forcing a smile. "Katie ... we call her Katie, after you ... is thriving. She's walking now and starting to talk as well."

"I'm so happy for you, Gavin," she said. "Please come in. Your squire is welcome too."

Gavin nodded and turned to the jug-eared lad. "Jamie, water

the horses and picket them in the meadow. Then you may join us in the house."

The boy sketched a quick bow. "Yes, m'lord."

Kaitlyn opened the door to her small cottage and ushered her brother inside. Unusually aware of her surroundings, she gazed at the familiar room. Light streamed through diamond-paned windows and shone on a scrubbed oak work table and sturdy wooden chairs. The hearth was clean-swept, wood neatly laid, ready to be kindled later that evening. Bunches of lavender and thyme hung from the rafters, scenting the air with spicy sweetness.

Gavin took a seat at the table while Kaitlyn poured mugs of cider. Placing one before her brother, she settled in her favorite chair and sipped from her own mug. The cool liquid was tart, sweet and refreshing.

"I suppose you're wondering why I've come," Gavin said. He tasted his cider and nodded his approval.

"Not really," she said. "I assume Lorien sent you to bring me to court. He'll need a new wizard now that Aelfric is gone."

Gavin's eyebrows shot up and his eyes widened. "You know about Aelfric? But how?"

She gave him a pitying glance. "I'm a sorceress, remember? He was my teacher. I felt him pass."

"Oh. I didn't … I'm sorry." He took another drink of cider and stared at the well-used table, fingering an old scar left by a chopping knife. "I was dreading having to tell you."

"He was a good man," Kaitlyn said, resisting the urge to reach for his hand. "A far better master than I deserved. Too bad I didn't heed his teaching more closely."

Gavin glanced up and met her eyes. "I'm so sorry, Katie," he said quietly. "About everything."

She dropped her gaze, unable to bear the love and tenderness she saw in his eyes. "I know. So am I, but it's my own doing and I've learned to live with it." She held up her gold-encased hand. "It hasn't mastered me. I've learned to control it."

He nodded. "Will you come? To court, I mean."

Taking another sip of cider, she considered.

Gavin waited a moment, then continued, "King Lorien bade me say that he recognizes he has no ability to compel you, but if you're willing, he would greatly appreciate your counsel."

A wry smile twisted her lips. "My counsel? The woman who cursed herself to a solitary life?"

Gavin frowned. "The woman who sacrificed herself for the realm," he said. His expression softened. "Who sacrificed herself for love of her brother."

She shuddered and covered her face with her hands.

"Katie, you were brave beyond your years. You may not have understood exactly what the cost would be, but you knew one would have to be paid, and you acted anyway."

The door opened and Gavin's squire sidled in.

Gavin nodded to the jug of cider on the sideboard. "Pour yourself a mug and wait on the bench outside."

The boy did as he was bid and escaped their company.

"Besides," Gavin said when the door closed behind the boy, "you've had years of secluded study, and Aelfric was sure that in learning to control both yourself and the Firestone, you'd've learned many other lessons as well."

"He said that?"

Gavin nodded. "I was with him when he died, as was the king. He said that you were by far the wisest and most powerful magic user in the realm. That Lorien would be lucky to have your counsel — if he could persuade you to return to court."

"And the king sent you to plead his case."

He shrugged. "He figured I'd stand the best chance."

She sighed. "He was right." She stood and walked to the window. Looking out over the neat rows of vegetables and herbs in her kitchen garden, she pondered her life. She had indeed learned control, and many other bits of arcane lore in the years since she'd left Aelfric and the king's court. Her master had gifted her with his most treasured gramarye and she had studied it well. She knew her art and she knew herself. What she didn't know was how to handle the company of people she could never touch.

She was afraid.

This self-imposed isolation allowed her to forget her handicap. She didn't miss what wasn't available.

But if she returned to court, her isolation would be tangible. She'd constantly be reminded of that which she could never have ... the simple touch of a hand, a kiss, a hug. Physical intimacy was forever beyond her reach.

Could she endure being adrift in a sea of courtiers?

Was she a coward to be ruled by her fears?

Turning from the window, Kaitlyn met her brother's gaze.

"I will come."

CHAPTER 3

KAITLYN MOVED into Aelfric's quarters. Wistfulness accompanied her as she walked through the workroom where she'd toiled as a witchling. She examined the shelves, still a jumble of crocks, jars of herbs, models of castles, desiccated rodents, and the odd skull or bone. She stepped to the small sitting room that lay between the workroom and bedchamber and stroked the back of his favorite chair.

So many memories.

She smiled. The Firestone had robbed her of human touch, but she could enjoy these artifacts of Aelfric's life. She sat in his chair, hers now, and rested her hands on wood polished smooth by his hands.

She would make these rooms her own, but they would always retain Aelfric's aura. She was content.

Gavin acted as her guide at court. He introduced her to those who had gained prominence in her absence and reminded her of folk she had known as a witchling. Everyone regarded her with awe, avoiding her eyes, but gazing avidly at the golden glove encasing her right hand and forearm.

No one attempted to touch her, but bowed and curtsied from a safe distance.

Lydia, Gavin's wife, welcomed Kaitlyn to the quarters she and Gavin shared with their child.

Little Katie provided the cruelest test of Kaitlyn's composure. The tiny girl was adorable, with wide blue eyes and sweet blonde curls. She toddled unsteadily to Kaitlyn with pudgy arms upheld.

Gavin stepped forward and swooped the little one into his arms, holding her up for Kaitlyn's inspection.

"This is your Auntie Kaitlyn, Katie," he said. "She a very great sorceress, so you mustn't bother her. Don't be begging for sweets or kisses."

Kaitlyn's eyes brimmed with tears, but she laughed and smiled at the little girl. "Oh, she can ask for sweets anytime she likes, just not for hugs or kisses. Will that be all right, Katie?"

Producing the sugar plum she had brought for this purpose, Kaitlyn dropped it in Katie's outstretched hand.

The child smiled, and Kaitlyn breathed a sigh of relief.

After sharing a quiet meal with Gavin and his family, Kaitlyn strolled back to her quarters in the Wizard's Tower. She didn't feel as alone as she'd expected. Wasn't as miserable as anticipated. Living in Aelfric's old rooms gave her a sense of peace and she enjoyed seeing Gavin again. Even watching the sweet interplay of his family hadn't upset her as she'd feared. She relished her brother's happiness, treasured the memories of their shared childhood that his interactions with Lydia and little Katie had brought to the surface.

She'd always known that she was different. Magic had marked her for its own early in her life and Aelfric had cautioned her that choosing to pursue her gift would pull her from the homely joys her girlhood friends would find.

Her path had simply taken a more radical twist than even her mentor had imagined.

Now, as a full-fledged sorceress, she found she was comfortable at court. The king and his nobles treated her with respect. She had ample time to pursue her studies and experiment with new brews and potions to the betterment of her people, and if she had no one with whom to share her life, well, neither had Aelfric. At least not until he'd taken on a certain wayward young witchling.

She rounded a corner and was jolted from her reverie by the sight of a man she'd yet to meet standing a few feet down the corridor. He leaned against an embrasure, gazing out, eyes hooded with concentration. A dark-haired man in his prime, he was well-muscled and sleek. Not like the soft-bodied courtiers with which King Lorien surrounded himself. A warrior, then. Perhaps one of the castle guard? No. He looked too at ease to be an off-duty guard.

Kaitlyn frowned. Something about the shape of his face — wide brow, high cheekbones, narrow nose — something was familiar. But what?

He glanced up, noted her, his gaze moving past, and then he looked at her again, frowned, and straightened from the wall.

"Kaitlyn?" he asked, stepping toward her. "Katie? Is that you?"

And his voice pulled him sharply into focus. Conall. Gavin's best friend, the boy she'd idolized as a girl. Conall. A boy no longer, but a well-grown man.

She glanced away, drew a calming breath, then met his gaze and stepped forward to meet him in the center of the corridor.

"Conall! How good to see you again. Do you live nearby?"

A smile spread across his handsome face. "As I live and breathe," he said, reaching for her hands. "It is you, Katie! How long has it been?"

Kaitlyn side-stepped, avoiding his grasp. If she were still the girl he remembered, nothing would have been more natural than to clasp his hands in welcome. But she was no longer simply Katie, Gavin's little sister. She was the Solitary Sorceress, and this moment brought that realization home with the force of a gut punch.

Clasping her hands behind her back, she turned to resume her walk, nodding her head to invite him to join her.

He frowned at her evasion, but put his own hands behind his back and walked beside her, sliding sidelong glances at her as they went.

"Are you staying with Gavin, Katie?" he asked, his tone curious, but mild. "Or perhaps you and your husband have chambers here?"

A small smile played around her lips and she glanced at the stone-flagged floor. "I've never married. Perhaps you didn't know that I was apprenticed to Aelfric, the King's wizard."

He nodded. "Yes, now I remember. Gavin did tell me you'd gone to court to study magic."

He stopped and turned to face her. "I understand Aelfric recently passed from this life." He inclined his head and lowered his eyes. "I am sorry for your loss."

Tears threatened, but she willed them away. "Thank you, Conall. He was a great man, but it had been many years since I'd seen him."

He looked up, startled. "Then why are you here, if you were no longer studying with Aelfric?"

"The king called me to replace Aelfric. I am the new King's Wizard."

"But..." He stopped abruptly, drew himself up to his full height and gave her a courtly bow. "Forgive me, my lady," he said, his voice suddenly stiff. "I didn't realize with whom I spoke."

Kaitlyn's mouth was suddenly as dry and cracked as a desert streamed in full summer. She'd been enjoying chatting with an old friend. Now, as though the man had been transformed by magic, a stiff and formal courtier stood before her.

"There is nothing to forgive, my lord," she said quietly, and gesturing forward with her right hand, she turned to continue their walk.

A strangled sound caused her to turn back to Conall.

His gaze was fixed on the golden glove encasing her right fore-arm. Her cheeks heated as he turned a wide-eyed stare upon her face.

"It's you?" he asked, his voice strained. "You're the Solitary Sorceress? The hero who saved my life?"

She blinked. "What? How could I have saved your life? I had no idea where you were!"

"But it was you?" he pressed.

"Yes," she sighed. "It was me. In a moment of total idiocy I claimed a magic that should have killed me. Instead, it turned me into who I am, the Solitary Sorceress."

He passed a hand over his eyes, and then turned to walk on. "I never dreamed it was you, Katie," he said quietly. "I heard the stories, of course, but it never occurred to me that I could know such a legendary sorceress."

She nodded and resumed walking at his side. "Believe me, I never intended to become the Solitary Sorceress. When I called the Firestone, I thought only to give it to Aelfric. I expected him to be the hero. Never myself. Even in my youthful arrogance, I understood that I lacked the knowledge to control such a powerful object." She lapsed into miserable silence.

After a moment, she roused herself. "But tell me, how did my actions save your life? I'm sure you must be attributing your skill at arms to my foolishness."

He smiled ruefully. "Skill at arms? You forget, ten years ago Gavin and I were rank amateurs. Neither of us would have lived to gain skill if not for your so-called foolishness."

He shook himself and made a warding gesture before continuing. "I was at the mercy of an enemy soldier, flat on my back, unarmed, my head ringing from the force of his last blow. He stood over me, his blade at my throat, ready to deliver the killing stroke."

"What happened?" Kaitlyn asked, wide-eyed, breathless with anticipation.

He grinned. "You happened. Whatever you did caused the warrior to ... I don't know ... it was like he woke up. He shuddered, looked around the battlefield, then lowered his weapon. He just stared at me. After a moment he offered me his hand and helped me to my feet. It was the strangest moment of my life."

She nodded. "After the Firestone defeated Darius..."

"After *you* defeated Darius," Conall interrupted with a fierce glare.

Frowning back at him, she said, "Fine. After *I* defeated Darius, Aelfric said that many, if not most, of his soldiers had been ensorcelled. That they would surrender without further violence."

Conall nodded. "Aelfric was a wise counselor. That's just what happened. The knight who nearly killed me surrendered immediately. The poor man didn't even know where he was or who he was fighting."

They walked on in silence for a few moments before Conall spoke again.

"Since the other things I've heard are true," he said, "is it also true that you are untouchable."

She cast him a sidelong glance, then schooled her features, stared straight ahead and nodded. "It was the Firestone's price."

He stopped. She walked on for a pace or two, then turned to face him.

"You'll think me impudent," he said, stepping closer to her, "but may I try?"

She gazed at him for a long moment. Conall. Her childhood friend. The boy whom she could have loved, grown to manhood. Was it possible? Could he end the enchantment? Would the Firestone bend to their combined wills?

She held out her encased hand to him. "I'd like that … very much."

Their gazes locked and both of them held their breaths as Conall slowly reached for her hand …

… only to have his fingers stopped by an invisible barrier an inch from her flesh.

She read the outcome in his eyes, in the furrow of his brow, and exhaled her disappointment.

He looked away. "I'm sorry, Katie," he murmured. "It's just that …" he paused, then looking embarrassed turned to walk. "I hoped that perhaps the Firestone had spared me for this moment."

Tears welled in Kaitlyn's eyes, but she clasped her hands behind her back again, raised her chin, and strode forward.

"You've always been special to me, Conall, and I'm glad to know I had a part in your survival, but the Firestone will not be cheated of its due."

They'd arrived at the door to the Wizard's Tower. Kaitlyn

turned to Conall and gave him a brave smile. "This is where I leave you, my lord. It's been a pleasure to see you again."

Conall gazed at her as intently as though he wanted to take up residence in her soul. With the suddenness of a striking viper, he unsheathed his sword and bent to one knee, the blade tip upright on the stone flag, his hands on the pommel.

"My life is yours, Lady Kaitlyn," he said, eyes on the floor at the sword's tip. "Will you accept my service?"

Kaitlyn glanced around the passageway where other courtiers were pausing to watch the scene Conall was creating. This wouldn't do. Her heart hammered, heating her cheeks. Kaitlyn had no desire to be party to even more court gossip.

Rubbing sweaty palms on regal velvet skirts, Kaitlyn whispered, "Get up, Conall. You're making a scene."

Conall remained as still as though he'd been turned to stone. "Answer the question, m'lady," he murmured without looking up.

"I don't need your life or your service," she cried in irritation.

He raised his gaze and their eyes locked. She saw sorrow, no, *anguish* in their depths and knew that she had wounded him.

Inspiration struck, and she smiled gently.

"Rise, Conall. I have no need of guardian, protector, or servant," she said, her voice gaining strength as her conviction deepened, "but I do have need of a friend. The Solitary Sorceress grows weary of seclusion. Will you be my friend, Conall?"

Relief and hope mingled in a sunburst of surprise, the light originating in his eyes and spreading across his handsome features. He grinned, climbed to his feet, and sheathed his sword. "It will be my honor, Lady Kaitlyn."

She grinned back. "Katie will do, Conall. I said *friend*, not *courtier*."

He nodded. "And you shall have one. Until tomorrow, Katie," he said, then giving her a small bow, he turned and strode away.

Kaitlyn watched him go, feeling lighter than she had in years.

A friend. What a gift he'd given her.

A friend. She hadn't known she'd needed one.

Opening the tower door, she fairly flew up the stairs to her quarters. A friend. Someone who knew her of old, someone she could talk to without worrying about the impression she gave. A confidant.

She had a friend, and that friend was Conall. A man she might have loved had the Firestone not existed. A man who would surely have died without the Firestone.

Touching the golden glove with her left hand, she acknowledged her gratitude. The first she'd ever felt.

Slender tendrils extended and crawled toward her elbow.

She laughed and clamped her iron will over the Firestone. "I may be grateful for his life," she said, "but not that grateful. You will not advance."

The Firestone re-absorbed the tendrils, exuding instead an aura of peace.

"Yes. Let us be at ease with each other." She stroked the warm surface of the living sheath encasing her forearm. "You have a mind and an arm to wield your power, and I … I have a friend. Let us agree to be content."

ABOUT THE AUTHOR

Debbie Mumford specializes in speculative fiction—fantasy, para-normal romance, and science fiction. Author of the popular Sorcha's Children series, Debbie loves the unknown, whether it's the lure of space or earthbound mythology. Her work has been published in multiple volumes of *Fiction River,* as well as in *Heart's Kiss Magazine, Spinetingler Magazine,* and other popular markets. She writes about dragon-shifters, time-traveling lovers, and ghostly detectives for adults as Debbie Mumford, and science fiction and fantasy tales for children and young adults as Deb Logan.

Find out more about Debbie at:
debbiemumford.com

goodreads.com/debbie_mumford
facebook.com/DebbieMumfordWrites
twitter.com/deborah_mumford
bookbub.com/authors/debbie-mumford
amazon.com/Debbie-Mumford/e/B004S3GGEY

THE FIXER

ANNIE REED

A BLAST of arctic air along with the smell of something not quite right assaulted Amelia when she stepped off the elevator into the lobby of her apartment building.

"Holy crap," she muttered to herself, pulling her sweater tightly around her shoulders and wrinkling her nose.

Moretown Bay in June wasn't the warmest place on the planet—the days were overcast and the offshore breezes blew in chilly, humid air from the bay—but usually a light coat or windbreaker was sufficient. The city wasn't Juneau, Alaska, for goodness sake.

Amelia didn't even own a down jacket. In all her years living in Moretown Bay, she'd never needed one. Raincoat? Oh my, yes. She had three, but no down jackets.

Today had dawned sunny and warm—for once—and she thought she'd be fine with a light sweater. The weather shouldn't have changed *that* much during the short elevator ride from her apartment on the ninth floor to the lobby.Strictly speaking, it shouldn't have changed at all.

Although her apartment building wasn't in the ritziest part of town, the lobby wasn't an open-air affair. The last time she'd checked, the building's heating system had been working just fine. The lobby shouldn't make her feel like she'd stepped into a walk-in freezer.

And the smell? Moretown Bay usually smelled like any other big coastal city—exhaust fumes from cars and busses, cooking smells from restaurants and those little hibachi things people used on their apartment balconies, and the smell of people (washed, unwashed, or perfumed and body-sprayed within an inch of their lives)—overlaid with the musty odor of the bay.

None of those odors quite described the smell in the lobby. More like an undercurrent of something horrible, like a combination of overripe skunk and fermented garbage pit dialed down to a level that barely registered.

Even trolls and goblins didn't smell quite like that

Magic. It had to be.

Someone had cast a singularly disturbing spell in the lobby. Just lovely. Didn't they realize other beings and just plain non-magical folk had to walk through the lobby on their way to work? And that smells just naturally clung to clothing? Amelia had worked for people who'd been fired from their jobs for smelling like the inside of this lobby.

And the scent was likely to attach to her clothing as well.

People tended to forget about other people when they were upset. Maybe a particularly bad breakup had happened in the lobby, or someone hadn't quite been able to sneak out as unnoticed as they'd hoped—talk about the morning walk of shame—and someone else had used magic to exact a little (mostly) harmless revenge.

Amelia considered casting a small shielding spell around herself. She had at least a good dozen prepaid spells on her license, but she hated to waste them. The lobby was smaller than her living room, and her living room was just big enough for a couch, a coffee table, her television, and her cat. She might be freezing and her stomach might be thinking about rebelling—the smell seemed to be getting stronger somehow—but after a couple dozen steps she'd be outside in the blessedly stench-free if only moderately warmer air.

She could hold her breath that long, right?

"Excuse me, are you Amelia Burke?"

The question nearly made Amelia jump out of her skin. She'd thought she was alone in the lobby, but someone—apparently a female someone, by the sound of the voice—was hiding behind a pretty decent veil.

She fumbled in the pocket of her sweater for the small smooth stone she carried with her everywhere. Non-magical folk called them "worry stones," but Amelia's was made specifically to hold a spell. In her case, a powerful disabling spell, the magical equivalent of the tasers some non-magical folk carried for protection.

When you were only four foot two in a city teeming with "normal" sized beings, you learned to watch out for yourself.

Especially when you thought you were alone and voices were coming out of thin air.

"It's not polite to hide yourself when you're trying to start a conversation," Amelia said.

"Oh," the unseen woman said. "Right."

The wall to the right of the lobby seemed to shiver, and then a woman stepped out of a rift in the air only a few feet away from Amelia.

The woman appeared to be human, a good foot and a half taller than Amelia, but painfully thin where Amelia considered herself pleasingly plump. She was dressed in a simple denim skirt and navy blue checkered blouse, with a pale blue silk scarf tied around her neck. Her hair was dark brown, worn in loose curls to her shoulders, and her eyes were vivid blue.

Amelia took a few steps away from her.

And not only because she'd been hiding behind a veil, which was never a good sign. The odd smell and the arctic air were practically pouring off the woman.

Maybe buying at least one down jacket wouldn't be such a bad idea after all.

"You are Amelia Burke, right?" the woman asked. "I really need your help."

She sounded desperate.

Gooseflesh crept up Amelia's arms, and a shiver ran down her spine. She tried breathing through her mouth to minimize the smell, then decided that whatever was causing the smell—a spell, no doubt, if the woman was looking for her—wasn't something Amelia wanted to taste.

"Most people make an appointment with my office," Amelia said.

"I'm really sorry, but I couldn't wait." The woman rubbed her hands up and down her arms. She must really be freezing, too. "I used up the best veil I had so I wouldn't bother any of your neighbors. I really need your help."

Of course, she did. Everyone who came to see Amelia really needed her help.

Amelia specialized in reversing spells. Nasty spells. Annoying spells. Spells cast by people who refused (or couldn't) cast a reversing spell themselves.

Officially the process was called "spell reclamation," and Amelia ran the most successful spell reclamation business in town. She even had three apprentices working for her now, which was why she could take the occasional morning to enjoy an unexpected sunny day.

Privately, Amelia thought of her job as something akin to running a magical eraser over the unintended consequences and allowing the spellcaster to start over.

The process wasn't as simple as most non-magical folks thought. If the original spellcaster took the recipe for the spell with them after they cast it, or the spell crafter forgot to write down the list of ingredients and incantations—which happened a lot (go figure; it wasn't like people were messing with something important like *magic* or anything)—the process of trying to develop a reversing spell was like trying to reverse engineer a recipe for rocket fuel so that the spaceship wouldn't blow up before it ever left the launchpad.

In other words, developing a reversing spell without the original spell was pretty much like doing rocket science with one hand tied behind your back and cheesecloth wrapped around your eyes.

"Well, you're bothering me," Amelia said to the rather fragrant woman. "Do you mind if we go outside so I can stand in the sunshine and get a breath of fresh air?"

A flush bloomed on the woman's cheeks. "Sorry," she said.

She started to rush for the front door—presumably to hold it open for Amelia—but Amelia held up one hand to stop her.

"I've got it," she said.

That wasn't the first time something like that had happened.

Amelia stood four foot two inches tall in her stocking feet, and she hated wearing heels, so she was usually four foot three inches tall at most.

The rest of Amelia's family were what was considered "normal" height-wise for humans. Which meant that somewhere along the line, someone in her family tree must have had a jolly old time with a halfling. That story, if there ever was one, had been long since forgotten. The halfling genes, however, had survived and decided to reappear in the form of a perfectly proportioned blonde-haired, blue-eyed baby girl who'd just never grown to normal height.

Amelia had come to terms with being an especially short person in a world full of beings that were a good foot or two taller than she was. The problem was with other people. They tended to think she couldn't do things for herself, so they rushed to do them for her.

Things like opening doors.

The flush deepened the woman's cheeks to a deep red. "I'm sorry. I didn't mean…"

Amelia took a deep breath to steady herself, and immediately wished she hadn't. Without the veil to conceal the smell, the disgusting odor had gotten much stronger.

Which made her wonder what the smell was like from this woman's perspective. Horrible, no doubt. Plus she was obviously freezing. No wonder she couldn't wait for Amelia's help.

And wasn't that what Amelia did, after all? Help people?

Even if they invaded her personal space?

Yes, that was exactly what she did. So why was she so cranky about this particular person?

Maybe it was the prospect of missing out on enjoying the unexpected sunny morning.

If that was the case, perhaps she'd lived in the cloud-covered Pacific Northwest for far too long. She'd have to see if Southern California—or maybe Florida—needed a crackerjack spell reclamation expert. Her business could always open a satellite branch.

Amelia forced herself to smile, and then surprised herself when she realized the smile was more genuine than forced. Never underestimate the value of a good internal pep talk.

"Don't worry," Amelia said. "It happens to me a lot."

She opened the door to the lobby for herself and was immediately refreshed by a good strong whiff of diesel as a city bus passed by. You'd think that Moretown Bay, of all places, would have replaced the old diesel buses with electric models given that the city's motto was *The Jewel of the Pacific Northwest*.

Jewels didn't belch diesel fumes.

"So," Amelia said once they were both outside and basking in the sunshine. "How exactly did you end up in this situation?"

The woman sighed. "I signed up for an online course. The spells were all guaranteed not to fail. Lots of five-star reviews. Great testimonials. They even sold me a license and everything."

Amelia stifled a sigh. Internet websites were the worst at duping wannabe wizards and witches into buying spells that only worked sometimes. If you were lucky.

And they'd even sell the poor dupe a license for spell crafting if he or she didn't already have one.

Anyone—magical folk or plain vanilla mortals—could buy a ready-made spell and cast it. The cost of the permit to cast the spell was part of the purchase price. The more serious the spell—say you wanted to turn someone into a giant rabbit for the day—the higher the price.

Higher prices were supposed to discourage people from casting spells with more serious consequences willy-nilly. But in reality, all the pricing scheme meant was that rich people could afford to cast asshole spells more often than those in Amelia's much more modest tax bracket.

Creating spells, though—that was a whole different ballgame. If someone actually wanted to make their own spell, they needed a spell crafting license, and those didn't come cheap. Even over the Internet. They also needed months and months of practice, preferably as an apprentice to a powerful wizard with years of experience under his or her belt.

All in all, it was much cheaper just to buy a ready-made spell. Amelia never could understand why someone who hadn't apprenticed to a licensed wizard or witch would shell out the kind of money just to be able to legally engage in a little DIY spell craft.

Especially, like in the case of this poor woman, when the spell backfired so spectacularly.

"Well, I'm going to need to see the recipe for the spell," Amelia told her.

"Why?" the woman asked. "Can't I just tell you the name of the spell?"

Amelia blinked. This woman was so new to the world of spell crafting, she didn't even know the procedure for reversing a spell.

"Well, I need to know the particulars of the spell, not just the name," Amelia said.

It was the woman's turn to blink at Amelia, although her blink looked more like an especially vigorous shiver.

"Why wouldn't you already know?" the woman asked. "It was *your* spell. That's why I need your help."

AMELIA HAD CREATED and cast her first spell when she was eleven years old. She'd turned her Barbie doll into a zombie doll, complete with plastic rotting flesh and the requisite broken ankle on which to hobble.

She'd been grounded for a week, her parents had had to pay a fine for permitting a minor to practice magic without a license, and she'd had to promise to never ever *ever* do that again.

Of course, that's all she'd wanted to do.

She'd been born with a case of the stubborns, according to her mother. Amelia's stubborns were in fine form where magic was concerned.

She'd pestered her parents relentlessly about getting her a magic tutor. Creating that spell had been fun, and she wanted to do more of that kind of stuff. She'd spent the week she'd been grounded on her computer in her room learning all she could about how to get a spell crafting license.

She'd discovered that would-be wizards, even if they could already cast spells, needed a period of apprenticeship with a wizard licensed as a tutor by the state. So she could either tutor with a real-life witch or wizard—incredibly expensive according to her parents—or she could enroll in an after-school program that did essentially the same thing—far cheaper, if quite a bit slower, because she'd have to share the magical tutor with the rest of her class.

Amelia's family wasn't wealthy, so the private tutor was definitely out. After quite a bit of pestering on her part, Amelia's parents finally relented and allowed her to enroll in the after-school program.

On her third day in the after-school program, she'd turned one of her classmates blue. The instructor, a no-nonsense wizard who was about a hundred-fifty years old with the bushiest white eyebrows Amelia had ever seen, had made Amelia create a reversing spell before he let her go home for the night.

Amelia's parents had called the school when she didn't come home for dinner. They'd been waiting in the hallway for her when she finally got the reversing spell right at eight that night and the old wizard finally let her go home.

"Your daughter," the old wizard had told her parents, "has a natural talent. You would do well to nurture it." He'd raised one of his bushy eyebrows in a way that somehow made him appear even more no-nonsense. "Carefully," he added.

From there on out, Amelia had been hooked on learning how to reverse spells. Reversing spells was like figuring out a giant puzzle made entirely of magic. In other words, it was about the best and most challenging work a spell crafter could undertake.

The hardest part was figuring out what cancelled out what, which wasn't at all intuitive.

For instance, if a spell called for "two drops of sweat from a hardworking man's brow," the ingredient to cancel out that ingredient wasn't the sweat from a hardworking woman's brow.

No. The cancelling ingredient was two drops of sweat from the armpit stain of a lazy man's undershirt. A lazy man being the opposite of a hardworking man. And an armpit stain earned from hours of sitting in a lounge chair watching game shows on television roughly being the opposite thing from a brow slick with sweat from a hard job done well. Two drops of the stuff? So much harder to obtain than brow sweat. The ingredients for most cancelling spells were.

And so on.

Each distinctive spell had its own weirdly logical counter spell. Amelia liked the mystery of discovering exactly what worked and what didn't.

Her parents had been supportive, if a little wary, but Amelia announced that reversing spells was what she wanted to do for a living. She'd even discovered the job had a neat-sounding name: spell reclamation.

Her parents had paid for the best education they could afford. When it became clear Amelia had far out-paced her classmates in the after-school program—and only the best potential wizards were eligible for the program to begin with—Amelia's parents paid the wizard in charge of the program to take Amelia on as an apprentice. It wasn't long before she was out-wizarding her mentor where reclamation spells were concerned. She'd graduated from both her formal education and her apprenticeship with flying colors, and opened her own business doing what she loved best.

Fixing broken spells.

She still created spells from time to time, mostly as a by-product of trying to reverse a spell. But she'd never, ever, *ever* created a spell that would make someone smell like a subdued garbage dump or radiate an arctic cold front.

The woman who was currently suffering from both conditions introduced herself as Darcy Peak. She lived in a modest apartment in a neighborhood that hadn't yet been hit with urban redevelopment.

Amelia currently sat at Darcy's dining room table, tapping away at the keys on Darcy's laptop computer. Darcy had given Amelia the website address where she'd purchased both a wizarding license and the spell that had made her the pariah of her apartment building.

"Do you know how many people, the same ones who passed me in the halls every day without glancing at me or even knowing my name, suddenly glared at me for daring to invade their space with my cold body or my…" Darcy paused, her hands fluttering in front of her face, like she was trying to blow away the smell. "Let's just call it the world's worst body odor. Nothing covers this up, and believe me when I tell you I've tried everything."

Amelia could believe her. Now that she'd spent more time with Darcy, she'd caught the scent of half a dozen different body sprays combined with a spray meant to get rid of offensive odors on furniture.

"Why would you invent a spell like this?" Darcy asked.

"I didn't think I had," Amelia said.

She'd recognized the spell, of course, as soon as Darcy had shown Amelia how to pull it up on the laptop. Amelia had created the spell when she'd still been an apprentice to the old wizard from her after-school program.

But she'd never allowed anyone to put the spell online. Especially not someone who ran a scam wizarding school for the sole intent of bilking people out of their money.

The website practically screamed "scam" in the brilliant purple letters that graced every page and link. Amelia's name was plastered all over the place. She could see why someone might mistake this website as something she'd endorsed, and that made her angry.

Her entire life, all she'd done was try to help people. This website was doing the exact opposite.

The homepage had at least a dozen links to various subpages, some of which required a login. Darcy had logged in on her account, and then clicked on a recipe for the offending spell. A second level spell, which the website assured wannabe wizards they could master "in no time!"

Not likely.

Amelia had been near the end of her apprenticeship when she'd crafted this particular spell. It certainly wasn't made for newbie wizards who hadn't had a few years of practice under their belts.

Sure, the list of ingredients made the spell look easy. Most of them were things people had around the house: two threads from their favorite piece of clothing; the mist from one pump of the spray from their favorite cologne, or half a drop of their favorite perfume (men could substitute aftershave or body spray); a dog-eared corner from a page in their favorite book; two drops of their favorite beverage; and two tablespoons of distilled water.

The finer touches, though—they took a practiced hand. Like needing the exact ratio of sunlight to shadow in the room where the spell's ingredients were mixed. Or collecting the proper amount of emotional energy from the person who was the intended beneficiary of the spell.

But how did the spell end up on this particular website? Amelia hadn't looked at the spell in years. Her original notes were part of her spell book, which was locked in her safe back at the office.

Wasn't it?

Amelia couldn't be sure. All her work involved *removing* spells created by others, not casting her own. Looking back over her old work these days would be the equivalent of pulling out her high school yearbook just to look at all the weird old hairstyles all her friends used to have back then.

"So you didn't actually endorse this website, did you?" Darcy asked.

Amelia shook her head. "I didn't even know it existed, or I would have sent my lawyers after them."

She had very good lawyers on retainer. Most working wizards did.

At least she knew how to counteract this spell. Or her version of the spell. Something minor might have been changed, and if it had, Amelia wasn't sure she'd know just by looking at the online version. She needed to compare it to the original.

She took out her cell and called her office. The receptionist put Amelia through to her assistant, the only other person who had a combination to Amelia's safe.

Amelia's assistant had no magical abilities whatsoever, nor did she have any desire to learn how to cast spells. She was a gamer girl who looked like a fashion model, and she delighted at beating gamer boys who thought women didn't belong in the gaming world. She thought using magic to enhance her abilities was cheating.

"Why would I need to cheat?" she'd told Amelia once. "I want to win fair and square. Otherwise, I don't deserve it."

Amelia wished more people felt that way, but the world was full of people who felt they needed a little extra to get ahead.

Like Darcy.

The spell she'd tried to cast was a confidence spell. Amelia had created the spell to work like a simple charm. All it was supposed to do was give the user a little more of the positive qualities the person already possessed. A big part of the spell was the person's perception of themselves. If the spellcaster thought she was pleasant-looking, the spell amped up her beauty from merely pleasant to unforgettable. If the spellcaster thought her hair was her best feature, the spell was supposed to make her hair look like those shampoo models on TV whose hair flowed in the wind and fell back perfectly into place.

In other words, the spell was supposed to give the user a fantasy version of themselves for a short period of time before it wore off.

Amelia could understand a person wanting a little more of themselves from time to time. She'd used the spell herself on a few first dates when she'd been younger before she'd figured out that someone who only liked the amped-up version of her would be disappointed when the real version showed up after the spell wore off.

Amelia waited on hold while her assistant went to unlock her safe and get out the original spell. While she waited, she asked Darcy why she'd tried to cast the spell in the first place.

Darcy glanced down at her shoes. Simple low-heeled pumps in a nondescript navy blue. They pretty much described Darcy perfectly, from what Amelia had seen so far.

"My boss put me in charge of a big project," Darcy said. "I have a team of six working with me, and I've never been in charge of anything before. I was supposed to start the project today, so I practiced on some other little spells first until I got pretty good at them."

She turned her attention to a candle sitting on her desk off to one side of her laptop. She stared hard at the candle, muttered a short incantation under her breath, snapped her fingers, and the candle flame flickered to life.

"Not bad," Amelia said.

Not everyone could do that. Fire was a tricky spell to learn, especially aiming fire to a finely pinpointed area.

"You learned that by yourself?" Amelia asked.

"Well…" Darcy's face flushed a rosy color, and then she shrugged. "I used to have an actual cabinet for my television."

Darcy's flat screen television was tucked into one corner of her living room across from her desk. The television sat on an unfinished wooden crate. Amelia could see a faint indent in the patterned brown-and-beige carpeting where the television cabinet used to be, along with a few faint scorch marks in the carpeting that she'd initially thought were just part of the pattern.

"You burned up your cabinet," Amelia said.

"Yeah." Darcy sighed. "At least I was smart enough to have a fire extinguisher right next to me when I tried the spell, and it was localized just to the cabinet. The television still works and everything, but that was the last time I practiced in my living room."

Which meant that she'd practiced elsewhere, and Amelia thought she might know where that "elsewhere" had been.

"Bathtub?" she asked.

Darcy blinked at her. "How did you know?"

"How do you think I learned?" Amelia snapped her fingers at the candle, and the flame flickered out. "I burned my eyebrows off the first few times I tried fire spells, but I'd been warned about collateral damage, so I practiced in my parents' bathtub. I nearly set the shower curtain on fire once."

Darcy relaxed a little for the first time since they'd met.

Good. It meant Amelia was finally building a bit of camaraderie with her. Amelia would need it in order to reverse the botched-up confidence spell.

That was the thing about the confidence spell she'd come up with as a teenager. Like every other teenage girl in history, she'd had absolutely no self-confidence when it came to boys she liked. But Amelia already knew what areas she felt were her weak points. She'd need to find out what areas about herself Darcy had been trying to amp up, and people didn't like to admit their shortcomings to strangers.

Especially not a wannabe wizard who knew she'd screwed up badly.

"I tried this spell last night," Darcy said, gesturing at the laptop which was currently displaying Amelia's confidence spell. "And this happened. I mean, I have to smell pretty bad if I can't stand it, you know? People aren't supposed to be able to smell their own b.o. But the instructions said the spell only worked for a short time, so I thought it would wear off."

Her eyes were getting shiny bright with unshed tears. Amelia was pretty sure they were tears of frustration, not self-pity.

"I actually had to call out sick today!" Darcy said. "I haven't called out sick in over two years. I never get sick."

"What type of work do you do?" Amelia asked.

"I work for the city."

That didn't really answer the question, and Darcy knew that, if the way she broke eye contact with Amelia was any indication.

"Kinda need to know the specifics here," Amelia said.

Darcy blew out a frustrated breath. "I work for the licensing bureau. I started out processing renewals, but last year I transferred over to citations."

She worked for the department in the city that handled the licensing of magical practitioners.

Spell crafters. Wizards. Witches. Any sort of magical or mortal folk who used spells.

The very type of license she'd gone to a shady website to obtain.

Darcy gave Amelia a sheepish look. "Yeah, I know. With my background, why didn't I go to a reputable school?"

"The thought did cross my mind," Amelia said.

"The only licensed wizards in the department are the department heads. If I started going to a local school to get my license, all my coworkers would think I'm bucking for a promotion. Especially since I got put in charge of this team."

"And you don't want a promotion?"

Darcy actually shuddered. "Good lord, no. Do you have any idea what kind of trouble an annoyed wizard can make when the department issues a citation for some infraction? And that's not even the worst. Heaven forbid we have to pull someone's license. I *do not* want to make a wizard angry at me."

"But you work in the citations department."

"I do paperwork," Darcy said. "I'm just a clerk. I have no decision-making ability whatsoever."

"What about the new team? What will your team be doing?"

"Going through old records," Darcy said. "Some of the old records are a mess, so we're transferring them over to new databases

that will make it easier to cross-check names against previous infractions. Strictly paperwork. I don't expect that we'll find anything
useful, but someone with a higher pay grade than mine decided it
was important."

Amelia had gotten so lost in her conversation with Darcy that
she'd almost forgotten that she was on hold with her office. When
Amelia's assistant picked up the line again, it was almost a shock.

"I can't find the spell," Amelia's assistant said. "I'm sorry I had
you on hold for so long, but I thumbed through your whole spell
book, and it's just not there."

A cold knot of dread settled in Amelia's belly. "What do you
mean it's not there?"

"I mean it's not there. It's not in the index, it's not in the book,
there isn't even a blank page where the spell should be. It's just
gone."

AMELIA WAS GOING to need to give her assistant a bonus. Or a new
videogame system. Or maybe a week in Tahiti.

Darcy currently sat in a small conference room next to the
assistant's office. Even behind closed doors, Darcy still radiated
smelly arctic air. Amelia's assistant had shot her a long-suffering look
as she put on the jacket she'd worn to work that day and turned on
a space heater near her feet.

Amelia had no other alternative but to take Darcy and her
laptop to her office. Whatever was going on, some powerful
wizardry was involved, and Darcy had clearly stumbled into it by
accident. Amelia couldn't leave her alone in her apartment unpro-
tected, and Amelia couldn't do what she needed to do outside of her
office.

Someone had tampered with Amelia's spell book. She needed to
find out who and if they were connected in any way with the
website Darcy had used to create the spell. She needed to reverse
the stinky/freezing spell Darcy had inadvertently cast on herself.
And Amelia needed to figure out who was behind the scam website

using her name to lure in unsuspecting victims and then zap them with fake versions of Amelia's own spells.

Amelia had her IT department—two very competent computer gurus, one a licensed wizard, the other just a natural with all things electronic—start going over Darcy's laptop and the website.

"Find out who's behind the privacy settings," she'd told her IT guys. Any half-baked scam artist would pony up enough money for not only the standard privacy setting for their website's URL but a few magical privacy walls as well, but her IT guys were up to the challenge. "I want to know everything about them because I'm going postal on their respective asses."

Then she called her very good lawyer to get him started on the paperwork necessary to shut the website down—at least temporarily—once her IT guys came up with the person or persons behind the scam. She might not be able to put them out of business period, but she could make sure they never used her name and her spells to con another student ever again.

Once she got the wheels rolling, she took her spell book and returned to her office and locked the door after herself.

To the casual observer, her corner office looked like a well-deserved perk for the wizard in charge of the most successful spell reclamation business in Moretown Bay. Furnished in dark, heavy wooden furniture specifically crafted for Amelia's smaller stature, the office had the sedate look of old money and older power. Amelia had softened the dark tones with potted plants and tapestries in muted tones hung on the walls.

The safe that housed her spell book was concealed in the credenza behind her desk. Both the credenza and her desk had been made by the elves who lived on Marlette Island, a thickly forested island in the middle of the bay that gave the city of Moretown Bay its name.

The Marlette elves had lived on the island for untold generations. They harvested just enough lumber from the island to keep the forest healthy. When fog didn't blanket the city, like today, Amelia had a fantastic view of the island from the two floor-to-ceiling windows that made up the outside walls of her corner office.

The spectacular view wasn't the only reason Amelia was thankful for today's rare clear skies.

The Marlette elves infused magic into the forest as they cared for it. Enough of that magic remained in the lumber they harvested from the forest to be useful to magic folk who had the skill to use it. Amelia did, but it took a clear line of sight from her office for the wood's magic to work.

Like most magic, the wood's magic needed a connection to something else. For the wood, that connection was to the island of its birth. When the wood could "see" the forest on Marlette Island, the connection grew so strong it became, in effect, its own ley line.

The natural ley lines in Moretown Bay had been mapped by wizards employed by the city decades ago. Most wizards learned their locations and properties during the first month of their apprenticeship. It took hours of practice to learn the skills necessary to use the ley lines properly.

Amelia had specifically crafted her office to create a space where magic was more powerful. She'd learned this particular trick from the wizard who'd been her mentor during her apprenticeship.

"It's not cheating?" she'd asked him.

"It's using the magical world to your advantage," he'd said. "It only enhances your natural ability."

"But isn't that cheating?"

He'd shrugged. "You call it cheating. I call it using your skills to become the best wizard you can without violating any of the laws that apply to the use of magic."

The study of the laws of magic had been part of Amelia's apprenticeship, and that, more than the crafting of spelling, had made her head spin.

The various permutations of the laws that applied to the use of magic would have filled an entire library. Luckily they all boiled down to two things: the prohibition against spell crafting without a license, and the prohibition against doing any person, whether magical or non-magical, any harm.

"Harm," of course, had so many different definitions depending on the situation involved that Amelia wondered if the wizards who had crafted the laws of magic had been lawyers in a former life.

The spell that Darcy had inflicted on herself had certainly caused her harm. Not life-threatening harm, but the results of the spell had certainly impacted her life just the same.

She needed to reverse the spell as quickly—and safely—as she could. The first thing she needed to do was see if the original spell was still in her spell book, just hidden somehow.

She opened her spell book to the index page. Amelia had made entries on the index at the time she wrote the spell, and she wrote all new spells on the next blank page of her spell book following the last completed spell. That resulted in a chronological index of the magic she'd worked on and learned during her apprenticeship.

Some of the early spells were really rough, and Amelia wished she could delete them from the spell book. But this was her education in a nutshell, warts and all, and Amelia would never erase them.

She found the section of the index where the confidence spell should have been, but her assistant had been right—there was nothing there. Not even a blank line. Amelia turned to the page for the spell in front of the confidence spell, and then thumbed to the beginning of the next spell. None of the page numbers were missing.

Someone had spelled her book to make it *appear* like the spell was missing. That had to be it.

Amelia removed a sachet packet from the top drawer of her desk, opened the top, and dipped in the little finger of her right hand. She closed her eyes and concentrated, said a simple incantation, and then touched each of her eyelids with the little finger of her right hand.

Then she opened her eyes.

The spell she'd just cast was a revealing spell. She used it sometimes before meeting with a difficult client in her office. The spell let her see through any charms, glamours, or veils to let her observe the person beneath the magic.

It should have revealed the missing spell.

It didn't.

Instead of the spell, a blank page appeared where the spell should have been.

No writing. No drawings. No list of ingredients. Not even any doodles scribbled in the margins, which Amelia used to do when she was younger.

She stared at the page without fully comprehending it.

Her spell book had been locked in her safe. Her safe had been protected by wards specifically designed to prevent anyone from stealing the spell book—or anything else inside the safe.

How could the spell just be *gone?*

She hadn't written the spell in disappearing ink. She didn't use tricks like that. Disappearing ink was for stage magicians, just like flash paper and slight-of-hand tricks. Real wizards used the magic in the world around them.

Like the ley line created by the wooden furniture in her office.

Amelia repeated the spell, only this time when she touched her closed eyelids with the little finger of her right hand, she rested her left hand on the surface of her desk, her palm flat against the wood. She reached out to the magic living in the wood and felt it flow through her, making the spell grow stronger.

This time when she opened her eyes, she saw something on the page.

Not her spell. That had been irrevocably stolen from her, but the thief had left something behind.

A symbol she hadn't seen in years.

Not since she'd walked into an after-school program run by a wizard with the bushiest eyebrows she'd ever seen and turned one of her classmates blue.

It took Amelia's IT people nearly four hours to break through all the privacy settings, firewalls, shell companies, and bank accounts to track down the wizard who'd stolen Amelia's spell and then sold it to not one, but a myriad of online wizarding schools.

Each online school had a slightly different version of her confidence spell on their website. Once her IT guys had found the websites and hacked into them, Amelia's assistant had printed out each version of the spell and charted the differences.

With that chart, Amelia was able to figure out the recipe for her original spell. Which in turn let her create a reversing spell for the version of the spell Darcy had used.

Or so Amelia hoped.

"I can fix this," Amelia told a shivering Darcy. "I just want to make sure that when I do the reclamation spell, you don't end up with anything worse."

For all Amelia knew, the wizard who'd stolen her spell had built some type of safety mechanism into the spell that not only let the wizard know when the spell was being used and by whom, but also when someone attempted to reverse the spell. Amelia didn't want to put Darcy in any more danger than she was already in.

"You mean there's something worse than this?" Darcy asked.

"You have no idea," Amelia said.

She did, but she didn't want to frighten Darcy out of her wits.

Amelia's assistant had tracked down a space heater for the small conference room. The temperature in the conference room was currently somewhere between toasty and tropical rain forest, but Darcy was still shivering. The gooseflesh on her arms had gooseflesh of its own, and her lips were starting to turn a dusty shade of blue that matched the color of her denim skirt.

As for the smell, Amelia barely noticed it anymore. She chalked up the lack of stench to nose blindness on her part. When one of the IT guys knocked on the conference room door and poked his head inside, he turned an alarming shade of green. He handed Amelia a note and backed out of the conference room, clearly holding his breath, and shut the door firmly behind himself.

The paper had two handwritten lines of text. Two names and corresponding addresses.

One of the names didn't surprise Amelia. She had seen the symbol the wizard had left behind in her spell book. But the addresses? Those did surprise her. They were both in Moretown Bay.

The first was in the financial district according to the note. Amelia didn't go to the financial district often—her offices were closer to the bay and chosen specifically for the view of Marlette Island—but a lot of wizards had offices in that section of the city.

She stared for a long minute at the second address.

She'd been surprised when she saw the second name. But now, combined with the address—which she knew well—the whole thing brought tears to her eyes.

Technically she had enough information to have her lawyer contact the police about the theft, not to mention get restraining orders against all the websites who used her name to advertise their slightly altered version of her confidence spell.

But the theft had been personal. The thief had been too good. She couldn't just assume the symbol had been an unintended by-product of the theft of her spell *out of her own spell book.*

The thief had been calling her out, as the kids used to say in school. And more than that, the thief had been patient enough to wait for someone like Darcy to try the spell and then go to Amelia to fix it.

She was the best fixer in town, after all. Wasn't that what all her advertising said?

Well, it was time she fixed this mess, too.

Amelia crumpled up the piece of paper. "Okay, then," she said to Darcy. "I need to pay someone a visit."

"You're leaving?" The shrill tone of Darcy's voice betrayed just how scared she really was. "What if something happens to you? I can't go through life stuck like this."

"You won't."

Amelia stood up, and for the first time noticed she was only a little taller than Darcy even though Darcy was sitting in one of the conference room chairs. And she wasn't even sitting up straight.

"You came to me for a reason," Amelia said. "Your instincts told you I could reverse the spell, and you're right. I can."

Or at least she hoped she could. She'd had a couple of failures over the years, and she'd never run up against a wizard powerful enough to do what had been done to Amelia's spell book.

"You have good instincts," she told Darcy. "That's something every wizard learns—to follow their instincts. You did that, and I'm guessing your online licensing class didn't cover that part of magic. Sometimes your gut knows things your head hasn't quite caught on to yet."

Darcy tried to smile, although her teeth were chattering too much for the smile to really work. "Are you trying to teach me about the way magic works?"

The question surprised Amelia, but she supposed that's what she'd just been doing.

"Because I could really use someone to teach me about magic," Darcy said. "I mean, I have a license, but I clearly don't know what I'm doing. I could use a little help, you know?"

In all the years since Amelia had received her own wizard's license, she'd never taken on an apprentice. She advertised herself as the best reclamation wizard in the city, but that was just advertising. Deep down, she still felt like that awkward teenage girl who needed to create a confidence spell just to talk to boys.

Maybe all wizards—the good ones anyway—had that core of self-doubt living in the deepest, most secret places of their hearts.

She couldn't ask her own mentor, not anymore. She didn't know anyone else she could ask. Darcy was in the same boat. She had no one to discuss magic with either.

Maybe they could learn from each other.

But first she had work to do.

"Let me take care of this first," Amelia said. "Then we'll talk."

THE ADDRESS in the financial district led Amelia to a side street that was little more than an alley. Concrete-and-steel monstrosities rose high around her, making her feel small. The sound of late afternoon traffic echoed oddly in the small space, and paper trash caught in a late afternoon breeze eddied around her feet.

For the most part, Amelia had come to terms with her size. She had magic to protect herself when she needed to, but most of the time she simply relied on attitude. The "as if" lesson she'd learned early in life.

Walk as if you belonged somewhere, and people assumed you did.

Create spells as if you knew exactly what you're doing, and that attitude would infuse itself into the spell, thereby producing the desired effect.

Confront a long-standing enemy you didn't even know you'd made as if you never did anything to deserve their ire.

That one? She was having trouble with that attitude.

She stood in front of a small door to a shop that was well-disguised among the surrounding office buildings. The shop looked like it had been carved out of a forgotten corner at the back of the building, shoved in among the machines that controlled the heat and air conditioning and ran the elevators and electricity and phones.

A simple veil hid the door—and no doubt the shop on the other side of the door—from the general public, but Amelia had no trouble piercing it. The veil had been specifically designed to allow any wizard worth half his or her weight in salt to break through.

This kind of place wouldn't be licensed. The entire feel of this area had the rundown, scammy aura of an off-the-books operation, and for the first time in her life, Amelia felt unsure that her magic would protect her.

But she needed to confront the wizard on the other side of the door, if for no other reason than to ask, "Why?"

She started to reach for the doorknob when the door opened by itself.

Another spell? Who would waste the cost of a spell on opening a door?

"Come on in, Amelia," called a voice from inside the shop. "I've been expecting you."

A chill ran down Amelia's spine and settled in the small of her back.

She shouldn't have been surprised that this wizard would recognize her by the feel of her magic even though the only magic she'd used was to break the veil.

As if, she reminded herself. Walk as if you belong here.

She held her head high and walked inside.

If she'd been at all claustrophobic, she would have run screaming back outside to the relative expanse of the alley.

The shop was crammed floor to very-low ceiling with all sorts of supplies, books, and accessories necessary for the creating and casting of spells. Herbs filled gallon-sized glass jars snugged up against each other on shelves just beyond Amelia's reach. Various dried body parts from all sorts of animals—mammals, reptiles, insects, fish, crustaceans; you name it, the shop had it—filled shelves and bins and plastic bags.

Filing boxes the mortals used to store comic books shared space with books of all varieties—handwritten journals, leather bound spell books, and hardback tomes detailing the history of magic and its integration into the mortal world, not to mention biographies of famous wizards known to magic folk the world over. The filing boxes were filled with individual handwritten spells, each carefully sleeved with a pressboard backing to protect the fragile nature of the paper on which they'd been written.

And those were just a few of the shop's wares that Amelia could see in the dim light shining down through the dusty air from recessed lights in the ceiling.

The shop smelled like sage and rosemary combined with dust and the slightly moldy odor of old paper and books.

And coffee.

Amelia couldn't see anyone in the shop, but she followed the aroma of a well-brewed cup of coffee through the narrow aisles between the shop's wares until she reached a display case near the back of the store.

The case held a variety of high-end merchandise: wands made of carved ivory or smoky crystal; insignias from the old European wizarding families who'd fled their homelands during the mortals' world wars; a complete spell book encased in a clear acrylic box, sealed to protect it from the elements.

Under other circumstances, Amelia might have been tempted to spend time looking through all these things. Her parents hadn't been magical folk, and she hadn't grown up with a tradition of magic that went back generations. Her only magical family had been the wizard who'd been her mentor, first in the after-school program and then in private instruction, and the other kids in the program.

Like the classmate she'd turned blue without meaning to.

He sat on a stool behind the glass display case. Lewis Tempe.

She'd forgotten all about him until she saw his name on the note from her IT guy, but he apparently hadn't forgotten about her.

"Good to see you, Lewis," she said.

"And you," he said.

It was clear neither of them meant it.

Amelia remembered Lewis as a tall, skinny kid with bad skin, thick glasses, and a kind smile that could light up a room. He'd been two years older than Amelia when she joined the after-school program, and he'd already been well on his way to developing his own spells.

And she'd turned him blue.

She'd told everyone it had been a mistake, that she hadn't meant to do it, but that wasn't the truth.

The truth was that Lewis had been an insufferable know-it-all. He'd been smart as a whip, and he'd known it and wanted to make sure everyone else did, too. He got away with being obnoxious most of the time because he'd smile and say he really didn't mean anything by it, and everyone would forgive him.

By the second day, Amelia had wanted to kill him.

By the third day, she wanted to teach him a lesson.

So she'd cast a spell that turned him blue.

Both of them had to stay until she'd created a spell that reversed the color spell and returned Lewis to normal.

He'd complained about it the whole time. He said the blue skin itched and that it was going to make his face break out even more, as if the blue pigment was body paint or something toxic.

Amelia had never been so glad to cast a spell in her life as she'd been to cast a reversing spell that actually worked and turned Lewis normal again.

Lewis had only gone to the after-school program twice after that. The following week the wizard who taught the program announced that Lewis wouldn't be back and that he'd decided to pursue his magic in a different direction.

A direction that had led him here, to this cramped little store where things like licenses didn't matter, only the amount a person was willing to pay.

By the looks of him, Lewis had paid dearly, and not with money.

He was still thin, but his shoulders were stooped and a silver cane with a dragon's head carved in the handle leaned against his side of the display case. His skin had cleared up but left behind deep scars. Those scars were buried in wrinkles that lined his forehead and made his cheeks look sallow and sunken. His hair was mostly gone. He still wore thick glasses, but the corners of his mouth had pulled downward.

When was the last time he'd smiled? His kind smile had been his one saving grace, and Amelia realized that she missed it.

She also realized why there'd been two names on the list her IT guy had handed her.

"You apprenticed with him, too," she said.

She was always under the impression that she'd been the only apprentice the old wizard with the bushy eyebrows who'd taught her after-school program had taken.

"I did," Lewis said. "He agreed to teach me because he said I had potential." He shot her a poisonous glance. "I just didn't have yours."

Amelia almost winced, but she caught herself just in time. She'd come here to find out why, and it looked like Lewis was going to tell her without having to ask him the question.

"It was never a competition," she said. "We were all just there to learn."

"Of course, it was a competition!"

The words came out so forcefully that spittle flew from his thin lips.

Amelia took an involuntary step backwards as he coughed. After a few moments, he seemed to get himself under control.

"It was always a competition," Lewis said. "And he encouraged it. He always used to tell me about how well you were doing, all the advanced techniques you were learning. 'And for someone so young, just remarkable,' he'd say. And then he'd look at me like I was a bug he found wanting." Lewis nodded as if to himself. It was the mannerism of a man decades older. "He thought the competition would bring out the best in me. Make me the best wizard I could be. And it did. For a little while."

He coughed again. Amelia was tempted to use her revealing spell to see what was wrong with him, but she didn't really need to know the particulars.

He was dying. That much was clear. Now that she'd been near him for a while, the decaying odor emanating from his body overcame the rest of the smells in the shop.

She didn't need to know what disease would be blamed for his death. The real cause was the dark magic he'd used to finally beat her.

That's how he'd stolen her spell from her spell book even through her wards. Dark magic. She should have realized it earlier, but she didn't run into dark magic often. It always left footprints, like the symbol the amped-up version of her revealing spell let her see. Or like the changes to her spell that had turned Darcy into a stinky, arctic version of herself.

But using dark magic exacted a heavy price, and Lewis was paying it.

Had her old teacher paid it, too? Or had Lewis…

"What happened to him?" she asked. "Professor—"

"Don't say his name!"

This outburst brought on another coughing fit. It took Lewis longer this time to get his coughs under control. When he spoke again, his voice was raspy and faint.

"Where do you think I learned it from?" he asked. "Our teacher was not nearly as pure and squeaky clean as he portrayed to the school and our parents. He was a jealous old man on a downward spiral. While he encouraged the best in you, he encouraged far different things in me. Things that made us both wealthy." He glanced over her shoulder at the overstuffed shelves and narrow aisles of his shop. "For a while."

Amelia shook her head. "I don't believe you."

Lewis smiled at her, but it wasn't his kind smile. "The beauty of it is that you don't have to. The only thing that matters is that I finally beat you. I stole from you and you never knew it. I sold what I stole to websites I knew would splash your name all over the place, and you never knew it. I wanted to *ruin* you, you sanctimonious bitch, but it turned out your spell was so lame no one ever wanted to try it."

No one except one poor wizard wannabe who worked for the city, and who'd been put in charge of a team that would be researching old licensing infractions and possibly pulling the licenses of wizards who had too many but had escaped detection.

Someone like Lewis?

"Do you know who tried to use that spell?" Amelia asked.

Lewis shrugged. "Does it matter? It finally brought you here. I've lived long enough to see you realize that you've never been the best. That you could be brought down, and I'm the one who did it."

He'd tried to ruin Darcy's life, and it didn't matter to him. She'd only been a pawn in his petty game of revenge.

He'd tried to take Amelia down, too, but as smart as he was, he didn't realize he could never win. Not this way. She might have lost business if people actually believed she endorsed the websites that hosted her altered spell, but he hadn't put her out of business.

Now that she knew dark magic was involved, she knew she could reverse the spell and return Darcy to normal. Her lawyer would make sure her spell was taken off the internet, and she'd cast her own (very expensive) spell to make sure no caches of the spell remained online.

Lewis had lost, but the sad thing was, he'd thought he'd won.

Amelia didn't care. She'd never been in this for the competition. She simply loved working with magic. Feeling the energy between the wood in her office and the forest on Marlette Island. Helping reverse the mistakes people made when they grew careless with magic.

Helping them reclaim the same love of magic that had made them want to learn to create and cast spells in the first place.

Lewis would never understand any of that, and Amelia was suddenly too tired to try to explain it to him. He wouldn't listen anyway.

"I wish you well, Lewis," she said. "You probably don't believe that, but I do."

She left the shop without saying anything else. As she closed the door behind herself, she heard him start to cough.

THE MORNING AIR was crisp and clean, but clouds to the west promised rain that afternoon. Amelia had an umbrella with her just in case. She didn't expect to be here long. She just needed to pay her respects to someone she still held in high regard, whether he deserved it or not.

Her old professor had been buried in the same cemetery where Amelia's mother and father had been buried after they died in a car crash. Amelia had been twenty-four. Their deaths had left her all alone in the world, and she'd thought about contacting him then but she hadn't.

His tombstone was a modest affair that simply listed the dates of his birth and death along with the inscription *Mentor and Friend.*

He had been her mentor, but he'd never been her friend. That more than anything had kept her from reaching out to him after her parents died. What could she say? He'd taught her to stand on her own two feet. To take responsibility for her actions. To be accountable to herself and to magic.

"It will respect you if you respect it," he'd told her more than once.

"I don't believe him," she said to the grave. "I think that's what I came here to say. I don't believe that you helped him do what he did to me."

Amelia had had her team look into the professor's life while she took care of reversing the spell Darcy had cast on herself. The dates on his tombstone put the professor's age at nearly two hundred when he'd died nearly six months ago, which correlated with what her team was able to discover.

For the last ten years of his life, the professor had lived in a retirement home for elderly wizards. Amelia had spoken with one of the aides who knew the professor. The aide had given Amelia his condolences, which she didn't feel she deserved, and told her how much he'd enjoyed spending time with the professor.

"His mind had started to go a little near the end," the aide told her. "But he was a truly pleasant man, if a little irascible at times. We finally had to cast a dampening bracelet on him, otherwise we found our dinner dishes floating in the air and dancing to disco playing on the sound system."

A dampening bracelet would have prevented the professor from using any magic at all, including dark magic.

The website where Darcy had found Amelia's stolen confidence spell hadn't been around all that long. Shady online wizarding schools rarely were. The professor's name had been one of two names listed behind the privacy walls as an owner of the website. The other owner was Lewis. But by that time the professor was nearing the end of his own life, and he probably didn't even know what Lewis was doing.

Had the professor shown Lewis how to work with dark magic? Amelia would never know for certain, but she doubted it. The professor had lived a long life. Lewis wouldn't live to see the end of the year.

Amelia's lawyers were working on the paperwork, which would be filed later in the day. For now, Amelia had an appointment with Darcy in a few hours to discuss a possible apprenticeship. It would be a big step for both of them, but maybe it was time for Amelia to take that step.

To act as if she knew enough to mentor a new wizard. To follow in the professor's footsteps, but never to take his place.

No one could ever do that.

Amelia laid her hand on the professor's tombstone. Someone had put flowers on the grave next to his. A beautiful arrangement full of yellow daisies and white roses and little blue buds she didn't know the name of. The scent of flowers mixed with the smell of fresh-cut grass and the smell of the approaching rain.

She should have brought flowers with her. She brought flowers to her parents' graves when she visited, but for some reason she hadn't thought about bringing them with her today.

She laid her hand on the professor's tombstone intending to say her final goodbyes. The first drops of rain started to fall splashing across the words "Mentor and Friend."

Did it have to be a final goodbye? What was the saying—a person never dies as long as you remember them?

Amelia was about to embark on a new part of her magical career. She could use some advice, and she could use someone to talk to. What better place to get it than from her old mentor? Maybe along the way they'd become friends.

She thought he might like that.

She opened her umbrella. Maybe while she was here she'd go visit her parents, let them know how their girl—who would always be their "little" girl—was doing.

She patted the tombstone one more time. "Until next time," she said to the professor.

And she'd be sure to bring flowers.

ABOUT THE AUTHOR

A prolific and versatile writer, Annie's a frequent contributor to both *Fiction River* and *Pulphouse Fiction Magazine*. Her recent work includes the near-future science fiction short novel *In Dreams*, the gritty urban fantasy novel *Iris & Ivy*, and the superhero novel *Faster*. Annie's stories appear regularly on Tangent Online's recommended reading lists, and "The Color of Guilt," originally published in *Fiction River: Hidden in Crime*, was selected as one of *The Best Crime and Mystery Stories 2016*. She's even had a story selected for inclusion in study materials for Japanese college entrance exams.

Annie also writes sweet romance under the name Liz McKnight, and is a founding member and contributor to the innovative Uncollected Anthology series of themed urban and contemporary fantasy anthologies.

Find out more about Annie at:
annie-reed.com

BB bookbub.com/authors/annie-reed
a amazon.com/Annie-Reed/e/B006G1P9YO

A WORTHWHILE SACRIFICE

REI ROSENQUIST

THE WOLVES COME EVERY NIGHT. Right after dusk. As the sky becomes deep purple-gray and the air fills with the heavy scent of damp grass, we wait with piqued ears for the horn blasts that signal the beasts' approach. Sealed up in our huts, with our magical locks drawn on every door in time, we watch their ferocity slam useless against meager wooden structures their strong bodies should—by all rights—break. But the magic protects our flesh and blood. A complex set of simple sigils drawn in charcoal on the back of the main door is all it takes to keep the monsters away. But, should any of us fail this one simple task, we are guaranteed a gruesome death.

At the first signs of the sun growing low, the entire town gathers together. Master Lock Maker and five skilled assistants draw the necessary locks on the main doors. The doors click shut just as the sun flashes and disappears. The whole town harbors all together in the sitting rooms of the most central homes. We sit beside the fire, eat and drink, knit or weave, read old scrolls, and talk story. We do everything but delay in our coming to this mandatory nightly gathering.

Today, foolishly, I've delayed.

TARRY, our Master Lock Maker and my dearest friend, came to me personally around breakfast time. A clump of autumn-red hair fell across their pepper-colored face. Their stark green eyes sparkled at me, full of trust. "Cedar. I have a vital task for you."

"Yes?"

"Well before dusk, get water from the northern well and bring it back. We have barely two barrels left. Hardly enough for even one more night."

"Not a problem."

The recent earthquake had ruined the inner-town well. It'd be a trek from the center of town to the hill on the northern-most tip, where the other well sat beside a cabin that overlooked the whole valley. It was a place I remembered from childhood. A place Gram

—my genetic originator and birth-maker—used to take me for quietude and private instruction.

I'd left my room straight after, the morning air still fresh with sweet honeysuckle and the night's wood smoke. I ran through town with much haste, grabbing all the necessary trekking gear, and made record time to the northern cabin.

And then, I'd dawdled.

Finding scrolls handwritten by Gram, I got myself caught up in the snare of nostalgia. My vision blurred behind the heavy clouds of longing for times gone. Happier days sitting in soft sweet grass under tall emerald trees, my body pressed alongside Gram. I'd listen for hours on end to stories of how modern humans came to be. Born without mothers and fathers, dwelling in small villages, our genes replicated using sigils enclosed in wooden eggs.

Gram had claimed the good masters of the past did away with sex for all its blood and hormones and pheromones to try and save us. When it worked, humans everywhere believed again in magic. The idea was always funny—a world without magic. But Gram said it once was that way, and I believed everything Gram said to me.

I'd gotten up, then, and stumbled across the room, my belly hot and heavy with sorrow. I bumped mindlessly into Gram's working desk and out tumbled Gram's drawings of what the world used to be like. Towers of metal and glass. Bridges that spanned massive rivers flowing from high mountains. Then, under those pages, I found Gram's notes on the last known sigils that made up the all-important door locks. Beneath those, I found my own old poorly recreated sigils.

What a mess my hand was, then. No better now, despite Tarry's encouragement.

I carefully laid all these papers in a fire built for the purpose of forgetting the past. Quietly, as I watched the flames devour the past, I re-promised I'd never return to sigil-making. I wasn't cut out for it. Besides, Tarry was a much better Master Lock Maker—no questions asked.

A cloud of bitter black smoke blew into my eyes. As if waking from a dream, I'd remembered: I was meant to gather water for the town! And while the embers crackled down to a dull orange glow, I looked out the small window and started with shock. The sky was deep blue-gray, the clouds already peppered with pink and orange.

Cursing myself, I'd grabbed the bucket and charged out of the cabin.

As MY FEET run across dead leaves and small stones, the pines high overhead begin to shift and warp in the lengthening rays of sunlight. Their needles brush together in the wind, whispering in a soft hush of creaking limbs. The wind kicks up and presses against my back. I shiver and quickly climb the dirt path to the high hilly clearing where the well sits.

"Being out before the day's end is a perfectly safe activity," Gram's voice bubbles up in my mind, encouraging me. Gram-- Master Lock Master before Tarry--always encouraged everyone in town. Gram was everyone's best friend before…

The accident, everyone calls it.

It was no accident, and we all know it. Suicide, that's what it was. Even if none of us know why Gram wanted to die.

I shudder, the memory of Gram's blood pooling on the middle floor of our cabin twisting up my gut. The sting of that unexpected discovery--Gram dead on the ground of their hut--never hurts any less. No matter how many eras go by.

I breathe out, readjusting the empty bucket on my shoulder, and calm myself with an ancient mantra: "Light hits the pine; the forest is mine. Shadow wraps the trunk; my time is done."

The pine needles still glow green-yellow. I have time.

Approaching the old stone rim of the well, I survey the grounds for damage. The big earthquake a few moon cycles ago really shook things up, but from what I can see, everything is stable. No major structural damage. No big trees fell to block either the path or the clearing here.

Along the tree line, shadows thicken as I lift the age-warped well cover. The thick cedar rope is frayed and rotted. I have to be watchful of the abrading fibers, so I don't end up with two palms full of splinters.

Just as the bucket's about to breach the stone lip of the well, it comes.

The ear-splitting blast of the wolf horn.

My whole body goes rigid. It's too soon. The sun isn't down. The trunks aren't wrapped in shadow. I should have time.

But the wolf horn is an unmistakable sound. Step one in our warning system. That horn always blows from the far southern watch tower. It means someone in the tower has seen the flash of black-gray fur. The sparkle of a yellow eye. A long body moving stealthily.

The second horn blows, confirming the wolves' approach. I scramble for the bucket, determined to complete my task like an idiot. Sometimes, in the face of overwhelming danger, we humans do the damnedest things. Like finishing up drawing water from a well when we ought to run.

When I get the bucket up, the third horn blows.

A third horn? Impossible! It's far too close and off to my left. It has to be from the eastern watch tower. The one protected by the river. The one wolves can't get to. The one that's protected.

Something is horribly wrong.

My grip slips and down goes the bucket of water. I leave it. My eyes dart to the undergrowth, imagining the red glow of wolf eyes closing in. I see no such thing.

Time to run.

Sweat beads my brow as I take off for the town. Crowded together, cedars, pines, and false firs become blurs of confusion. In the darkening shadows, I keep thinking there's movement. I force my eyes open wide like tea cup saucers, try to both see where my feet are slamming into the ground and the surrounding forest. But my wide-angle view keeps collapsing into tunnel vision.

I can't do it. Won't make it. I stop, lungs burning, huffing, vision going blurry.

Catching my breath takes too long. Every tree and every plant looks as if it's a wolf, ready to devour me. Every leaf transforms into a sharp tooth. Every branch, a snarling muzzle. I can't move, can't run, can't stop the wolves from killing everyone I love.

"Don't give up," Gram's voice rises up inside me.

Gram always said that.

And then, out of nowhere, they'd killed themself.

It didn't add up.

What if Gram hadn't killed themself? What if it'd been a sneak wolf attack? No one would have believed it. No one will believe it now. But, the wolves are still coming.

I have to warn Tarry.

Tarry's face in my mind forces my body to move.

The fourth horn blast goes off from the eastern tower, confirming the wolves there too. As I run, a sickening realization slaps me in the face. The eastern wolves have to be a new pack. No wolf has ever crossed the river and lived. Long ago, the original pack tried once. Our scouts found scores of bodies. The wolves are anything but dumb. They don't ever try again what the pack failed to accomplish. As proof, the watchers in the east tower haven't needed to blast their horn in--

My whole life.

The watchers there aren't even trained in lock making. Instead, every afternoon, Tarry goes by before the first south horn blows and locks the door for them.

My gut clenches, another realization punching me in the chest.

Tarry lives in the last hut nearest the river on the eastern edge of town. Their yard is right beside the sleepy eastern watch tower that's blowing its horns right now. Gathering the locking supplies in preparation of the early coming of the southern wolves, Tarry will by all rights still be there. And their hut will be the first hut hit, unprepared, door standing wide open.

No matter how fast Tarry is at lock making, nobody is that fast.

In the distance, I think I hear the snarling of wolves coming. I can smell their stench. I can feel the vibrations in the ground of their feet pounding the earth. I can hear their huffing breath sniffing me out. Their noses could rise up out of the underbrush, through the thick needles and rotting leaves any second. Their ugly, scabby, black-gray blood-smeared faces will burst forth, snarling, baring hideous yellow-white glistening teeth dripping in saliva, hungry for me.

I will not give up.

I force myself to run faster. My long, thin blades of legs snap through air like whips tied to my hips. The forest flies by. I push harder, tightening my whole body into a lightning bolt slicing across the spongy ground. I don't even bother with stealth. Maybe the wolves will hear the ruckus and wonder if I'm something dangerous, buying me necessary seconds.

They won't, though. I smell human. Of treats. Of a fresh meal.

Branches snap behind me. A cacophony of snarls.

I don't stop or look back. I crash through the last of the trees. Some hundred meters away, I can see the beginning of the huts. Mine is small and thatched, old and oddly antique. Off to my left, at the farthest eastern edge, is Tarry's. Small and modest, in need of repair. The hand-tiled roof always needs patching, and the white-washed walls always need cleaning. The scrubby grass is dead and needs pulling, which makes for bad lunch picnics but nice for color balance.

As I hit the gravel where the footpath ends, I come up short.

Right in front of me stands a huge, snarling, drool-dripping wolf.

I'm about to do what nobody alive has ever done. I'm about to face this fucker down. Hand to tooth. I'm a fool, but here we go.

The wolf's slender body ripples, full of tight muscle. The thick, sleek fur is blue in the haze light of the dying day. A white halo of fur surrounds a dangerous mouth and bright yellow, perfectly round eyes. A wide red-and-purple panting mouth, jaws full of sharp teeth. Puffs of white breath evaporate into the chill of the humid evening.

This is it, then.

Might as well go down with a crash.

I stomp out into the clearing that forms the first outer ring of the town. I'm still a goddamn long way from Tarry's hut, I know. But this is me improvising, doing the best I can.

"Hey blood face!" I scream, waving my arms wildly above my head.

The Leader of the Pack cocks their grisly head and approaches me languidly. Glowing yellow-green forest eyes swallow me whole.

Drink up, furry fucker.

"That's right, over here," I bellow.

All around me, wet wolves pad out of the woodwork and begin doing just as I predicted they will. They've crossed the river like I've guessed, and now they circle up around their hulking Pack Leader, closing in, waiting for the cue.

I pick up a rock and throw it.

Pack Leader snarls. A low growl is born up from the massive throat that could, if it wanted, swallow my head whole up to the shoulders. Instead, it bristles the back ridge of its fur.

Screams come from the town. Doors slam. I don't see Tarry anywhere, but now the town knows. I snarl back at the wolves to keep them distracted and throw another stone.

A roar goes up from the whole pack and the leader bolts for me.

Not *at* me. The wolves don't ever charge right for us. They're more clever about it. Pack Leader whips around a massive craggy red cedar three times the width of me and disappears. The rest of the pack follow pattern, splitting up and dashing into the trees and shadows.

I shoot straight forward as if I'm running to the middle of town then, in true wolf fashion, I cut off. Sharp and to the left. I hear the wolves panting, and their paws scratching at the dead leaves and tiny stones underfoot. They aren't anticipating my behavior because we humans don't run like they do. Only, right now, I have to. Keep them guessing before they close in around me.

After the third maneuver like this, a plan comes to me. It relies on the one thing I know. These river-crossing wolves are new to these parts. They're a break-off group from somewhere else. They don't know the first thing about our town.

So, if I keep running straight, I can get this new pack to follow me all the way back to the well. If they take the bait, which they will, Tarry and the others stand a chance to react before our usual predators descend on the town.

If the old pack come in from the old angle—no reason why they shouldn't—Tarry and the other handful of skilled lock makers might even be able to get the whole innermost ring of huts secure before the attack gears up. The innermost ring is hugely important. Food and water stores, the records, everything that keeps us alive is inside that ring. If someone is smart enough to send in the little ones first and get those huts locked down—the town might actually stand a chance at surviving tonight.

Of course, I'll be out at the well with the new eastern pack. But if saving the town means dying tonight, so be it. Maybe that's why Gram died too.

I scrabble up the last slope of the footpath, stumbling occasionally in the deepening shadows. Luckily, I know this path by memory. Soon, the low black ring of the well is within my sights. All I have to do now is...

What?

I hadn't actually thought this far ahead. I kind of thought I'd already be dead.

I go to make a final sharp turn maneuver, a last-ditch effort to confuse the pack, but then run smack into--

"Tarry?!"

All the breath zaps out of my lungs, but I regain my legs quickly. I gape into the familiar face, dark as a shadow. Eyes wide and round as the sun, and just as orange, stare back at me. High, steep cheeks make no expression, but a nose like a charcoal-smudged button mushroom flares in and out showing both determination and exhaustion. Sweat beads along a course line of plaited hair, woven into three thick braids of red rope. Dressed in the dappled forest-colored tight knit, close hugging one-piece suit of a hunter-gatherer, Tarry stands on toes as if ready to leap. Not a stitch of gear, but a rough stick in one hand.

Tarry points with the stick back toward town. "Run."

And we do.

Tarry pulls away easily, my legs an aching jelly. It's all I can do to keep my body moving, legs scissoring forward. My mind scrambles for hope, but I find none.

Everything I've just done—the sacrifice I made bringing the wolves in heated chase after me—didn't matter. Not a scratch. My plan depended on Tarry coming out alive, not being here by my side!

Without our Master Lock Maker, the town goes extinct. It doesn't matter how many secondary lock makers we have. How many kids, eggs, and resources we tuck away. Even if everyone has fight and bite in them. Even if the innermost ring is safe and all the huts outward from it are saved. There's no point.

Without a master, the magic is dead.

And without the magical locks, the wolves are unstoppable. They can tear a human head right off. They can break through any structure that isn't sealed up with a magical lock drawn on the inside of the main door. They can and will devour everything.

Supposedly, both the wolves and the locks came from the same failed experiment. Something about resetting ecological balance. The details are vague in the records, but the truth is the same. Our ancestors of old tried to fix the damage their ancestors had done, and in doing so ruined the whole world.

Our little town--all that's left of people on this planet--lives in the shadow of that curse.

I don't believe in gods or manifest destiny or any of that bullshit. But I believe in curses from the universe. Maybe, I'm the one whose cursed in all this. It explains why Gram's dead. Why the wolves found me first. Why Tarry's about to die, despite all my effort.

Gram, who I found face-up dead one night after hutting up with Tarry, practicing our sigils and lock replication based on Gram's careful instructions. And now, Tarry, who's locks are the most artistic and perfect replications I've ever seen.

As my feet pound the ground below me, I stare at Tarry's muscular back. I silently curse them for not just staying put, goddamn it, and let me play hero for once.

Who I am I to save, after all? I'd already given up on my birth maker's legacy by proving I was too weak to face down the big dangers. Too untalented to become Master Lock Maker. And when I said I wouldn't keep trying to learn locking, I'd shown I was a quitter. But then, I hadn't done it out of fear.

I'd done it to let Tarry—the truly masterful artist—shine brighter.

Because even though Gram's death had stopped me dead in the tracks of my life, I was still in love with Tarry. And, I'd promised myself I would always do whatever it took to help Tarry rise high. I might not be a blazing savior, but I know what's in my heart. And I try to follow that impulse with all I am.

"High or low water," as the saying goes. "Come whatever."

I hear a snapping of sticks on my right. Then on my left. The air suddenly smells of rotting flesh, wet fur, and blood. My eyes and nose burn, joining up with my lungs, and I'm caught in a snag of coughs. But I manage to hurl myself over a fallen log, throw my cough straight up, and carry on.

I've hit that point in running when the burn is all gone. Every muscle is a knot, a fist clenched tight. I barely feel the sweat dripping down my brow, the middle of my back, in the crack of my ass. Only the slickness and the occasional blur in the corner of my vision remind me its there at all.

At my heels, there's the echo of violent sounds. Snarling and growling. Snapping, champing razor blades of teeth. I know the wolves are closer than I dare admit to myself. But lucky for me (I guess), I can't see the cursed things.

They're flanking. They're playing. If they wanted us dead, we would be already.

That gives us half a chance to make it to wherever Tarry is running.

It can't be my hut. Oh gods, say it's not my hut. That's too goddamn far away, and at this rate, the wolves will get tired of this game before we even get close.

The growling, champing, and yapping goes silent just as I break into the first small clearing which means we've cleared three quarters of the route.

My heart freezes up.

That silence is our impending doom.

The wolves are done playing. They're now maneuvering. It's kill time and we've got zero cover. They were waiting for this moment. What the fuck had I been thinking? I should have seen this coming.

Ahead of me, there's a skidding, sliding sound. And I know the worst of what's just happened in a flash. Tarry's gone down. There's no snarl or howl, so I bet it's from a bad step, not a mouth full of teeth.

I can hope.

I don't slow, and rush to where the sound originated. Tarry is on the ground, tangled in a matrix of branches.

"Get up!" I scream, as if that's helpful. I know it's not, but I'm short circuiting here.

"Get down!" Tarry contradicts.

I whip my neck around so fast it's shocking my head doesn't fly off. I expect to see a black-gray body in mid-leap.

Nothing. Trees and falling leaves.

"Get down!" Tarry screams again.

I crouch uncertainly. "What the…"

"Inside the circle."

I whip back around and see a complicated series of unfamiliar sigils drawn into the sand. It's not a lock, but some kind of magic I don't recognize. Before I can respond, Tarry's hand closes around my collar and two strong arms yank me backwards hard. My legs flail and kick up debris, but I manage to clank my lips between my teeth to sever off the scream.

That's a little trick we're all taught as little ones. The adults scare us in the safety of daylight, so we learn to cut off our screams before it's night and those bright sharp sounds can bring the wolves out.

"Don't move while I finish it," Tarry whispers against my ear.

I obey, concentrating on my hammering heart, and on slowing my erratic breath. The sweat covering my tight, flushed skin slowly grows cold again. The sensation of Tarry's prickly arms is the center of my meditation. I focus all I am around the sensation. The itchiness of each rough wiry hair as it rubs and catches against mine.

Tarry's hands, moving in directions I don't understand. Hesitating, starting again.

"There," comes out hushed and strangely sharp.

"You okay?" I ask.

There's a hesitation and a shudder. Fear. Yes, even Tarry fears the wolves.

"Yes," Tarry says in a forced tone. "This should work. Stay close."

I lean my head against theirs, trying to be comforting. Our sweat mingles, our heartbeats skipping over one another through bursting veins in our foreheads.

Stay close hammers through my blood, blasting through my dilated veins, and flooding my heart. If there is anyone I could handle dying alongside, it's Tarry.

Stealthy footfalls. Four, eight, sixteen, twenty-eight in total. Seven wolves. Lucky number to some mythologies. Meaningless to others. Bad for us. Seven is an unfinished pack. Which means one of two things: a broken pack that's over-hungry, or a paired pack with the other half yet to descend on us.

I feel fingers interlace with mine. Our palms are as sweaty as our foreheads. Tarry's is shockingly chilled. Like the night itself. The sensation is both grounding and terrifying. At least we're together.

Shouts rise, pop-corning from all over the forest.

"That'll be the others," Tarry says, voice oddly shaky.

The others?

I suddenly remember the first trumpet blast of the day. The one that sounded the incoming of Pack Old Holler. Our usual wolves. They'd been thundering toward town all this time, and I'd completely forgotten because I was certain Tarry was in danger. And I'd convinced myself these eastern wolves were a separate pack. Their joint arrival was merely unlucky coincidence.

Clearly, Tarry hasn't made the same mistakes.

"This pack—" I start, then choke on the words and phlegm in my throat.

Tarry nods shakily, confirming I've been wrong about the eastern pack.

They aren't new.

They're Pack Old Holler, split in two.

Our worst fears are coming true. The wolves aren't slowly dying off. They're expanding. Soon, there'll be enough to end our pathetic little settlement, locking magic or not. Already, the wolves feel flush enough in resources to play with us. Test us. Take risks.

Hence the pre-dusk coming.

"But fording the river? How…" I try to make sense of it.

"The wolves saw what happened to the river," Tarry whispers suddenly.

"The river?" I have no idea what they mean.

"The earthquake. It sub-ducted a major portion of the water flow. With the recent lack of rain, it's low. Crossable. The wolves have been scouting back and forth. Testing how aware we are of our surroundings."

"Why didn't you tell anyone?" I growl, spine stabbed with betrayal.

"I only just found the tracks this morning. And by then, it was too late to rally everyone. I could only get to the lock makers."

"You had a plan," I say, and the betrayal melts away.

Of course Tarry had a plan. What was I thinking? That our Master Lock Maker would let us silently slip into the night without a fight? I meet Tarry's eyes, and my shoulders hunch up in a new sensation. Strength suspended between fear and determination. Whatever that chemical cocktail is in my brain, it makes me buzz all over.

I'm ready to flow.

"What do we do now?" I ask with new resolve.

"Trick them back," Tarry says, then shudders violently as if freezing to death.

"How?"

"By hiding here in the forest."

"It'll never work. They can smell us."

"That's true, but we're locked here." The words come out oddly thin, almost a gasp. As if Tarry has been in incredible pain, and only now is losing the ability to hid it.

"What's wrong?" I want to ask, but instead am distracted by the sigils in the dirt. "That'll never work either. There's no door. No wood. No frame."

The three rules. I can just hear Gram's voice repeating them. "Place the lock in the center of the appropriate location and the wolves can't get in. But try it any other place—your body, clothes, the window or the floor—and no go."

People have tried.

Hundred percent fail.

Tarry's face is stone lit by the scraps of shadowy silver night light. "This is a special code. It'll work."

As much as I want to trust them, I don't. Special codes don't exist. We all know that. There is only the one. Because when the humans made their deals with the devils and demons, no one thought to ask for a toolbox of spells that would be useful.

Too bad it turns out magic is actually the only thing that keeps us alive.

Maybe humans past could have been a little more diligent.

I look around frantic for a sharp rock, long stick, heavy log, strong bone. Anything I can repurpose into a weapon. I'm going down fighting.

Not like Gram.

My eye catches on the long arching curve of Tarry's lock design. For what it's worth, the shape is all new. It's not even a circle like it's supposed to be. It's a cube inside a cube, with the core sigil trapped inside a series of triangles and spheres. My eye gets lost in it. My belly lurches like I'm diving underground. My ears starting ringing.

Then, bam. Flash.

I'm back in the past.

Before me, Gram bleeding. Hand trembling. Reaching. Gram is about to die. Then, the door rattles. There's a howl. A scraping snarl snap against the jamb. A scratching pounding, heavy paws trying to get a landing on the handle. Another howl, more aggravated than the first.

The door bursts inward, and there stands a massive wolf. Mouth, a red froth of gore. Bits of tendon dangling from dripping teeth. Blood stains thick and black, meat so torn up it's pulp. The stench of death, tangy metallic and grotesque. It fills present-me up. I want to scream, but all I do is stare. Gram's hand in my vision. Trembling.

The wolf closes in, sniffing and huffing. Sniffing and huffing.

This flashback is all wrong. Gram wasn't taken down. We all know that. Zero signs of attack. Gram's death was the town's only suicide to date. The sheer confusion of it will never let us forget.

Then, in my vision, the wolf backs off. Eyes squinting like something is offensive to the senses. A whimpering, not a growl.

I have never heard a wolf sound afraid. But here it is, in this odd vision memory.

Images jolt across my mind like a flickering flashlight.

The blade, the cutting, and Gram's head lolling like a rag doll.

All I can think is—all that blood…

I come to and my face is slapped with the sharp smell of rust.

I jolt upright. Not rust, I realize in a sickening twisting off of the thought.

Blood.

I stare at the ground and finally see it. The glint of a long razor blade beside our feet. Tarry smiles faintly, an expression full of sadness and regret. A bloody wrist rises into view. And then the other.

I can't move. "The fuck did you do?" are not words, but a gasp.

"It takes sacrifice," Tarry mumbles distantly.

The dripping splats against the ground. It sounds like the laughter of the world.

"No…" I start to protest, but know it's way too late. The shaking, the funny way Tarry had of talking. It all makes sense. In my exhaustion and confusion of being pulled into the circle, I hadn't even seen Tarry cut both wrists. They'd done it so quietly.

I stare down at what I realize is not simply damp, spongy forest ground.

All that blood…

"Gram's death wasn't suicide," I say breathlessly, putting it together.

Gram did go down fighting. Just not like I'd imagined. Gram's fight was a bloody sacrifice. A new kind of locking magic. A new chance for everyone.

"This…is…the…only…way…" Tarry manages.

What's happening clicks in my brain. The blood is replacing wood. The door is the ground. The frame is the two of us. Somehow, all these elements are good enough. Each one connected magically to the root source of energy in the world. I don't understand, but it's working.

It's not magic, just science we don't know yet, Gram's ghost recites from the stories.

Both Gram and Tarry figured out a piece of it.

I long to ask, needing to know. But Tarry shudders, gasps, and lolls to the side.

I'm too late

I stare down into glassy, glossed -over eyes. That dark shadow of a face turns pale as the midday sun. Everything is shaking. Tarry's body and my resolve. Nothing holds. I force myself to look at the two crimson rivers mid-wrist. The cuts hang open like two meaty mouths, spewing out Tarry's life force.

The world closes in, narrowing to a prick of light just as the wolves approach. Their noses sniff and huff. Sniff and huff.

Something in their presence focuses my energy. I suck in lungful after lungful of air, tightening my belly. I can't pass out. I can't die here. The town is relying on me to…to…

To do what?

Panic makes me illogical, and I give Tarry's body a shake.

"Hey!"

Nothing.

My throat closes up, my heart bursts with pain, the breath squeezes from my lungs.

We don't give up, Gram's ghost echoes in my ear. And maybe I don't understand everything about what they meant or what they did, but I understand this.

This is my fight. And I have to win.

Wolves young and old circle me. Sniff, huff. They draw in close.

I stare them down. Their noses get so close I could slap them. Eyes squint, lips draw back. I scream in their face. They all flinch and move away. As if my breath is disgusting. I scream again. They pad around in tight circles, trying to figure me out.

Tarry, smart and quick, must have seen Gram's experimental notes and made heads and tails of them. Now I have to.

I study the lock around me in the silver light. It's almost identical to Gram's. A few noticeable changes. More circles, less squares. A central triangle within a triangle. It's oddly beautiful. Except for the last ounces of Tarry's blood pooling into the crevices and our clothes.

I study the lines until I hear the unthinkable.

The wolves give up, padded feet echoing a slow retreat.

I don't know if I'm happy or not.

I've lost my best friend. The town's lost our Master Lock Maker. The wolves, multiplying, are now two cooperative packs. As far as the future goes, it's looking bleak as fuck.

And yet…the wolves left. And there's new magic.

And the town?

I hear footfalls through the dark and the trees. The footfalls are human, easily recognizable. Some run, some pick their way. Eventually, the townspeople surround me in twos and threes, their red solar torches hanging by their sides.

We meet each other's eyes, saying nothing. I see the same busted expression on each terse face. The exact same emotion flits across their almost smiling lips, almost crying eyes.

Unexpected victory tucked cleverly inside painful defeat.

I stand up, knowing I have to ask the question nobody wants to answer.

"The other locks—" I start.

The town collectively chokes.

"It was the same for all of them, wasn't it?" I don't have to say: someone killed themselves to make the locks work. It's obvious. What else would I mean?

From the back, I see Sayer slip forward, covered like me in

blood. Only now the color is a faded clay-like red. It's crusty and crackles as Sayer comes to my side.

"A worthwhile sacrifice," Sayer whispers, touching Tarry's blank eyes.

I don't reply, because those words aren't for me.

Sayer reaches into Tarry's pocket. Withdrawing, I think, the notes that will explain how the new locks work. How we can use our blood to ground the magic instead of wood. Tarry will have made perfectly detailed drawings. I have no doubt about that.

"It's for you," Sayer says, sounding not surprised, but matter-of-fact.

"What is?"

"The notes. Gram's and Tarry's. And a map to where the source material is stored."

I reach out for the slip of noting and unfold it. Sure enough, there's my name in fancy dancing lettering. I hiccup to cover the rising sensation from my belly. More bile, a scream, a sob? I don't want to find out. Not right now.

I hold the noting out under Sayer's red night-sight torch light. It's shaking so bad I can hardly make out the note at the top, right under my name.

I have to use both hands to steady it, pressing it firmly against some dirt that's not soaked through. The words jump up and grab me by the lungs.

Cedar,

I'll come for you even if this fails.

Love Always, your Tarry

Nothing more needed to be writ. It's clear what they mean.

Meant.

Even if the lock hadn't saved us, Tarry would have come running. Just like I did at first in my ill-conceived plan when I heard the eastern trumpet sound.

"I'd have thrown myself before the muzzle of the wolves for you," this note says.

But Tarry went one step further, in the end, and didn't go blindly into danger like I had. No, of course. They took the time to put the right pieces together. The pieces I too had, but had failed to align. Tarry took the right measures, the right view, and the right amount of time.

And Tarry saved us all when I'd merely managed to run myself into the ground.

I have a lot to learn. About life. About love.

And now, about how locks work.

This new lock can't require suicide, like everything thinks it does. I refuse to believe that. There's another way; we just don't know it yet. Gram and Tarry died to save me. They would want me to figure it out so no one else need die.

It's time to stop hiding.

I roll up the notes and slip them into the now crackling fabric of my shirt. I slide it in right over my heart. I know I can't bring Gram or Tarry back, but I'll do my damnedest to keep the rest of us alive.

Sayer reaches out and touches my shoulder. "Cedar, will you be the next Master Lock Maker?"

"Without a doubt, I will."

ABOUT THE AUTHOR

Rei Rosenquist is a queer agender (they/them) speculative fiction and romance writer who depicts a wide variety of identities struggling to find a place in a wide variety of worlds. They are also a barista, baker, musician, and lifelong semi-nomad.

Rei first remembers life as seen out the high window of a hotel balcony. Down below is a courtyard, swarms of brightly dressed tourists, and the beach. The memory is nothing but a blue-green washed image. Warmth and sunlight. Here, they are three years old, and this is the beginning of a storyteller's life. Over the years, Rei has traveled to many countries, engaged many peoples, picked up new habits, and learned new languages. Across lands, they find constant inspiration in the stories we tell each other, the food we share with one another, the music we make together, and the world we can build when we allow ourselves to dream.

Find out more about Rei at:
reirosenquist.com

facebook.com/reirosenquist

twitter.com/rylrosenquist

instagram.com/rylrosenquist

goodreads.com/reirosenquist

amazon.com/Rei-Rosenquist/e/B06XQQRPK4

CAMPBELL COUNTY COOK-OFF

ALICIA CAY

"BREAKING AND ENTERING is not what I had in mind today, Rebecca." Leah stood on the front porch of their older sister's blue clapboard house, keys in hand.

Rebecca rolled her eyes at her younger sister. "It's not exactly breaking and entering when we're related to the homeowner."

A humid breeze ruffled through the pink gardenias in the oversized terra cotta pots along the porch stairs. It was a typical summer day in central Texas, the air thick enough to swim through, and hotter than Hades at noon. Rebecca set her handbag on one of the white wicker chairs, dug around in it for a handkerchief, then mopped the sweat from her brow.

"I guess," Leah said. "It's just that Elizabeth left me in charge while she's gone."

"Of feeding the cat!" Rebecca huffed. "She'd let me in if she was here. She's my sister too."

"Yes, but she didn't give *you* the password to get through her wards."

Rebecca shook her head. "I left the door open accidentally, Leah! I wasn't trying to let her cat out on purpose. That was two hundred years ago, don't either of you ever let anything go?" She held her hand out. "Give me the keys, I'll do it."

"No." Leah snatched her hand away. "You can't enter, you'll set off her spell."

"Fine, I'll wait out here and make sure Taco doesn't get out. Dumb name for a familiar anyway, if you ask me."

Leah propped open the wooden screen door with her butt, placed the key into the lock, then murmured the magic word under her breath. The deadbolt slid in its mechanism and the front door opened.

"I don't know," she said, as she entered the house. "I think it's a cute name for a kitty."

"Says the old lady who named her cat Banana," Rebecca muttered under her breath. She'd spent a thousand years with her sisters, and they still annoyed the ever-loving dust out of her.

Leah called back from the kitchen, "What am I looking for again?"

"Her recipe book!"

"She's got a bunch of them," Leah said, sounding panicked. "How am I supposed to know which one it is?"

Rebecca sighed. In her opinion they had coddled their younger sister to the point where the woman couldn't tell a frog lip from an eye of newt. "I don't know, Sister," Rebecca said. "I can't come in, remember?" She fiddled with the hem of her housecoat; patience was not her strong suit. "Read out the names of the cookbooks, maybe I can tell—"

A red station wagon drove by, slowing to pull into a nearby driveway. Rebecca put on her best Sunday smile and raised a hand in greeting. "Nothing to see here, mortals, just two gray-haired old ladies robbing their sister's house." She turned back to the front door as Leah called out again.

"*Summer Salads*?"

"No," Rebecca said. "Chili is not a salad. Think, you old ding-bat!" She tugged on the loose string hanging from one of her buttons and smiled to herself. For the past three years, Elizabeth's chili recipe had taken the blue ribbon at the County Fair's chili cook-off. *Not this year, big sister. That blue ribbon is mine.* Elizabeth was in need of being taken down a peg or two. But first, Rebecca needed to get her hands on that recipe.

She had considered just snatching the recipe and adding an unusual ingredient onto the card, but Elizabeth would notice that right away. Elizabeth was too smart for that, and didn't she think so, too. Their sister had gotten a little too big for her britches recently, in more ways than one. So yesterday, when Elizabeth mentioned she was taking an overnight trip to San Antonio to get the *better* tomatoes, whatever that meant, Rebecca had come up with a plan. She convinced Leah to get a copy of the recipe from Elizabeth's house. Not a hard thing to do, as both women harbored some resentment toward their big sister. Just because she was the oldest didn't give her the right to be so bossy all the time.

Leah was still reading cookbook titles out loud. "*Jell-O Molds, Autumn Squash Dishes, Louisiana Roadkill: Recipes to Die For.*"

"It's not going to be in some Betty Crocker book." Rebecca snorted. Betty Crocker—what a terrible witch. Who used her spells to enchant a nation into buying books bound in picnic tablecloth pattern, anyway? Not a single frog or child in any of them either. Total lack of imagination. "Look for a handwritten card or something. It won't be in a regular book."

"Here's something," Leah said. "This one looks handwritten. Chili, chili… where is the chili recipe? Oh, Becks, I think I found it! It says Chil-*ite* Wyner. That's probably some kind of code she wrote it in, right?"

"I don't know," Rebecca said. "Hurry up, what in tarred-hide is taking you so long?"

"I'm trying to take a picture of it with my phone," Leah said.

Rebecca noticed a black shadow at her feet, trying to ease its way out the front door. "No, Taco, stay!" Rebecca said. She bent down and pushed the midnight-colored cat back inside the house. Her arm passed the threshold, activating the ward.

White rags flowed off the ghostly image that appeared at the top of the staircase inside the house. The banshee's hair stood on end, floating in an imaginary breeze. It rushed down the stairs in a flurry of blue and white light, screeching at a decibel intended to make any intruder's bowels evacuate.

"Rebecca!" Leah hollered. "What did you do?"

"Come on, old woman!" Rebecca yelled back, the banshee's yowls ringing in her head like a bell. The neighborhood dogs sent up calls in unison, barking and yowling. Taco settled beneath the dining room table and licked a paw

Leah put the book back and rushed out the front door. She slammed it closed, pushed the key into the lock, and whispered the magical word again. The noise inside the house ceased. The cell phone in her other hand buzzed. She glared at Rebecca. "Great. Elizabeth is calling."

AFTER ASSURING Elizabeth that Taco was still in the house and that it had been Rebecca who set off the ward, the two sisters hurried home to the cozy, mid-century bungalow they shared three streets over.

They sat at the kitchen table in the breakfast nook where the light was good, and poured over the fuzzy cell phone picture of the cookbook page.

"Why is it so blurry?" Rebecca asked.

"You were rushing me," Leah said. "I hate this new-fangled technology. I can't get used to it."

Rebecca rolled her eyes. "We've moved on from the past, Sister. The days of cauldrons and love potions are long gone."

Leah cackled. "Ahh, those were my favorite. Watching those women drink sheep musk and fisheye stew just to get John the farmer-boy to look their way." She sighed. "I miss those days."

Rebecca put her hands on her hips. "Until they found out the stuff didn't work and came looking for us with torches and pitch-forks. Now come on, I need you to focus, we've got work to do."

The smile slid from Leah's face. She stuck her tongue out at her older sister. Rebecca ignored her and took the cell phone into the study to print out the picture. .

Back at the table with Leah, Rebecca stared at the photo. "Must be a foreign language. Just like that witch to make it unreadable. Sneaky, like she doesn't trust us or something."

It was Leah's turn to roll her eyes. "Jeez, I can't imagine why."

"Don't get sassy with me," Rebecca said. "Pull up Google. We can get it to translate this for us." She bustled into the kitchen. The stockpot sat cold on the stove burner. Rebecca clicked the switch over until the gaslight *whoompfed* to life and the blue-white flame ignited. She lined up the ingredients on her kitchen counter: chili powder, red pepper flakes, garlic, onions, ground beef, and her favorite—red kidney beans. They reminded her of the old days, when their homebrews had contained more...personal...ingredients. "Alright, Sister, what do we do first?"

Leah's fingers pecked at the laptop's keyboard. "It wants to know what language to translate. Do you think this will work if Elizabeth wrote it in the old language?"

"Try Latin," Rebecca said. Elizabeth had always taken top marks in Latin when they were young girls in the Middle Ages, and still never let her sisters forget it.

Leah cocked an eyebrow. "It wants to know if I mean 'chill out'."

"You can't say 'chill out' in Latin." Rebecca threw the chopped onions and ground beef into the pot. "Just enter one of the words from the picture, and see what comes up."

"Hmm…" Leah bit her lower lip and tried another word. "Oh, Becks, it says 'fire', like spicy, right? I think we've got it." She danced in her chair and continued on to the next word, translating the chili recipe as best she could using modern technology. "It doesn't know what daemonium is. What do you think it means?"

Rebecca shrugged. "Doesn't sound like something we can find at the Stop & Shop. Just scratch it out and go to the next word."

After an hour of translating, with Rebecca filling in the gaps with her best guesses, the pot on the stove simmered and bubbled with a lovely reddish-brown stew. "Now, for some heat." Rebecca added a generous amount of red pepper flakes to the concoction. Her own special ingredient. In her opinion, Elizabeth's version had always lacked kick.

Leah stood and stretched. "It does smell good."

Rebecca grinned and tapped the wooden spoon on the pot's edge, then replaced the lid. "Now, Sister, if you'll whip up a batch of your honey cornbread to tame the heat in this monster, we'll be set." She rubbed her hands together. Tomorrow that satin blue ribbon would be hanging on her wall, and Elizabeth was going to be simply green with envy.

REBECCA AND LEAH lugged the large stock pot into the Fairground's exhibition hall. Other contestants were setting up on the long line of tables around the main room, and the chatter of gossip and smells of Texas chili filled the air. Mayor Ari was making his usual rounds, picking at the baked goods. Every good contestant knew to include something sweet for him to munch on, as much a good old-fashioned bribe as a necessary part of the judging.

The Mayor spotted the two sisters and headed over. His silver-dappled beard hung to his chest, and he wore a neatly pressed gray suit with a dashing blue bow tie. He bent slightly at the waist in greeting. "Good morning, ladies. I see you're entering this year. Going to give your sister some competition?"

Leah smiled shyly. She uncovered her plate of honey cornbread muffins and offered him one. "Rebecca made the stew, but I made these special."

Mayor Ari selected one of the muffins. "Oh, Ms. Leah, you've outdone yourself. These smell heavenly." He winked at her then moved on to the next table.

Rebecca knocked Leah in the ribs with an elbow. "Quit your flirting and help me set up. Get the bowls and spoons out."

"That hurt," Leah said, pressing a hand to her ribs. "And I was not flirting. He just reminds me of someone, is all."

The pot's lid rattled as the contents bubbled within, and steam leaked out. Leah pressed a hand against the side of the pot and yanked it back with a gasp. "How long ago did you take this off the burner? It's going to be overcooked."

"It's fine." Rebecca flapped a hand at her sister. "I tasted it this morning. Anyway, it'll be nice and hot for the judges."

Elizabeth entered through the double doors at the far end of the room. She wore a green sun dress that matched her jade-colored eyes, and pushed a cart that carried her cast iron pot.

Rebecca smacked Leah in the ribs again. "Looks like our big sister got herself a new dress." She snorted. "Good for her, she'll need all the help she can get this year."

Leah sighed. "Stop hitting me, Rebecca. It hurts, you know."

Elizabeth spotted them, frowned, and wheeled her cart over. "What are you two doing here?" She eyed the steaming pot on the table and placed a hand on her hip.

"Ms. Elizabeth," Mayor Ari's voice cut in. "Our returning

champion." He took one of Elizabeth's hands in his. "I'm looking forward to your chili, as always. It's so good, one might think you've enchanted the stuff." He laughed a big guffaw, then turned to greet another woman who had come up behind him.

Rebecca's eyes widened. "That's why you always win, isn't it? You're using your spellbook to cheat."

Elizabeth clutched at her pearl necklace. "Why, I never——"

"Oh, don't give me that innocent act, we're not in the Inquisition anymore. Don't think I don't know your tricks, you old bat."

Elizabeth pointed to Rebecca's still steaming pot. "If anything is suspicious, it's *that*. Why's it still steaming even though it's off the burner?"

Rebecca sniffed. "Unlike your chili, mine is good. It's got some heat to it. Prepare your hankie for tears, Sister." She shooed Elizabeth away with a hand. "Go on now, get on over to your own table. I've got a blue ribbon to win."

"Ha!" Elizabeth said. "Good luck with that."

"Attention, everyone," Mayor Ari called out. "I believe all the contestants have arrived, and my stomach is telling me it's time to begin the tasting."

He tucked a white cloth napkin over his long beard, and made his way along the tables with the other three judges. They tasted, nodded, and scribbled notes. Soon they stood before Elizabeth's table, talking, tasting, and making little golf pencil marks on their scoring cards.

Rebecca leaned over and whispered in Leah's ear, "Did you see that? Ms. Emerson just gave Elizabeth a look."

Leah nodded. "She did? Wait, who's Ms. Emerson?"

"The elementary school principal," Rebecca said. "Mean old biddy, too. If I didn't know better, I'd guess she's the one who ate those Hansel and Gretel kids back in the day."

"*Ahh*, the good ol' days." Leah grinned, a look of nostalgia in her eyes.

"That's how she's doing it," Rebecca said. "She's got one of the judges in her pocket. Damn her to Hades, I knew she was cheating somehow."

Finally, the judges approached Rebecca and Leah's table. "We've got a combined effort here this year," Mayor Ari said. He grabbed another cornbread muffin and smiled. "These, Ms. Leah, should be honored in a category all their own, they're so good."

Leah's blush deepened. Ms. Emerson stood across the table from the sisters. She scowled and picked up a spoon.

"Old biddy," Rebecca muttered under her breath.

"We ready?" Mayor Ari asked. He leaned over the table and lifted the lid off Rebecca's chili.

A tower of flame erupted from the stock pot, instantly tarnishing the stainless steel into a burnt black. The volcanic eruption pushed Rebecca, Leah, and the three judges off their feet. The Mayor was knocked onto his butt and slid across the floor into the opposite wall. His eyes were circles of surprise, and the bottom of his beard was singed and smoking. He smacked at the sparks in his beard to put them out. "What in the hell was that?"

The answer unfurled its wings from the burnt stock pot that teetered on the edge of the table. The wings, brown and red and webbed, were followed by a gnarled creature covered in scales. It slowly pulled itself from the pot's narrow confines. The thing looked like a mix between a baby dragon, a newborn kitten, and the daemon Leah had accidentally summoned from the Unders in the 12th Century.

Its body was the color of campfire chili, and its kidney bean scales clinked against the pot as the chili-daemon stepped onto the table. Red chili pepper flakes dotted its flesh and clumped into its slitted eyes—red, tan, and full of heat. It grabbed the stock pot with a beak formed of ground beef and launched the pot across the room. The chili-daemon screeched out a roar, another plume of flame spewing from its mouth. The pink and yellow flowered drapes on the community center windows burst into flames.

The silent shock in the room erupted into chaos. Suddenly, everyone was screaming, but the towers of fire surrounding each window made escape through them impossible. This sent everyone in the same direction:toward the double doors. A walker flew through the air, and old Ms. Emerson was pushed to the floor in the kerfuffle. In the rush, several pots of chili were bumped or pulled off their tables. Pots clattered, and beef and beans pooled onto the floor. Folks slipped and slid their way away from the rapidly growing chili-daemon, their Sunday-best clothing covered in stains that no amount of club soda would ever render wearable again.

Elizabeth made her way over to her sisters and pulled them both to their feet. "You okay?"

"I'm fine," Leah said. There were tears in her eyes.

Rebecca opened her mouth to answer, then ducked as the creature aimed another spout of flame in her direction. Her crocheted tablecloth caught fire and began to curl at the edges.

Mayor Ari got to his feet, dodging a rogue wing that expanded above his head, and hurried over to Ms. Emerson. He pulled her up and pushed her toward the exit, then turned to help the others.

Elizabeth grabbed her sisters and yanked them over to her table. They all crawled beneath it. "What have you two dingbats done?"

"Don't blame us." Rebecca had to yell to be heard over the cacophony of chaos. "It was *your* recipe!"

"*My* recipe?" Elizabeth yelled back. "My recipe isn't trying to eat the judges!"

Leah burst into sobs. "We got the recipe from your cookbook while you were out of town. I let her talk me into it, this is all my fault!"

"Oh, shut up," Rebecca said.

Leah's elbow snapped out and hit Rebecca square in the ribs, payback. "*You* shut up! I take it back. I may have translated her recipe, but you're the one who kept crossing out words. This is *your* fault."

"*Translated* my recipe?" Elizabeth said. "What are you—"

The chili-daemon spun toward the doors, its claws of hardened beef scratching trenches in the concrete. The thing flung its neck sideways and snapped at Mr. Phil, the owner of the local hardware store. Mr. Phil lost his toupee, but managed to keep his head. He screamed and dove out the doors, landing on top of Mrs. Palmapple, the preacher's wife, who looked like she enjoyed it more than she would ever admit.

"You don't mean you got this recipe from the old book on my kitchen shelf, do you?" Elizabeth glared at Rebecca.

"Where else?" Rebecca said. "It was with all the other recipe books."

Elizabeth raised her voice. "That isn't a recipe book, it's Grandmama's Grimoire!"

Mayor Ari pushed the last straggler out the doors, then slammed them closed, trying to contain the chili-daemon. The creature whirled a barbed tail at him. The Mayor flung himself to the ground and crawled over to the sisters on his hands and knees.

The chili-daemon lowered its head and smashed through the exit. Its kidney bean scales ripped through metal and drywall as it hammered itself free, escaping onto the county fairgrounds. The community center room was quiet, save for the flickering of the burning drapes.

Mayor Ari stood up next to the sisters' table and pulled a willow branch switch, complete with a single leaf on the end, out of his pocket. With a flick of his wrist, water poured from the end of his wand and doused the flaming drapes. He turned in slow circles, watering the room until all the fires were extinguished.

The sisters emerged from beneath the table. Elizabeth, brushing off her knees, asked, "Just who in Hades are *you*?"

Mayor Ari smirked. "I guess the ruse is up." He slid a hand up over his face and across the top of his head. As the glamour fell away, his beard pulled up into his chin, leaving a neatly trimmed goatee; a deep chestnut color ran down the length of his hair, erasing all traces of gray. In an instant, the Mayor had lost 30 years.

Leah yipped. "Merlin! I knew I recognized something about you. Didn't I tell you, Rebecca?" She threw her arms around Merlin's neck.

Elizabeth and Rebecca exchanged glances. It seemed a mere 450 years ago that Merlin had pulled his little disappearing act and broken their younger sister's heart.

"Well, if you aren't just the cherry on a shit sundae," Elizabeth said.

Merlin stepped back from Leah and looked at the women. "I see trouble still comes in threes."

"Jokes?" Elizabeth snapped. "You've got time for jokes when…" She pointed out the window. "The whole town is about to be set on fire, then eaten." She lowered her hand and smoothed her dress down. "Hopefully in that order."

"Ah, that," Merlin said. "Well, the thing appears to be made of food. Eventually the organic material will rot and fall apart. Problem solved." He grinned.

Elizabeth placed a hand on her hip. "Helpful as always."

Rebecca shook a finger in Merlin's face. "You've got some nerve being here, after what you did to our little sister."

"Of course you're right, Rebecca." Merlin shuffled his feet and managed to look appropriately remorseful. "But I didn't leave because I wanted to. I got mixed up in some bad business with Henry VIII, and well… a woman lost her head and I had to get out of the city quickly." He took both of Leah's hands in his. "I haven't stopped thinking about you since. I searched for you for years, until I found you, here."

"Why didn't you tell me, Merlin?" Leah asked.

"I worried what might happen if I revealed myself too soon." He darted a look at Elizabeth and Rebecca.

Rebecca snorted.

"You do understand, don't you, my darling?" Merlin placed a small kiss on Leah's hand.

Leah smiled and twirled slightly in place. Had she still the thick eyelashes of her youth, she would have batted them.

Elizabeth threw her hands up. "Right now, there are more pressing matters at hand. Half the town is going up while you two make lovey-dovey eyes at each other."

Merlin squeezed Leah's hands. "Your sister is right." He cleared his throat. "Perhaps the four of us together can send that thing back into the abyss. What say you all, one more collaboration?" He extended an elbow to Leah. "Shall we?" They began walking toward the torn-out hole in the wall.

Leah reached into her bra and pulled out her wand, a delicate twig of willow from the same tree as Merlin's. With a curtsy, she took Merlin's arm. "We shall."

Rebecca cocked an eyebrow at Elizabeth. "Because the last time we joined forces with him, everything went just swimmingly."

"That was one hell of a flood." Elizabeth smirked before letting the scowl settle on her face again.

Rebecca and Elizabeth dug through the rubble to locate their massive old lady purses and pulled out their wands. Elizabeth's wand was thick and made of mahogany with a single whisker plucked from a tiger stuck from the end. Rebecca's wand was unadorned, but curled, and made from the wood of an ancient species of oak that no longer grew in this world.

Leah pulled Merlin to a stop. "But if we do this, everyone will know what we are."

"True," Merlin said. "But at least we'll get to do it together." Then he grabbed Leah around the waist, pulled her in, and kissed her hard.

Rebecca leaned toward Elizabeth as they followed Merlin and Leah outside. "Know what we are?" She snorted. "I think the daemon is out of the pot on that one."

ONCE OUTSIDE, the witches and Merlin dodged fiery bursts of anger from the chili-daemon, and hurled banishment spells at its kidney bean-covered hide until they had to stop and catch their breaths.

"We're not even slowing it down," Rebecca said. "What do we do?" She looked at Elizabeth.

"*Now* you ask me?" Elizabeth wore a hurt look on her face. "After you two went against me in the cook-off?"

Leah put a hand on her oldest sister's arm. "I'm sorry, Liz."

Rebecca said, "It's just... you're so good at *everything*. Do you have to rub it in our faces all the time?"

The chili-daemon turned and spewed a spigot of burning rage at Merlin's head. He countered with a deft deflection spell. The fireball bounced off and the carriages on the Ferris wheel burst into flame.

"Ummm," Merlin said. "Ladies, perhaps you could do this another time?"

"Rub what?" Elizabeth asked.

"We get jealous sometimes, is all," Leah said. "You're so good at—"

"At what? Making chili?" Elizabeth asked.

"At everything!" Rebecca said.

Elizabeth looked truly injured then. "I was just getting into the Southern spirit. Things have changed so much over the years and, well, you girls are all I have. I don't want some cook-off to come between us."

Leah rubbed Elizabeth's arm. "We know. We're really sorry." She glared at Rebecca. "Aren't we, Rebecca?"

Rebecca sighed.

"Ladies!" Merlin called. The chili-daemon had cornered him against the back of the livestock building. "I could use a little—"

The creature leaned its neck against the burning Ferris wheel, metal crunched and began to twist under its weight.

"Help!"

"Come on, girls," Leah said. "We're sisters. We've always been stronger together."

Rebecca smiled at Elizabeth. "She's right." She held out an arm to her big sister.

Elizabeth linked arms with Rebecca, then looked at Leah. "Looks like your boyfriend could use a little assistance. Shall we?"

Leah smiled and linked arms with Elizabeth. "We shall."

Together, the sisters threw streams of power from the ends of their wands. Rebecca and Leah lassoed the chili-daemon around its neck and tail with white fire, then Elizabeth cast her best magenta-colored spell at the creature's chest.

Purple flames lit the early evening sky up like the 4th of July. Merlin threw himself on the ground and covered his head as sparks flew in every direction.

The chili-daemon thrashed under the weight of the combined

spells, its dying screech rumbled the buildings around them. Finally, it collapsed on the ground in front of the bent and burning Ferris wheel, in a giant, steaming heap of chili.

SIRENS WAILED THROUGH THE AIR. The four of them cast their best memory-replacement spells on the weeping mob of chili cook-off contestants; they would recall the smell of gas and the subsequent explosion, but little else. The foursome headed to the parking lot.

"Oh shoot." Elizabeth pulled at her green dress. "My new dress got burned." She shrugged. "At least we stopped that thing before it got out of hand, unlike that time in Chicago."

Rebecca frowned. "One practice spell on a cow gets away from me, and I have to hear about it for the next bajillion years. Don't you two ever let anything go?"

Leah giggled. "How about the fire in London before that?"

"Yeah, ha-ha, we get it," Rebecca said. She shook her head. Her sisters really did annoy the ever-loving dust out of her. "Since we've worn out our welcome in the U.K., the Midwest, and now the South, where do we go next?"

"Oh!" Leah clapped her hands. "Can we go to California, please?" She looked at Merlin.

Merlin took Leah's hand. "As long as I'm with you, my sweet, we can go anywhere."

Elizabeth and Rebecca made faces at each other.

"I guess California would be okay," Elizabeth said. "If there's another mishap..." She looked at Rebecca. "We could always blame it on an earthquake or—"

"A wildfire," Merlin said.

Rebecca raised her wand at Merlin's back. Elizabeth shook her head and grabbed Rebecca's arm.

"The bigger question," Elizabeth said, "is how you two dingbats could confuse Grandmama's Grimoire for a recipe book?"

Leah huffed. "How was I supposed to know? It was on the shelf with all the other cookbooks."

"It's bound in human skin, for one thing," Elizabeth said.

"Looked like old leather to me," Leah said.

"It is!" Rebecca said.

The Wyrd sisters broke into cackles of laughter, then headed home to pack.

ABOUT THE AUTHOR

Alicia Cay is a writer of Speculative and Mystery stories. Her short fiction has been published in several anthologies including "Hold Your Fire" from WordFire Press, and "The Wild Hunt" by Air and Nothingness Press. In 2020 she was awarded a scholarship to attend SuperStars Writing Seminars. She suffers from wanderlust, crochets, collects quotes, and lives beneath the shadows of the Rocky Mountains with a corgi, a kitty, and a lot of fur.

Find out more about Alicia at:
aliciacay.com

goodreads.com/aliciacay

facebook.com/aliciacaywrites

twitter.com/AliciaCayWrites

instagram.com/aliciacaywrites

pinterest.com/aliciacay

NO PLACE LIKE HOME

JAMES PYLES

AFTER ALL THEIR ADVENTURES, the dangers, the terrors…after the Yellow Brick Road, the poppy field, the witch's castle—and most importantly, confronting the wizard—Dorothy regarded her closest friends, the Cowardly Lion, the Tin Woodsman, and her dearest friend, the Scarecrow. Each had received their heart's desire (though no one was sure co-ruling Oz was part of that). Now, in the throne room of the Wizard of Oz in the palace at the center of the Emerald City, it was her turn—she was supposed to finally get her wish and return home.

But…how?

The Wizard would have taken her home in the same hot air balloon that had brought him to Oz. But just as they were about to climb aboard Toto had wriggled out of her arms, and when she ran after him the balloon took off with the Wizard—and without the two of them.

The large, chamber they all stood within was green, the citizens of Oz were dressed in green, and even the munchkins wore green little hats and jackets. Everything was green in keeping with the city's name except for Dorothy, her friends, and her ruby slippers. Then a soft, shimmering crimson glow warmed the room, and as it vanished, Glinda the Good Witch of the North appeared.

How like an angel she appeared, albeit one with a very long wand and very tall crown. All the subjects present bowed toward her. Glinda gently ascended the platform where Dorothy and her companions had stood and watched the Wizard ascend heavenward.

Dorothy, though trembling, gave a polite curtsey, and then wailed, "The Wizard's gone, Glinda, flown off in his balloon! How am I supposed to get back home?" The witch was powerful, but even she couldn't conjure up another big balloon and make it sail to Kansas.

Dorothy expected to cry, but the tears didn't come—which frankly, was quite a surprise. She stood shivering in the center of the jade throne room, her tiny black terrier held tightly in her arms, along with Wicked's captured golden cap. Her three friends no longer seemed outlandish, or even foolish.

"You've had the power to return to your cherished aunt and uncle all this while, Dorothy." Glinda, the good witch, dressed in an overbearingly fluffy white-and-pink dress made out of clouds, smiled kindly down at Dorothy. The tall, cotton candy crown on her head, magically held in place, didn't even wiggle. She spoke precisely, as if her every word was part of a prepared speech to be presented before royalty.

"I have?"

"Then why didn't you tell her about it?" the Scarecrow asked, a hint of suspicion in his voice.

Dorothy saw a twinkle in Glinda's eyes, just for an instant, an unpleasant glint she had never seen before. The Wizard said he needed Wicked's broomstick, but it turned out he didn't really want it at all—it was just an excuse to get Dorothy and her friends to kill the witch. Except for her three friends, Dorothy wondered if she could trust anyone in Oz.

"What is it, Dorothy? What's the matter, huh?" The Lion put a large, gentle paw on her shoulder. The Tin Woodsman, wearing his heart on his chest, if not his sleeve, bent down over her, while the wise Scarecrow smiled knowingly, using a finger to tuck some escaping stuffing back into his left ear.

"It's quite simple," Glinda said. Dorothy thought she heard a hint of annoyance behind the witch's soothing words. "Merely close your eyes, and click the heels of your ruby slippers together three times while repeating 'There's no place like home.' Have you got that?"

Dorothy looked down at her occult footwear. As she did, she caught an expression of uncharacteristic greed on Glinda's face as she eyed the bright red shoes. Dorothy shivered.

"That's all I need to do?" she asked. She bit her lip and thought about her home on the plains, the love she felt for her Aunt and Uncle, the antics of farm hands Hunk, Hickory, and Zeke, and how Auntie Em might actually have worried herself sick because her niece went missing.

Then she remembered getting up before dawn, and freezing

half to death as she made her way from her warm bed out to the barn to milk the cow and then feed the chickens. She remembered stepping in pig poo and ruining her brand-new shoes, even if that pair hadn't been as beautiful as the ruby red slippers. And there was that time awful Billy Johnson, who sat right behind her in school, dipped her freshly washed curls in his inkwell. Most of all, she remembered that dirty, good-for-nothing Miss Almira daring to have her precious dog Toto killed just because he bit the old woman (and she'd deserved it, too).

"No place like home?"

"That's right, my dear." The white witch's tone now sounded phony, and too-sweet maple syrupy. Had she sounded like that all along, and Dorothy and her friends just hadn't noticed? "Here, let me help."

The witch reached for the girl's shoulders as the Lion, who seemed somewhat intimidated by Glinda, removed his paw and stepped back. Apparently fear hadn't completely failed him.

"No!" This time hot tears really did stream down Dorothy's face as she ducked under Glinda's arms and ran around behind the witch.

"Wait! What are you doing? Damn it, come back here. I mean, I only want to help." The witch spun on her heels as Dorothy, clutching dog and cap, dashed across the room, away from her three friends, inspiring gasps from the aghast crowds of the Emerald City.

"Getting away from you!" Her little legs trembled and spun as Dorothy scurried over to the one thing the so-called wizard had left behind; Wicked's broomstick, the bewitching artifact she and the others had vainly risked their lives for.

Dorothy whisked it up from the foot of the stairs that led to where the phony baloney floating wizard's head had previously appeared. Crouching down like the squirrels Toto used to chase, she clutched her dog and the stick in one arm, while donning the forbidden golden cap with the other. She didn't know why Glinda wanted her slippers, but the witch was sprinting toward Dorothy, her face screwed up so she looked evil, just like Wicked.

Tugging the cap tighter on her head, Dorothy began hear a chittering sound coming from it, like from a radio. The monkeys! She could use the cap to call them! The idea was crazy and scary, but as long as she wore the cap, they wouldn't hurt her - instead, they'd obey her. Dorothy made her decision and called to the monkeys.

Glinda slowed to a stately stroll and composed her features so she looked kind and good again. "Please, give the cap to me, precious one."

"You want to send me back home, take the ruby slippers, and run...everything, all this. You want to take Oz away from my friends, and be the ruler of everyone. You're worse than the wizard, worse than even Wicked."

" I want nothing of the sort, child." Glinda's eyes flickered back to Dorothy's companions for an instant, then to the crowd. "I just want to send you back to your family, Dorothy. After all, you said it's your heart's desire. Didn't you tell me that your dear Auntie was ill and dying? If you hurry, you might return to Kansas in time to save her."

"Who cares about Auntie Em and Uncle Henry? When the Sheriff came to take Toto away and kill him, they didn't say or do anything. They never cared about me, they just wanted me around to do chores."

Dorothy kept one hand tight on the floppy golden cap firmly on top of her head and desperately kept trying to summon Wicked's monkeys, although she was not unsure if she was using the cap right. Her fingers, still wrapped around the now shuddering broomstick, were white and bloodless. Somehow she managed to keep a hold of Toto, but if the squirming dog ever managed to escape, the witch would grab him and hold him for hostage or something.

Glinda crept steadily closer. "Come now. Don't be so stubborn." A low growl, rising from the back of her throat, accompanied her words. "And you don't need to dig your heels in that way. You might ruin the slippers. Now, let's just get you sent back to your aunt and uncle."

"No! Please, no!" She was going to send Dorothy back to Kansas. Life there was so ordinary, so plain, so boring.

"It's for your own good."

Dorothy was literally backed against a wall, confronted by the greatest evil she had ever known in this strange, magical land. Where were her so-called friends? They'd stuck by her like glue when they'd faced down Wicked and her monkey minions. What were they waiting for? Why weren't they trying to save her now?

Her gaze darted around the room. The inhabitants of Oz were still bowing, and the faces Scarecrow, Lion, and Tin Woodsman were frozen in confusion and indecision. Had Glinda's magic done something to them, or were they just shocked at Glinda's abrupt transformation?

Toto barked at the witch like a maniac, but mercifully, didn't try to escape Dorothy's grasp. The broomstick competed with Dorothy's legs as to which could shake faster and harder. If the monkeys didn't arrive soon, Glinda would grab Dorothy and send her back home. Dorothy could try to ride the broomstick back to Wicked's castle, where she knew the monkeys were sure to take her if they'd ever show up. But she'd never ridden a broomstick before. What if she fell - or worse, dropped Toto?

At once, Glinda, the Scarecrow, the Tin Woodsman, the Lion, and the colorful, friendly, and terrified citizens of the Emerald City, looked up. There was nothing to see, not yet, but a multitude of chattering voices, the gibbering of monkeys and the fluttering of a congregation of wings was getting closer. Wicked's flying monkeys were arriving, and there were a lot of them.

Glinda leapt toward Dorothy, but the girl wielded the now ener-gized broomstick like a sword, poking the witch between her two modest breasts. Repelled by the dark magic, Glinda staggered backward.

Frantically imploring her fuzzy saviors, Dorothy stared upward as a thousand swarming specters blocked the sunlight above. The horde of flying monkeys descended, all thick gray fur, their wings of coordinating colors looking too small to lift their ponderous weight, but managing nicely anyway. The fez on each one's head matched their short jackets of turquoise and scarlet, trimmed elegantly with golden yellow. Their eyes glowed with frightening malevolence for everyone in the Emerald City. Everyone except Dorothy.

Glinda, face set with determination, raised her wand, a long staff tipped with a five-pointed star, but it was too late. She was inundated, fuzzily flooded by chattering, spinning, flapping apish masses. Strong hands and deft fingers pulled and tugged at every bit of her. Her hat went one way, the wand another, and her puffy white-and-pink cloudy dress was reduced to shreds. The good and kindly citizens of the Emerald City panicked, some running willy-nilly into walls, but most of them managed to dash through the great doorway leading out of the throne room and disappeared into the verdant recesses of the city. Dorothy wanted to blot out her screams with her hands during the simian assault, but holding the broomstick and the frantically wiggling Toto made this impossible.

Amid the chaos, only the Lion ran forward, probably as a test of his new courage, valor, and sense of chivalry. Oddly, the Scarecrow didn't join his friend. What had his new intelligence done to change him so? The Tin Woodsman, Dorothy felt, must be overflowing with compassion over her plight, but he wasn't doing anything either. Why weren't they trying to help her? Was it because of the monkeys?

Dorothy cried out as the Lion, who was positively and heroically fierce, beat back a phalanx of the monkeys attacking Glinda.

"But I called them, I want them! Lion, why are you defending her and not me?"

The Lion continued swatting at the monkeys like enormous, hairy flies. Each wave of his mighty paws, ferocious claws extended, sent half a dozen of the demonic simians scattering away from the white witch, fur and blood careening through the air like grenade shrapnel.

He was saving the witch…not helping Dorothy. Why weren't her friends helping her? Were they really her friends after all?

Dorothy took a deep breath, grasped Toto even more tightly, and then commanded the monkeys to take her to her new home.

SECONDS later the monkeys took to the air. Glinda glanced toward the ceiling and watched as the hundreds of flying monkeys rose upward toward the opening above, then gasped as she realized they were carrying Dorothy. The child clutched Toto in one arm and the somewhat scorched, broomstick in the other. Wicked's golden cap was stuck firmly on her head. She had gotten away, with the cap, the broomstick…and most importantly, the ruby slippers.

"No!" Glinda yelled, but her voice came out as a croak. Without the slippers, she'd never escape her dreary, icebound castle and rule Oz! And she couldn't cast a spell to stop the girl because she was pinned on the floor by the Lion, who had fallen on top of her.

"Get off me, you oaf," she said. She was seized by a series of sneezes, and feared that she had suddenly become allergic to cat hair. Later, she would realize it was his cologne, which could be easily changed.

The Lion didn't move. He was apparently transfixed by the aerial monkeys who rose higher and higher in the air, and then flew westward and out of sight. The raucous noise of their voices and the flapping of their wings became fainter and fainter, and then everything was silent.

"I said…" she heaved upward, attempting to dislodge his tremendous, furry bulk, but to no avail. "…get off me. You're crushing…"

"Oh, dear. I am so sorry. Please allow me to…"

"Don't be sorry, just *move*."

Glinda scrambled to her knees as the great cat finally moved. She immediately realized her condition of undress, and desperately grabbed at the tatters that remained of her clothing. The Lion might be noble, but he kept stealing glances at her long, exposed and shapely legs, her small, pouting breasts, and particularly the miniature, star-shaped mole on her left buttocks. She glared at him.

"At least pretend to be a gentleman."

The Lion shook his head, mane swirling like a cyclone, and redoubled his efforts not to notice.

She turned her back on him and began to search for her wand. Where had it gone?

The metal boots of the Tin Woodsman clanked on the stone floor as he hurried over to join them. Tears were in his eyes, presumably at the loss of Dorothy, but he quickly wiped them away.

The witch scanned the room, empty now except for her and Dorothy's three friends. The scarecrow had been granted intelligence, but apparently not class, since he was seemingly cataloging the various elements and attributes of her beauty now being generously displayed.

"Woodsman, don't just stand around looking heartbroken," she snapped. "Find something to clothe me in."

"At once, your witchness." He clomped across the hall, picked up a green cloak discarded by one of the city's denizens in their haste to escape, and carried it over to Glinda.

The Lion grabbed the cloak from him and wrapped it around her shoulders. His paws were soft and gentle. Glinda met his eyes and, to her great surprise, blushed, even though the cloak now covered her body. She reached out a hand and stroked his soft, silky fur. She'd find her wand eventually. And if not, she would let her fierce protector mete out punishment upon anyone foolish enough to make off with it. After all, she had plans for both the Lion and the wand.

THE TIN WOODSMAN followed his cloth and straw friend to the back of the room near the exit. The Emerald City citizens had still not returned, not even one of them, and those who had been trapped in the chamber during the attack were now nowhere to be seen.

"So, what makes you think Dorothy wants to come back?" the Scarecrow whispered to the Woodsmans, although there was no one around to hear except the Lion and Glinda.

The Woodsman restrained his tears, trying to forestall more rust. "Those horrible monkeys…"

"Did not kidnap her, they *rescued* her."

"From what? Us?"

"From going home. Think, that is if you can, with that empty tin can on your shoulders."

"I am not empty," the metal man said with great indignity. "I am full of love." He felt his metal frame become nearly aglow with emotion.

"You're full of something, all right" The Scarecrow rolled his eyes.

Woodsman didn't like what being smart had done to his friend, but he still couldn't help but adore him.

"You saw the same thing I did. When Glinda told Dorothy how to get back home using the slippers, the kid practically had a panic attack. She was crying, sweating, trembling. It's amazing she didn't wet her bloomers out of sheer terror."

"But all this time, over and over again, she's been saying how she needed to get back home to Kansas, to her sick Aunt. Why would she change her mind right when she got what she wanted all along?"

"You still don't get it, do you, Mr. Metal Head? None of us really got what we wanted. We just thought we did."

"What do you mean? You got smart, the Lion's brave now, and I have a loving and tender heart." The Woodsman's eyes fluttered romantically, though they still creaked slightly.

"What about running Oz, did you get that action from the wizard, huh, did you?"

"Well I…"

"He was looking for a way out, back to Kansas, and we provided the fall guys. What did he give us? A piece of paper, that cheap trinket around your neck, and the Lion got a medal. He gave us just enough so we'd tumble for this scam to rule Oz after he got away. Nothing doing. I don't need the headache, and you don't either. I promise that you and the Lion wouldn't last a day of attending boring council meetings, reviewing ordinances, and listening to the complaints of the public. You know, the real business of being the boss. It's not all floating heads and thundering voices."

"You know, I never thought of it that way."

"That's because you can't think. Fortunately, I can."

The Scarecrow took a step to one side, and his foot errantly nudged the staff of Glinda's wand. He quickly bent over and picked it up. Then he looked side to side and at the witch, making sure his act was unobserved., and jammed it inside his overalls.

"What are you going to do with that?"

"Not give it back to Glinda, that's for sure."

"But why? It belongs to her."

"As long as she has its power, she'll make another one of those bubbles and fly after Dorothy to get the ruby slippers."

"Don't you want to go after her?"

"Follow the Courageous Lion on some damn, foolish crusade if you want to, but I've had enough of witches, good and otherwise. And now that Glinda's revealed her true colors, none of which are white, I, for one, don't want to give her a second shot at those slippers or the role of dictator."

"Then who will be the ruler of Oz?"

"Who cares, as long as it's not her or me, savvy?"

Without waiting for a response, the Scarecrow, wand firmly in hand, turned and left the room. His soft leather shoes made almost no sound, but his straw had a tendency to crinkle.

The Tin Woodsman looked back at Glinda, who was still being comforted by the Lion. His heart felt warm as he watched the big lug cuddle her like an enormous teddy bear. He couldn't help noticing how she smiled as she nuzzled his fur. Tin made note of a budding romance, and in time, maybe wedding plans would be in order. Of course, given everything else the Scarecrow had just told him, he might be letting his feelings run away with him, now that he had feelings.

"When Glinda can't find her wand, she's going to be pissed," he muttered. Then, having nothing better to do, he walked toward the Lion and Glinda to see if there was anything he could do to render comfort.

DOROTHY SAT GLOOMILY on her throne in the Wicked Witch's castle, as she had for the past ten years. As they had for her predecessor, the guards continued to march tirelessly in front of its only entrance —or at least the only entrance accessible via land. Dressed in a grandeur that made the famed Swiss Guards seem unpretentious by comparison, they were each armed with a vicious-looking halberd. They sang a low, marching chant as they defended the barred entrance to her sanctuary. The stone bridge was clear of traffic, it being half past midnight, but these days the span was almost always empty, even at high noon.

She had buried her beloved Toto in the haunted forest below, his loyal heart finally stilled by the passage of time. Her only attendants now were the monkeys. She kept a favorite, of course, and even named him Toto, but there was no real love between them. He could only offer her his fear and obedience.

Dorothy sometimes chose to express her displeasure on some local town, but never troubled herself with the Emerald City. It was now ruled by Glinda, with those three deserters serving as her advisers. Her spies told her the Scarecrow eventually "found" Glinda's wand and returned it to her in exchange for certain favors for the trio. That may well have included the Scarecrow's ability to woo the local wenches, and Lion becoming the consort of the sorceress. Supposedly, the Woodsman requested nothing, spending most of his time consuming tawdry romance fiction.

Dorothy shunned all of those bright and welcoming lands, and absolutely avoided having anything to do with munchkins and Yellow Brick Roads.

She always dressed in black, the cloth tightly hugging her newly developed curves. Occasionally, she'd have Toto and a few of his mates kidnap a boy, some farm lad or an innkeeper's son, so she could slake an appetite she had never known when she was first spirited out of Kansas. Not being quite as murderous as the old Wicked, she made sure the boys were returned from whence they came, though more than a few asked if they'd be invited back.

She no longer needed the golden cap she'd taken from Wicked to control the monkeys. Like the guards, they had found their brief freedom from Wicked's rule exhausting, boring, and confusing, and were happy to have her rule them in Wicked's stead.

Dorothy adjusted the wide-brimmed, conical hat she wore, and her hand tightened around the burned but functional broomstick she held in one hand as if it were a staff. She stared down at the ruby slippers she still wore. The shoes were both her salvation and her curse. With their power, even Glinda and the combined armies of Oz could not breach her borders, although they'd certainly tried.

"Someday, there'll be war."

Several monkeys moved a step or two forward and bowed as if she had issued a command they had missed. She ignored them, and they resumed their places.

The crystal ball on the dais at the room's murky center began to glow. Dorothy was surprised to see the image of the Kansas farmhouse appear in the crystal. She banished the visions with a wave of her broom. "Go away."

She had meant to sound stern, but her voice came out small, the voice of the terrified little girl who still lived somewhere inside of her, afraid she'd someday be sent back to the regular world.

"I won't go back." Dorothy's bladder felt weak, and her mouth went dry. She gripped the broomstick tighter, as if it was an anchor that could prevent her from being swept away by the tornado of rising panic.

"I'll never go back! It's so horrible, so cruel, so ordinary."

The monkey Toto edged up to her left side and laid his head on her arm. She reached back and scratched behind his ear. He panted in satisfaction as she stroked the fur on his neck.

"That's a good boy." Dorothy the Wicked Witch of the West regarded the crystal, the dark hall, and the castle where she ruled with a will of iron. Her will kept at bay her dread of a plodding life, a plain, dull existence in a world without magic, without flying monkeys and mystic crystals, without scarecrows who talked and lions who cried.

"Come on, monkeys." She grinned and stood, her sheer ebony skirt falling down across her thighs. "Let's go have some fun."

She sat astride her broomstick, and flew across the midnight sky like an ebony comet as she and her airborne warriors cast away from the castle in search of a new adventure.

Far below, the terrified inhabitants of humble hamlets shuddered in their beds as they heard her distant cry from above, "There's no place like home."

ABOUT THE AUTHOR

James Pyles is a published science fiction and fantasy writer. He is also an Information Technology textbook author and editor, and technical writer for the IT department of a multi-state corporation located in the U.S. northwest. A growing number of his short stories have been published in anthologies and periodicals since 2019. He also is working on more interesting and compelling projects for 2021.

Find out more about James at:
poweredbyrobots.com

goodreads.com/jamespyles
facebook.com/jamespylesauthor
twitter.com/jamespyles
bookbub.com/authors/james-pyles
amazon.com/James-Pyles/e/B001IQXL38

TERMINAL SORCERY

GRAYSON TOWLER

MANY YEARS AGO, this chamber at the top of my tower was filled with the glow of my magical crystals. Travelers could see the light from miles away, all the way to the borders of Greensward in the east and the Relentless Straits in the west. They would see that eldritch glow, and would know they looked upon the sanctuary of the greatest sorcerer for a thousand miles.

Kings begged for permission to ascend and treat with me. Fae lords paid me tribute in coin and service to add to the splendor of my tower. Dragons brought me gifts from their hoards and set them upon the immaculate marble of my balcony.

Now the only light comes from the meager fire in the crude hearth near my sickbed.

I tilt my head, peering through clouded eyes at the gold-framed mirror a few yards away, the one I once used to scry into distant lands and other worlds. The glass is grimy and dull.

I don't want to look in a mirror anyway. The ancient, withered thing in the reflection would just depress me. I let my gaze drift to the vaulted ceiling. Cobwebs up there. My useless apprentice has let them get out of hand again. She's going to get an earful, the dullard.

This room used to clean itself. Servitor spirits swept away every speck of dust, leaving all gleaming and pristine. The spirits are gone now.

There's no magic left in this place.

I'm going to die here.

Why? Why would the legendary Kenryk the Magnificent, he who cast demon princes back to the darkness and brought demigods to their knees, be trapped here in his own tower, shivering under a stack of grey, threadbare blankets?

Because I can't get down the damned steps, that's why.

I used to be able to levitate up and down my tower at will. Or teleport where I wanted to go. The steps were for guests and supplicants and apprentices, not for me.

Wait.

Didn't…didn't I have a magic carpet once?

Someone gave that to me. An Ifrit noblewoman, was it? Yes, that was it. A fiery kiss of gratitude for my aid, a night of spiced wine and passion that would have turned a normal man to ash…and the gifts. Including a magic carpet.

Even in my state, I should be able to use something as simple as a magic carpet. I could ride it wherever I wanted to go. Not be stuck here. Should have thought of this years ago!

I just need to remember where I put it.

No…I don't have to remember where it is, just the command word! I can make the carpet come to me. Obey me. Just have to remember the right word.

I mumble a few possibilities. The right side of my face is slack these days, and I slur my words. Can't slur. Incantations must be crisp and precise.

Precise. Yes.

What was the word I was looking for?

I lift my head to gaze around the chamber, searching for something to remind me what I'd been trying to do. Cobwebs on rafters. A filthy mirror. A sullen glow in the crudely-built hearth my apprentice made from broken stone.

I'm trapped here. Trapped in my lifeless tower, trapped in my decaying body.

Why is it so much effort to lift my head?

I let my eyes close and flop back down.

I don't want to look at this room anymore.

"Master?"

For a moment, I don't recognize the voice. Then the haze clears, and I remember it's Brei, my fool of an apprentice. She sits there on her stool beside my bed, staring at me with those absurd doe-eyes of hers. She looks more like a kitchen maid than a sorceress, with that ruddy scarf tied around her head, and her grease-stained apron.

But she's an apprentice, all right. She's got the aged grimoire on seasonal magic open on her lap, and is waiting patiently for me to continue the lesson.

Lessons every day. I may be old, but I'm still the master here. I'm not about to start letting an apprentice slack off, even a useless one.

I clear my throat, rearranging the pillows that she's propped under me so I can sit up.

"Seasonal magic," I say. I hate my voice these days. Used to have a thunderous baritone that could stop an ogre in its tracks. Now I sound like a sick toad. To hell with it. "Every season has a purpose. Its own power."

I pause. She nods, like I've said something valuable. Maybe I did?

Brei doesn't usually ask questions in lessons. She's not stupid… she can recite the chapters I've assigned her by heart…but where's her drive? Her ambition? She never questions, never challenges me, never tries to do a spell before I give her permission.

She's going to be my last apprentice. Pathetic.

I'll drum *some* kind of learning into her if it's the last thing I do.

I clear my throat again. She passes me a cup, and I take a sip of the warm tea, flavored with honey. Brei's a good enough cook, I'll give her that.

"We are in the season of winter," I say. "The common man is afraid of winter. Barren time. Cold kills, he thinks. And he's right enough, sure." I remember the time I called down a blight of ice upon the army of a would-be conqueror. Steel swords shattering in the cold, men begging for their lives as the snow piled up around their waists, their chests. A great working, that one. I smile.

"Yes, Master," Brei says softly.

I blink, coming back to the present. "Yes. Cold kills. But cold also preserves!" I raise a finger. "Every year, I've done rituals of preservation in midwinter. Sealing spells to talismans, binding contracts with spirits. Any sorcerer who wishes to extend his life will learn to harness the power of cold, girl. Remember that."

She nods her head dutifully, the mousy curls not held in place by her scarf bobbing like loose springs.

"Think I wouldn't have lived this long if I didn't know how to wield winter's strength?" I say, as if she's doubted me. "I'm 475 years old! I'd have made it to 500, longer even, if that little snake Lir hadn't poisoned me!" The century-old memory still makes my blood boil. He'd been such a promising student, but he'd *betrayed* me. Nearly killed me.

Or had that been Roarke?

Doesn't matter. Have to stick to the lesson. "So tell me what your book says about winter magic," I demand. "Go on."

Brei's round face deflates like dough without enough yeast. She bows her head and thumbs at her book. "Yes, Master. May I refresh my memory for a moment?"

I scowl. Brei can *usually* be counted on to read the material, if little else. "What's the matter with you?" I jab a finger at her. "I gave you an assignment. Can't you see winter's here? You want to waste all this power just because you couldn't be bothered to read your——"

I look past her, out the window overlooking the valley.

Even with my clouded vision, I see the forest stretching across the valley, green and brilliant with the new leaves. On far mountains, only modest caps of snow cover the highest peaks.

This isn't winter. It's spring.

Why did I think…?

Why…?

Why didn't that stupid cow of an apprentice *tell* me I was talking about the wrong season? Fury rages in me as I glare at Brei. She sees where my gaze has gone, knows I've finally twigged to my lapse. I could take it if there was contempt in her eyes. But no, not her.

Her amber eyes are glimmering. She's holding back tears.

My knuckles crack like old twigs as I ball my hands into useless fists. "No wonder I thought it was winter!" I growl. "Cold as a Jotun's balls in this room! Get that fire going, damn it. I'm freezing in here."

Brei stands up so quickly that her grimoire falls to the floor. I bark an angry word at her—books should be treated with care! She stammers an apology, then hurries to the hearth, grabbing wood and twigs and dry grass to pile onto the ashes.

In her haste, she smothers the few remaining coals.

Brei apologizes some more and fumbles in her apron for flint and tinder.

"No," I say, and my voice is steady with command. My anger has kindled a new strength in me, and it feels good. "Not like some common serving wench. Light it with magic."

My apprentice trembles.

"What are you waiting for?" I ask. "I was lighting fires with sorcery when I was barely out of diapers, girl."

She flinches and ducks her head...and of course, I understand why. I'm back in diapers now, as she knows all too well. The humiliating reminder stokes my anger even higher.

"You know the incantation!" I shout, an echo of my old thunder coming back into my voice. "Speak it! Light the fire, apprentice!"

Brei takes a deep breath and squares her shoulders to the hearth. She extends her hand, fingers spread in the proper gesture, and pronounces the simple incantation in a squeak: "*Pira!*"

"You sound like a frightened mouse," I say. "To work magic is to impose your will on reality. Again, with authority!"

"*Pira!*" Like she's scolding a puppy.

Her gestures are correct, her breathing and stance are all as they should be, and even her pronunciation is without flaw. And I know she has a gift for magic...I'm not so far gone that I can't sense it. The problem is in her head. Her attitude.

A weakling can never command the fundamental forces of the cosmos.

I wave my hand at the fire. "*Pira,*" I say, and the familiar sizzle of power dances through my nerves. A spark ignites in the dry grass—really, the spell couldn't be any easier with such kindling—and within moments, a robust flame roars in the hearth.

Brei's shoulders slump. She refuses to look at me.

"Go," I tell her. "Leave me."

She obeys, and runs to the door as if I plan to set her on fire next.

For once, I don't just collapse back into my bed after the lesson. Too agitated, too angry...and too excited. I haven't done much magic lately. Lighting that fire didn't tire me out at all! I'm ready for more.

I know what I will do.

I'll create a replacement for Brei.

Not another apprentice, of course. Even at the height of my power with the Conclave of Archmagi behind me, creating a living human would have been impossible. Sorcery has its limits. Besides, I don't want an apprentice anymore. Too much work.

All I need is a golem. That I can do.

I pull myself all the way up and haul the blankets off. The marble of the floor is cold as ice on my feet, but I feel steady enough for this. I have my staff by my bed—little more than firewood itself right now, since I haven't renewed its enchantment for a decade, but it will serve me as a walking stick.

I haul myself out of bed. Shouldn't take so much effort. I weighed more as a boy than I do now.

What was I doing?

A golem. Yes. That's it. Make a golem out of these sticks and firewood. One that can tend to all the needs of this stupid, traitorous old body. Won't need Brei anymore for that stuff...can send her away. Let her find another master. Someone who can teach her how to start a fire.

Takes a few steps to get over to the hearth. My feet threaten to slip out from under me. Hard to keep the staff in the right place to support my weight. I hobble over, my knees quaking, and sit down on the edge of the hearth.

There's a good, warm fire at my back. Burning nicely.

Brei can set up firewood, at least. Just can't make it burn.

Why not?

What's the matter with her?

The room feels like it's swaying slowly around me. I'm not... feeling so strong anymore. Just need a little more rest. The fire's warmth is so relaxing.

My gaze wanders down to the pile of firewood. Had I been planning to do something with that? Can't remember.

The edge of the hearth is wide enough to lay down on. Hard and lumpy, though. Not soft, like my bed. I won't stay for very long.

I just need to lay here where it's warm. Get my strength back. Then I'll...

I'll...

"Here you go, Master. Time to eat."

The voice seems to come from a long, long way off. For a long moment, I can't place it. A soft voice, gentle.

Something smells good.

I force my eyes open. For a while, all I see are blurs in the darkness. She sits beside my bed on her stool, and the lovely smell is coming from the bowl in her hands. My apprentice—that's who it is—extends a spoon toward me.

When I turn my head, a spike of pain jabs me in the neck.

"Aah...no!" I cry. Terror grips me. Has someone stabbed me?

Brei's hand reaches for me, but I'm too slow to move away. For a horrible moment, I'm sure she's here to kill me. I'm helpless, ruined, powerless to defend myself...but then she cups my bald head gently in her hand and supports my head.

"Easy, sir," she says. "I found you sleeping on the hearth. That must be how you hurt your neck. I'm sorry you were so cold."

My bony chest flutters as I get my breath back under control. No danger. I'm safe.

Why should I even be afraid? I chide myself for panicking. Kenryk the Magnificent, Master Archmage, wailing like a frightened lamb.

Death would be a release right now. I should welcome it.

Brei holds my head just so until the pain in my neck fades, then spoons the chicken soup carefully into my mouth. A mild soup, with carrot and onion and rice, all softened up by a long stay in the broth. I have dined upon the egg of a phoenix at the table of a god, and I cannot remember anything more welcome than this simple, wholesome soup.

"There," Brei says. Her round cheeks lift as she smiles. "Looks like I got the soup right, at least."

She did. She always does. The meal slowly feeds strength back into me...and with it, comes the shameful memory of my plan to make a golem to replace her. Foolish, foolish old man. Even if it wasn't far beyond my current powers to craft a golem, I know better than to believe a mindless automaton could do the things this girl does. Golems are for battle and crude labor. No golem ever made could cook a good chicken soup.

"How do you feel?" she asks. "Do you hurt anywhere else?"

I let my attention wander down my body. My hip is sore, but it's always sore. Nothing new there. I do notice I'm wearing clean diapers. Brei has performed that repulsive task once again. She prefers to do it when I sleep...to spare me the shame of having to witness my degradation.

"I am...fine," I say, though we both know how untrue that is.

She settles me carefully back on my pillow, making sure not to jostle my head.

The fire crackles in its hearth, the sole source of light in the room. She sits beside me, mostly a silhouette backlit by the steady glow.

"Why do you stay?" I ask her.

"I'm your apprentice," says Brei.

I start to shake my head, but my neck twinges and I hold still again. "No. I'm worthless as a master. I am not teaching you anything."

She takes in a breath as if she's about to say something, then subsides.

"I have scant inheritance for you," I say. "Most of my treasures of any value have been sold long ago." A flicker of a memory—I'd been thinking about that flying carpet the other day, forgetting I'd sold it off already some fifteen years ago. Another tiny moment of humiliation. "You may take the books...what coin I have left...the mirror, if you can get the vulgar old thing down the stairs. My staff, even."

She lets out a gasp, as if I'd blasphemed.

"I would leave you the tower," I say. "But it is worthless. I had to move it every time the ley lines shift, but last time I didn't have the strength. All the greater enchantments failed then."

"You…could move the *whole* tower?" she asks with wonder in her voice.

For some reason, this makes me smile. I know I've spoken of my truly great deeds to her before, and by comparison moving this tower is barely worth mentioning. Perhaps in Brei's mind, old stories about magical wonders are too abstract to truly sink in. But she knows this tower. Thirty flights of stairs, thousands of tons of marble and granite…yes, to her, the concept of moving such a mass would seem like an impossible feat.

"Take what you can of value," I tell her. "Find another master. One who can teach you…teach you to light a fire."

She shakes her head, her curls whisking over the coarse wool of her tunic. "I can't," she says.

A long sigh escapes me. If she leaves, I will die. That's why she "can't."

Brei has a tender heart…and it makes me afraid for her. The path of magic is not a place for softness. I want to warn her…to tell her of the hags and necromancers and gibbering nameless things that care nothing for kindness or charity…they will eat her alive if they smell weakness on her. The fire will burn her, the waters will swallow her whole…how can someone so gentle hope to assert her will over these primal energies?

I try to tell her, but a coughing fit seizes me. All I manage is: "You…too kind…too kind…"

"Drink, Master," she says, and holds cup to my lips. More of her tea, mint and honey, soothing on the throat.

My cough settles slowly as I sip the tea.

"I'm not kind," Brei says quietly as I drink. "You give me too much credit, Master. I don't have anywhere else to go. No other teacher would take me. A stupid girl who can't even light dried grass."

She sees me wince as my neck gives another pang, eases me back into a more comfortable position.

"I was a burden as a daughter," she says. "The fifth girl in a family that needed boys to carry on the farm. All I could hope for is to marry someone worth his salt someday." A soft, rueful laugh. "Then the wise woman of our village said I had the spark. I could be a sorceress. And for a moment...I actually thought I could."

I want to say something. Can't think of what. Brei never talks about herself. And I never ask.

"But that was all a fool's dream," she says. "Real sorceresses don't come from common stock. Everyone knows that."

What? Who filled her head with that idiocy? I was a miller's son! My own master's father was a farrier!

But of course I know what happened. These sorts of beliefs cycle around every few decades. Imbecilic twaddle about pure blood or the divine right of aristocratic lines. Might even have been my sniveling ex-apprentice Roarke behind the latest incarnation of the prejudice. He was from a noble family.

Or had that been Lir?

Doesn't matter. If it wasn't one of the traitorous little shits, it was some other snotty rich brat who didn't want to have to train a grubby peasant for an apprentice.

Brei is still talking, though I've missed some of what she said. "...so they sent me here. Traded me for that self-spinning wheel of yours. My father laughed at what a good deal he'd made. He was sure the wheel would make him rich."

I snort. I can't even remember that agreement now. I *do* remember that the spinning wheel was cursed, though, so I doubt very much that her father thinks he'd made such a fine bargain anymore, wherever he is.

My apprentice shrugs and takes my empty tea cup away. "That's why I can't make fire, or move objects with my mind, or do anything with magic. It's not your fault, sir. It's me."

Weariness threatens to overtake me. I fight against it, but this is a foe that has the measure of me these days. "You...*do* have the gift," I manage to say.

In the warm glow of the fire, I see the sad smile on her face. "Thank you, Master," she says, but she doesn't believe me. I am an old man who shits into a diaper and cannot remember what season it is. Why would she believe me?

What can I do to make her believe, with this little time I have left?

THE DAYS BLUR TOGETHER. I am losing track of time.

I am forced to admit to myself that my daily lessons with Brei have not been "daily" for some time. Hours can slip by in a heartbeat. I know I have missed whole days when I was supposed to be teaching.

Not that I have much to teach.

One morning—or is it afternoon?—I awaken to see Brei sweeping broken glass into a bin. My mirror...destroyed, as if hurled across the vast chamber by a raging giant. The remains of the frame are splintered, the glass smashed. Did Brei do this?

She looks at me as I watch her. "Master?" A tremble of fear in her voice.

"Did...I break the mirror?" I ask. Hellfire, my voice is so weak.

"You had a seizure," she says. "There was a wind, like a tornado..."

A seizure? I have no memory of it, nothing at all. My magic has become as incontinent as my body.

Exhaustion pulls my eyes shut. Using that much magic in my condition, I'm surprised it didn't kill me outright.

Death is so very, very close. Won't be long now.

I OPEN my eyes and see my chamber in sharp relief. Outside the window, the night sky is filled with stars—and I can *see* them. My vision is as sharp as it was in my youth.

And my mind is even sharper.

I sit up. My body responds easily.

A quick inventory of my condition tells me the aches and pains are still there, but at some remove that allows me to disregard them as mere information. Though my flesh is as wasted and dry as before, what's left of my musculature responds without protest.

So does my magic.

Without the slightest effort, I levitate out of bed and hover a few inches off the floor. I make a simple gesture, and my staff leaps into my hand. Long-dormant runes burst to life, filling the room with ruby radiance.

I am not confused. I am under no illusions that this is some sort of miraculous recovery. I know exactly what is happening to me.

My memory, which until so recently has failed and betrayed me at every turn, is as perfect as it was in my prime. The name of this phenomenon springs to mind, as noted in the Fifth Epoch by the great Archmage Ibn Sina in his *Canon of Medicinal Magic.* "Terminal lucidity," he dubbed it on page 417 of the second volume, in subsection Thanatology. I mentally flip through his many citations, all describing incidents in which the dying patient demonstrates an unexpected and dramatic return of their mental and/or physical faculties just before death.

I laugh in full-throated joy. So this is what it feels like to be on the inside of a great medical mystery!

A mystery? No, no. It makes such perfect sense.

The mind interfaces with this material reality through the brain and body. The body is like a window through which our true essence, our consciousness, peers into the realm of form and substance. Over time, that window becomes smudged and grimy with age, disease, decay. My own window had caked over with such a layer of filth it had almost become opaque.

Now, in my final hours, the window has broken. I am seeing without obstruction into this world. My mind has absolute freedom.

Yet such perfect, unrestricted vision cannot be sustained. The window between worlds has become a breach, and the breach must close. The last reserves of my body are burning away as the ancient vessel of flesh yields its final gift.

I will die soon. Very, very soon. But I am no longer afraid.

My magic is *back.* And I have enough time for one final working.

Possibilities whirl in my mind. I might craft an inescapable curse that would expunge my faithless ex-apprentices from the world wherever they might be hiding—Lir, who robbed me and took credit for my work; Roarke, who poisoned me and fled when I survived. Or I might perform some feat thought to be unachievable, like capturing the throne of a god or penetrating the dreams of a dragon, something that would leave my name forever blazing in the annals of history. I even might be able to restore youth to my limbs and vitals, to purchase myself another century...or another five.

All these grandiose ideas flare and die away like the embers from the makeshift hearth.

"Brei!" I call, and the tower rings with my voice. "To me, Brei!"

She is close, of course. She has made her bed in my old library, just one flight down, and she always keeps a wary ear for a cough or a moan from my chamber. Seconds after my summons, she bursts through the door and skids to a stop. Her eyes widen to near-perfect circles as she sees me, for the first time, in my full power.

"Master?" she gasps, her face aglow with the reflected light from my staff. "What's happening?"

"There is not much time," I say. "I have one final lesson for you."

I work a spell I have never even contemplated before, but in this state of final grace the words and gestures flow effortlessly. Now that my mind is clear—finally, *finally* clear again—I understand what is holding Brei back as a sorceress.

I only hope my solution will be enough.

For the first time in decades, I am afraid for something other than myself. I will not have another chance to get this right...and if I fail, Brei will never reach the great potential locked inside her.

The working is ready. "Now, Brei!" I say, and extend my hand to a spot just a few yards in front of her. "Look!"

As she looks, I call forth the image of a child.

It's a young girl, perhaps eight years old. She huddles on the ground, knees drawn up tight to her chest as if she is concealing herself in a small space. She's dressed in plain roughspun, flecks of straw and dirt on her ill-fitting clothes. Her back is turned to Brei, but my apprentice can see the girl's body shaking with sobs, and hear the muffled whimpers as she weeps in the abject misery only a child can feel.

Brei's eyes fix on the girl. Her whole being softens, as I knew it would, and she does what her deepest instinct tells her to do. She steps forward to comfort the crying girl.

Then a wall appears in front of my apprentice, blocking her.

The barrier appears to be made of heavy stones—translucent, so Brei can still see and hear the distressed girl, but as solid as the walls of this tower. Brei slaps a hand against it, quite fruitlessly.

"Break that wall," I tell her. "Break it, apprentice."

"I don't know how!" Brei cries. "Master, I can't even make a spark!"

"You *can!*" I thunder.

"How?" She smacks her hands against the unyielding barrier. "What spell, Master?"

I shake my head. "Magic is an act of will. The gestures and words and symbols are all tools, but the *will* is all! Reach into yourself, Brei. Find what is within you, and the wall will not stand. I promise you, apprentice, it *will not stand!*"

That is all I can do to help her. I have given her what she needs —in my feeble way, through six years of training, I have prepared her as well as she can be prepared. She has read the tomes and learned the gestures and practiced the meditations. Now she must put it all together herself…or not at all.

I watch my apprentice close her eyes and gain control over her breathing. My time is rushing away, roaring away like a river in flood, but I wait in silence.

The image of the child sobs and wails. Brei's hands move as if to cover her ears…no, no, not like that! She must turn toward the child's pain, not shut it out!

I keep my lips sealed, waiting for her to understand.

She lowers her hands.

My heart leaps in joy as Brei opens her eyes—fierce eyes, the eyes of a mother bear defending her cub—and I know she has found her strength.

Brei places her palms against the wall. She fixes her gaze on the child before her, the suffering girl sobbing in some dark corner of some faraway barn that I have never seen…but that Brei has.

The young sorceress speaks a word of power, and the wall shatters.

The stones were never stones. They were memories, drawn from Brei's own mind. A father's rough knuckles, a cousin's cruel pinches and indignities, a mother's sullen disappointment—as well as the contemptuous words of a vain old man too blind and too afraid to spare a kind thought for the finest apprentice he has ever taught.

She could not have broken such a barrier for her own sake. But for another's? I'd gambled everything she could do that.

And I was right.

Brei rushes to the child and sweeps her up in strong, gentle arms. I wonder if Brei even sees that the child was also drawn from her own memory, a younger version of herself grieving in the dark as one of her dreams was stepped on. Perhaps she does. If she doesn't now, she will realize it someday. I have faith in her.

The light from my staff fades. The power that held me aloft suddenly drains away.

My body crumples like a rag to the floor.

The magically-crafted image of the girl in Brei's arms dwindles out of being, and my apprentice's attention snaps to me. She scrambles to my side, and in moments she is cradling me with the same tenderness she showed to the crying child.

I am surrounded in warmth and light. The lingering radiance does not come from my magic, for that has all been spent. It is all Brei.

"Master?" she says. "Can you hear me? Oh, Master, speak to me, please."

She is weeping for me. Where, oh where, did Brei get that magnificent heart of hers?

I hold her hand in my feeble, fading grip. So little breath left, but enough to finish the lesson. "Power," I say. "It was power you feared. Because you have never seen it used except to inflict harm." Her parents, her neighbors—and me. "But there is…a *good* use of power, Brei. There is. And you will have the wisdom to find it. Far more wisdom than I ever had…"

She strokes my head, and I hear her muttering the words to a healing spell. With her newly awakened magic, she is going to try to bring me back from the edge.

"Hush," I say, and she does as I bid. "There are some things beyond sorcery. As they should be."

Her tears drop onto my face, like a blessing. Even as the world fades away, I smile. If this is the last thing my body is allowed to feel, then I am fortunate beyond my desserts.

"Sing to me, please," I ask.

Brei's lullaby follows me through the closing breach, as all dissolves into light.

THE SORCERESS LOCKS the door of a great but ancient tower behind her, and slips the large iron key into her traveling pouch.

The pouch holds considerably more than a casual observer might expect. Within it, there is a decent stash of coin, some artifacts that were once enchanted and might be again with the proper care, and a few humble pieces of personal memorabilia that are significant to this young woman. The greatest treasure by far is the collection of books, some of which would be the envy of any Archmage's library.

Starlight casts its dim silver glow upon the ground. Ahead of the woman is a long climb down mountain paths, difficult to make in the dark.

"*Pira*," says the sorceress.

The staff in her hand, a length of wood far older than she is, alights with a golden flame at its tip. The wood is not even singed by this enchanted flame, which gives off plenty of light for the sorceress to find her way.

She does not really know where she's going next. But that's all right.

The sorceress turns and looks at the tower, craning her neck to make out the outline of the distant uppermost prominence against the star-filled sky.

"Goodbye, Master," she says. "Thank you for everything."

Brei makes her way down the mountain path, step by step, toward her future.

ABOUT THE AUTHOR

Grayson Towler is the author of *The Dragon Waking* (Albert Whitman & Co., 2016), along with many published works of short fiction. He is an editor of speculative fiction for ElectricSpec magazine, and is a marketing writer and editor of non-fiction for Sounds True. He is also an illustrator, and writes and illustrates the urban fantasy comic, Thunderstruck. He and his wife, Candi, live in a house owned by three relatively benevolent cats in Longmont, Colorado.

Find out more about Grayson at:
graysontowler.com

f facebook.com/GraysonTowler

a amazon.com/Grayson-Towler/e/B07NV3C2D7

BB bookbub.com/authors/grayson-towler

DIAMOND BETTY

JAMIE FERGUSON

I LEANED against a pillar of marble, tucked a stray curl behind my ear, and took as deep a breath possible given the ridiculously tight corset I wore. I rummaged through my beaded satin handbag, pushing aside the tiny, ribbon-wrapped spells I'd prepared ahead of time as I pretended to look for something—but I was really watching my target out of the corner of my eye.

Elizabeth Mercy Lévesque—or, as she was known here in Denver, Colorado, Diamond Betty—stood in the center of the mezzanine of the opera house, light glinting off the giant blue diamond that was the centerpiece of her necklace. Her flame-red hair stood out against her ermine opera cloak like a splotch of wine on a white linen tablecloth. She held a flute of champagne in one hand; her other hand rested on the arm of her new husband, Cornelius Montgomery. Betty said something I couldn't make out from this distance, and then tossed her head back with a laugh like the pealing of bells. The crowd of well-dressed, well-coiffed, and well-to-do ladies and gentlemen surrounding her joined in, a few giving soft, polite claps.

Cornelius started a silver mining company right after he left the Union Army, invested in real estate and other mining holdings, and by the mid-1870s he was worth well over five million dollars. He'd met Betty in Leadville. She'd been part of a traveling theater troupe, a singer, or perhaps a seamstress; no one seemed clear on exactly what. There was, however, no doubt about what had happened next: Cornelius left his wife of twenty-seven years, set up extravagantly appointed hotel suites in both Leadville and Denver for Betty, and began what turned into a two-year battle to get a divorce from his wife. Somewhere along the way he'd acquired an elaborate necklace studded with diamonds and sapphires, with a large, dark blue diamond pendant; Betty had worn it at their lavish midsummer wedding a few months earlier. The newspapers said the necklace cost close to $100,000.

I'd come here for the necklace. Not because of how much it was worth, but because the blue diamond contained a demon.

"Pardon me," a man's voice said from behind my left shoulder.

I jumped and turned around. A handsome, dark-haired, broad-shouldered man stood in front of me. He wore a charcoal tail coat, a white bow tie, and solid silver cufflinks. His brownish-yellow eyes were warm, almost the color of amber, and there were little lines in the corners, as if he smiled often.

"You startled me," I said, pressing a hand against the ridiculous amount of lace that decorated my bodice. My heart thumped like mad. There was no way he could know why I was really at the opera house, of course, but I felt as though I'd been caught in the act of thievery even though Betty and her necklace were at least fifty feet away.

"My apologies, miss," he said. He raised one hand to his head as if to tip his hat, then blinked and lowered his arm as he remembered he wasn't wearing it. He held out his other hand toward me. "You dropped this."

A chill ran down my back as I realized one of my spells lay in the middle of his outstretched palm.

"Thank you," I said, resisting the urge to snatch the colorful bundle and run away. I reached out and plucked it up as gracefully as I could, given that my entire body was trembling. It was a sleep spell, wrapped in pale blue silk and tied up with navy and white satin ribbons. I opened my handbag, dropped the spell inside, and snapped the clasp of my bag shut. "It must have fallen out while I was…"

I stopped in mid-sentence, unable to come up with a plausible response on the spur of the moment. I couldn't exactly say a magic spell had fallen out of my bag while I was spying on a woman whose diamond necklace I intended to steal tonight.

"I'm happy I noticed it," he said. He gave me a grin so infectious I could feel my own mouth curving into a smile. "With so many people milling about, it would certainly have gotten trampled. I don't believe we've met before. My name is Thomas Hughes."

"Penelope Jones," I said. That wasn't completely a lie, as my first name really was Penelope. I took a deep breath, grateful that my heart rate appeared to be subsiding. There was no way he could possibly realize what I'd dropped, nor what I was really doing at the opera house. I held out my hand. "I'm only in town for a few days. It's a pleasure to meet you."

"And you as well, Miss Jones," he said, taking my hand in his. His grip was firm but gentle. I found myself noticing the warmth and softness of his skin more than was appropriate for a lady at an opera. He relinquished my hand politely.

"I love the opera," I said, trying to keep my voice steady. I could still feel the touch of his skin on mine, even though both of my hands now clutched my handbag so tightly my knuckles ached. I straightened my shoulders. I was just being hypersensitive because of Betty. That was all. "My uncle and I are traveling from Boston to San Francisco, and planned to spend a few days in Denver. Unfortunately, he took ill, but he insisted I leave him at the hotel and come to the opera this evening."

"That's a shame," he said. "Are you enjoying tonight's performance?"

"Yes, it's quite lovely," I said. A soft, melodious chime rang, the sound carrying through the mezzanine. People began to head toward the entrances to the opera hall. "It was a pleasure to meet you, Mr. Hughes."

"And you as well, Miss Jones," he said. "Enjoy the rest of the show, and I hope your uncle recovers quickly."

"Thank you."

He gave a brief nod, and turned and headed to the far side of the lobby.

I joined the crowd, walked back into the hall, and headed down the rich crimson carpet to my plush mohair seat—and the empty one next to it that I'd paid for to keep up the story about my "uncle." I sat down and glanced up to my left. Diamond Betty sat in a box seat made of Japanese cherry, her flame-red hair gleaming in the light. Even from this distance I could see the blue glint of her pendant.

The gas lamps began to dim. I set my purse in my lap and faced the stage just as the orchestra began to play.

Betty's suite was on the top floor of the same hotel I was staying in. In a few hours I'd make my way upstairs, put her to sleep with the spell that Mr. Hughes had—thankfully!—noticed I'd dropped in the lobby, and I'd take the necklace. She wouldn't realize what had happened until well after I'd left town.

By this time tomorrow evening I'd be in my first-class berth in a Pullman car, halfway to San Francisco, necklace—and demon—in hand.

FOUR HOURS later I was back in my suite at the extravagant Winston hotel. I'd recovered from wearing that hideously tight corset, taken a short nap, and was ready to go. I put on a simple maid's uniform, pulled on a pair of black slippers, and plaited my unruly hair into two thick braids that I wrapped around my head and pinned in place. I added a cap crocheted from white yarn, and tied a white cotton apron around my waist. I took the spells from my handbag and placed all but one of them in the deep pockets of the apron.

I untied the ribbons on the last spell and shook it free from its wrapping of golden-green silk. It looked like a collection of leaves and tiny bits of twigs in a bag of muslin, which was exactly what it was. But it was also a look-away spell, designed to encourage the eyes of those born without magic to slide over something—or someone—without consciously noticing it. Being dressed as a servant worked similarly, of course. I'd found that the well-to-do in particular tended to ignore maids and porters and the like, as if they were armchairs, or doorknobs, instead of living, breathing, thinking people. This fact often worked to my advantage, but given the importance of what I was about to steal, I wanted the extra certainty that my spell would provide.

Besides, it would be dark in the posh, over-decorated suite Betty and the necklace were in, and if she or her husband woke up, they were likely to wonder what I was doing there in the middle of the night, even if I was dressed as a maid.

I sprinkled the contents of the look-away spell—dried lavender, marigold seeds, slivers of burdock root, and twigs from a blueberry bush—into my hair, grinding them into tiny bits to make sure the spell took full effect. I turned off the gas lamp, slipped out of my room into the dimly lit hallway, and waited a moment while my eyes adjusted to the dimness. Moonlight streamed in through the tall window at the end of the hall.

I padded down the carpet and around the corner to the servant's stairs, then climbed the two flights up to the top floor and walked down the thick carpet of the hall to room 505. I knelt down and found the thin piece of wood leaning up against their door in exactly the same position I'd placed it a few hours earlier. As much as I loved using magic, this was a much simpler way to be sure no one had left the suite that evening—which meant the necklace had to be inside. I picked the lock with the ease of long practice, took a deep breath, and then turned the polished brass doorknob and ducked inside, pulling the heavy wooden door shut behind me.

The large and spacious Montgomery suite was as dimly lit as the hallway, although not as quiet; I could hear the faint but unmistakable sound of Cornelius snoring. My heartbeat sounded loud in my ears. I pressed my lips together and waited for a moment, just to make sure I hadn't been heard, and then made my way across the polished wooden floor toward the parlor, tiptoeing around the armchairs that loomed up in the darkness like chunks of granite. They were actually covered in rich green velvet, which I'd seen the three times I'd ventured into the suite when the couple had been out. Each time I'd searched their entire suite, and each time I'd found a large assortment of jewelry, coins, bank notes, and more rich, sumptuous clothing than I'd seen in my entire life. But each time the necklace was nowhere to be found.

I'd thought perhaps Betty kept it locked in the hotel safe, but after breaking into the safe myself two nights ago, I'd discovered this was not actually the case. I'd tagged along behind her on a shopping trip the other day, careful to keep my distance lest she realize she was being followed, but she hadn't been wearing the necklace. Last night at the opera house was the first time I'd actually seen her with the pendant. I'd searched their entire suite, so all I could think of was that Cornelius had taken the necklace to be cleaned.

Either way, I knew it had to be here tonight. I'd stood in a corner of the fourth-floor hallway and watched as the couple climbed the wooden staircase and entered their suite. And, thanks to my simple trick with the sliver of wood, I knew no one had entered or left the suite.

Now I just needed to find the necklace.

There was no shortage of places to look. The opulent suite consisted of three large bedrooms, a parlor, a dining room, a study, a sitting room, and three private bathrooms—one with a giant bathtub gilded with gold leaf. Everything in the lavish Winston hotel seemed a little over the top; the Montgomerys' suite even more so.

Moonlight streamed through the windows in the parlor and dining room, and the silver light illuminated my way as I walked as quietly as I could down the carpeted hallway to the bedroom. The door hung slightly ajar. I peeked in at the large shape of the snoring Cornelius, and the smaller one of Betty.

I pulled the sleep spell out of my apron, untied it, and then tossed it onto the bed. I gave the spell a moment to settle, then lit the oil lamp in the sconce on the wall near the door. The couple would sleep through 'til morning, and by then the tiny bundle of leaves and silk thread would have disintegrated, leaving no trace it had ever even existed. Cornelius continued to snore away. One of his arms was wrapped around Betty, so all I could see was her bright red hair spilling out on the cream pillowcase.

For the fourth time, I searched their bedchamber. I found the same things in Betty's large and elaborately carved jewelry chest that I'd seen before—necklaces, bracelets, gem-covered hair clips, cufflinks—but no necklace. I rummaged through the mahogany chest of drawers, pushing aside Betty's large assortment of hand-made lace undergarments, looking under her silk stockings, and pawing through Cornelius' much less extensive collection of socks and shorts. I looked in every hat box in the closet, went through the pockets of each suit jacket and pair of trousers, and even shook out all of their shoes. I got on my hands and knees and crawled around the room, looking underneath the bed, the dressers, and the overstuffed chair in the corner by the window. Finally, I pushed myself to my feet and wiped my hands off on my cotton apron. The necklace had to be somewhere else in the suite.

I extinguished the lamp and headed back to the parlor, which was surprisingly bright with the light from the moon, and then froze as I saw something out of the corner of my eye. I shook my head as I realized I'd seen my own reflection in the mirror hanging on one wall. It was a diamond dust mirror which, in spite of the name and the opulence of the hotel, was actually backed with silver, not diamonds. All of the suites in the Winston contained mirrors like this, although the Montgomerys' had been set in an elaborately carved frame of silver, as befitted a couple whose wealth had come from mining. I stared at the frame for a moment. I knew there wasn't a safe in the suite—I'd looked everywhere and found no trace of one. But...what if the necklace had been hidden in plain sight, like in a secret panel on the back of a mirror?

I turned to the mirror and reached my hands up, hoping the silver frame wasn't as heavy as it looked.

The room brightened. I spun around, one hand held up to shield my eyes from the brilliance of the lit paraffin lamp that sat on the mantel.

Diamond Betty sat on one of the green velvet armchairs. She wore a long robe of pale peach satin trimmed with cream-colored lace. Her skin looked as if it were made of porcelain, and her long red hair glowed like fire in the lamplight. The unmistakable shape of the necklace I'd been searching for was around her neck.

I shot a glance back toward the bedroom. She was asleep. She had to be. I'd made the sleep spell myself. Unless...there was someone else in bed with Cornelius? I blinked and reminded myself about the look-away spell I'd used earlier. She couldn't actually see me.

"Won't you sit down?" Betty waved a pale, perfectly manicured hand at the chair I stood next to.

I swallowed as I realized she could see me after all.

I'd cast this spell hundreds of times, and only in a few cases had someone noticed me. But that was not out of the realm of possibility. The spell was designed to distract and deceive, and we were the

227

only people in a brightly lit room in the middle of the night, so it was not unreasonable to think that its potency could be a bit diminished. All I had to do would be to give her a plausible story, then I'd be able to sneak back to my room and she'd forget the entire event within minutes. My spells always worked.

"I was sent up to check on the grate in the fireplace, ma'am," I said. "I'll just be on my way."

I sidled past the armchair and started toward the door.

She stood up, her emerald eyes fixed on me. I stopped in mid-step. My spell wasn't working at all, but how was that even possible? It had always, *always* worked before. Unless...

A jolt ran through my body as I realized Diamond Betty was a witch.

A witch who wore a necklace that contained a demon.

"Please sit down," she said. There was a hard edge in her voice that hadn't been there before.

I walked the few steps back to the armchair and took a seat, sinking into the plush fabric that covered the soft cushions. Betty sat back down.

"Thank you," she said. We stared at each other for a moment. This close up, I could see tiny flecks of gold in the green of her eyes. "Perhaps you could tell me why you're here."

"I'm sorry, I don't understand," I said, my mind racing as I tried to figure out what to do.

Betty rolled her eyes. "Don't play games. You broke into my suite, cast a sleep spell over my husband, and went through my belongings. At least you had the decency to put everything back."

I took a deep breath and ran a hand through my hair, the bits of crumbled leaves catching on my skin.

"How did you keep from falling under the spell?" I asked. Unlike the look-away spell, the sleep spell should have worked on her even though she was clearly a witch.

"I wasn't in the bedroom," she said. She gave a little laugh. "I rolled up a few blankets, added a red scarf so that it would look like my hair, and then pulled the sheet up."

I wrinkled my nose. One of the oldest tricks in the book, and I'd fallen for it. I was used to assuming my targets didn't have magic. I should have—

My jaw tightened as I realized the ramifications of what she'd just said.

"How did you know I was coming?" I asked.

"I didn't, actually," she said. "At least, I didn't know who to expect. But I did know someone had searched through my things several times in the past few days. Since nothing had been taken, I figured it had to be someone after my necklace. I've kept it with me for the past few weeks, either around my neck, or in a silk bag hidden inside my dress."

I pressed my lips together and nodded. "You're right. I'm here for the necklace."

My mind raced. Not only was Betty a witch, she had prepared for my arrival ahead of time. There was no telling what kinds of defensive enchantments she might have at the ready. Whatever they were, they'd certainly be significantly more useful than what I had in my apron: a second sleep spell in case I'd found Cornelius and Betty in separate rooms; a follow-me spell, to tuck in Betty's purse if I hadn't found the necklace and needed to track her in the morning; and a light spell, in case one of the lamps had been low on paraffin. All very practical spells which had made perfect sense when I'd been planning for contingencies, but which wouldn't help at all against an angry witch.

And since Betty was clearly a witch, by now she might have realized the pendant contained a demon. She'd said she'd kept the necklace with her for the past few weeks, long before I'd arrived in town. What if she'd found a way to release the demon and harness its powers?

Prickles ran down the back of my neck. I'd come prepared to steal a diamond pendant, not have a magical duel with a demon.

"I'm obviously not going to give my necklace to you," she said. "It was my wedding gift from my dear husband."

"I understand," I said.

We sat there and stared at each other, in a momentary stalemate. If she'd bonded with the demon, wouldn't she have taken action against me by now? What if she truly didn't know the diamond contained a demon? Was that even possible? What if—

"I love diamonds," Betty said. "I couldn't afford any of my own when I was younger, of course. My mother was killed in an accident on my thirteenth birthday, and her diamond necklace was the only thing left to give me. It had just a small stone, but I found it enhanced my magic. And, of course, one of the properties of diamonds is protection, which was useful because I didn't have any other relatives, and had to live on my own."

"I'm sorry," I said, unsure how to respond. I had more relatives than I could shake a stick at, and couldn't imagine being family-free, much less having to fend for myself at such a young age.

"I learned to speak to the stones, to pull power from them," she said. She fingered the diamond pendant. "This one is different, somehow. I haven't been able to see all the way through it yet."

Did she really not know about the demon?

"There's something bad in that diamond," I said, the words coming out in a rush. "A demon. That's why I'm here. The necklace was put in a vault in Paris in the fourteenth century, and was stolen about five years ago. When I saw your wedding photo in the paper I recognized the pendant, and I came here to take it back to the vault."

"A demon?" She rested her pale fingers on the blue diamond in the pendant. "Ah... I see, now. That's what I've been sensing. I've never encountered a demon before."

A shadowy figure appeared behind Betty, a finger raised to its lips. I blinked as I recognized Mr. Thomas Hughes, the man I'd met at the opera earlier in the evening. He began to move toward Betty, his steps soundless. Was he, too, here to return the necklace to safety? Or did he intend to control the demon and harness its power for himself?

Either way, I had to figure out how to get the necklace from Betty.

"It was imprisoned in the stone," I said. "It can't leave the diamond on its own. But it's very dangerous. Please, give me the necklace so I can return it to safety."

"It doesn't sound like that vault is very safe, if someone was able to steal the necklace," she said. A smile flitted across her lips, but her eyes were cold and serious. "And it belongs to me now. The diamonds I wear enhance my magic and give me power. I'm not afraid of the demon."

Mr. Hughes had almost reached Betty. His hands were outstretched as he reached toward the clasp on the back of the necklace.

"You should be afraid," I said.

"Why?"

"Because it's…it's a *demon*."

"That doesn't mean it's malevolent," she said. "What did it do that made someone put it in the diamond?"

I kept my eyes locked on Betty's and tried not to look at Mr. Hughes.

"I don't know," I said finally. "I'm assuming it killed people, or possessed them, or something. A warlock called it into our world a few hundred years ago with the intention of using the demon to take over the throne of France, and a witch found out and stopped him and put the demon in the diamond."

"So, you don't really know," she said. She glanced down at the stone. "I can sense it more clearly now. It's as if it was hiding in the facets, but now I can see it. It's—"

Mr. Hughes grabbed the back of the necklace. Betty leapt up and spun around, but he managed to keep his fingers on the necklace long enough to undo the clasp. The ends of the necklace fell, but Betty still held the diamond, which glowed with a brilliant blue light. I jumped up, ready to grab the necklace, but the glow grew larger and brighter, so bright I had to screw my eyes shut. And then the light was gone.

The demon stood in the center of the parlor.

It stood at least six feet tall, maybe seven. It had the shape of a man, but its skin was covered with black and gray scales. Dark wings extended from its back. Its face was the color of coal, and its eyes glowed amber.

I took a step backward, then another, and then bumped into the cool brick of the fireplace.

"I thank you, madam," the creature said in a low, deep rumble that vibrated through my very bones. It gave Betty a little bow, its wings rustling together. It turned to face Mr. Hughes, and then me, as if taking our measure.

"I order you to get back in this diamond," Betty said, holding out the necklace in front of her, her left hand wrapped around the blue diamond.

The demon chuckled. "I am not yours to command," it said.

"But...I'm holding the diamond," she said. She looked at the stone in her hand, a puzzled look on her face.

The demon raised an eyebrow the color of night.

"I don't think it's in your power," Mr. Hughes said, keeping his eyes on the demon. He pulled a small silver ball out of his pocket and placed it in his palm, where it began to glow with a soft green light. He tucked the ball back in his pocket.

"And whose fault is that?" Betty asked. She put the pendant back around her neck and did the clasp. "I was trying to talk with it when you attacked me. Who are you, anyway?"

"Thomas Hughes, Pinkerton detective," he said. "I'm here for the same reason Miss Jones is. To take the necklace and the demon and lock them away, for everyone's safety."

The demon shook out its wings, and then furled them. It looked at each of us again, and then its eyes slid around the room, as if evaluating the situation and weighing its options. What if it possessed—or killed—one of us?

I put my hands in my apron pocket and fingered the spells I'd prepared, identifying them by the texture of the fabric I'd used to wrap each. If only I'd crafted something that would have been more useful in this type of situation, although I wasn't sure would be effective in battling a demon. How had that long-ago witch managed to capture it in the diamond?

"You can have the demon," Betty said. She shrugged. "But the necklace is mine."

The demon snorted and headed toward the door, moving faster

than any creature I'd ever seen before. Mr. Hughes pulled something out of his pocket and shot a beam of golden light at the creature; the demon skidded to a stop and batted the light away with one giant paw. The light shot into the chandelier in the dining room, knocking the elaborate crystal contraption to the floor with a loud crash. Oil from the lamp spilled out onto the plush red and white carpet.

Betty stepped in front of the demon and clasped her diamond necklace with both hands. The demon froze, its own hands clenched into fists, and its jaw tight. It stood there for a moment, and then suddenly flew backward, as if pushed up into the air by an unseen force. I pulled the sleep spell out of my pocket and flung it at the demon; it smacked the creature right in the center of its forehead. The demon collapsed, falling asleep right before hitting the diamond dust mirror. But instead of breaking the mirror, the sleeping demon went *into* the mirror itself.

And then it was gone.

The three of us stood there for a moment. Warm, rosy red rays from the rising sun began to stream in through the east-facing window of the dining room.

"Where did it go?" I asked, my voice cracking.

Betty walked across the parlor and placed one hand on the glass of the mirror, the other still wrapped around the diamond pendant.

"It's in there," she said finally.

I let out the breath I'd been holding in a loud whoosh. "It will be more work to get the mirror back to the vault in France, but it will be doable."

"Excuse me," Mr. Hughes said. "But I'm taking the mirror to Fort Knox."

"No, you're not," I said. I glared at him. "This is not a chunk of gold for the government to add to its collection. It's a mirror with a demon in it! It's got to go back to the Grand Council's vault."

"Where it was stolen from," he said. He shook his head. "The vault is obviously not sufficiently secure."

"It is *now*," I said. I crossed my arms. "Why do you care about this anyway?"

He straightened his shoulders. "I'm working on behalf of the government of the United States."

"Why is a warlock working as a detective? Shouldn't you be off chasing criminals, or stopping a train robbery or something instead?"

"Why is a witch tracking down a diamond necklace that contains a demon, instead of making potions or poultices or something?"

"Are you trying to imply that a witch can't do the same things a warlock can?" I gritted my teeth. "Maybe women don't have the right to vote—*yet*. But I can cast spells at least as good as any man, if not better. You're—"

I snapped my mouth shut as Betty swung her necklace at the mirror.

"No!" I cried, just as the blue diamond in the pendant hit the glass. The mirror shattered with a loud crash. Slivers of glass flew through the air, landing on the stuffed armchairs, the carpet, and clanked off the glass cover of the gas lamp.

Betty turned toward us, and I gasped. Blood streamed down her face, and shards of glass jutted out from her cheeks and forehead. She put the necklace around her neck, snapped the clasp into place, then rested her blood-streaked fingers on the diamond pendant. My breath caught as I watched the slivers of glass in her skin slide out and fall to the floor. The jagged cuts in her skin closed up on their own, and the bright red of her blood faded, as if erased. In a moment her face was the same perfect porcelain white it had been before.

Diamond Betty smiled.

A chill ran down my spine. I'd never had an affinity for stones, and didn't use them in my own witchcraft. But even if I had, Betty's magic seemed far beyond my comprehension.

"My husband will be up soon," she said. She narrowed her eyes at me. "As soon as the sleep spell wears off, that is. Would the two of you please leave so I can get this mess cleaned up before he wakes? Or at least try to. I have no idea what I'm going to do about the oil on the carpet in my dining room."

"The demon—" Mr. Hughes began.

"Do you see a demon?" Betty gestured at the blood-spattered shards of glass at her feet. "It's gone."

"But where did it go to?" I asked.

She shrugged. "I have no idea. Perhaps it was sent back to its own world. Perhaps it was destroyed. Whatever happened to it, it's not here. I couldn't let it escape into our world, so I pulled all the power I could from the diamond that had imprisoned it, and threw that power at the demon."

Mr. Hughes pulled the small silver ball out of his pocket again, and held it in the palm of his hand for a moment. This time it didn't glow. He nodded.

"She's right," he said. "It's gone."

"Thank you, Betty," I said. I glanced at the shards of glass on the floor, and then at her emerald eyes. "We'll leave."

"Thank you, ma'am," Mr. Hughes said, nodding at Betty.

The two of us walked across toward the door. I glanced back over my shoulder at Diamond Betty. The morning sun shone in through the large window next to her and glinted off the diamond in her pendant. Her red hair glowed as if it was made of fire.

I shivered and hurried through the door; Mr. Hughes pulled it to. We stood in the hallway, the warm light of the early morning sun coming through the tall window at one end of the hall and shining on the polished wooden floor.

"I apologize for saying you should be making potions instead of tracking down a demon," he said. He pressed his lips together. "Truly. I believe women should have the same rights as men. Not just voting, everything should be the same. I shouldn't have said anything that implied otherwise."

"Thank you, Mr. Hughes," I said. "I'm sorry I said you should be stopping crimes instead of tracking down a demon. Although I suspect stopping crimes might be less dramatic."

"You'd be surprised," he said with a chuckle. "And please call me Tom."

"Please call me Penelope," I said. I held my hand out and he took it in his, my skin tingling where we touched. We stared at each other for a moment. My heart thumped so loudly I felt he must be able to hear it.

"I'd better go," I said, pulling my hand free. "I'm catching the 10 o'clock train to San Francisco."

He raised his eyebrows. "Coincidentally, I'm on that train myself. Would you be interested in joining me in the dining car for lunch?"

I grinned. "I'd love to."

We headed down the wide wooden staircase. I glanced over my shoulder at the Montgomerys' door, and then hurried down the stairs, happy to leave Diamond Betty and all of her diamonds behind.

I had a train to catch, and a very interesting man to meet for lunch.

ABOUT THE AUTHOR

Jamie focuses on getting into the minds and hearts of her characters, whether she's writing about a saloon girl in the American West, a man who discovers the barista he's in love with is a naiad, or a ghost who haunts the house she was killed in—even though that house no longer exists. Jamie lives in Colorado, and spends her free time in a futile quest to wear out her two border collies since she hasn't given in and gotten them their own herd of sheep.

Find out more about Jamie at:
jamieferguson.com

- **f** facebook.com/jamie.ferguson.author
- **y** twitter.com/jamie_ferguson
- **O** instagram.com/jamie.ferguson.author
- **g** goodreads.com/jamieferguson
- **P** pinterest.com/jamieauthor
- **BB** bookbub.com/authors/jamie-ferguson
- **a** amazon.com/Jamie-Ferguson/e/B004SVIP3G

TELLING THE BEES

DAYLE A. DERMATIS

THE AMULET WAS A SIMPLE, teardrop-shaped amethyst edged with tiny silver spirals. I wasn't a jewelry maker; I bought the items with which to make the amulets my sister, Willow, and I sold in our Portland shop.

Stone, wood, metal. Simple elements, but part of the earth.

Part of the interwoven magic of the world.

Willow and I don't sell to casual passers-by. Our clientele are true magic users. The shop comprises the front rooms of a purple-and-slate-blue Victorian home, on a side street in the trendy Hawthorne District. Not as easy to find, especially with the wards on it. Sometimes we had to work stronger magic, magic that might be visible or audible or otherwise noticeable to the average person, so we had spells to prevent that.

My workspace was in a second-floor bedroom. The walls were painted a deep, rich blue, like the sky at twilight, but the natural wood trim glowed a dark reddish-brown in the sunlight. Glass-fronted wood cabinets between the windows and doors held tools and supplies. In the center of the room, a round wooden table, close to bistro height, with Celtic knot work etched around the rim, served as my work table.

It was a sunny spring day, still cool, but warm enough that I could lift the double-hung windows for a bit of fresh air. The breeze occasionally guttered the flames of the fat white candles ringed on the floor around me, but it wasn't enough to blow them out. The candles helped me focus my magic, allowing me to define and doubly bless my space before I started.

Willow and I are hedgewitches. Willow's talents are with earth, water and plants, so she handles the herbs, potions, tisanes, and other concoctions. Amulets and charms are my purview: air, fire, auras, and protection spells.

Now, gathering up magic from within and around me, I traced invisible symbols on the amethyst, reciting a cantrip as I did. The amethyst shimmered, then glowed as the magic infused it. Amethysts are known for their emotional and spiritual healing properties, and the magic I used was to enhance that, allowing the user to benefit even more from meditations and cleansing rituals. There was a level of protection, too.

Right now, in the world, it felt like everyone needed a little protection from the vast negativity battering at them from all sides.

I finished, closing my eyes and hold my hands, palms up, at waist height for a moment, giving thanks to the universe for my abilities. Then I set the amethyst next to the previous amulet I'd worked on: a flat, polished disk of wood, with a simple triskele etched on it (adding the element of Fire). Into that I'd imbued solidity, groundedness to go along with the already present slow, patient strength of the tree.

I shook out my hands and reached for the next project when a soft knock sounded at the door, followed by Willow's light voice.

"Holly? Sorry to bother you…"

I huffed through my nose. Magic work took preparation, and being interrupted meant I'd have to start over before I could work on anything else.

But I also knew Willow wouldn't interrupt me unless it was important. Really important.

"Come in."

The door opened. Willow's long, light brown hair, streaked with pale green, was piled on her head in a wispy, Gibson-girl style. She wore a floaty, wine-colored skirt edged in crocheted lace, a scoop-neck white shirt, a choker made of crocheted leaves, and a sage-green, open jacket, the light fabric embroidered with burgundy and darker green.

In contrast, my short, darker hair is shot through with dark green, and is spiky like my personality. (Very few people are allowed to say that and live.) I wore skinny jeans, a Prussian-blue top, and dangling peacock-feather earrings.

I leaned back, elbows on my work table. "What's going on?"

"Jayden called," Willow said. "He sounded pretty worried."

Jayden. I mouthed the name. It sounded familiar, but I couldn't place it.

"From West Linn," Willow said. When I obviously still wasn't getting it, she added, "The protection bubble?"

Oh, Jayden. The annoying kid. The barely trained witch and unlicensed boob who'd botched a protection spell and made my life hell for a day. I let my emotions show on my face. "What's he done now?"

"I'm not sure," Willow said. "He asked for you, and said he really needed help. That it would take too long to explain, and it was urgent."

I held out a hand and pinched my thumb and forefinger together. The candles on the floor went out, leaving behind the sharp scent of trailing smoke.

"Guess I have to go, then."

Our job is to help, not to judge. And yes, I was being my usual cranky self, but it wasn't entirely Jayden's fault that he hadn't been getting the proper training or that his familiar had gone walkabout because he wasn't ready for her.

Mostly his fault, but not entirely.

"I'll go with you," Willow said.

"You sure?"

"I saw how monumentally Jayden can screw up," she said wryly. "I have a feeling this is going to need all of us."

By all of us, she meant the two of us and my familiar, Cam.

For some reason, the story of what a familiar is to a witch got mutated and morphed by the non-magical, like a legendary game of telephone, down through the ages. Now people think familiars are magical animal companions, or animal-shaped spirits, or something along those lines. Sure, Cam could shift into any type of creature he chose, as well as mist, water, a tree, a rock...you name it, Cam can become it.

Because Cam is magic. He's one of the Fae folk, and that's what witches' familiars are. We can do magic, but the Fae folk can't. They're aligned with the earth, with nature—they're simply pure magic, and we tap that magical essence to help weave and create our spells.

It's a symbiotic relationship, not a master/servant one like the stories of witches and familiars that ordinary people believe. We're partners, equals. Each witch connects with a Fae whose magical essence closely dovetails with his or her personal energy, and for lack of a better way to phrase it, we bond for life—although the Fae live longer than humans, and can have multiple such relationships throughout their existence. There are a few things that can break the bond, but they're rare. In fact, some familiars stay within a family, although that wasn't the case with Cam.

He wore dark grey trousers and a white button-down shirt. He was tall and slender, but there was a steely core strength to him. His hair was the color of goldenrod, his eyes were stormy blue, and his cheekbones wouldn't cut just glass, but diamonds.

A Fae's true name is private, and can change, and is a part of them in a way human names simply aren't. Even though Cam's power was entwined with mine, for him to share his true name with me would be to give up a deep part of himself. Fae didn't do that, and witches didn't ask them to.

Also, their names are impossible for humans to pronounce.

So I called him Cam, short for Camelot, because he has this posh accent that sounds la-di-dah upper-crust British. Because he puts up with me, he's not even offended.

Willow's familiar, Eoin, was missing. She wouldn't talk about it, not even to me.

And Jayden's had decided he needed more training before they could truly form their bond, so she'd ditched him.

So Cam was all we had.

We got in my car, and I cut across Portland to I-205 and headed south.

West Linn was essentially a suburb of Portland, most of it lying along the banks of the Willamette River. The town is known for its falls, its trees, and the massive paper mill that had just closed after more than 120 years of operation. (All of those things were related.) Now, it was also known for being a safe and tony place to live, as McMansions had been built in the hills to take advantage of the great views.

The first thing I noticed when I took Exit 8 off the freeway was that there were no cars on the road. It was the morning of a work day, not quite lunch time, but there should have been some. Maybe there was construction somewhere.

Except there were no signs to that effect.

I pulled into the parking lot of the Market of Choice, an Oregon-based grocery chain that wasn't quite as hoity-toity as New Seasons or Whole Foods, but significantly above Safeway and the like.

I'd been here once before, seeking out Jayden. It had been in the middle of an unusually heavy snow season, but even then, there had been shoppers around. The market was behind a row of businesses, from a backyard bird shop to a Vietnamese pho place to a martial arts dojo. A Starbucks, of course. Can't have a business area without a Starbucks. The local library and Post Office were nearby, too. The whole area was surrounded by tall trees, making it feel less strip-mall-y.

There were a few cars in the parking lot and along the street, but no pedestrians.

On a beautiful spring day like this, the area should have been teeming with soccer moms in yoga pants.

We opened our car doors, and as one, froze.

The sound…was wrong.

No cars, obviously, except the faint ones on the freeway bridge crossing the river, less than a mile away. No voices.

Only…humming.

Like a thousand—no, a million voices humming together, a wordless tune. Barely a tune, because each note lasted so long, and eased into the next without a pause or break.

I looked around, then closed my eyes. I couldn't pinpoint a source. I looked at Willow and Cam. They shook their heads.

For some reason, none of us wanted to speak.

The humming wasn't unpleasant. In many ways, it was soothing.

Which did not mean it wasn't entirely weird.

I hate weird.

Jayden had told Willow he'd be inside the market. The glass doors, which had a large sign letting us know we could purchase reusable shopping bags if we'd forgotten ours, parted automatically.

The grocery store was so quiet, I could hear the faint buzz of the fluorescent lights, which normally wouldn't have been obvious over the regular noises of chatting shoppers and check-out people, shelves being stacked, and the cooking going on behind the freshly made food counter along the right.

I could've gone for a slice of pizza, myself, or maybe a wok bowl, but there were more pressing problems.

Like, where were all the people in the middle of the day?

And what was that humming noise outside, which I felt like I could still faintly hear?

Feeding myself came in a reluctant third right now. Which gave me extra motivation to solve questions one and two.

Jayden had been sitting at a black table by the front window, near the espresso bar, to our right behind a cooler of individual bottles of juice and kombucha and snooty water. Because of the silence, I heard the scrape of his chair as he stood.

He was a lanky kid, barely into his twenties, still with a smattering of acne that stood out when he went pale from nervousness. He wore jeans that were torn at the hem, scuffed hiking boots, and a black T-shirt with a faded Led Zeppelin logo.

"What did you do?" I demanded by way of greeting.

He swallowed, his prominent Adam's apple bobbing. "I didn't do anything, I swear! At least...I can't think of anything I might have done that would have caused this."

He was scared of me. This fact brought me great pleasure.

"Caused what?" Willow's voice was gentler than mine. We had Soothing Witch/Cranky Witch thing down pat.

He threw his hand out to indicate the store, or maybe the whole town. "This!"

"The fact that nobody's shopping?" I asked. "You have stock in Market of Choice or something?"

"It's not that," he said. "Everyone's asleep."

"Everyone?" Willow asked, looking alarmed.

"Everyone," he repeated. "The whole town." He bit his lip. "I think we've been cursed."

CURSES DON'T WORK that way, but this was definitely something bad and wrong.

According to Jayden, the day had started out normally, and then…well, as best he could tell, everyone went home and went back to bed, or curled up beneath their desks, or in the break room here in the store. (There was also a meeting room upstairs here. Some employees had stretched out on the floor and table.) He couldn't wake up his parents, his friends.

It seemed to be limited to West Linn. Across the river, in Oregon City, life was going on as normal.

"And you're not affected," I said. "That makes it look like you did something."

"I swear I didn't," he said. "I've been practicing magic—your friend Burke has been mentoring me—but really low-key and carefully. I didn't do anything yesterday or today."

Unless a deliberate time-release factor was part of a spell, magic was instantaneous.

"We need to find the source of the humming," Willow said. Which was obvious, but I didn't say so. Plus, I could stand here all day blaming Jayden, and that wasn't going to make things better.

My stomach grumbled.

"Let's go, then," I said, waving a hand at the glass doors. "Once more unto the breach."

IT DIDN'T TAKE us very long. One of my magical affinities is for animals, so once I sat still and grounded myself and cast out, I found them.

All the many, many, many bees.

They were all over West Linn. I mean, all over. They were spread out enough that they hadn't been visibly obvious when we'd arrived, and I sensed that the clustered swarms were in the woods and various parks scattered through the small city.

We sat at the openwork metal tables outside the Starbucks. I really wanted to go inside and get a snack, but I refrained.

Plus I'd have to make my drink myself.

Because Cam was pure magic and, essentially, part of nature, I connected with him to communicate with the bees.

I felt his essence dovetail with mine, slide into me—charging me up, so to speak. I took that pure magic and formed it into the tools I needed, and then I reached out to find the nearest queen.

I know enough about bees that you had to go directly to the source.

I frowned. I could sense all the bees—well, not each individual bee as if I were counting them, but I felt their numbers. I found quite a few queens, which also surprised me, because queens didn't usually hang out together. Well, there were a few species that did, but not our happy American honeybees.

I wasn't sure which queen to address. Would I offend them if I spoke to the wrong one? None stood out.

I made a decision, and hoped it was the right one.

Cam gave me a…I'm not sure "word" is a strong enough concept for the almost overwhelming power it carried. It was in the language of the Fae, an ancient language of the earth and air and fire and water that binds the world together.

That word was for the bees. Not a command, but a respectful request.

Without knowing which queen to choose, I had to talk to all of them. At once.

And they responded. All at once. Not just the queens, but all the damn bees.

At first it was deafening, but together Cam and I managed to modulate the sound so it was not painful and was easier to understand, and we looped in Willow and Jayden so they could hear, too.

The bees came.

The air cooled as they blocked out the sky, blotted out the sun, before turning every building around us, and the cars and the roads and the parking lots black as they settled. We still couldn't see all of them, I knew; some remained behind, or tucked into the nearby trees.

You can hear usss, the bees said.

"We can," I said. I introduced us, three witches and a familiar.

I got the sense the bees genuflected a tiny bit, but it was hard to say.

"What are you doing?" I asked. "Why have you put the town to sleep?"

It is our ssssong. We are sssso very tired.

"Did the people here do something to you?" I didn't ask if Jayden was responsible. I really couldn't see how he was, and the bees would point fingers—er, antennae—if it came to that.

All people, the bees said. Sssso many people. Then our Queen died, and we could not take any more.

"Any more what?" I could see this was going to take a while. Which made me grumpy. Why couldn't they have at least brought me some honey?

Telling. Telling ussss. The telling of the beesss.

Oh, yeah, like that was a lot of help. I tamped down my annoyance in case they could sense it—I really didn't want this to turn into a 1950s low-budget horror movie—and pondered how to frame my next question when Jayden said, "Oh, I've heard of that!"

Then he added sheepishly, probably because of the expression on my face, "I read a lot."

"Fill us in, please," I said.

"In many cultures, they believed that when something happened in a beekeeper's life, someone had to tell the bees. A marriage, the birth of a child, and especially death. A hive could die out, or stop making honey, or leave because nobody properly told them about their keeper's death."

Sssso many tellingsss. Sssso many ssstoriesss.

Bit by bit, Jayden and I got the bees to explain the real problem.

The bees remembered the stories, and many more—it turned out the "telling" didn't have to be direct, or even only about their own beekeeper. Each hive in turn told their queens, who "carried" the stories with her, and passed them on to future queens. The worker bees collected the stories but could only hold so many; the queens were the only ones who could keep all of them.

The queens, in essence, were the ones with the big hard drives. The workers were more like little thumb drives.

And then there was the matter of the Queen. The Queen of the queens. The biggest memory chip of all.

Who had died.

Now the queens were full, and the workers were full, and they couldn't handle any more stories. They couldn't process any more deaths.

Then Cam dropped the bomb that it went deeper than that, in terms of it being a problem for everyone, not just the bees.

"The bees bridge the natural world with the afterlife," he said. "Without their work, there could be…" He spread his hands. "I'm not even sure how to describe it without it taking days. But it could affect your world, and mine as well, permanently."

"I believe you that it would be really bad," I said. "I think we can move to a solution without knowing all those details, yes?"

Willow and Jayden nodded. The bees hummed in agreement. Good, because I wasn't waiting days for food.

So the bees had put everyone to sleep because they were full of stories and couldn't take any more, even though the stories were banging at them, trying to get in.

Right now, only West Linn had been taken out. There was no telling how fast this would spread, or how far. We could be in deep doo-doo very soon.

We might be battered by negativity from all sides, and in some ways, being lulled to sleep by buzzing bees sounded kind of peaceful, but the world was going to end up a lot worse if we all crashed out.

"How long will it take for you to find a new Queen?" I asked.

Wwe don't knowww.

Damn. "Can you tell the stories to someone else? Something else? In other words, can you store the stories while waiting for a new Queen?"

The bees buzzed amongst themselves, the sound rising and falling. I hoped I hadn't said the wrong thing. They didn't sound agitated.

Yesss. We believe that will work.

I pointed. "How about him?"

"Me?" Jayden yelped. "Why me?"

"Because you need training," I said. "You need experience. This is a way for you to learn about people, other people's lives. Not just stuff from books."

"Hey, his book knowledge helped here," Willow pointed out. "But what you're saying makes a lot of sense, actually."

"Sometimes I come up with good ideas," I said.

She shook her head and a ghost of a smile whispered across her lips.

I focused back to the bees. "This man will take your stories, hold them for you," I said. "But first, I need to go to my house and get something for him, to help with the process. Is that acceptable?"

Yesss. And thank you.

I LEFT Cam and Willow in West Linn to hash out any final details with the bees, and drove back north and into Portland. The cars and people were almost startling. There was something to be said for silence, for having only the song of the bees.

When I'd worked on the amethyst amulet earlier this morning, I hadn't been thinking of anyone in particular. Some amulets were commissions, but not this one. This one...when I'd picked up the silver-edged stone, I'd known what it needed to be.

I curled my fingers around it, feeling the magic pulse like a heartbeat.

Like the hum of bees telling their stories.

The amulet would help Jayden process the stories, because the stories were about emotion. The happiest and saddest days of people's lives.

I had a feeling he and the bees were going to be good for each other.

ABOUT THE AUTHOR

Dayle A. Dermatis is the author or coauthor of many novels (including snarky urban fantasies *Ghosted*, *Shaded*, and *Spectered*) and more than a hundred short stories in multiple genres, appearing in such venues as *Fiction River*, *Alfred Hitchcock's Mystery Magazine*, and DAW Books.

Called the mastermind behind the Uncollected Anthology project, she also guest edits anthologies for *Fiction River*, and her own short fiction has been lauded in many year's best anthologies in erotica, mystery, and horror.

She lives in a book- and cat-filled historic English-style cottage in the wild greenscapes of the Pacific Northwest. In her spare time she follows Styx around the country and travels the world, which inspires her writing.

Find out more about Dayle at:
https://dayledermatis.com

facebook.com/dayledermatis

twitter.com/dayledermatis

goodreads.com/DayleDermatis

bookbub.com/authors/dayle-a-dermatis

amazon.com/Dayle-A.-Dermatis/e/B004W5KAZY

THE FINAL INITIATION

THEA HUTCHESON

SINDAL STARED down at the scruffy mud-brick village from the top of the rocky hill as she sipped stale water from the leather skin, clearing the dust from her throat. She sighed heavily, shifted her walking stick to her left hand, and let her leather pack slide down to the travel-worn trail.

She'd fled this place eight years ago to escape Tirlan, in shame and tears, with a lump of hatred burning in her throat. The buildings had looked much larger when she'd run away, but the pall of smoke was exactly as she remembered. So was the stench of the midden, the odor of roasting meat from the cook fires, and the smell of bread from the clay ovens.

She studied the six double-hands of huts as she contemplated the quest that had brought her back here. The pale mud-brick hovels, all clustered up against each other, looked not so much worn as smaller, meaner than she remembered. A few dirty goats and a stray tan-and-black dog wandered between the cramped buildings.

A gaggle of boys wearing rags suddenly burst out from one of the crooked alleys and ran, shouting, out toward the fields that lay to the east of the clusters of huts. She smiled to see their nearly completely shaven heads, one lone forelock hanging over each of their foreheads. So they'd had the annual outbreak of lice, then.

Sindal glanced over the fields, the crop of lentils thick and verdant, the golden wheat bent over nearly double as the harvest grew near. The orchards beyond were heavy with apples, almonds, and olives, and in the distance the grapevines seemed to glow in the late afternoon sun. It was beautiful and welcoming, but she wanted only to have her revenge on Tirlan and go back to Garlis, her witch mistress, to receive her marks.

He'd be the final initiation into the fullness of her witchcraft.

Sindal had wanted babies to care for and a hearth to call her own, the same as any little girl. Her mother had begged her father to wait another year before marrying her off. He'd seen the dowry of fat sheep and goats and the breeding bitch to herd them, though, and told Tirlan he could have her before she'd even bled.

She'd often wondered, as she toiled in Garlis' dank, dark cave, preparing brews and potions and charms, whether Tirlan had made her father give back the dowry.

Well, she'd find out now.

Best to see her mother before she killed the bastard.

Brushing her hands across her travel-stained face and down the dusty woolen tunic, she muttered a see-me-not spell, picked up her pack, slung it on her back, and made her way down into the village.

Toya, her tawny lioness animal spirit, followed her down the hill, the late afternoon sun shining through her hide.

The children ran past Sindalin a knot, Toya invisible to them, as she reached the bottom of the trail that let out into the valley. She smiled at the memories they raised; her running the same path, carefree and wild in the late summer days, before the hard work of the harvest set in.

The rutted path was dusty from the generations of villagers and their livestock traipsing along it, and she walked carefully. It wouldn't do to lame herself before she got her revenge. Her fingers touched the symbols she'd carved about the head of her walking stick, now smooth and shiny from her hand and the oils it left behind.

SHE'D BEEN eleven when she'd run away. After a week spent scratching and scrabbling in the wilderness, Garlis had caught her raiding the garden just below the mouth of the cave. Sindal had stared, a piece of arugula halfway to her drooling mouth. The thin woman had wild hair, woven with bits of bone, flowers, and carved stone. Her sharp, piercing eyes seemed to see right into Sindal's soul.

"What've we here?" she asked, although Sindal hadn't understood the witch's tongue then.

The crone reached out a scrawny hand tipped with ragged, dirty nails and gestured sharply while muttering in a sing -song voice. Sindal froze, unable to move anything except for her eyeballs. The woman, who was surely a witch, studied her, then reached out to gently touch the bruises at the corner of Sindal's mouth, above her eye, and stared at her sex as if she could see through the wool.

All at once, she took Sindal by the arm and began to drag her down the hill. Sindal tried to fight, but the old woman was strong, and her nails dug into Sindal's wrist. She gave up and submitted, following the woman to the spring that bubbled up at the bottom of the hill. The witch began to pull at the filthy dress.

Taking the hint, Sindal removed it, and then stepped into the pool when the woman gestured at her to do so. The woman turned to go after making sure Sindal knew to wash herself with the fine sand at the bottom, scrub her scalp, and work the mud from her hair.

Sindal got out and pulled grass to dry herself. The woman returned with a small blanket and mimed wrapping it around her. Clothed in the blanket, Sindal washed her dress, beating it on the rocks beside the pool and laying it over a bush to dry in the sun.

The woman led her back up and into the cave after she'd untangled Sindal's hair and plaited it, tying it off with threads from her shift. It was dark and cool inside, and smelled of fragrant leaves and mud and something else, probably from whatever was in the red clay pots and roughly carved boxes lining the shelves along the sides of the cave. She sat Sindal down on a small three-legged stool at a low wooden table that looked like someone had fought with it and come out the better. The woman gave her watered wine in a chipped clay cup and a hand carved wooden bowl with a bit of rabbit mixed with grain and greens.

Sindal's belly clenched at the smell of cooked food. She'd been scavenging the few berries and tubers the bears had left behind. She tried to eat slowly, giving her belly time to embrace the cooked food, and succeeded, mostly. She drank the cup dry and the woman refilled it. The second cup went down more leisurely and Sindal belched loudly afterward. The woman nodded, pleased. After she ate, Sindal sat nodding until the woman nudged her and pointed at a pile of sheepskins. Sindal fell onto them, and slept deeply for the first time since she run away from Tirlan.

Over the next few months Sindal learned the crone's tongue, an ancient-sounding language, discovered her name was Garlis, and helped her work a spell for another woman who made her way to the cave.

She found Garlis kind and caring, which meant a much better life than she would have had with Tirlan. She wanted to learn the woman's spellcraft, and made that clear. With that kind of power at her beck and call, she'd never need fear Tirlan again, and she could pay him back for all the indignities and horrors he'd visited upon her during the year of their marriage.

Garlis had agreed and set to teaching her the basics of her trade. Which mostly meant picking roots and leaves, snaring animals and preparing them, and making bread with the grain people left Garlis in return for the charms and potions she made them. Garlis never beat her unless she made a mistake in a potion or missed a step in a charm - never just for fun, or to humiliate her or force her to something.

The old witch had seen her through six initiations. This one was the magical seventh, the binding of all Sindal had learned and the one that would open the door, revealing the path she'd follow ever after.

"Go see to yer heart's desire then, woman," Garlis had said after Sindal returned from her spirit walk, a lion spirit trailing behind. "Ye've power to bring that kind of helper, ye've got to find yer direction. And ye can only do that once ye've settled yer heart."

SINDAL STOPPED, her hand shading her eyes. There, at the far edge of the field, urging the pair of oxen pulling the wagon, was Tirlan. She'd recognize his shout anywhere. Her heart froze and she clenched the walking stick tightly, feeling the magical symbols impress themselves into her hand.

"Breathe, woman," she muttered, "you're a blooded witch, tried and marked. You've nothing to fear from that little prick of a man."

She relaxed, breathing Tan Ro as Garlis had taught, gathering her strength back into her chest, the seat of her power. When her spirit eye saw the yellow-colored breath chuffing out of her mouth, she stopped, in control again.

Her feet took her to her parents' home. She knew before she even arrived that it was empty. The mud-bricks were scorched to a ruddy brown where they showed from beneath the blackened lime plaster. The villagers would have torched it when her parents died, releasing its sacred hearth back to heaven.

Sindal swallowed. The purpose of the ritualistic burning brought a welter of thoughts. Had it been pestilence? Where was her sister?

Her feet knew what to do, though; they walked purposefully toward Tirlan's house, the walking stick tapping at each step. The smoke hole at his house bled dung smoke. She peered in the narrow door. The beaten clay floor was spotless, the bright woolen blankets folded neatly on the wooden benches that lined three sides of the room, the ladder led up to roof on the fourth. The altar niche holding the household gods looked well-tended. A small, bright wick burned in a cleverly-incised red clay oil lamp.

Men's voices from behind her made Sindal jerk back and away. The spell would keep the casual glance sliding off her, but a direct sighting could penetrate the glamour. She melted around the corner, found a niche in the sun-warmed mud-brick walls between two of the small houses, and stood tensely, her breath high in her chest, her hands clenched tight on the stick.

Tirlan. His voice brought back memories she'd forgotten.

But her body hadn't. She began to shake, and tears rose up to block her throat.

"Wife, bring me water," she heard Tirlan say from inside the house. "And some cheese and bread."

She despised the sound of his voice: arrogant, with the slightly feminine pitch he'd always hated. The men in the village had made fun of him, calling him "boy", even after he'd grown his beard. She'd paid for the humiliation they had visited upon him for that too, as she'd paid for every slight he suffered or thought he suffered. The women at the well had commiserated with her, casting pitying looks and shaking their heads when she brought fresh bruises along with her water jar.

"Clumsy bitch," Sindal heard from inside the hut, followed by a slap.

Anger and embarrassment rose up in her heart for the woman who suffered Tirlan's anger. She strode quickly around the corner and back to the door. Once there, she stood, heart thumping fear and anticipation warring in her chest at the thought of confronting the husband who'd humiliated and beaten her.

She had to be strong. This was her initiation.

Sindal stepped into the hut.

She heard noise in the next room, the women's space of the small house, but her eye was draw to the man who lounged on the bench to her right, drinking from a clay cup and eating goat cheese with flat bread wrapped around it.

Tirlan was the same spindly man she remembered, dark hair cropped short except for a queue on the crown of his head. His skull was paler than his arms from the headcloth that hung in its customary spot next to the door, and dirt creased the lines in his face.

His loin cloth was dusty, and his shanks were skinnier than she remembered. She looked at his gnarled hands. She hated those hands, hated the way they'd touched her, hated the way he'd known it and gone to pains to touch her often—on the shoulder, the arm, the breast, lifting her chin so he could see her fear.

She set her pack down, straightened her shoulders, and shed the spell.

"Tirlan," she said, and smiled in pleasure as he startled, falling off the bench.

"Who are you? How come you to be in my house?" He shouted as he stood up, squinting at her.

Sindal smiled wider as recognition lit his beady eyes.

A woman came out from the small doorway leading into the woman's side of the house, wiping her eyes. Sindal paid no mind, her attention focused on the twig of a man who'd ruled her life and made it miserable, and who would now pay the way for her last initiation.

"Sindal," he breathed.

He was shorter, or she was taller. She lifted her chin as he took in her now womanly figure, her fine tunic, her leather cloak.

"Wife," he said, pulling himself up. "Come home to do your duty at last."

"No, Tirlan. I have not come back to be your wife again. I've come to take my revenge."

She heard a gasp behind her and turned to see her younger sister, now a grown woman, her eyes open wide in shock.

"Lian? Lian, my sister," she said softly.

"Sindal, can it be?"

"It is. I am here."

Sindal opened her arms to embrace her sister. Lian smelled of flour and sweat, her woolen shift patched and threadbare. Her eyes were lined at the corners already, an old bruise fading under the right. Anger rose up as Sindal took in the livid red mark on her sister's cheek where Tindal had slapped her.

"Sister, how do you come to be in Tirlan's house?"

Lian frowned, and her eyes darkened as she took in the leather pack, the new woolen tunic Sindal had woven for her seventh trial, and the leather cloak she carried.

"Can you not guess, Wife?" Tirlan said. "When you ran away from me, I went to your father and demanded my bride price back. In the end he kept it and gave me her to take your place. She's been a much better wife. I should have taken her in the first place."

Sindal's face colored, and she felt ice in her belly. Lian had been nine then, when Tirlan took her.

Lian nodded, dropping her gaze to the floor. Her calloused hands clenched into fists. "I've been his wife these eight years."

"Lian, I am so sorry. I didn't know."

"Didn't know what? That he'd want his bride price back, that father would give me instead, to replace you?" Lian let out a sharp, bitter laugh. "It was a good deal for Tirlan. He got me, plus the bride price animals back when Mother and Father died of the sickness three years ago. But then the animals died of another sickness two summers ago. And now we have our children to feed as well as ourselves."

That confirmation of the burned house and the hearth broken open made Sindal gasp. Tirlan laughed. She tried to remember to breathe, concentrating on her chest and the yellow sun that Garlis taught her to gather there, awaiting her bidding.

Except that it wouldn't coalesce. The power fled in tatters under the lash of his laughter and the memories it brought.

"I—"

"Why did you come?" Lian asked. "We thought you died."

Sindal couldn't say that she'd come to kill Tirlan. That would leave her sister a widow, with no one to care for her and their children.

But if she didn't kill him, she'd fail her initiation. Garlis wouldn't give her the sorceress' cheek scars, and Toya, Sindal's lioness spirit, would leave her.

"I came to see Mother."

"She's dead and gone, buried with Father under the floor of her house." Lian's eyes misted over in remembrance. "Six polluted houses burned that day, and the smoke rose up to heaven in great black clouds. The village sacrificed a new he goat and three lambs, and feasted the entire night after we gave the offerings to the gods."

Sindal smiled to see her sister's pleasure at the offering. She looked back to see Tirlan smug on his bench, cup held carelessly in his hand. She hadn't expected to find Tirlan with a new wife, much less her own sister, and didn't know what to do.

"Then I'll take my leave of this house," she said.

Tirlan leaped up. "But you've just come home, Wife. Lian, get her food."

He reached for Sindal, but she lifted her pack and her stick, dancing away from his dirty hand, and ran through the door. Tirlan's laughter followed her out onto the packed-dirt street. She cast the see-me-not spell again, half afraid the fear and anger rising up in her throat would foul the spell.

At last she drew up along the river. The smells of mud and rotting grass were as thick as the brambles, reeds, and brush that grew along it. She found a tall willow and climbed it, leaning back against the rough trunk as she looked out over the water dyed ruddy red in the dying day.

She couldn't kill Tirlan, no matter her hate. Lian and her children would die without him to provide for them. The villagers, struggling themselves, would do what they could, but Lian would be reduced to begging, and the children would starve if she couldn't find a new husband. Sindal could not take her sister with her to the cave—she and Garlis often had barely enough food for the two of them.

But if Sindal didn't kill him, her hopes and all the work she struggled to master over the last eight years would be as dust before the wind.

She pulled the walking stick across her thighs, and stroked the symbols as her thoughts chased themselves round and round like a dog chasing his tail. When the sun set and her spirit animal, Toya's eyes gleamed like tiny fires as the lioness watched and waited at the base of the willow.

Sindal woke the next morning in the willow tree, her cloak wrapped around her. She watched the mist rise off the river, and the cranes wake the sky with their calls.

When the men had reached the fields, she crept back to the village and knocked on her sister's door.

Lian answered it, her pleasure at the sight of her sister making Sindal's heart rise.

"Come in and have bread and tea. Meet my children."

Sindal followed her into the woman's side of the house; Toya walked behind her, tail lashing, invisible to everyone but Sindal. The room smelled faintly of the dough Lian had made, cheese, and the herbs that hung from the ceiling beams. The lime-washed walls were covered by shelves laden with dishes and wheels of cheese, dried fruits, and hanks of wool waiting to be spun. The lioness lay down along one wall and idly licked one paw.

Sindal smiled at the baby fussing in a rush basket, and the

toddler playing on the floor with her small doll. A small boy, one of the racing children she'd seen yesterday, sat near the hearth, a blanket wrapped around him against the morning chill.

Lian knelt back on the immaculate, beaten clay floor and resumed shaping loaves of bread. She patted them into flat rounds, and gestured to Sindal to open the hearth door so she could slide them in.

"May I?" Sindal asked once the hearth was closed, gesturing to the baby.

Lian smiled proudly as she lifted the dusky boy out of the basket and handed him to her.

"Cais," she said.

He had Tirlan's mouth and spindly legs, but the rest was Lian's blood. Sindal nodded at her sister. "He has Father's eyes, just like you."

"And your cowlick, see?" Lian lifted the shock of black hair that hung down over the child's high forehead. Sindal laughed to see the lick of hair that stood up to one side of the peak. She rocked the baby and cooed. He had good energy, strong and well-colored. The toddler, though, had a clot of blackish-purple in her third eye, between her brows. After handing the baby to her sister, Sindal gestured to the girl. The toddler swayed on her feet, holding on to a basket that sat against the wall near Toya.

"Merta, go to your auntie." Lain shrugged. "She's always been slow. Tirlan doesn't help. He teases her and scolds her all the time."

Sindal smiled and waggled her fingers at the girl, pulling the child gently with her will. The girl's big eyes were just starting to show some fear when she reached her aunt. Sindal opened her pack and took out a comb of honey, wrapped in waxed cloth.

"Want a taste, Merta?" She brushed her finger across a golden tear that trickled from the broken wax, and held it to the toddler's lips. The girl licked Sindal's finger and reached for the comb.

"Here, then," she said, breaking off a piece for Merta and another for the boy, who'd stood and dropped his blanket. She gave a piece to Lian as well, who took it with many thanks.

Merta seemed happy to sit in her aunt's lap as she ate the honey.

Sindal ran her hands up and down the girl, tracing the root of the clot. There was power in her, but the threads knotted in the child's throat. She massaged the girl's neck until it unraveled, the clot turning pale and disappearing as she murmured a release spell against the back of the girl's head. She smelled of smoke and wool and little girl.

Merta pulled away, rubbed her forehead, and then slid down on to the floor. She stared at Toya for a long moment.

She sees true. She has my blood.

"Give me another piece, Auntie," the boy said.

"Tiras," Lian said, laying her hand on the boy's shoulder. "That's not the way you ask for something."

He pushed his mother's hand away with a disgusted scowl. Lian flushed and looked down.

"No," Sindal said. "I don't share with brats who have no manners."

"Give me a piece, *now*," he demanded, staring at her.

Sindal raised her eyebrows and narrowed her eyes.

Go on. Push me, Tirlan's get.

Whatever he saw chastened him, and he shuffled his feet and looked away. "Please, may I have another piece?"

"Yes, boy. You may."

He took it quickly and ran out of the room.

"Oh, Lian, I'm so sorry. I never thought of anything but getting away from Tirlan. I hated him so much. I never thought of what he'd do."

"Don't Sindal. I've not been unhappy. He mellowed after his first son died, and the midwife said I almost died too, because I was too young to bear children."

"Yes, I can see he mellowed," Sindal said, brushing at the old bruise beneath her sister's eye, and the cheek he'd slapped yesterday.

Lain shrugged. "He waited for a long time before he took me again, and then waited again after the second one died. We've made a life, and I have two fine sons, and only one daughter to sell for more goats."

"Lian, I—"

"Really, Sindal. You have nothing to feel bad about."

But she did. She was the reason Lian was here. And she was the reason Lian would suffer if she took her revenge on Tirlan.

But she wanted the power. She wanted the ability to help them with a charm, or a dream interpretation, or a bit of healing like she'd done for Merta. She wanted the gifts the people brought to Garlis for those workings.

And to have that she had to kill Tirlan.

And ruin Lian's life.

"Why don't you come with me?"

Lian scoffed. "What would we do, you with no husband, me with three children? No, the knucklebones have been cast. We have to live with what we've made for ourselves."

That brought the heat back into Sindal's chest, made the yellow sun grow inside of her.

"No, we don't. We just have to choose."

"You choose. I can't choose differently."

They both smelled the bread at the same time. Lian threw the door open and pulled the loaves out just as they would have been too done.

The sisters caught each other's eyes and smiled.

For the rest of the morning they spun and shared stories and jokes. When Tirlan came home for the midday meal, they were both laughing at a story Sindal had told about a dog and piglet.

"What's so funny, Wife?"

They both started and scrambled to their feet as he put his head in the door.

"So, you're back, Sindal."

She could see the pleasure of his thoughts in his eyes, and she cringed at the thought of his hands on her. Toya stared at Tirlan from her spot on the floor. Sindal picked up her stick.

"Yes, I'm back."

"Good."

Sindal could see the plans forming in his mind, the status two wives would give him.

Now was the time. Lian was still young and fertile. Another man would marry her and adopt her children. It had to be.

"I've not come to stay. I've come to kill you, Tirlan."

He stared at her as if a goat had asked to spend the night outside the pen. Then he laughed.

"Oh, little potter, that's rich," he gasped.

Rage grew in Sindal's heart, stoked by each guffaw.

"But you always were silly. First rugs, then pots, now this."

His hand lashed out suddenly and cuffed her hard. She stumbled and crashed into the shelves. They tipped over, hitting her hard on the head and the shoulder as everything fell to the floor.

"Now look what you've done, clumsy bitch."

Fear flooded into her then, knowing that he would hit her again while she was down and helpless. Memories of other beatings filled her head and she was frozen in their midst, a frightened, beaten eleven-year-old girl again.

The yellow power she held in her chest fled.

All her dreams curdled as Tirlan stood over her, deciding what to do next to her. His smile revealed a gap where a front tooth had fallen out.

He lifted his foot lazily.

Sindal heard Lian shout, saw her throw herself at her husband. Tirlan threw her off casually and turn back to Sindal.

He lifted his foot and kicked her. She managed to roll and took the blow on her back, over her kidney, instead of in her aching belly. Pain flared and she gasped.

"That'll teach you, Wife, to obey your Husband. I see you have need of lessons. I'll be pleased to school you."

School her. Thoughts of lessons Garlis set her to flickered through her mind. Sindal had faced the spirits of the underworld, battled mages for their power and won. She'd followed the kindly ones down to the River Styx as they went about their business, reaping souls to fill Hades.

He had no idea.

The rage filled her chest, her throat, and she gathered the strands of that power along with her conviction as she stood.

She'd have her revenge. She'd have her place in the world, Toya would follow her yet. Lian would find a new husband.

Sindal let a trickle of the burning sun flow into her right hand and let it pool there, taking satisfaction as his eyes grew round as he saw what she did.

She held it in front of her and rolled it around her hand, knowing it illuminated her face, shadowing her eyes, making her look ghastly. Goddess knew it had scared the piss out of her when Garlis had done it during her first initiation.

Tirlan stood, mesmerized by the power in her hand.

"You think I'm the same cowed girl you used to kick in the corner of your house, but I'm not. Why would I fear you, spiteful little man? You're the last price I'll pay to earn my place."

Those words stung him, and he reached for her with his filthy hands.

"No," Lian cried as Sindal let the ball of fire fly. Her sister's shout ruined Sindal's aim and it flew past Tirlan, close enough it singed his hair, and exploded against the mud-brick wall. The hut filled with the scents of scorched lime and straw.

"No, Sindal. You can't come back here and take your revenge." Lian saw to Tirlan's singed hair, and brushed him off.

Sindal stared at them. All of the anger went out of her, replaced by despair, knowing Lian would pay the price. But Sindal would fail, lose everything she had worked for.

Tirlan smirked from behind her sister.

"You see? She's a better wife. You were never a good wife, and you're a terrible witch, just like you were a terrible potter and a worse weaver."

He was wrong. She'd been a good potter, and a better weaver, and she had six initiations and the sacred marks to prove she was adept at witchery.

No, no. I will have this. I have only to finish this and I can claim my full power.

She raised her hand again, felt the power flow at her command. Lian braced herself, tears sparkling in her eyes.

"Will you kill your sister to have your revenge on me?"

No. She couldn't.

Her dream fluttered up from her chest, shredding along with the power in her hand. She dropped her pack and pulled twigs of herbs from the clumps hanging above her, breathing over them as she twisted them together. She pulled a hair and a thread out of Tirlan's headcloth where it lay on the floor.

"Here, now, what are you doing?"

The fear in Tirlan's voice as he spoke was a nice reward for the loss of her dream. Her knowledge of what Lian's life would be now was an even better reward. She muttered a curse on the charm and, as it lay in her palm, let a bit of energy flow into her palm and ignite the working. She dropped it on the floor where it sputtered and smoked.

Toya stood then and stretched lazily, her golden eyes flicking over Sindal as she padded out of the room.

Sindal's spirit animal had abandoned her. She didn't deserve to be a witch. All her gains gone. All she had left was this small revenge on Tirlan, which would in turn create a great gift for her sister.

"Hear me, Tirlan. I'll not kill you for my sister's sake." She let him have his smirk, knowing that she'd have the greater pleasure after he'd heard her words.

"But I've laid a curse on you, and a blessing on my sister."

"What? How? You took hair and thread from my head scarf."

"Your hair, but her work; her hand spinning the wool, her hand on the loom."

Tirlan's eyes flickered with the first sign of doubt.

"From now on, my blessing on Lian will work on her house and her family, bringing luck and fortune upon them. Her love and industry for them will stoke the charm. Any hatred and pettiness and violence you engender or teach cannot touch it, and will only bounce back upon you. If you wish to bask in the fullness she brings to your house, you will do well to put your anger away, lest the misery you bring down on your head crush you."

She looked to Lian. "Do you understand, sister?"

Lian nodded her head and stepped forward. "My sister, thank

you for this gift. Better, thank yourself for not weighting yourself with such a crime on your heart."

Sindal embraced her sister before picking up her cloak, flinging it over her, shouldering the pack, and lifting her walking stick.

As she left, Tirlan came for her. She didn't look back, but flung a ball of fire over her shoulder, grinning as she heard him swear and move out of its way.

She walked for a week, trudging along the dusty trail dotted with dung under the hot sun, telling herself Lian was right. It was better to lose all that she'd worked for than bear the weight of his death for the rest of her days.

If only she believed it.

Garlis, shriveled like an old fig, sat napping on her stool in the late afternoon sun at the mouth of the cave. Toya lay sprawled at the entrance.

Sindal felt a spike of sadness as she looked at the creature's beautiful, tawny fur. Toya had abandoned her for Garlis.

Garlis opened her eyes and nodded.

"Ye've returned then. Welcome back, Sindal. Come, share bread and salt with an old woman."

At least she was gracious. Sindal would share guest rites and then go.

The old woman got up and went into the cave. Sindal crouched down beside her stool and shed her pack and cloak, laying the stick beside her. Toya stretched and yawned widely, the sun shining through her sharp teeth.

Sindal looked away, her heart in her throat, her eyes pricking with tears. She had been so proud when the great cat had told Sindal her name, and then followed her home. Garlis had been pleased, and had patted Sindal on the shoulder as she prepared ashes and sharpened the knife to make the mark on Sindal's left arm, above the blackened crooked tree that climbed up from her elbow.

Garlis returned, carrying a polished oak tray laden with a round flat loaf of bread, a small black clay bowl of coarse salt, and a matching bowl of oil. She tore a bit of bread from the loaf, dipped it in the oil, and then the salt. She offered it up to the Queen of Heaven, then tossed it to the earth.

"I greet ye, sister Sindal," she said offering the tray.

Sindal blushed.

She believes I did it. She thinks I killed Tirlan.

Her throat tightened as she tore off a bit of bread, knowing she'd have to tell her mentor the truth. The morsel was tasteless and her throat refused to open. She nearly gagged trying to swallow it.

"I'm pleased to see yer path shines with light and honor."

"But Mother Garlis," Sindal blurted. "I failed. I tried to kill him, but he'd married my sister, Lian, and she would've been alone with her three children, and none are old enough to care for her."

Garlis smiled. "I told ye only to go see to yer heart's desire. And ye've done that. I see it in yer heart."

"But I didn't kill him!"

Garlis laughed. "No. I don't see how ye could. Yer heart has never been dark. Full of anger, yes, but never dark enough to murder."

Sindal shook her head. "But didn't I fail?"

"Whenever ye've spoken of yer husband, yer heart cried out for revenge. Did ye not have revenge on him?"

She stopped. She had. And in the end, either he'd hurt himself, or turn his heart around and embrace the gifts his wife brought to their home. She hoped he embraced them, but also that he'd be galled by the knowledge she'd rendered his anger impotent.

Toya stood and stretched hugely, her sharp teeth shining in the late afternoon sun. She strode over and rubbed her spirit face across Sindal's legs, scenting her.

"Then you didn't leave me," she said to the great cat.

"The spirits cleave to power, and to the ones who wield it with confidence. She sensed the turmoil in ye. But she knew ye'd won whether ye knew it yourself or not, and came here to wait for ye."

The despair that had coiled in Sindal's heart unraveled, and she felt the inrush of bright yellow power fill the center of her chest.

"Ye passed yer trial. And I must say I am glad ye chose this path.

If ye'd murdered him, the furies would prey on ye forever more, and all yer deeds would take ye down a steadily darker path."

Garlis smiled, her wrinkled face swallowing her eyes. Her mouth parted, and Sindal noticed she'd lost another tooth.

"We'll wait till dark and then I'll give ye yer mark. Tomorrow ye can see the petitioners that come up the hill."

"Tomorrow? But that's too soon. What will you do?"

"Me? I'll take my ease. About time."

Sindal stroked the lioness' head and grinned.

The marks on her cheeks would tell everyone she was a sorceress, able to heal and bless with either hand.

Yes, this was the better path. And one day she'd pay a dowry to Lian and bring Merta here as an apprentice even as Garlis had apprenticed her.

It was good to be a sorceress. Better to be a sorceress with a light heart, and a bright path to walk upon.

ABOUT THE AUTHOR

Thea Hutcheson's story in *Realms of Fantasy's* 100th issue prompted Lois Tilton of Locus to say her work "is sensual, fertile, with seed quickening on every page. Well done…" She has appeared in such publications as *Hot Blood XI, Fatal Attractions, Baen's Universe Issue 4, Vol. 1,* Amazing Monster Tales: *It Came From Outer Space, Nuns with Guns, Water Fairies,* and several of the critically acclaimed *Fiction River* anthologies.

She lives in an unscenic, nearly historic small city in Colorado with a 1000 books, four rescued cats and one understanding partner. When she's not working diligently as a Planning Commissioner to change that, she writes, and fills the time between bouts at the computer as a factotum and an event planner.

Find out more about Thea at:
theahutcheson.com

 twitter.com/theah1771

 amazon.com/Thea-Hutcheson/e/B0068RQ8Q4

 bookbub.com/authors/thea-hutcheson

FIGHT OR FLIGHT

LESLIE CLAIRE WALKER

THE MIDNIGHT MOON hung low and huge in the black velvet sky, stars winking all around. I could not only see the glow that flowed over the city and cast a silver halo over the Rockies to the west, I could smell it. I could taste it like a spark on the back of my tongue. It tasted like magic.

Magic wasn't supposed to exist.

The moon was just a moon. The city was just a city. People drove by in their Chevys and Fords, on their way home to love and warmth. Gas lamps split the streets into pockets of light and shadow. The light claimed respectable folks.

The shadows ate everyone else.

I blinked that thought away, then winced when the dull ache behind my left eye sharpened to a point. Nothing to do for a black eye except wait until the bruise healed. If it hurt bad enough to wonder whether something was broken? Well, I couldn't do anything about that. I didn't have the kind of money it took to see a doctor. I barely had enough dough to scrounge the half a roast beef sandwich I'd eaten for dinner. I'd had to wolf it down before the diner waitress kicked me out. Nobody wanted my kind. Not for long.

The wind kicked up, bringing with it the stink of motor oil and cigarette smoke, threatening to pull off my hat and send it flying. I planted a palm on top of the hat, pressing it to my sweaty head until the wind changed its mind. The last of the August day's warmth seeped from the rooftop through the seat of my trousers and into my skin.

I could hardly stand the feeling—I hated to be hot. It always felt like a prelude to Hell, where I would certainly be going after I finally, actually died, given that my list of sins was long and included stealing and coveting, among other things.

But the view was too slick, and I wanted to savor the spark of magic and I had nowhere else to go. So I stayed and pulled off my dusty, brown shoes with their patched laces and the matching socks with the holes in the toes, setting them beside me. With bruised and aching hands, I rolled up my trouser legs to my knees and dangled my feet in their scuffed shoes free and easy three stories above the grimy street. I rolled up the sleeves of my pinstriped shirt that had been white once upon a time, hooked my suspenders with my thumbs, and watched the moon.

The stairwell door opened and two sets of footfalls clocked across the roof, heading toward me. I knew who they were without looking. I knew who they were before either of them opened their mouths.

Doogie Smokes cleared his throat. He sounded like he had a mouth full of marbles when he talked. My handiwork, from last night. I had a mean left hook.

"Hey, Charlie," he said. "Missed you at the warehouse today."

Not because I hadn't showed for my shift, but because Doogie hadn't. It wasn't that he had a problem with rolling kegs of illegal booze into the backs of plain, nondescript trucks. He didn't object to the shady deal-making our bosses engaged in by selling alcohol to certain establishments, even if sometimes it ended with men in the hospital or dead in back alleys. He just had a problem with work of any kind, and a giant chip on his shoulder with my name on it.

He'd come up here to take the coin I'd earned pulling his load along with my own, sure. But he'd come up here for another reason. Like magic, I wasn't supposed to exist.

I sighed as I stood up, brushing asphalt pebbles from the seat of my pants as I turned to look at him. He had one year and thirty-nine days on me, but he seemed older—as if he were a full-grown eighteen instead of the fifteen I knew him to be. He wore his black hair slicked back and cut tight over his great, big ears. His eyes were flinty.

He wore the same shirt and trousers as me, only his were clean and pressed, and they stretched over thick slabs of muscle. He'd tucked a pack of smokes in his shirt pocket, like always. I could practically see my reflection in the spit-shine of his shoes, even from ten feet away.

He'd kicked me with those shoes last night.

He caught me looking and flashed an angry grin.

His buddy, whom I didn't recognize, stood at his left flank. Could've been anybody. There were a lot of anybodies, guys who wanted to get in good with Doogie. Guys who thought they'd get a leg up by doing so. Every single one thought of himself as ambitious. I thought of them as delusional.

This one had blond hair, dull brown eyes, carefully pressed clothes. This one wore a peacock blue tie like an arrogant noose around his neck. He'd have a name like Biff, or Geordie, or Ramsey. Something that felt carefree rolling off the tongue.

The new guy slid his hands into his pants pockets casual-like, as if he didn't expect any guff from me. Beating me to a pulp wouldn't be hard. I was a runt, after all. Runty Charlie Nobody.

I raised my chin. "Doogie here tell you about me?"

The new guy shrugged. "Said you owe him."

"And he's paying you to help him come after me. There's a breakdown in your logic," I said. "What's he supposed to pay you with?"

The new guy blinked at me, then shook his head. "Said you were a bastard."

So we were getting right down to brass tacks. "He told you we got the same father?"

The new guy blinked again.

"Guess that's a no," I said. "Makes me his daddy's bastard, and he hates to be reminded."

"Shut up," Doogie said.

I smiled and took a step forward. "He tell you I'm a pugilist?"

The new guy stared at me. "You? You couldn't lay a hand on me."

"Necessity is the mother of invention," I said.

The new guy took a step toward me.

Doogie held out a thick arm in front of him. "We want to take whatever he's got on him first."

"What difference does it make?" the new guy asked. "We can take it off him after we knock him out."

"Something might happen," Doogie said. "It happened last night."

It had only happened the once. I'd lost consciousness.

Something had happened.

Doogie had seen it.

"What're you talking about?" the new guy asked.

Doogie glanced at him sideways. "Just do what I said."

Doogie was the boss.

The new guy ran straight for me, the soles of his shoes scuffing the roof.

I sidestepped. I considered during the space between heartbeats letting the guy's momentum carry him off the edge and into thin air. He didn't mean anything to me.

He read the thought as it crossed my face. His eyes widened with fear.

Because of that, I stuck out my foot. Tripped him instead.

He sprawled face-first onto the deck and skidded to within an inch of the edge, skinning the heels of his hands bloody.

During the space of the breath I took while he did that, Doogie rushed me.

He grabbed me by the left arm, paralyzing my left hook. I still had my right hand, though. And I had a mean uppercut.

The impact of my fist against his jaw reverberated through my bones all the way to my shoulder. Doogie staggered back. Miraculously, he kept his balance. He turned his head, keeping his gaze fixed on me, and spat red.

"You're gonna die," he said.

"You said that last night."

He curled his hands into fists. "I don't know how you got away. You shouldn't have. It was—"

"Impossible?" I said.

"It's all wrong, just like you."

I punched him the gut.

Doogie let out a whistle like a deflating balloon. He dropped to his knees.

"You can't beat me," I said. "Whatever you do, it just makes me stronger."

"No." He pushed to his feet through what seemed like sheer force of will. When he opened his mouth again, he spoke in a series of grunts. "You don't belong in this world."

He was right. He knew it. I knew it. But here I was, in the world.

No home. No bed. No one to care whether I lived or died—except Doogie, it seemed. Still, I didn't want to die. I just didn't want to stay here. Maybe I wouldn't have to.

Last night, Doogie had landed a lucky punch. I'd fallen flat on my back, knocking my head against the pebbled ground. The world had turned gray and fuzzy and then black. And cold. I'd felt cold like I'd never felt before, not even in February with six inches of snow on the ground, when the only prospect for warmth was a barrel fire I had to fight to get close to.

This new cold, it felt like I imagined the space between the stars felt: the empty space between breaths, and the icy air stabbing my lungs like knives. Frost coating my eyelashes. A shiver so deep and so wide, it wasn't something I felt or did, but something I fell into.

A heartbeat later, my eyes opened on the big ugly of Doogie's face. His eyes had gone huge, like the moon. The corners of his mouth turned down. His mouth trembled. Like a baby's, right before it cried. A damn sad sight. An infuriating sight.

I'd managed to land the punch that made him talk funny, but then he'd knocked me out for real with the fist that had blackened my eye. That time, I hadn't felt any cold. I hadn't felt anything at all until I woke up in the wee, small hours with the silence of the whole world heavy on me like a smothering blanket.

Like déjà vu, Doogie's fist hit my face, shattering the memory running through my mind. The force of the blow rocked me back on my heels. I lost my balance. Fell back onto the rooftop. It knocked the air out of me with an *oomph*.

He loomed over me for a second, eyes narrowed, fists ready. "Where did you go last night, you freak?" he asked.

"I'm the freak? Have you looked in the mirror lately?"

He grabbed my shoulders and shook me. My eyes rolled around in my head like marbles. "Answer the goddamn question."

I didn't have time, even if I'd felt inclined—even if I'd had an answer, which I didn't. Doogie shook me harder and slammed my head back against the asphalt.

The moon ballooned suddenly until it seemed to take up the

whole night, until there was nothing else. Then it shrank to a pinpoint as the darkness that ate people like me rushed in. A roar filled my ears. Cold darkness took me whole.

The last thing I heard was Doogie's scream. "Charlie!"

I came to with my teeth chattering, shaking like a beaten dog, feeling like I'd died and come back to life—like maybe part of me might still be dead.

I froze at the thought. Not a rational thought. But God strike me down if it didn't feel true.

I drew a deep inhale that stank of car exhaust and tasted like a greasy spoon and hurt my lungs. When I blew it out, my breath frosted the air.

The moon hovered above, big and creamy and filled with magic.

The surface under me felt different than the rooftop. It didn't have the give of asphalt. It didn't smell like it either. I braced my palms against it on either side, holding myself in place, trying to understand what had happened. Pebbles dug into the heels of my hands. Whatever it was underneath them—concrete—scratched my skin.

The halo of a streetlamp spotlighted me. Red brick walls grew out of the ground on either side of me. White paint splattered the brick in big, billowy letters that made no sense to me. A foreign language? Had I fetched up someplace across the world?

I shook my head and felt immediately sorry. I saw stars. My roast beef dinner climbed halfway up the pipe it'd gone down. I swallowed hard and I squeezed my eyes shut until the feeling went away.

When I looked out again, a giant shadow stood to my right. I blinked, trying to focus on it. It seemed to shape shift, or maybe I just saw more clearly. It wasn't a giant. It was Doogie, hugging himself against the chill.

He hitched in a breath. "Charlie? Charlie, where are we?"

It was the friendliest thing he'd ever said to me. I didn't know whether to feel grateful or suspicious. I pushed up on my elbows very carefully.

A vehicle hugged the curb on the far side of the streetlamp's light. It looked vaguely like a car, but not like any car I'd ever seen. No footboards. The front grille slanted the wrong way. This one was wider and lower to the ground and enhanced the foreign feeling of wherever we'd ended up.

And why *we?* Why the hell had Doogie ended up with me, wherever we were?

He glanced over his shoulder and down at me. "Charlie?"

"No idea," I said.

"If you're lying——"

"Why would I lie?" I asked.

"It's like last night," he said.

I shook my head, more gently this time. "No, it's not. I didn't come here last night."

"You disappeared from the street where you were laying," he said. "You vanished. Who does that?"

"Yeah, but I didn't go anywhere. Or at least I don't remember it. I certainly don't remember this place."

Charlie took a shuddering breath. "This is a dream."

"No offense, but you don't usually star in my dreams—or my nightmares." I rose slowly to my feet.

"I hate you," he said.

"That makes two of us."

He snorted like an angry boar. Not that I'd ever heard an angry boar, but I could imagine the sound one of them would make.

We stood in some kind of alley, from the looks of it. But it didn't smell like piss or trash or drunks. The brick walls on either side of us belonged to buildings, though since they didn't have windows or stenches emanating from them, I had no way to tell what sort of buildings or who, if anyone, might be inside.

I had no reference for where we were. It looked enough like the world I understood to seem at least a little familiar, but it looked strange enough so that unease bloomed like a flower in the pit of my belly, the petals soft and enticing, but singed around the edges.

"Take me back." Doogie spun on his heel to face me. The confusion on his face mirrored mine, but then his expression hardened. "Back to the roof."

"I don't know how."

His face flushed. He pointed a finger at me. "This whole thing—it's all your fault."

I could neither confirm nor deny. There was definitely something unusual going on, but I didn't know why. "Maybe."

"You did this on purpose."

I held up a hand. "Wait a minute."

"No." He curled his pointing hand into a fist.

I raised a brow. "Really? More fighting?"

"Isn't that what you like, pugilist?" he asked.

"No," I said. "I just never had a choice."

He thinned his mouth into a purple line that clashed with his now beet-red face. He didn't have a comeback. He hated not having a comeback.

"I got no idea why we're here," I said. "I swear on my mother's grave."

The words had been automatic. My heart sank, because I'd given him another round of ammunition.

"Who told you she was dead?" Doogie asked. "You see her kick it?"

My heart beat faster. Pressure built behind my ribs. He knew I hadn't seen my mom die. I hadn't been there when she was taken to the hospital. It'd taken me a lot of grief—grief I didn't have to spare—to pry out of the place what had happened to her.

They'd said she died. They'd buried her in a pauper's grave. Whoever *they* were. I hated them.

"Ever think she just left you?" he asked. "Ever think she hated you enough to do that?"

All the time. But damned if I'd ever admit something like that to Doogie Smokes. I glared at him.

The corners of his mouth curved into a smirk.

"Who's the bastard now?" I asked.

He raised his fist.

I caught movement in an alley that crossed ours about twenty feet in front of us. Someone poked their head around the corner of the red brick building there, the one that stood to my left side. I jumped half an inch off the concrete.

Doogie was observant enough to understand he didn't have what it took to make me do such a thing. He turned around to follow my gaze.

Whoever had looked around the corner didn't flinch or back away. I couldn't see them clearly since the light didn't illuminate them enough, but a moment later, as they stepped fully into our alley, the mystery someone resolved into a child's shape.

A girl's voice flowed toward us. It bounced off the brick walls. The words dropped in front of us like a stone into still water, ripples rolling over us. "Who are you?"

The voice felt disconcerting. She wasn't wearing a dress, after all. And she didn't seem quite…right. No reason not to tell her our names, though. She knew where we were, but we sure didn't. I didn't like being at a disadvantage, and maybe she could help us. If she wasn't afraid of us, that was.

"Charlie," I said. "The other guy is Doogie."

She looked from me to Doogie and back again. "You're the interesting one."

"Hey," Doogie said, with a little affront.

She shrugged. "You're the normal. Charlie's anything but."

Doogie took a step toward her. "You want to come closer and say that?"

She answered his threat with a step forward of her own. Definitely not afraid.

That was the first thought I had about her, and the last thought I had for a good, long minute as I stared at her. She had blond curls that cascaded down to the middle of her back and flowed over her shoulders like a golden river. Ice blue eyes studied us from behind coal-black lashes. A pink spot dotted each cheek, and her lips were blood red. She wore a white shirt with no buttons that I could see and a puffy black coat over the top of it, but the coat came only to her waist. She wore pants that looked a little like mine, and black boots without laces.

She might as well have been an alien.

She was a girl. She was my age. Maybe a year older.

"Give me a break," she said. "You want to come in out of the cold?"

"Where's in?" I asked.

Casually, she cocked her head toward the corner she'd come from. Her tone was anything but casual. "Now."

I followed. I didn't look back to see whether Doogie did, but I heard his footfalls, reluctant behind me.

The girl led the way down her alley. I hurried to catch her, coming to pace with her as she turned up the short sidewalk that led to a steel door in the red brick building. She moved with purpose, her gaze roaming side-to-side and even over her shoulder without her turning her head much. Up close, she still looked little, but also wiry and strong. She looked like someone used to handling herself.

"What's your name?" I asked.

"Sunday," she said.

"That's a day, not a name."

"Whatever."

"What's that mean?" I asked.

"Whatever you want it to," she said. "Hurry up, will you? And tell your friend to haul ass. There's something happening out here that's dangerous and I don't know what it is."

She had me up until she said she didn't know. Unlike when I'd said the same thing to Doogie a minute ago, she was lying.

"What's inside?" I asked.

"Shelter from the storm." She looked at me, studying me with her icy eyes, not missing a step as she did.

The sound of Doogie's steps drew closer. He panted a little as he ran. "What storm?" he asked.

"The kind you might not live through," she said.

The closer we got to the building, the more it looked like a fortress. One way in and out. No windows over on this side either. Talk of danger and shelter. For a second, the big moon above seemed reflected in the flat steel of the door in front of us. Then Sunday reached for the handle and pulled open the door, and the reflection fled.

It was dark inside. The door looked like a mouth. I froze in my tracks.

"Inside," she said, her voice taking on an urgent cast. "Now."

The rawness in her voice propelled me forward, across the threshold and onto a hard concrete floor. That much I could tell without being able to see anything. Doogie plowed into the back of me, forcing me in further. Behind him, Sunday shut the door. A lock clicked into place with a sound that sent a flash of panic from the bottom of my spine up and out through the top of my head.

A match strike against sandpaper was followed by the familiar stink of sulfur, then the spark of a candlewick catching flame. Sunday held the fat, white candle with one hand just beneath her chin, turning her face into a ghost story for a moment. Then the moment passed. She spun on her heel and waved us to follow her across the big room.

"This way," she said.

Our footfalls echoed like gunshots. My eyes adjusted as best they could on the way through what appeared to be a big, empty room that had maybe been a warehouse. My nose picked up the smell of wood and old paper. And the smell of ancient cigarette butts.

I didn't catch a glimpse of any machinery, nor of any other people. I didn't hear anyone else breathing. But the hairs at the nape of my neck stood straight up. I was an animal, and I was being hunted. We all were.

Sunday ducked into the first side room we came to, shutting the windowless steel door to it, behind us and flipping the lock. She blew out the candle then, with a small spray of beeswax and the bitter sting of smoke, and flicked on the overhead light, which buzzed and creaked inside its long, white coffin. The way it flickered mesmerized.

Doogie whispered—the situation seemed to call for it. "What is this place?"

Sunday snapped her fingers.

I tore my eyes away from the strange light and met her gaze. Doogie stared at me, then at her.

"We don't have much time," she said. "I don't know how you and your friend got here, Charlie—"

Doogie scowled. "We're not friends."

"Whatever," she said. "I don't know how you got here, but I need to know what year you're from, how much you know, and why you came."

The room was empty except for an empty metal desk that had been shoved against the wall. The walls had once been white, but had grayed with time and grime, except for the bright patches where pictures had once hung. The nails they'd hung from remained in the walls. The whole room was a ghost. Standing in here, it felt as if we were ghosts already, too.

"What year?" Doogie's eyebrows climbed to his hairline.

"Yeah," she said.

Doogie's voice rose an octave with each syllable of my name. "Charlie."

"What?" The room started to gray out.

"It's Charlie's fault. He did it."

"I know." Sunday watched me. "Charlie, take a breath."

I did. What color there was washed back into the room. I walked over to the desk and leaned against it, wrapping my fingers right around the edge.

"What year, Charlie?" Sunday asked gently.

"1933."

"Shit. No kidding?"

I blinked at her. "When is this?"

"2003," she said.

I whistled.

Doogie started to shake like a tree under the saw. Any second now, he'd topple over and crush one of us.

"I don't know anything," I said, answering her questions down the line. "I don't even know how we got here. Or where here is."

"Denver," she said.

"Same city, then. Fine. But there is no why."

She chewed her bottom lip. "This is your first time."

"My first time what?" I asked.

"Flying. You know, time travel."

Flying. Traveling. Through time. And she wanted me to breathe. I didn't think I'd ever be able to breathe again. "So that's why I'm interesting."

She shook her head. "I didn't know what kind of power you had, just that you had power."

"Power," I said evenly.

"Magic," she said.

Doogie looked from her to me and back again. "What a load of bull crap."

"You got another explanation?" she asked.

He opened his mouth to respond, but nothing came out.

"You look like a fish."

He snapped his mouth shut.

"I don't know what I'm supposed to do here, okay?" Sunday said. "I thought you were here to help me, but you don't even know how to do what you do. We're in deep shit and it's getting deeper by the minute. There's an assassin out there looking to take me—us—out. I don't think I can take him on my own. My own power isn't what you'd call dependable."

Assassins: I knew from assassins, I just didn't usually hear them referred to using that word.

"You do something to a boss? You in a boss's way?" I asked.

She looked at me as if I had two heads. "I'm fifteen. I don't have a boss. I don't even have parents anymore."

Maybe she'd done something and didn't realize. No one put out a hit for no reason, not on a fifteen-year-old girl. And not on someone like me. I was invisible. I was literally nobody. I was fourteen, and I wasn't stupid.

The reason was square in front of my face: magic. No matter how impossible that sounded, I couldn't ignore what I heard and saw, what I knew to be true in my gut.

Sunday had undependable powers, she said. "What powers?"

"Mine?"

I nodded.

"It's my eyes," she said.

"You can see through things?" Doogie asked.

"No," she said. "I can blind other people by looking at them."

He stared at her.

"It just doesn't always work," she said. "Not yet. I think it will, eventually. For now, though, I never know. And that's just not good enough."

I pressed the heel of my hand against my forehead, trying to focus. "Do you know where the hit man is?"

"A couple of blocks away," she said. "He came at me and I—I hurt him. It gave me a window to go outside and get you. He's older and stronger, and whatever I did, it won't stop him for long."

Doogie re-planted his feet firmly on the floor and set his hands on his hips. "What kind of gun has he got?"

"No gun," Sunday said.

"Then how's he gonna assassinate us?" Doogie asked.

"He eats."

Doogie cocked his head. "What?"

"He's closing in," she said.

She couldn't see that—none of us could see a damn thing outside of the windowless room. No noise filtered in through the steel door, either. No crash of glass breaking. No creaking of hinges. Nothing at all.

But those hairs on the back of my neck, the ones that had stood straight up, they pulled so tight, it was as if they were trying to break off and run away. My heart raced.

"What does he eat?" I asked.

"Everything," she said.

Everything. My imagination took that word and built a nightmare out of it. An assassin who could eat the whole world. My skin went clammy.

Sunday laid a hand on my arm. A wave of electricity shot from her skin to mine. I sucked in a breath.

"Can you take us out of here?" she asked.

"I don't know." My stomach wanted to turn inside out. I thought of my sandwich. I pushed the thought away fast. "I have to be knocked out."

"He's a pugilist," Doogie said.

I steamrolled over his words. "That's how it worked before."

She wrapped her fingers around my arm in a vise-grip and swung before I had a chance to flinch.

Her fist hit my temple at frightening speed with a smack that shook me to my core. Stars floated behind my eyes. I toppled over like tree in a storm.

"Doogie!" Sunday shouted.

He grabbed my free arm. He twisted to put himself between me and the shape of certain death.

Surprise zinged through me, too fast to leave more than a taste. And fear—fear roared like the rush of blood in my ears.

Doogie had a hold of me. Sunday, too. They would not let go.

The three of us fell together fast, but it seemed slow, as if we fell through molasses.

Darkness filled my sight—not the nothing and nowhere of unconsciousness, but a shape that passed through the steel door that had sheltered us—darkness in the shape of a man. Stars shone inside the black velvet maw of his body, their light barely bright, as if whatever he was tried to eat that, too.

He'd stepped through the door and the steel where he'd touched it was just—gone.

He eats.

He'd do that to us. He'd make us gone, vanished without a trace.

Doogie hit the floor behind me, breaking my fall. Then cold, cold darkness finally did reach up to swallow me.

The last coherent thought that fluttered across my mind was a prayer for flight. Then I knew nothing. Not where or when we were. Not whether we lived or died.

A sound rushed toward me like a speeding train, running me over and leaving me flattened in its wake. It crashed over me again and again until the sound began to take shape, and the shape became my name.

"Charlie," Sunday said, in the calmest, clearest voice that reminded me of bells.

What a weird thing to think on waking.

Waking.

I was alive. We were alive.

I opened my eyes. For a second, I couldn't see anything except gray, and fear wrapped itself around my heart. What if Sunday had blinded me by accident? What if—

"Charlie," she said again.

The gray resolved itself into more shapes: Sunday's ice-blue eyes, the curve of her cheek, the curl of her blond hair. She knelt over me, her hair like a curtain all around me. Her cheeks were flushed.

My words came out more like a croak. "Did I do it?"

"Yeah," she said.

Thank God. "Doogie?"

"He's fine."

But he wasn't kneeling over me like she was, and I didn't hear him throwing insults at me either. "Where?"

"He's sitting on a bench not five feet away."

Something about the way she said that made me furrow my brow. "Why?"

"The assassin got a hand on him."

I tried to sit up. Sunday pressed her hand against my chest and used her weight to hold me down. She kept her voice low. "There's things you need to know. Like the assassin—he could've followed us here."

The scent of frying burgers and onion rings perfumed the air. I tasted them when I opened my mouth to copy Sunday's whisper. "Did he? Follow us?"

She glanced up and to the right, as if listening or looking for something I couldn't see or hear. "I don't sense him."

"So the answer's no," I said.

"He could still follow us."

"He's not here now," I said. "We are."

She shook her head. Water filled her eyes. She blinked back the tears that wanted to fall.

She was worried about me. About us. I wasn't just someone who happened to be convenient in a fight. I held her gaze until I could no longer handle the dawning wonder I saw on her face.

"Move, Sunday." I placed my hand over hers. "Now."

She studied my face. Then she pulled her hand back and rose, reaching down to help me up. I let her.

It was a simple thing, my hand in hers. And it wasn't so simple. Another electric shock sparked through us both. She squeezed my hand and then let it go.

We stood on asphalt, near the back of a parking lot behind a greasy spoon with faded, red brick walls. The back door was shut tight against the cold and the big, back windows were papered over. Busy shadows moved behind the paper. Cooks, from the frantic look of their silhouettes.

A trash bin crouched in the far corner, staring at us, its black rubber top like an eyelid. A chain link fence emerged from behind it to run the length of the lot, dandelions standing guard at its feet. Doogie sat with his back to the fence, hands curled around his knees, rocking back and forth. The squeak of the chain link made me want to crawl out of my skin.

He looked…wrong.

I took a deep breath and blew it out slow. "You get in the boss's way?"

He glanced at me through his lashes. "Never been a boss like that one."

"What'd he do to you?" I asked.

Doogie motioned with a tip of his head for me to come closer. He shifted his weight as I walked over, my shoes scuffing the black-top. He turned all the way around so that I could see his back.

There was a hole between the widest part of the upside-down V his shoulder blades formed. The hole went halfway to his chest. Everything the assassin had touched was gone. Doogie's shirt. His skin. And probably a rib or two, along with part of his heart and lungs. In their place, black velvet darkness and the pinpoint lights that looked like stars.

My mouth fell open.

His voice shook. "How am I still alive?"

"I don't know." I didn't know what else to say.

He frowned. "Your three favorite words, Charlie. I hate you."

It made no sense to believe he'd be fine. How could he be? But hating me was what Doogie did. It was normal. "Good to know you haven't lost your sense of humor."

"I should've pushed you off the roof, Charlie."

"Back atcha," I said.

Sunday snapped her fingers to get our attention. "Anyone hungry?"

Unbelievably, I was. I just didn't have two pennies to rub together.

"I'm buying." Sunday shrugged out of her coat and handed it to Doogie. "Wear that—we shouldn't draw attention."

Doogie laughed. It was nervous and almost hysterical, but it was a laugh all the same.

We walked around to the front of the greasy spoon. No traffic on the street at this hour, but a handful of people sat in red vinyl booths on the other side of the windows, eating messy, juicy burgers and washing them down with milkshakes or coffee. They looked good. They looked normal.

Sunday dug five quarters from her front pocket and shoved them into the slot in the glass-front, blue box by the front door and pulled out a newspaper.

A dollar twenty-five. For a newspaper. "That's a fortune," I said.

"Not anymore." She checked the date in the upper right corner and froze.

"What?" I asked.

"Nothing." She folded the paper under her arm and led the way inside.

Warmth from the heaters washed over us. The smell of meat and grease and onions made my mouth water.

Photographs of the city in brilliant color hung on the walls. The black-and-white check floors gleamed. A stick-thin waitress with red hair shorter than Doogie's and my dad's hurried past, balancing enough food for an army on a single, brown tray. She carried the tray stand in her other hand like the potential weapon it was.

She didn't so much as look at us, but she spoke from the corner of her mouth. "Be right with ya."

It was as close to heaven as I'd ever felt.

I ate like my stomach had never contained a roast beef sandwich. The whole time, Sunday watched me like she had something to say, but she never uttered a word—none of us did—not until Doogie went to the bathroom.

We watched him walk away until he vanished from sight. The waitress came and silently dropped off a slip of paper, which I took to be the bill, and scooped up a handful of our dirty dishes.

Sunday wiped her mouth with the last remaining white paper napkin and crumpled it in her fist, setting her elbows on the table. "You took us back a year," she said. "That's good control."

"I wasn't trying to focus. I was trying not to die," I said.

"Well, still."

I thought about the way she froze when she saw the date. "What's bad that happened in 2002?"

She threw the napkin onto the tabletop and considered her answer. "My parents kicked me out."

I knew that feeling in my bones. It was part of who I was. "You're like me."

"I guess I am," she said.

I had questions. A lot of questions. But since I didn't know how to ask them, I held my tongue.

She cleared her throat. "You could stay here."

I wanted nothing more. I didn't want to go back to my own time. My own shitty life. If I stayed here with Sunday, we would have each other. We would both have someone who cared whether we lived or died.

But this wasn't just about her and me.

"Doogie has to go back," I said. "Our dad will miss him."

She caught my drift. She leaned back in her seat. "You sure? You want to ask him when he gets back?"

"I know him pretty well," I said. "I know what he'll say."

"He's an asshole," she said.

No denying it. "Yep."

"You'll take him back to your time. You can leave him and come back here. Can't you?" The wonder had returned to her face.

"What?" I asked.

She glanced down at the table before looking up again to meet my gaze. "I never cared about anybody before. I don't want you to go."

I blinked at her. "No one's ever said anything like that to me before."

"It's a selfish thing to say."

I shook my head. "No. It's perfect."

"Only because you don't know what it might cost you," she said.

I started to ask her what she meant by that, but then Doogie's shadow loomed over the table. "What'd I miss?"

Sunday sighed. "Time to go home."

One look at Doogie's face told me he needed to go home like a dying man needed a priest. Sunday saw it, too.

She walked us out and back to the parking lot, which seemed like as good a place as any to work the bit of magic that would take Doogie and me back where we'd come from. The air tasted less like grease and more like sunrise. My full belly sloshed as I walked—courtesy of the world's largest strawberry milkshake. A breeze kicked up, lifting the hair from the nape of my neck and dropping straight down the back of my shirt.

Sunday moved to stand in front of me. She took my hands in hers. "You understand what you are, don't you?"

I shook my head. "I don't understand anything about any of this."

"You can fly. You can enter the future or the past. You can learn secrets. You can know things other people will never know."

"What—I'm the world's most clueless and dangerous fortune teller? You want me to tell you your fortune?"

She had powers that others would kill to possess. Also, she had an immense gift for pugilism—I could tell already.

"You are that," she said. "Kinda clueless, kinda dangerous. And it's killing you."

She wasn't joking. Her eyes were serious.

I thought about the feeling that I'd died and come back. That part of me remained dead. If I kept doing the flying, one day I might not come back.

I'd never asked for this, not for any of it. What was I supposed to do with it?

"What makes us what we are?" I asked.

"The Devil," she said.

I could believe that if we were talking about me, or if we were talking about Doogie. But no power of evil had made Sunday, in spite of what she could do with her eyes.

"Maybe the other one," I said. Maybe God.

She wrapped her arms around me. After an awkward minute, I hugged her, too. This close, she smelled like vanilla and coffee. I breathed in her scent. I memorized it until she let me go.

"All right," she said. "Let's make it happen."

Doogie started to take off Sunday's coat. "You want this back?"

She shook her head. "Keep it. You need it more."

"Can you get a new one?" he asked.

"Don't worry about me," she said to both of us.

But I did. I did worry.

Doogie grabbed my arm. He held on for dear life.

I put on my best, bravest face. "You gonna hit me again?" I asked Sunday.

She grinned, but the smile didn't touch her sad eyes. She punched me so hard and so fast, I barely had time to see it coming.

When I came too again, Doogie was hunkered down beside me, watching me for signs of consciousness. He helped me up and held me steady while my legs decided whether they planned to hold me on their own.

The rooftop looked exactly like it had when we'd left it, except that the new guy was nowhere to be seen. The moon hung huge and bright in the night sky, though pink and gold stained the horizon, as if the sunrise had followed us from the future.

I took a deep breath of tar and darkness, letting the stink settle me, letting it tell my body as much as it told my mind where and when I was.

"We should check to see you got us back to the right time," Doogie said.

I nodded. "Go downstairs and see."

"You should come with," he said.

"I'm tired." I'd never felt more tired in my life. I had no idea what the new day would bring, only that I'd never be the same.

"I don't know what to tell my dad about what happened," Doogie said.

"You think I do?"

Whatever the reason, it would be my fault. It was always my fault.

"Maybe I won't say anything," he said. "I just don't want to do it —or not do it—by myself. Not anymore."

I studied his face. His clear eyes. The determined set of his mouth. He wasn't lying. The thread of surprise in his voice testified to it, too.

"You still hate me, right?" I asked.

"I'll hate you every day," he said.

Okay. "What are we gonna do about Dad? I mean, where I'm concerned."

"We can figure it out, Charlie."

What would it be like not to be Nobody anymore? One more thing I didn't know, but I desperately wanted to find out. I didn't trust Doogie as far as I could throw him, but he'd saved my life and Sunday's. I'd never in a million years figured Doogie for a good guy.

Maybe he wasn't. Maybe he'd be less of an asshole from here on out.

I had no idea what the future could bring, but I had the ability to find out. Maybe I'd even be able to get back to Sunday someday, even knowing that if I tried, it might kill me. But then what was life about? We were all dying, a little more every day. Maybe that didn't matter as much as how we lived.

We'd figure it out. We had the power.

We carried the moon inside of us. We carried the magic.

ABOUT THE AUTHOR

Since the age of seven, Leslie Claire Walker has wanted to be Princess Leia—wise and brave and never afraid of a fight, no matter the odds.

Leslie hails from the concrete and steel canyons and lush bayous of southeast Texas—a long way from Alderaan. Now, she lives in the rain-drenched Pacific Northwest with a cast of spectacular characters, including cats, harps, fantastic pieces of art that may or may not be doorways to other realms, and too many fantasy novels to count.

She is the author of the *Awakened Magic Saga*, a collected series of urban fantasy novels, novellas, and stories filled with magical assassins, fallen angels, faeries, demons, and complex, heroic humans. The primary series in the saga are the *Soul Forge*, set in Portland, Oregon, and the *Faery Chronicles*, set in Houston Texas. She has also authored stories for *The Uncollected Anthology* on a mission to redefine the boundaries of contemporary and urban fantasy.

Leslie takes her inspiration from the dark beauty of the city, the power of myth, strong coffee, whisky, and music ranging from Celtic harp to jazz to heavy metal. Rock on!

Find out more about Leslie at:
leslieclairewalker.com

WITCHES OF COLOGNE

SHARON KAE REAMER

THE SUN HAD shone hot that afternoon, just like today. Gwen slid her fingers across the dry skin on her face. The rough patches on her arms were open sores from lack of bathing and vermin. Those unseen creatures ate her skin when she slept, curled up on the pale and damp and dirty pile of straw in the farthest corner of the dark room that stank of prisoners come and gone. She smiled as she recalled that day of sunshine and the time she had spent as a foolish girl before she made the choice that she could never undo, the choice that had aged her instantly and irrevocably.

GWEN'S TEETH ground together while she fought to steer the wagon clear of the deepest ruts along the track. She still couldn't glimpse the Cologne city walls. The sun burned through thick clouds, warming her face, although her nose told her the air still carried a fair bit of moisture.

She stared at her uncle who, oblivious to her labors, sang a cheerful hymn in their ancient dialect, a sullied mix of French and Breton. After a hard pull on the mule's reins, the worn leather rasping against her calluses, she pushed out the words, needing to ask her question one more time.

"But why is it so hard to make a bargain with the Raven Queen? Can't it be worded...very carefully? Worded to avoid trouble or a wrong result?"

Uncle Aemil cut off his song and placed his broad callused hands across his knees. It was the pose he always used to lecture her. "Who is easiest to cheat?"

Gwen sat straighter, holding the reins loosely. "The church elite."

Uncle Aemil chuckled. "Depends on who's doing the swindling. Go on," he said with a wave of his hand.

"Then there's the Jews. They're not easy at all. Except for Faigel. She trusts me because she's my friend. Then there's foreigners. They're the easiest, I'd guess, until they've been in the city for a while."

"You've forgotten the most easiest-easiest," he said, his broad infectious smile breaking out as he ran a hand through his thick blonde hair.

She shook her head and shrugged.

Uncle Aemil pointed at her. "The cheater."

She laid a hand on his. "But if the person is aware they can be tricked?"

His voice softened. "I'm just warning you, lass. What is it you want from her? Nothing good can come of it."

NONE OF THE SORES, a product of the lack of cleanliness in their dank prison cell, were indicative of the Great Death, not that it would matter now. Faigel stared at the pitted and scarred stone wall in front of her, as if she could make it disappear with her gaze. Gwen stepped down from the three-legged stool she had tilted against the wall to watch the progress of the townsfolk building and shaping the wood into rough pyramids for the bonefire.

The flurry of activity and buzz of conversation and laughter made Gwen feel oddly comfortable, as if she were to take part in a huge pageantry, until terror seized her insides again. Her empty stomach tried to disgorge. She stepped down and bent over double to keep from retching, bile burning her throat.

She took a deep breath and stood, brushing tendrils of dingy gray hair from her face. It was time. Faigel needed to know, to understand the truth. Despite everything that had happened, her friend deserved to hear it. And she needed to hear it now because there would be no tomorrow for Gwen to ponder, no other time left to them. Gwen sighed out before speaking. "Uncle Aemil was my mother's brother."

Faigel scratched at her nose. "He was a charming man, your uncle, both in looks and word. Why didn't he marry?"

Gwen shrugged. "Made a promise to my mother, to look after me. He took it seriously." She settled the stool against the wall and sank onto it. "He warned me not to make a deal with her."

"Seems like ages ago," Faigel said. "And yet, as if we were just girls, just yesterday."

"We…" Banging her head on the wall didn't do anything to relieve Gwen's frustration. She began again. "Do you remember anything in between that day and today?"

Faigel rubbed her palms on her plain wool dress, pushed herself upwards. Gwen heard her bones creak. "I should have memories… of my life…of Cologne." She paced. "We're not young girls anymore."

The truth was not one Gwen wanted to force on Faigel. But she couldn't give up, at least not before she heard and smelled the flames. But then, Gwen had to face her own truth…couldn't she just…go away, escape to Ande-dubnos, to the Otherworld? She could. She'd have to leave Faigel, the silly cow. Why—and how—had Faigel followed her that day? Everything would have been so different.

"Why didn't you just stay home?" Gwen asked in a heavy whisper.

"I was afraid. I thought you were going to do something stupid." Faigel brushed her hands down her dress again. "It was the least I could do."

Gwen leaned forward. "I *was* going to do something stupid, but that didn't mean you had to reap my folly."

"Doesn't matter now. Are they done building it?" Faigel stood on her tiptoes, but the top of her head didn't even reach to the windowsill.

"No. Well, maybe it does matter. Do you believe in your God?"

Faigel turned quickly, pressing her back against the wall. "Gwenifree, how can you ask that?"

"That's what they're burning us for—consorting with the Devil and bringing down the Great Death on the city—doesn't matter if you're a Jew or just an everyday sort of pagan as I am. As if Cologne wasn't rife with wickedness without any help from us."

"But why? Why did Henri denounce us?"

"Because he recognized us. Maybe he used that iron-tipped whip one too many times. I don't know. And since Gwen and Faigel, the *girls*, disappeared, replaced by Gwen and Faigel, the *hags*, they think we sacrificed—or hexed—the younger versions of ourselves. Not at all incorrect."

Gwen's memories intruded again. She couldn't help but picture the Raven Queen's face, so vibrant and beautiful, as she had looked that day. Cathubodua's dark hair and fair skin had made Gwen blush. So intent was she on her quest to save Henri, she hadn't seen the flaw in her plan: Faigel.

"You remember how he looked—that first public display they made after he joined the Brothers of the Cross, half naked in the square?" Faigel asked.

She was remembering. Good. Gwen would tell her—continue to tell her—and so wouldn't have to take the guilt of an ignorant Faigel with her. If Gwen escaped the flames, guilt would remain that she'd abandoned her friend; it would be an additional dark smudge, perhaps, to be left behind.

"He had magnificent smooth skin, until the lesions showed up." She brushed her fingers along her aged skin, no longer smooth. "Neither of us could have won him," Gwen said, trying to laugh, but it came out as a cackle. "Look at us. We really do look like witches now. My uncle was right."

The deal Gwen had forged with the Raven Queen had been sealed in Gwen's own blood, and she could still feel the pain of the sword entering her heart. Her youth, her health in exchange for Henri's healing. She loved him more than her own life, although she hadn't told anyone but Faigel that.

It had been easy to confess to Faigel. Besides friendship, they had little in common except for their devotion to Henri, a man in turn devoted to his God and willing to forsake all earthly pleasures for it. That made Faigel and Gwen pine for Henri even more.

When the Great Death struck Cologne, neither girl contracted the illness. Henri was not so lucky. As the sickness swept through the city, they feared for him more each day. The vow he took with the

Brothers of the Cross forbade him to speak to women, but he'd known Gwen and Faigel since they were girls, and truth be told, they weren't much beyond that.

Henri had worked for Maria, the goldsmith near the Jewish quarter where Faigel lived, before joining the Brothers. Uncle Aemil had often done business near there, at the small marketplace near the ruins of the Praetorium just off the Haymarket, once a week, peddling whatever he'd been able to acquire. The three of them had come together. A friendship formed of opportunity and tolerance. It had been tolerated for a time until Henri took up his calling. But they still saw him. Gwen and Faigel remained devoted to Henri; his being the missing third in their threesome only intensified their feelings.

He met them by the river's edge that day, its bland grayness hiding the swiftness of its progress northward and contrasting with the bright blue of the spring sky. His tear-streaked face covered in bruises and cuts from the whip, his skin encrusted with the filth of not bathing; he stank heavily. He confessed to them his unworthiness. Why else would his God have struck him with the illness?

Gwen made her decision to bargain with Cathubodua, but was unsure because of what her uncle had said, that bargains made with the Raven Queen never turned out well. But when Uncle Aemil contracted the disease, his death coming a mere week afterwards, Gwen knew. It was the only way to save Henri.

"Why did you ask me about my God?" Faigel's voice pleaded.

"Maybe the burning won't be much worse than those night sweats." Gwen folded her hands in front of her. "Awful. I'm so awful hot all the time."

Faigel crossed her arms. Her girlish pout looked comical on her not-so-girlish face.

"It's because I am a witch, Faigel. A real honest one. Why do you think I could have Henri healed?"

Faigel shook her head. "It was her—that dark lady. She is...a demon."

"No, she's...one of my Gods, Faigel, even though I don't believe in her quite that way. It's what she is."

Faigel clapped a hand over her mouth. "You can't mean that."

"It's an old religion, far older than the Christians, a religion with many faces and many ways. Some believe because they want to, and some of us believe because we *have* to."

"But she did help Henri," Faigel said.

"And she cursed us—that was the price—our youth for Henri. Think back, Faigel, and you'll see the truth of it."

Faigel slumped to the floor and held her head in both hands. "You can see your Gods? Are they all beautiful demons?"

"Not all of them. I've seen Death before. He's taken everyone dear to me. He's ghastly. He'll be there to take me—from earthly bonefire to the Eternal Flame. Will your God be there for you?"

As they were led to the pyres, Gwen saw others. More Jews, a few beggars and a couple of Roma were to be sacrificed to the Christian God today. Each was tied to a central stake to keep them from escaping the fire. The August sun beat on Gwen's face, the rough wood hard on her back through the scanty covering. She wished she could have a cup of cool sweet wine to slake her thirst.

The priests motioned. The crowd grew momentarily silent. Even the birds had stopped. Gwen felt her breath go in and out and wished she could hold time still. Just a few moments more. Soon the flames licked the bottom of the dry wood.

Gwen hadn't wanted to give up her youth. She hadn't wanted to give up her chance at winning Henri. And she hadn't wanted to see Henri die horribly, not like Uncle Aemil. Most of all, she hadn't wanted to see her beautiful friend Faigel share her fate. She hadn't wanted this. The realization came to her, late but not too late. She and Faigel were true friends; they had remained friends *despite* Henri.

GWEN HID herself in a dark cloak as she tread the boards that took her over the bridge across the Rhine that morning, before the first light of day swept the city.

Once over the ancient creaking bridge she swept through the rowans to the glade, using paths her uncle had shown her. She hurried through the deep forest, her legs aching from her trek, and fell to her knees. A few minutes of deep mediation and she crossed into the Otherworld which her family called Ande-dubnos, from the ancient language of her ancestors. She was going to meet one of its equally ancient denizens, one of the gods once revered by her people.

After lowering her head and speaking the summons, again in the ancient Breton dialect, nothing happened. Not at first. But then a wan light grew, darkness crowned in a sickly moonlight. Cathu-bodua appeared. Not there and then there, framed within a leaden dark cloud. This *was* the Otherworld, where the power of shadow ruled.

Gwen had expected something more, scarier or louder maybe, but the Queen of Darkness's visage was scary enough. Cathubodua embodied everything her uncle had warned her about. Terrifying dark-haired beauty, and a will forged in iron and blood. This was no fairy queen, but a goddess who promised vengeance, and demanded everything in return.

She was flanked by her servants the crows, each one almost as big as Gwen and blacker than the pre-dawn darkness. Ragged beaks shone reddish gold in the dimness of the forest. Their black crow orbs were fixed on her, hungry and intelligent. Her uncle said the crows could turn themselves into men when they wanted to. The thought made Gwen shiver.

Forcing her lips to part, Gwen told her tale and after only a moment's hesitation, took the oath that would grant her deepest desire. Henri should live. He *must* live.

At the time, Gwen did not think the cost too great. Her uncle was no longer alive to tell her any differently.

After Cathubodua's sword pierced her heart, Gwen stumbled upright to await the metamorphosis from girl to crone—her price for the bargain—for the craft that would heal Henri.

Faigel burst from the trees, her chest heaving, and said, "Take me, too! She will not have him for herself!"

Gwen knew then that she'd been the one cheated. The taunting look in the Raven Queen's eyes confirmed the sin Gwen had committed. The sin of loving Henri too much. And of loving Faigel, too, of wanting to spare her a similar fate.

THE CROWD HAD SWELLED in the time it took them to finish raising the mound of wood. The pile of branches, both great and small, formed a low wall around the two women. For a moment, Gwen and Faigel were at peace, standing alone on an island of logs in the middle of the pile. Separate from the boisterous, chanting crowd, intent on their revelry. The burning itself was merely a culmination of the festivities.

There was a single truth in death, in the moments before. It freed the soul to be as it should be. Not young, not old, perfect in every way.

But that was before they lit the fire. It felt good at first, warmth that they hadn't had in days spent in a damp, mildewed room of putrid stone. Old bones needed heat. And her and Faigel's bones were old. Gwen had never felt more ancient. But the feeling wouldn't last for long.

She reached an arm towards Faigel, and the bonds fell away from the other woman's wrists. Gwen grabbed her friend's hand. She tried to breathe deeply but couldn't, her throat scorched with thirst. Soon it would just be scorched. Her mind fought the reek of evil, willed it away, willed all the badness away. She had always been good at doing that, Uncle Aemil had once told her.

Now was the time to call on Ankou to take her away. She could summon him here in the waking world as she had summoned Cathubodua in Ande-dubnos. The Lord of Death knew no boundaries save those he erected. Gwen could give the crowd the show they deserved. Confirm their worst fears. Once a *Hexe*, always a *Hexe. Catch me if you can.*

Faigel smiled over at her, a small brave smile, her face lit with sorrow. "I remember now, Gwenifree, and I'm sorry. But I am also glad, in a way, that you...that we are not alone." She lowered her head and whispered, "Henri wouldn't have deserved you."

The crowd roared in the way they always did, glad that others were suffering more than they were. But it all faded. Everything except the bright blue sky, as clear as the sky that day by the river. Faigel's small, sweaty, wrinkled hand shook.

Just a few eternally painful minutes remained.

The *other* truth, the deeper one she'd tried to deny, forced its way upward. There was no one she could trust in the Otherworld. And even if there was, she couldn't leave her friend to die alone.

Gwen stared out at the faces through a haze of smoke and falling ash. She caught a glimpse of Henri. Or had she imagined it? Was Henri's face streaked with tears?

She turned her head, unwilling to look at Henri, if it really was him at all. Gwen held tight onto Faigel's hand and chanted in the old tongue. A balm to take her friend to Death's door with the least amount of pain and suffering.

Instead of leaving Faigel to take her place with Ankou, Gwen would share her friend's fate and die in the waking world. It was the least she could do.

ABOUT THE AUTHOR

Now a full-time writer living near Cologne, Sharon Kae Reamer's speculative fiction is inspired by her participation in various archeo-seismology projects during her twenty-something years as a senior scientist at the University of Cologne. Locations that include the Praetorium and medieval Jewish settlement in Cologne, ancient Tiryns in Greece, and Greek ruins in Selinunte, Sicily, provide perfect backdrops for creating fantasy stories rich with history and mythology, such as her *Immortal Guardian* and *Schattenreich Mystery* novelette series and her five-book *Schattenreich* novel series.

Her love for mixing and mashing science fiction and fantasy continues unabated. *Night Shepherd*, in the *Schattenreich* universe is a spinoff (one of many) of her soon-to-be-published first novel in *The Sundered Veil* series, a further conception of science fantasy.

Sharon still pursues archeoseismology projects. She also cooks daily (German-English), gardens (chaotically, at best), knits (badly), does needlepoint (rather well) and reads (everything) all the damn time.

And, of course, she has cats.

Find out more about Sharon at:
sharonreamer.com

twitter.com/sharonkae
bookbub.com/authors/sharon-kae-reamer
amazon.com/Sharon-Kae-Reamer/e/B008J1Z0A2

TRAVIS ALAMO BOONE - WITCHHUNTER

STEVE VERNON

THE YEAR on the calendar in the eye doctor's waiting room said 2020, which I thought was kind of funny, given that was exactly what the eye doctor had told me a pair of glasses would give me.

"The right pair of glasses will give 20-20 vision," he'd said the first time I saw him. "I just need to give you a few more tests before we settle on a prescription."

My name is Travis Alamo Boone and I was twelve years old. I was there in that office because of the funny way I look at things. I can't really explain it to you, but it's like the world looks a little different to me than it does to ordinary people. I kind of see colors in between the lines this world has drawn around what is, and what ought to be. For example, I've got a dog named Rudy. Now if you were to look at Rudy you would see a mud-colored, tangle-furred, no-account mutt. But when I look at Rudy I see an eagle getting ready to fly, with golden wings and a shrieking beak. And I know what I see is the real honest truth of it, because I have seen Rudy chase a rabbit and catch it just as easily as you or I could pick up our toothbrush and give our teeth a gentle morning scrubbing.

Not that I had much use for teeth those days. Like I said, the year on the calendar said 2020, which meant everyone in the waiting room wore a mask over their faces—which made it hard to see their teeth, so you could get away with brushing your teeth once a month or so, and nobody would even notice. I mean, it wasn't as if anybody was going to get close enough to your face those days to smell your breath. Still, my Momma made it a point to have me brush my teeth at least three times a day—once after breakfast, once after lunchtime, and once after supper—whether they need brushing or not.

My Momma reminded me about a lot of things.

"Sit up straight, Travis," Momma reminded me. "You'll crook your spine until you look like a question mark if you sit like that for too darned long."

That was my Momma sitting beside me in one of those waiting room chairs; only she was about six feet away because that is how everybody was supposed to be those days until that Covid stuff went away. That Covid stuff had sure changed the way the world worked.

It's funny how something that you can't really see can change so very much so very quickly.

My Momma had her face buried in one of her housekeeping magazines, so I don't even know how she noticed that I was slouching like I was. I guess it was just the way Momma could use her eyes without even looking, like she had some kind of built-in radar where I was concerned. She brought the magazine with her to look at while we waited, on account of doctor's offices weren't allowed to have magazines laying around for you to look at anymore. So Momma made it a point to bring along a magazine from our home.

Momma likes to be prepared.

It was always a housekeeping magazine showing how some people like to dress up their living room, or bathroom, or their kitchen or dining room. I didn't really see the point in Momma looking at all of those housekeeping magazines like she does. Staring at all of those pictures and reading those words like they were magical gifts from heaven. I tried looking at the pictures and reading some of the words, but I was pretty sure they were nothing more than a bunch of stupid lies.

Oh sure, those words and pictures told you how all of fancy furniture and appliances were made out of space age modern materials all guaranteed not to fade or crack or wear out, but sooner or later if you breathed too hard, or just looked at them the wrong way, or if you even caught yourself thinking too many bad thoughts about those pieces of fancy furniture or appliances, then they would snap like a frozen frost-bit twig in a tree. So the way I saw things, I figure those pictures and words in my Mom's magazines were nothing more than a bunch of lies wrapped up in fancy wrapping paper.

I once told Momma my theory about her lying housekeeping magazines, and all Momma said back to me was, "Travis Alamo Boone—I'll bet you a shiny silver dollar if you keep on talking like you are talking to your Momma, a great big old darning needle dragonfly is going to fly straight through our kitchen window and stitch your lips up tighter than a rusty glued-on pickle jar lid."

I didn't take her up on her bet about darning needle justice. I just shut my mouth, because it seemed a whole lot safer by my way of thinking. My Momma never made a bet if she knew she might lose it, and I wasn't about to take a chance on her being wrong this time.

In any case, I never brought along anything much with me to read or look at, even if I knew I was going to be sitting for a while. I like a good comic book, but I did not want to run the risk of bringing a comic book to a doctor's office where somebody might cough on it or sneeze really hard, and then my Momma would most likely make me throw my comic book away just because you never could tell those days.

"There is a dangerous virus out there," Momma told me. "It can walk through walls and appear out of nowhere, and believe you me —it can kill a young boy like you quicker than a rat running down a hangman's rope."

"What's that virus look like, Momma?" I'd ask her, looking around like I had lost something important. "I don't see it anywhere."

"I can't rightly say what it looks like," Momma answered. "Danger always catches you when you don't expect to see it coming. I can tell you one thing for certain sure. It is a sneaky kind of virus, and it will hide on things you never think of worrying about. You might find it hiding on a door knob, or on a friend's good morning, or even on the keys of a cellphone. That virus hides in the same way evil hides where you don't expect. You might think a person you know is just as good as good can be—but you can't see inside of them— at least not with the eyes you wear on your face. The eyes you need to use are hidden deep inside of your soul."

My Momma could say an awful lot when the mood struck her, but other times she was as quiet as a mouse peeing on a bed of cotton—especially when she was reading one of her housekeeping magazines. So I just sat there on my doctor's office waiting chair that was supposed to be comfortable, but that was just another lie too, staring at the people sitting in the other office waiting chairs.

"I declare, Travis," Momma went on, flipping a page to read

another lie. "I don't know what is going to become of you. Do you have any idea what you want to do with your life?"

I didn't, to tell the truth. My future looked to me like a dark old road, but I was only twelve and I figured had years to go before I needed any sort of a compass bead on things, so I let Momma go back to her magazine dreaming and I got back to looking at other people, which wasn't any hardship. People-watching is something I have always enjoyed doing. People can teach you things about how they are inside themselves, and how the world works, and how people really are instead of what they look like on their outside.

Only I tried not to look like I was staring at the other people in the waiting room because that would be rude of me, so I had taught myself a long time before how to sort of sideways glimpse at other people and what they were doing and saying. You can learn an awful lot just by looking at other people when they didn't think you were really looking at them.

For example—there was a woman who probably weighed close to three hundred pounds, and I knew that because my Daddy raised sheep on our farm and he always needed to weigh them, and I helped him whenever I could by writing the weight numbers down as he called them out. Daddy had my kind of eyes too in that he could look at a sheep and say something like "That one weighs about 170 pounds. She's nearly fully grown."

Of course, he still weighed them on his big old set of barn scales, although he could also come pretty close to making a guess at any given sheep's actual weight with his old cloth measuring tape. He'd measure the sheep around, and measure how long it was from nose to tail, and how high it stood, and by tallying them out inside of his imagination he could come pretty close to what it actually said on the barn scales. So I guess what I am trying to tell you are that there are an awful lot of ways to look at a sheep and tell what it was made out of, just the same as you could tell what people were like inside of themselves if you looked hard enough long enough.

Like that woman over there who probably weighed close to three hundred pounds. She was peeking the corner of her mask down whenever she thought nobody was watching her gnaw on her fingernails, paying particular attention to one particular fingernail. I kind of had the feeling that she had eaten herself a big old chocolate bar right before she walked into this eye doctor's waiting room, and she had maybe found a little bit of chocolate still tucked beneath that fingernail like a memory that she just did not want to forget. On top of that, she was shifting her eyes whenever she bit into her fingernail, like she really wished chocolate bars hadn't ever been invented, and for the life of me I could not figure out why a person would feel that way because as far as I was concerned, chocolate bars were some of the best inventions on the planet.

So I stopped looking at her nail chewing, and I looked at that little boy, about three years old, who was playing with a few building blocks his mother had brought along with her. Two of them were putting together something that looked like it might either have been a carrot or a rocket ship.

A part of me thought it might have been fun to sit down and build that carrot rocket ship right along with them, but that little boy looked about three years old and I was twelve, and I was way too grown up to be playing with carrots, building blocks or rocket ships —and besides, it would have been rude of me to try and join in what with it being 2020 and that invisible Covid evil virus going around like it was. Still, those building blocks looked awfully fun, and I had to remind myself two or three times I was way too old and grown up to be messing with such things no matter how hard my imagination tried to tell me differently.

So I looked once more around the room, and that was when I saw the witch.

Now, you understand she wasn't there when I looked before. I'll swear she wasn't. I don't know where she came from. There wasn't a door behind her for her to have entered through. I sure don't think that she was hiding beneath her chair. It's just one moment she wasn't there, and when I looked again, there she was.

So how did I know she was a witch?

Well, I didn't know she was a witch at first.

I mean, she wasn't wearing one of those tall, floppy-brimmed, ice cream cone pointed black hats. She wasn't carrying a broom, and there wasn't a big old black cat curled up on her left shoulder blade. She wasn't wearing knee-high striped stockings, or spiky laced-up stiletto boots. She had a big old black handbag, but I was pretty sure she wasn't carrying a crystal ball or a Ouija board in it— and I didn't see a cauldron anywhere in sight. But I knew right away she was a witch.

The first thing I noticed about her was her long, jet-black hair that somehow looked as if she had combed her hair this morning with a corn broom dipped into a barrel of white flour. My Daddy's hair looked a bit like that, and my Momma always called it salt-and-pepper, except for the times she said it was just my Daddy's skunk blood coming out through his hairline—only the witch's hair looked more like an unexpected snowstorm blowing across a black asphalt highway.

Only it wasn't her hair that really caught my eye. It was her left eye, or rather her lack of it. She wore a dark black eyepatch over her left eye, just like a pirate might wear. She was wearing a mask over her mouth and nose too, just like everyone else in the eye doctor's waiting room, but her mask was solid black, darker than I had ever seen. It looked to me like the whole lower part of her face was painted with nothing but a bucketful of inky starless midnight sky.

"Momma," I asked quietly. "Did you see where that one-eyed woman came from?"

Only Momma didn't answer.

I looked up to see what was wrong.

Momma wasn't moving. In fact, I wasn't sure if Momma was even breathing. She just sat there in that eye doctor's waiting room chair like she had turned into some kind of Momma-shaped department store mannequin, sitting there and staring and not moving a single tiny bit. She looked to me like she had been frozen into some kind of a permanent no-melt ice statue.

I looked around, and it seemed to me as if everyone else in that eye doctor's waiting room were all playing that frozen statue game as well. The three-hundred-pound woman, and the carrot-rocket-building mother and her little boy. The lady at the desk hiding behind the Plexiglas shield while staring at a computer screen. I couldn't see him, but I wondered if the eye doctor was a statue too. And maybe the people outside on the sidewalk and the streets of our city. Maybe the whole big round world was all stuck frozen fast, playing statue.

For a moment I thought maybe that sneaky virus had crept onto the whole waiting room when nobody was looking, but then I realized I wasn't the only person who hadn't been frozen.

In fact, as far as I could tell the only two people who still could move in the waiting room were me and that one-eyed, creepy-looking witch lady.

"I see you, boy," the witch lady said, in a voice that sounded like a roll of tangled-up barbed wire being dragged along a long gravel road. "You've got something I want, and I can see it, too."

As she spoke, I could see her mouth moving beneath that midnight black virus-mask she was wearing. It was like watching a cartoon mouth laughing on a black television screen. I could see her long sharp teeth, picket-fencing like the teeth in a giant shark movie.

"Who are you?" I asked, trying to avoid the obvious question of: just what the heck could you possibly want that belonged to me, you creepy old lady.

"Who? Who? Now you are thinking you're a hoot owl, boy," the witch lady said. "But if it is my name you are wanting, well, you can call me Bracken. That's not my true name, you understand. True names are power, and a witch won't go very far giving away her power to any Tom, Dick, or Travis."

My eyes widened. How did she know my name was Travis? And then I remembered that Momma had called me by that name just a couple of minutes before I saw the witch. Maybe that old witch woman had been listening, maybe she heard my Momma use my name.

Only that wasn't it.

"Travis Alamo Boone," the witch lady said, rolling my name off of her tongue as if the name my family had given me was made out of freshly-tapped maple syrup. "Now, there is a name to conjure with. Your parents must have really hated you, hanging a name like that around your neck."

She stared at me, and as she stared I swear I could see her eyepatch staring straight at me. It had been black at first, but now it looked as if it were made out of a thousand-thousand tiny little eyes staring right at me, their eye dots gleaming like a fistful of raven diamonds.

"I want your eye, Travis Alamo Boone." She told me. "After all, you have got two of them in your head, now don't you? I figure you ought to be able to spare at least one of those two eyeballs for a little old lady with an eyepatch like mine, now ought you boy?"

No, I thought to myself. I ought not to be able to spare one of my eyes. Not even an eyelash.

The old witch woman grinned a big old hungry shark kind of grin, just as if she could hear what I was thinking.

"Just look at that color swimming in those eyeballs," she said. "Blue as the sky, which rhymes with lie. Did you know that was what the old buried people used to call blue eyes? They called them liar's eyes. Cheating eyes. Never you mind your people who try and tell you blue eyes are true eyes. No sir, sky eyes like yours, just as pale as frozen periwinkles, they tell you nothing but bold as brass lies."

Then she reached one long arm out towards me. I tried to take a step back, but I wasn't nearly fast enough, and she plucked out my left eye just as easily as you might pick up a shiny blue ocean aggie from out of a giggling brook.

I felt her long finger-claws tug out my left eye just as easy as that, and all at once an even fifty-percent half of my world went *pop* like a soap bubble hitting a thorn bush.

She pulled out what was left of her own eye and dropped it onto the ground like the pit of a spit-out olive. And then she screwed my stolen left eye into her eye pit and smiled at me like she was looking at a birthday cake with her name on it in sticky-sweet chocolate icing.

"You can have what's left of that old eye of mine," she told me. "I don't want it anymore. I don't need it, now that I've got *your* eye."

So what could I do?

I picked that spit-out olive pit eye seed up from the dirt where she had dropped it, and I screwed it into my own eye hole. And just that fast the whole world swam into bright blue colors, like a rainbow of gasoline spilled onto a puddle in your driveway. I drew in my breath in a long icicle inhale, feeling it chill and slice across my teeth, and all of a sudden I felt as if I were part eagle, my vision seemed to burn so sharp and clear.

"I can see you, old woman," I told her in a hard and confident voice full of truth. "I can see you, Bracken Sally Branwen. You can't turn your back and walk away from me just as easy as that."

Now her eyes—both of them, including the one she'd stolen from me, grew as wide as shiny aluminum pie pans hung in the trees to scare away the crows. She was looking through fear so big it was going to drown her.

"How do you know my true name?" that old witch woman asked in blatant astonishment. "I ain't never told that to anybody in the last two hundred years."

"I see your true name written on what's left of your miserable, wrinkled old soul," I said, using words and ideas way too big for me —but suddenly wearing that eye of hers, it was like I was looking at a cheat sheet for the whole wide universe. "Like a scribbled-up tombstone, I see your name written across your charcoal heart just as clear as clear can be."

Then I reached out and plucked my own eye out back out of her skull. It was like pulling a plug out of a bathtub, as all of the evil and misery glugged out of her empty eye socket, spilled out onto the tiled floor of the eye doctor's waiting room, and soaked away into nothingness.

I looked over at my Momma, and she wasn't frozen there anymore. She was sitting and shaking her head like she had just nodded off for a short afternoon nap.

"Goodness," she said. "I must have dozed off."

"You work too darned hard Momma," I told her. "You must have needed to have a little sleep."

I could see everybody else in the waiting room was looking around blinking and bewildered in same slow and fuzzy confused state my Momma found herself in. But, being my Momma, she shook off her confusion like a dog shaking the wet out of is rained-on pelt. She fixed her eye on me, and then she smiled.

"I declare, Travis, you look like you've got something stuck in your eye," she said. "Were you rubbing it too hard?"

I laughed just a little.

"The only thing I've got stuck in my eye is the picture of you and your smile, Momma," I said. "And in case you didn't notice, I'm smiling right back at you."

And I was smiling too, only it wasn't really because of Momma.

After I saw the eye doctor I smiled at him too, because he couldn't believe just how clear my eyes had got between the last time he had looked at them and now. My eyes were as clear and sharp as an inter-planetary telescope.

"I don't you think you needed glasses at all, young man."

And I smiled at that too, only what I was really smiling at was for the first time in my life I knew just exactly what I wanted to do with the rest of my life.

I wanted to be a witch hunter.

And that's how I started on the road I am still on today.

ABOUT THE AUTHOR

Steve is a writer and an oral tradition storyteller; he learned the storytelling tradition from his grandfather, and regularly tells stories to in-person audiences ranging from 5 to 5,000 spectators. He writes horror, paranormal, dark fantasy, and ghost stories, and specializes in the fine old art of booga-booga.

Think of Steve as that old dude at the campfire spinning out ghost stories and weird adventures and the grand epic saga of how Thud the Second stepped out of his cave with nothing more than a rock in his fist and slew the saber-tooth tiger.

Find out more about Steve at:
stevevernonstoryteller.wordpress.com

goodreads.com/stevevernon
facebook.com/SteveVernonsKindleYarns
twitter.com/StephenVernon
bookbub.com/authors/steve-vernon
amazon.com/Steve-Vernon/e/B002BMD282

ABOUT ENCHANTED TALES

Magicks & Enchantments is the first issue in the anthology series Enchanted Tales. Learn more about the series at:

https://blackbirdpublishing.com/series/enchanted-tales.

OTHER COLLECTIONS

If you enjoyed *Magicks & Enchantments*, check out A Procession of Faeries, an anthology series about the Fae.

https://blackbirdpublishing.com/series/a-procession-of-faeries/

www.ingramcontent.com/pod-product-compliance
Lightning Source LLC
Chambersburg PA
CBHW071048250626
47159CB00002B/399